Abigail Maskall spends lots of her time with books, whether project managing them at the educational publishing house that she works at, or with her nose stuck in one. She currently lives in England with her husband, their boxadore, and tortoise. *Lovers and Friends* is her debut novel.

For Nanny Sheila, who would love the romantic parts. And for Nanny Pat, who would just love that I did it.

Abigail Maskall

LOVERS AND FRIENDS

AUSTIN MACAULEY PUBLISHERS

LONDON * CAMBRIDGE * NEW YORK * SHARJAH

A CIP catalogue record for this title is available from the British Library.

ISBN 9781035867899 (Paperback)
ISBN 9781035867905 (ePub e-book)

www.austinmacauley.com

First Published 2024
Austin Macauley Publishers Ltd®
1 Canada Square
Canary Wharf
London
E14 5AA

Table of Contents

1993
Oliver

The first time that Oliver saw Nelly was at The Punter pub in Cambridge. The year was 1993 and the Free Smoking law was still something of the imagination, which meant that the smell filling the public house was a heady riddle of cigarettes and spilled lager. Oliver and his friends frequented this particular pub often, on account of it being close to their college and also because it charged only two pounds ninety-eight for a pint of beer. Many nights in a row, he and his friends would sit talking about life and women and definitely anything other than their studies, for which Oliver was grateful. He had moved from his family home in the Cotswolds to study in Cambridge three years previously, pursuing an education in French and economics. Economics had been his father's preference, which was why Oliver was particularly glad that he and his friends so seldom discussed their education during their frequent visits to The Punter.

To Oliver, the entire subject of economics was incredibly dull. It wasn't that he didn't have an interest in the global economy. It was just that he had no interest in working for it. His father, on the other hand, had other plans. Oliver was to finish his degree at Cambridge University and come to work for his investment banking firm as a junior broker. It was a good job. A safe job. For Oliver, at least. Which would pay very well and many people would be grateful for. However, for Oliver money was something that had always been a constant in his life, and he therefore neither longed for it nor worried about it. He didn't have the drive that his fellow students had to go out into the world and make their million. His financial fate was, as far as he was concerned, already somewhat secured by his sizeable inheritance and therefore eradicated the need to dwell on such things. He had the drive to make more money, but that was what it was; more money. He could always find it, if he really needed to. Still, it was what his father had wanted and therefore what Oliver had agreed to doing. There would be a year abroad somewhere—likely France—where Oliver could have one final stab at freedom and then he was to go into a life of investment and high-stakes monotony. It was for this very reason that Oliver was glad for the distraction of his evening trips to The Punter.

Oliver's sister, India, had also joined them that evening. She had followed Oliver from the Cotswolds to Cambridge under the vague veil of studying literature. Nobody had any real inclination to believe that she was interested in her studies any more than Oliver was interested in economics. But, as it was India, this didn't really matter. People assumed that Oliver would mind his younger sister tailing him from home in his years of freedom from his parents, but this wasn't something that bothered him.

Oliver and India had always been close. She was an untameable, flighty creature. Lovely and wild and prone to both laughing and crying and not very much in between. Life was an adventure whenever India was around, and so Oliver wasn't disappointed to have her joining his social circle. Oliver was also glad of his sister being in close proximity on account of the fact that he worried about her—which was strange, because Oliver seldom worried about anything—and so it was always fine with him when India tailed along to social gatherings, dragging some new friend or another along with her. India did so hate to be alone.

The friend she had brought with her this evening, however, was different from India's usual type. She was slight and practical looking, with a mass of curly dark hair and a fringe that stuck out at angles that indicated that she had cut it herself. Her face was hidden behind a large pair of glasses and a bottle-green cardigan was tugged tightly across her shoulders. She was the type of person that Oliver would associate with the words 'Academic' and 'Sensible'. Which was curious, as these were the last words that he would associate with India.

"Who's for another?" Oliver's friend Henry asked, standing up from the table to head back over to the dingy corner bar.

"Gin and tonic for me please. What would you like, Nel?" India trilled, casting her attention to her sensible-looking friend.

Nelly looked up somewhat nervously and Oliver noticed the top of her cheeks glowing pink, "A rum and coke, if that's alright please?"

Her accent was different from what Oliver had expected. Unlike his and his friends' lullingly flat southern English accents, Nelly's was harsh and travelling and gave away her routes to the east of London. It sounded to Oliver like someone clapping quite near to his ears.

"Oh that sounds nice, I'll have the same."

"Rum and coke for the girls," Henry winked smoothly, "Lads, beers all round?"

Oliver nodded lazily with the other boys, the sensation of the first two pints already warming the skin down the back of his neck.

"What happened with that blonde girl last night, Oliver, mate?" a boy called George shot from across the table.

Oliver shrugged, "Nothing too exciting."

"Not too exciting?" George scoffed, "She was bloody gorgeous, wasn't she? I don't know how you manage it!"

"I know how he manages it," Henry laughed as he trailed back over balancing pints of amber-coloured liquid on a sticky tray, "He's bloody gorgeous, isn't he!" Henry placed a beer in front of Oliver and rubbed his hair as if he were a show dog at Crufts.

Oliver smiled and shrugged. Like money, attention from women wasn't something that Oliver had ever lacked. He was handsome and just the right mixture of confident and aloof that for some reason seemed to make it very easy to seduce women without very much effort. He enjoyed the attention, but rarely enjoyed their company for any longer than one evening or two. They were always too eager. Too loud. Too something.

The boys laughed and India rolled her eyes, hiding her own smile. "Well, I don't know about that. Surely I'm the looker of the family, right Nel?" she laughed. India nudged her friend's arm playfully.

Nelly shrugged, the glow of pink on her cheeks now spreading to the side of her face close to her ears. "I dunno," she muttered simply.

"Go on, Nelly. Don't be shy," George grinned, "Tell us what you think. Do you reckon Oliver is God's gift, or what?"

"I reckon he thinks he is." The table erupted into laughter and Nelly smirked into her drink, seemingly pleased at the reaction to her joke and yet also embarrassed by the attention that it was bringing. Her response caught Oliver off guard. It was rare that someone, other than his father, said anything negative about him. It was like an elastic band snapping on the back of the wrist.

"Fair enough," Oliver responded, raising an eyebrow. The conversation turned back to the events of the evening previous and then dwindled into something that mocked at a deeper tone. Somewhere in the evening's events Oliver fought his way through the now busying pub to fetch more drinks for the table and, when he returned, found it vacant other than the sensible-looking girl—Nelly—still sat patiently in the corner.

"India and Henry are buying fags and George went to the loo," she told him almost apologetically when he returned, the same lilt in her accent carrying over the other voices that were filling the room.

"Ah," Oliver raised an eyebrow and took his place on the bench opposite Nelly, pushing a glass of rum and coke toward her.

"Thanks," she smiled so that her lips parted from her teeth. Judging from the rest of her appearance he had half been expecting Nelly to be wearing braces, and was mildly surprised to see that she wasn't. One of her front teeth slightly over-knocked the other. Like someone briefly crossing their fingers.

"No problem," he responded lightly, peering over his shoulder to see where the other table-mates had gotten to.

"I'm sorry if what I said before pissed you off," Nelly's voice brought him back to the table.

"Sorry?"

"What I said before. About you thinking that your God's gift to women, or whatever. I didn't mean it really. It was just a joke, you know? Although, to be fair, just about every girl on campus seems to have a story about you one way or another."

Oliver raised his eyebrows again, surprised by her sudden explosion of conversation. "It's fine. Don't worry about it."

She didn't seem satisfied by this response because she followed with, "It's just that I don't want you to think that I'm a dick."

Oliver looked up from his pint, "Well, you seem to think that I'm one."

"Mmm."

Oliver frowned, "Why would you care what I think about you, anyway?"

"Well, India's my best friend and you're her brother, so…" Nelly flushed again and Oliver noticed that it was beginning to travel down her neck, mottling the skin over her chest now that she had removed her heavy cardigan.

Feeling suddenly oddly sympathetic toward her, he replied, "Well, don't worry about it. I certainly don't think you're a dick."

Nelly smiled, apparently satisfied by this small effort, "Well, that's alright then."

"That's alright," Oliver agreed.

"So, you're studying economics?" She looked embarrassed again at revealing that she knew more about Oliver than he did her, but Oliver pretended not to notice.

"Yep. Economics and French."

"French? That's interesting."

"Really?"

"You just don't really look the type."

Oliver raised an eyebrow, "What do I look the type for?"

"I dunno. Economics or law or something, I suppose."

Oliver nodded, "Fair enough."

"I like that, though. I think it's cool, I mean. The French thing. I speak Italian."

"Yeah?"

"Yeah," she seemed pleased with herself suddenly, as if she had just found something that she had misplaced, "My parents are Italian. Not exactly shocking, I know. With a name like Strapelli."

Oliver smiled, "Nelly Strapelli?"

"Yep. It's awful, isn't it?" It seemed like a question rather than a statement.

"Not awful. Just… it sounds like a children's television presenter, or something."

Nelly rolled her eyes playfully, "Wow, come up with something original at least."

"Nelly Strapelli. It definitely has a ring to it." Nelly looked pleased about this and Oliver found himself continuing, "So then, Nelly Strapelli, what are you studying?"

"English. Well, literature. With India. We have Russian lit together."

"Ah right. Yeah," Oliver suddenly had visions of India somehow compelling Nelly into writing her literary assignments on her behalf.

"We've been doing *The Master and Margarita* recently. Although it definitely isn't for everyone."

Oliver nodded and craned his neck to see where his friends were. They seemed to be taking ages. "It's hard to give a fuck about Satan when there's a talking cat around," he quipped lazily.

He turned back and saw that Nelly looked pleased by his statement, "Exactly! That's exactly what I said to India. Well, not exactly because she hadn't read it.

But still." She smiled so as one dimple appeared on the left of her face and then reached a hand to cover her mouth. Oliver smiled back at her. He was just about to respond when India and Henry stumbled over with the drinks.

"It's bloody heaving over there!" India laughed, pulling open a packet of cigarettes and offering them to Nelly. Oliver was mildly surprised again when she took one.

"Bloody ridiculous," Henry agreed, sliding along the bench beside Nelly and leaning his arm back behind so as his hand rested on the wall beside her shoulder. Oliver noticed Nelly sit further forward in her seat, her dark eyes flitting to Henry's arm that had coiled around the edge of the bench.

"Hey, Oliver. That girl's over there, from last night."

"Oh."

Henry seemed to miss the disincline of Oliver's tone. "Yeah. She spotted me from the other end and came over asking for you. I reckon you should go over." He nodded emphatically, gesturing to someone behind Oliver's head. Oliver turned around to see the girl that he had met the night previously propped against the bar with her friend, her blonde hair flicking around her shoulders as she waved him over. Oliver sat for a moment, reluctant to make the effort to move from his chair, but then remembered the way that she had looked naked and decided that he would make the time. He pushed himself up from the seat and reached over to tap Henry's arm before he left the table.

"Typical," he heard Nelly say beneath her breath to India as he stood.

He turned and looked at her, but she was already looking the other way.

Oliver walked over to the girl at the bar and bought a drink for she and her friend. She had an accent the same as his—long and lulling—and asked him about his father's investment banking business and the job that he was going to do there when he graduated from university.

"Like the drink?" She asked when, on a whim, Oliver asked her if she had read *The Master and the Margarita.* By the end of the evening, she was eagerly draped around his arm ready to follow him back to his dormitory room.

The group stood in the night air to say their goodbyes, Oliver and the rest of the boys due to walk back to their college and India and Nelly to go back to theirs respectively. India kept laughing loudly and steadying herself on Nelly's far slighter shoulder and Oliver wondered whether they would be okay to walk home alone.

"We'll be fine," India slurred, smacking his arm lightly, "Stop worrying about me."

Oliver wasn't completely satisfied and found himself looking to Nelly for reassurance. She nodded lightly, "She'll be fine. I'll walk her back to her room."

India hugged Nelly tightly and smiled, "See, Oliver? Didn't I tell you that Nelly was the best person in the world?"

Oliver nodded before allowing the woman from the bar to drag him the opposite way along the path back to his dormitory. He wouldn't remember India's comment that night about Nelly Strapelli. But, one day soon, he would grow to develop the very same opinion.

1994
Nelly

Nelly didn't see Oliver for almost a full year after their encounter at The Punter in 1993. Or she hadn't spoken with him since then, at least. As she had done so before their last meeting, Nelly had seen glimpses of Oliver around Cambridge for a time. And of course she had heard news of him from India. Since graduating university, he had moved to France for a year, as he had planned, and was apparently working in some sort of photography studio. India had shown Nelly some of the photographs that Oliver had posted to her; beautiful, thick letters headed with exciting red and blue patterns. She had half expected them to be tasteless pictures of women sprawled over chaise longues, but they were much different from what she had anticipated. Black and white polaroids of all different types of people; sometimes from afar, like a stranger admiring from a distance, or sometimes so close that you could see each freckle and crevice on the person's face. Raw. Unabashed. Human. She had nodded politely when India raved over them and secretly told herself that she thought that they were pretentious and generic.

Since their last meeting, she had stubbornly convinced herself that she did not care for Oliver Matthews. He was snobbish and aloof and arrogant. Yes, there had been a brief conversation where she had allowed herself to think that he might be mildly interested in her. But then he had barely offered her a second glance when there was anyone else around to absorb his attention. Like a child when someone waves something colourful in front of their face. He was everything that she didn't like in men. Egotistical and aesthetic. She clung to this idea tightly, trying to persuade herself that this was her true opinion and ignoring the disconcerting way that her stomach flipped whenever his name was mentioned in a way that only a person experiencing unrequited feeling can. Contrastingly, her feelings for Oliver's sister were worn on her sleeve. Nelly adored India and blindly ignored all of her friend's negative qualities, refusing to believe that she was anything less than utterly wonderful. Because love is blind.

Nelly and India had moved in together in their third year of university. Together they shared a tiny flat overlooking Jesus Green. It was small and cramped and always smelled faintly like mildew, but it was their home and they both loved it dearly. Unlike the majority of India's acquaintances, Nelly wasn't only interested in her friendship for the elaborate nights out and dramatic rendezvous that India always seemed to somehow knot herself into. She enjoyed India's company for the person that she was; kind and creative and desperate, for some reason that felt so strange to Nelly, to be liked by everyone around her.

Nelly noticed the way that India might change her opinions or her accent or the way that she did her hair to fit in with certain social circles. Like a child trying to impress an absent parent. But when it was just Nelly and India in their flat, all of this seemed to melt away. They would haul up on the settee with a bottle of wine and speak for hours on end about life and love and music and art and everything in between. And Nelly, who had always been so shy and lonely, felt for the first time interesting and almost vibrant. They were yin and yang. Nelly somehow brought India back down to reality and India somehow dragged Nelly out from it.

The time in their flat had been nothing less than utterly wonderful for several months. Until India had sparked up a complicated relationship with a boy named Spencer and the long evenings spent laughing over the idea of love turned into long nights listening to India crying about the latest argument or break up that she was enduring. Several times Nelly had found India curled up on the tiny kitchen floor, almost shaking with tears. She had told her firmly that Spencer was no good for her many times and India had appeared to agree with each sentiment. But somehow, the two of them always seemed to make it up one way or another. And India spent the next six months between being gloriously happy and utterly devastated. As different as night and day and never anything in between. Indeed, there seldom was anything in between with India.

Still, people had toxic relationships when they were young. It was what happened. Nobody needed to worry.

And so, Nelly had bitten her tongue and continued to pick up the pieces each time the latest break up occurred, hoping secretly that this would be the last time but knowing from experience that it probably wouldn't be. It felt to her as if, very slowly, something in her friend was beginning to unravel. Like a thread that has just begun to come loose from a cardigan; she knew that, if it was pulled hard enough, the entire structure would likely fall apart. Of course, Nelly shared her feelings on the matter with her best friend. But India would just wave away the comment and tell Nelly that this was what love was supposed to feel like. Painful and blissful. Nelly couldn't disagree, not yet realising that she too was in love with a person. And so had to go along with the charade. Her own experiences of men were far less complicated.

Recently, perhaps from the boost in confidence that India's friendship had befitted her, Nelly had begun to experience attention from men for the first time. She had gone on a few awkward dates and fumbled through plenty of uncomfortable altercations after too many wines and too few inhibitions. None of them made her stomach flip in the way that the very mention of Oliver's name was prone to doing. But none of them made her cry or feel inadequate either, so she satisfied herself with being satisfied with this. For the time being.

When the term finished in the summer of 1994, India invited Nelly to stay at her family home in the Cotswolds for the holidays. The day that Nelly was arriving was also the day before India's twenty-first birthday and, as ever, there was a glorious party to mark the celebration. Nelly's feet dragged as she lugged her rucksack over her shoulder from the train station that afternoon. Having gotten the train from Kings Cross four hours ago, she was glad to finally see the long, slim figure of her friend perched against of the silver-blue Mercedes waiting for her.

"It's my mum's car," India smiled as Nelly dragged herself over, "Gosh, give me that bag. It's bloody enormous!" she hauled the luggage in mock-dramatics into the back seat and then sprung forward to pull Nelly into a tight hug. "I've missed you!"

"Me too," Nelly smiled into her friend's shoulder. She smelled like cigarettes and gardenias and also faintly like something alcoholic. The two of them drove along the winding Cotswolds roads back to India's parent's house. Nelly marvelled at the scene around her; the furthest that she had ventured from her home in London so far was to Cambridge where she lived currently, and the Cotswolds felt far removed from either of those places. Quiet and green, with washed-white stone walls that seemed to stretch for miles and miles. It was a wonder to Nelly why India would ever want to leave this place. They pulled over a gravelled drive in front of two tall gates and India nipped out of the car in a swift movement to pull them open.

"You just sit there, Nel," she laughed as she ran back to hop into the driver's seat. Nelly hadn't stayed sat on account of being purposefully unhelpful. It was more that she was shocked at how ginormous the house behind the iron gates was, and suddenly felt instinctively like she needed to scrub the chewing gum that was stuck to the bottom of her shoe before setting foot inside. It was the largest house that Nelly had ever seen. On a summer's day, it looked rather like something that might be featured in some terribly chic European film. Shuttered windows opened up over a long, green lawn where several cars were already parked neatly, as if on show. It was a far cry from their home by Jesus Green and Nelly suddenly felt conscious of her spiky London accent.

"People are arriving around seven," India explained as she dragged Nelly's rucksack up the steps toward the front door and pushed it open lazily, "So we've got about an hour to get things set up and get ourselves ready."

"Right. Okay," Nelly was barely listening. She suddenly felt terribly nervous.

"What are you going to wear?"

"Umm I dunno. This, probably," Nelly said, gesturing down to the t-shirt and jeans that she was wearing.

India looked perplexed, "No way. I don't think so. You must have something sexier in this bag of yours?"

"I don't know. Maybe," Nelly shrugged, knowing full well that the sexiest item that she had in her luggage was a pair of denim shorts that she only half intended on wearing this summer if it was terribly warm and she plucked up the courage.

India shook her head, "It's worse than I thought. Well then, setting up will have to wait. Let's get you sorted first, then we can worry about the rest." Nelly followed India up a flight of stairs and onto a long, cool landing that she was told was India's brother's floor. "My ensuite is getting re-done at the moment, so you can have a shower in Oliver's room." Nelly must have shot India a nervous expression because India laughed and said, "Don't worry. He's still isn't back from Paris."

Nelly nodded and felt herself ease slightly, both relieved and disappointed at the same time by the news that Oliver wouldn't be joining them for the summer. She was sure that it would be awkward to have to hang around with him for weeks on end. Although she was also certain that he would probably ignore her anyway if he were there. She followed India through to a large bedroom.

"It's as big as our entire flat!" she told India as she walked in.

India laughed and started flicking lights on around them. She continued chatting away avidly and gestured to the walls which Nelly now saw were covered in various photographs much akin to the ones that she had seen India pouring over before. There wasn't much cohesion to them—they were a mixture of black and white and colour, some of people, some of scenery, some of abstract objects. It was as if Oliver hadn't yet found the muse that he was looking for and wasn't quite certain where to channel his talent. It was a shame that even Nelly had to admit that he had talent. Some, at least.

India shrugged, "It's just a hobby, of course. He's going to work for Dad's firm when he's back, much to his displeasure." She rolled her eyes theatrically, "Honestly, you'd think he was being forced to work the mines. Right then, the shower's through there. I'll be back in a minute with drinks."

Nelly padded quietly through the bedroom and toward the small ensuite bathroom. It felt strange being inside Oliver's bedroom without him there. Personal. Almost intimate. Hoping her presence there would go unnoticed were he to return, she was careful not to disrupt anything as she stepped out of her underwear and twisted on the shower. She could smell her deodorant as she raised her arms. The water was cool and welcome after the journey and she spent longer in there than she had intended. India was already back in the room when she had finished, rifling through Nelly's bag and throwing various options on top of the bed.

"Have you not brought any dresses with you?" she asked.

"I don't think so."

"What about that green one I gave you? You look great in that."

Nelly shook her head, "I must have forgotten it." Her hair was wet from the shower and was dripping down the back of her neck. She reached down for the hand towel that India had laid out for her, ready to ruffle her hair dry, when India's eyes quickly whipped up.

"No, no, no. Don't do that. Your hair looks so much nicer when you let it dry naturally."

"Really?"

"Yeah! It's so wild and sexy. I wish mine was like that," she flicked at her own straight blonde hair and sighed in mock-dramatics. "I'll get you something from my room." Nelly waited for a brief moment before India reappeared holding two hangers of dresses.

"What do we think of the gold?" India asked. Nelly shook her head. India laughed, "I thought as much. Okay, what about this one?" She held out a black dress with spaghetti straps and a lower neckline than Nelly would have usually felt comfortable in.

"Do you think that will suit me?" she asked nervously, fingering the soft fabric.

"You'll look bloody gorgeous in it. I promise," India implored. "Now, you get dressed whilst I have a shower and then we'll start setting up, yeah?"

"Yep. Okay," Nelly nodded.

India beamed, "I'm so happy you're here, Nel. We're going to have the best summer. I promise."

Nelly nodded back, hoping that this statement would be true.

The party began to fill up at around 8 o'clock. True to form, India had invited more people than most would invite to a wedding. 'Friends of friends' was how she referred to them. But Nelly knew the truth was that the majority of the people at the party were acquaintances at best. People that India knew from her days at boarding school. Tall, confident girls that somehow looked and spoke exactly in the same way as India did. They were the types of people that Nelly could imagine playing hockey at school, or belonging to a riding club. The boys there were all vaguely similar to one another, also. With striped pastel shirts and loud guffawing laughs. It was as if everyone had been given a uniform to wear, which Nelly hadn't packed in her battered rucksack.

At some point in the evening, when the moon was beginning to rise and people's speech was beginning to slowly become more and more slurred, Nelly found herself padding quietly out from the garden and back into the kitchen. She had lost India when Spencer had arrived about an hour ago and had been loitering awkwardly with a group of people who were speaking very animatedly about a ski trip they had once all taken. Nelly, having holidayed mainly in Clacton when her parent's restaurant was doing well enough to allow them to take a few days off, couldn't relate to the conversation and felt somehow like an imposter at this lavish party with these lavish people. Pleased to be away from the excruciating awkwardness for a moment, she pretended to herself that she was looking for India and found herself tiptoeing back upstairs to Oliver's bedroom. She would just allow herself to hide in there for ten minutes or so. Nobody would miss her. She was sure that India wouldn't mind.

She pushed the door open quietly; the room completely dark save for the brief warm light that was filtering through the open shutters. The noise of someone's voice was travelling up from the garden beneath. "You know what they say. Rome really is a poor man's Vienna."

Nelly rolled her eyes, an urge that she had been fighting for the entirety of the evening. "Posh twat," she snapped to herself as she clicked the door shut behind her.

"I hope you aren't referring to me."

Nelly jumped. She fumbled for a light switch, but then a dim lamp flicked on in front of her and she saw the shape of Oliver leaning back lazily on the windowsill, one leg dangled out from the window into the world below.

"Oh. I'm sorry. I—No, I wasn't speaking to you. I didn't think you'd be in here," she stumbled quickly.

Oliver looked nonplussed, "It is my bedroom."

"Yes. Of course. I mean, I thought you were away still. India said that you were still in Paris."

"Mmm. I got back about an hour ago," he was staring at the wall as he spoke.

"Ah right. You must be tired. Shall I go and find India for you? Or do you want to be left alone?" Nelly wasn't sure why she was being so accommodating to him. Yes, it was his room and his parents' house. But she was behaving as if she was working for him. She felt annoyed with herself for it.

Oliver shook his head, "Were you hoping to escape the posh twats then?"

"Oh. Well, yes. To be honest."

"And here you go finding yourself locked in a room with one." He turned and half-smiled at her.

"Well… I didn't mean…"

"Do you want a drink?" He held a bottle of wine out toward her. Nelly thought for a moment. The idea of having to spend the rest of the evening navigating the awkwardness of her feelings for India's brother felt uncomfortable, but she also didn't want to have to go back downstairs and rejoin the obnoxious party. Oliver watched her expectantly, as if encountering something curious. "Unless you'd prefer to let Hugo tell you about the summer that he spent sailing Greece on Daddy's boat?"

Nelly laughed and then immediately put her hand to her mouth, feeling self-conscious of her smile. "Go on then," she shrugged, and padded over to the window toward Oliver. She took the bottle from him as she approached, noticing the tan on the skin of his forearms where his sleeves were rolled to his elbows. Oliver shuffled back slightly, allowing just enough space for Nelly to perch awkwardly on the side of the sill. Her dress rode up as she sat, revealing the flesh on the tops of her thighs, and she tugged at her skirt to hide them as she felt the familiar blush begin to creep over her cheeks.

"You'd be more comfortable if you straddled it," Oliver told her, nodding toward the windowsill beneath them.

"I'm fine," Nelly lied, wishing that she was still wearing her jeans. Oliver shrugged and then, apparently in an after-thought, reached out to pull the chair that was tucked beneath the desk over toward them. It squeaked slightly as it tugged across the wooden floor. He twisted it around with one hand so as the seat was facing them and then gestured to Nelly to put her feet onto it.

"Thanks," she said as she pulled the seat further forward. It was an oddly thoughtful gesture that didn't tally with the image of Oliver that she had built in her mind since their last encounter. She watched him out from the corner of her eye as she took a swig of the wine, feeling the warmth of the alcohol run down her throat. He looked the same as he had always done, except for that his hair was slightly longer and his skin had tanned so as tiny white lines fell from the corners of his eyes as if he had spent his time abroad smiling. He was almost irritatingly attractive.

"So, how's Russian lit?"

"Oh. It's fine. Or it was. I dropped it after first year and picked up American literature." She wasn't sure why it was coming out irritably. She didn't mean for it to. She was shocked that Oliver remembered what she had been studying when they had last seen each other, but then remembered that India must have spoken with him about it as she was on the same course. Nelly looked over to see if Oliver looked bothered by her sharpness, but he didn't seem to care. "How was Paris?"

Oliver took the wine back from her and took a gulp. "Paris was Paris," he shrugged. He said it with the glib of someone who had travelled a lot, but then seemed to catch himself. "Have you been?"

Nelly shook her head, "Me? No. I've never been abroad."

She felt the blush crawling down her neck, half-expecting Oliver to laugh at this confession. But he just nodded ever so slightly, allowing his eyes to dart to hers for the briefest of moments. "You're Italian though?"

"Yeah. Well, my parents are. From Bologna. But I've never been. Or I've never been back, I suppose. My mum and dad moved to London when I was two and brought my Nonna with them. And my aunts and cousins followed, so... We always speak about going back. But my parents are always so busy with work and... everything." She trailed off, feeling suddenly exposed.

"Your parents have a restaurant, right?"

"Yeah." She turned to look at Oliver and saw that he was already looking at her.

He raised his eyebrow slightly, saying as way of explanation, "India chats." He handed the bottle back over to her and leant back slightly, bringing his leg up so as his foot was resting on the edge of the chair that Nelly's was on. He was wearing socks but no shoes. "So, what sort of food does your parents' restaurant do?"

"Oh, well... mostly Italian."

Oliver grinned and Nelly realised that he had been joking. She rolled her eyes and fought the smile that was playing on the edges of her mouth. There was a noise from the scene below them and Nelly looked down to see India there, her arm clutching around Spencer's back as if she almost needed support to keep her upright.

"What do you think of him?" Oliver nodded to the scene below.

"Spencer? Mmm, a bit of a prick."

"A bit?"

Nelly shrugged, "India loves him."

"That doesn't mean he's not an utter wanker."

Nelly nodded in agreement, "No. That's definitely true."

"Did he genuinely leave her to walk home alone that night a few weeks ago?"

"After the theatre? Yeah. She was soaked when she got in."

"And pissed as a prostitute, no doubt."

"Let's not slag off sex workers, shall we?"

"Oh, it isn't the prostitutes I'm meaning to offend. I'd need to be thoroughly inebriated to get through those evenings too, I'm sure."

Nelly laughed and then covered her mouth again. "I'd have thought you'd quite enjoy it."

"What would give you that impression?"

Nelly opened her mouth to reply, suddenly anxious that she had said the wrong thing. "I just… heard things, I suppose. You're a tiny bit infamous on our campus."

Oliver watched her quietly for a moment, and she was worried she'd offended him. Then he half-smiled, shaking his head slightly and turning back to the window. "Lovely to know that you've followed my exploits so closely, Nelly Strapelli. Almost flattering."

"I've not *followed them closely*."

"Well, you just gave my sexual prowess a glowing review. *Famous*, I think you called it."

"Infamous."

"I heard famous."

"Shocking."

He blew a laugh out of his nose. Nelly smiled back slightly, watching the side of his face. He was quiet for a moment. "She's okay though, isn't she?" Something in the way that he said it sounded almost anxious. Worried.

"Yeah. She's okay. I mean, she spends half the nights crying over some argument or another, but I'm always there to look after her."

"Thank Christ for Nelly Strapelli, right?" He smiled again and she wasn't sure whether he was making fun of her or not.

She shrugged, "India's my best friend."

Oliver nodded. "Do you fancy a smoke?"

"Oh. Yeah. I've got cigarettes in my bag."

"No. I mean something a bit stronger." Oliver hopped off from the sill, the wood having created a long crease in his light blue shorts, and then produced something in a plastic sandwich bag from the desk drawer.

"Hiding marijuana in your bedroom. Are you sixteen?"

Oliver smiled again and Nelly could see where the white creases in the sides of his eyes had formed from. "You haven't met my father."

"Not yet," Nelly agreed. Oliver sat back down, his foot edging closer toward hers atop the chair, and began to roll a joint lazily on his lap. "You two must get on well though. You're going to work at his company, aren't you?"

"Ah, yes. Well, that's his plan."

"I'm surprised you didn't want to carry on with the photography."

Oliver glanced up as if she had just suggested that he run away to the circus, "Photography?"

"Yeah. Well, you know?" She gestured around them at the photographs that scattered the walls.

"Right, yeah." Oliver nodded as if just remembering, "Well, photography was never a steady career path. So, Dad had me study economics."

"Economics and French." The correction escaped Nelly's lips and she suddenly felt embarrassed that she had remembered his full degree.

"Ah yeah, well the French was really just an excuse for the photography." Oliver smiled up at her from beneath the hair that was flopping into his eyes. He stuck out his tongue briefly and dragged it along the edge of the thin paper.

"Right. Of course."

Oliver sat back up and lit the joint with a lighter from his pocket. He took a deep drag and then held it out toward Nelly, offering for her to take it from him. Nelly hesitated. She had smoked marijuana before with India, but it didn't seem to have the same effect on her as it did her friend. She worried that she would embarrass herself and then regret it in the morning. Oliver seemed to anticipate the concern because he said, "You don't have to. But don't worry, it's French, so its barely stronger than a cigar."

"That's assuming I know the strength of a cigar," Nelly smiled. She covered her mouth and then reached out to take the joint from Oliver's fingers.

Nelly felt the blush begin to travel to the tops of her ears and begged it not to show in the dim light of the lamp. "Why don't you want to go down to the party?"

Oliver raised his eyebrows, "Probably the same reason that you don't."

"I doubt that."

Oliver laughed. "Well, let's just say I have the entire summer to feign an interest in a life riding on my father's coat tails. Do your parents want you to work in their restaurant when you graduate?"

"I think they might have at one point. But they don't really mind what I do, I don't think."

"Wow. What's that like?" Oliver grinned again and Nelly couldn't help but smile back. "Do you not like your smile?"

The question was so abrasive that it caught Nelly off guard. "Not really," she shrugged nervously into her shoulder.

Someone would normally look away. But Oliver continued to watch her. Study her. His eyes locked onto her face curiously. "You should. You have quite a disarming smile."

If it was a compliment, he didn't show it freely. He turned and resumed his lazy gaze out of the window at the scene below, apparently oblivious to the fire that was beginning to burn in Nelly's chest.

The two of them slept in the same bed for the first time that night. The noise from the party below carried up to the room above as they settled down on Oliver's mattress. His breath smelled of tobacco and red wine as he fell asleep behind Nelly's head, his arm tucked just underneath the crook of her neck. It was uncomfortable, but she daren't move in case he retracted it. And so, she lay there for the remainder of the night in India's dress and in Oliver's arms. For the first time.

1994
Oliver

The morning after India's party, Oliver awoke with the aching muzzling of a hangover in the back of his head. Nelly was still asleep. Her dark, curling hair splayed across the pillow that they had shared like corkscrews across a counter. She was still wearing her dress from last night. The one that had made Oliver notice her. She had been standing in the garden when he had first seen her, her arms pulled across her chest as if she were cold despite the warmth of the summer air. He had watched her roll her eyes at the people below and it had made him smile that she seemed oblivious to how deceptive her face was to her thoughts. The art of networking and feigning interest that he had learned from a young age was apparently foreign to Nelly. She was different. Almost refreshing. He watched her sleeping now and wondered why he didn't feel the immediate pull to leave that usually settled in around this time. He had been with many beautiful women. But there was something about Nelly that he hadn't expected. It wasn't that she was now beautiful, necessarily. She had ditched the unflattering cardigans—possibly under India's influence—grown out that awful fringe, and had also fixed the small overlap that he had previously seen in the front of her teeth. She had definitely made an effort the previous evening to look attractive. But that wasn't necessarily what had cajoled Oliver's curiosity. He thought about this now as they lay there.

Perhaps it was in the chaotic way that her hair lay across the pillow, or the faint freckle above her lip that he had only noticed now that their faces were laying so closely together. She was different and yet familiar. Complex. Simple. Oliver wished that he could take a photo of her to capture this moment.

He had been mildly concerned when he had seen Nelly in his bedroom that she thought him an idiot, like she clearly did the rest of the party. This in itself had surprised him, as he didn't usually care what anyone else's opinions of him were. He knew that she fancied him. It was obvious from the way that she stole glances at him and blushed whenever he spoke to her. But she, at the same time, seemed set on disagreeing with him wherever possible. He had made the comment about the prostitute knowing that it would provoke a reaction and was pleased when it had. He enjoyed the way that her eyebrows knotted into the middle of her face when he said something that she didn't agree with.

It was challenging. Provocative. He also appreciated the way that Nelly took care of his sister. From what India had told him, her relationship with Spencer had been little short of a rollercoaster. And the only thing that had stopped him from returning from Paris on several occasions had been the knowledge that Nelly Strapelli had been there to pick up the pieces. He was grateful to her for that. And also intrigued by it. Kindness wasn't something that Oliver had been particularly accustomed to.

The sun had only just risen outside of the bedroom window. It could only be four, maybe five o'clock in the morning. His head still swam slightly from the wine and the smoking from the previous hours, and he let it rest down against the warm pillow again behind Nelly's head. It didn't take him long to fall back to sleep.

The sound of laughter travelled like an arrow through the air as Oliver padded down to the kitchen later that morning. When he had awoken again at around ten, Nelly had already slipped out from between his arms, taking her corkscrew curls and blushed cheeks with her. India was sat atop the work unit, a bottle of half-drunk champagne open beside her as she laughed heartily at what someone was saying. Oliver was mildly surprised to see that it was Nelly cracking eggs into a pan in his parents' kitchen.

"Hello stranger!" India called out as Oliver entered the room. There were still wine glasses and bottles cast around, leftover from the previous night. India hopped down from the work surface and stumbled her way over to Oliver, pulling him into a tight hug and then smacking him on the arm. "It's so good to see you."

"Then what's the smack for?"

"For not coming to find me last night, of course!" She laughed and stumbled over to the kitchen table where Spencer was sat nursing a glass of what looked like whisky.

Oliver shrugged, "I was pretty tired from the journey."

"Yeah. Nelly said," India rolled her eyes. "Oh, Oliver, this is my boyfriend, Spencer."

Oliver nodded and ignored the comment. He had heard enough about Spencer over the past months to have already made up his mind that this person wasn't good enough for his sister, and this had only been solidified by the behaviour that he had witnessed from his window last night. Spencer didn't seem fazed by the lack of introduction. "I've told you not to speak so loudly," he snapped at India, "I told you; I've got a headache."

"Ah yeah. Sorry babe."

"For fucks sake. How difficult is it to not shout about everything?"

Oliver was about to say something when Nelly's voice spoke from behind the counter, "I think India can shout all that she likes on her birthday, Spencer."

"Of course you bloody do." Spencer rolled his eyes and stood up, taking his whisky with him, "I'm going for a smoke."

Oliver smiled at Nelly from across the room, and then jutted a thumb toward Spencer's shape behind the glass French-doors. "Seriously, Ind? This is the arsehole you want to waste your summer with?"

"Oh, don't you two start ganging up on me," India said, slumping onto the kitchen chair and rubbing her eyes in fatigue.

"He's right though, India. Spencer is a class dickhead." The freedom of Nelly's comment brought Oliver's eyes up to look at her. She had always seemed so shy and demure, but it was as if a tiny piece of India's confidence had seeped into her. Nelly shrugged at the stares, "You know what I think about it, Ind."

"Ugh okay, okay. Do you know, I think I preferred it when you two didn't get along." She smirked at her comment and Nelly's face quickly flushed pink.

"When didn't we get along?" Oliver addressed the question to Nelly.

"Oh. She's just being daft," Nelly shot a stern look at India who was now laughing into a bottle of champagne. "Do you want any eggs?"

"I'm good. Thanks."

"Can you do me your special French toast, Nel?" India asked, following with, "It *is* my birthday."

Nelly laughed, "Whatever you say."

"You're the best," India grinned. "I'll go and find Spencer."

Oliver and Nelly were left alone in the kitchen. They had spent the entirety of the night before just the two of them, but suddenly the proximity felt stifling. Nelly busied herself with the eggs, tapping at them with a spatula more than necessary, which Oliver knew was to avoid having to look up and expose the flush that was beginning to mottle the skin of her neck. She had changed from the previous night. The dress that she had been wearing was now replaced by a baggy t-shirt with a slogan across it that read *Save the Rhino*. Her hair was wet, as if she had just showered, and was creating tiny freckle-like droplets across her shoulders.

Oliver thought for a moment about walking behind her and leaning his face into the crook of her neck and how the warm, wet hair might feel against his cheek, but instead trod over to the fridge and pulled out a carton of orange juice. He took the opportunity of standing behind her to watch her for a moment. Now that they were standing close to one another he found himself surprised at quite how small she was. Her head barely reached the height of his chest; her feet were on tiptoes to give her a better view of the pan she was busying herself with. His eyes travelled down her figure to her legs, which were exposed by a pair of denim shorts that he was slightly surprised that she was wearing. From the rigid way that she was holding her shoulders, Oliver knew that Nelly was aware that he was watching her. But this didn't embarrass him in the slightest.

Eventually, he said, "You know, you don't have to make everyone breakfast to pay your way."

She shot a look at him over her shoulder and Oliver smiled to see her eyebrows knotting in the middle of her face. Her tension eased at the sight of his amusement and she rolled her eyes, turning back to the pan. They stood in silence like this for another couple of long minutes. It was almost as if the previous night hadn't happened and they were seeing each other again for the first time. Awkward; the ease that had somehow lubricated the previous night's conversation now dispersed. An uncomfortable tension that Oliver somehow found enjoyable. The noise of the pan sizzled like a thunder-clap amidst their silence. Eventually, India and Spencer came back into the room and broke the spell. Oliver went back to sit down at the table and Nelly brought over plates for everyone. They ate and listened as India enthralled them with her plans for the day.

Every now and again, Oliver found himself glancing up at Nelly to see her reaction to something that he had said or done, but she kept her gaze fixed permanently to her plate. He wondered why he cared suddenly for this girl's approval and then decided that it was probably the challenge. She was more self-conscious than she had been the night previous. Always tugging her shorts further down over her thighs and covering her mouth with her hand every time she gave hint of a smile. He thought about what he had called her smile last night. Disarming. He wondered if she had taken the compliment as it were meant.

"Mummy and Daddy are coming back tonight at around nine," India told them as they digested, "So they'll get to meet you then." She smiled at Spencer and rubbed his arm.

"You say it like it's a bloody treat."

India laughed and glanced up at Oliver, who made an effort not to react.

In fairness, he hadn't much been looking forward to the idea of seeing his father. For a year in Paris, he had managed to dodge the idea of any visits with his family. It wasn't that he didn't love them—indeed, he adored India and his mother very much. And he held a fondness for his father. But it was an uneasy relationship between the two of them. A dynamic that had never quite settled. The only person that made him uncomfortable in his own skin.

He found Nelly's eyes watching him when he looked up, as if trying to gauge his reaction to this news. He raised his eyebrows noncommittally and stood from his chair. "I'm gonna go for a shower."

Later that day the four of them sat in the garden together, passing the time. Oliver was opening a bottle of sparkling wine and pouring it into glasses whilst he watched the girls fuss with two deck chairs, trying to make them face toward the sun. India was telling Nelly some story which Nelly was laughing at animatedly, all of the abash that usually flooded her face forgotten whilst she was alone with her friend. He remembered how the first time that he had seen them together he had thought it an odd friendship. But now it made perfect sense.

There seemed to be a trust between them—a kinship, almost. Both Oliver and India had grown up in a world of privilege, surrounded by people who called themselves friends but secretly hoped to overthrow them on the social ladder. Nelly was a different type of person. A different breed. There was none of the competition or the falsity that India's companions usually dripped with. She was genuine. Almost bravely so. But why was Nelly interested in a friendship with India? So uneven and unpredictable. He observed that Nelly didn't cover her mouth when she laughed in front of his sister, and concluded that it must be something to do with that.

"Would you like your present now, or later?" Nelly asked India when they were sat drinking their wine.

"You got me a present?" India shot up in her chair like an exuberant child, clapping her hands together.

"It is customary on a birthday."

"Oh my God. Now. Please!" She threw Spencer a gleeful look that he didn't reciprocate.

Nelly stood up from her chair and moved back toward the house. First slowly, and then more quickly once she was out from eyeshot. Oliver glanced behind him and then reached beneath his own wooden chair, pulling out a small, wrapped parcel. He had bought the present for India months ago from a tiny boutique in Paris. It was a small present. Far more about sentimentality than taste. And, for some reason that he did not quite comprehend, he suddenly felt embarrassed about selecting it. India pulled open the package gleefully, her face full of childish happiness.

"Oh my God, Oliver!" She held the tiny bracelet up against her palm, fingering the delicate twining. When they were young, India had developed a peculiar obsession with collecting bugs. Beetles were her particular favourite. She would pluck them from their garden in Toulouse and put them under glasses, watching them crawl up the sides inquisitively. She would always let them go and then cry when they did. And so, Oliver had called her his bug. And when he had seen the gold bracelet with the bug charm, he had immediately thought of her.

"A bug for a bug," he said as he picked back up the bottle of wine.

"I love it," India gleamed, jumping up from her seat to pull Oliver into a tight hug. "Nel, did you see what Oliver got me? Isn't it lovely?"

"It's gorgeous," Nelly agreed. She pronounced it 'Gawh-jus' and it made the corners of Oliver's mouth twitch. She let her eyes flit toward Oliver as she said it and then back again to her friend, "Really sweet."

India smiled. "Oh my God, is that for me too?"

"Yeah. It isn't anything big, though. It's just…" Nelly shrugged anxiously. The blush on her cheeks was just beginning to pink.

India pulled open the paper to reveal a thin, rather dog-eared book. Nelly bit on the end of her thumb, stealing glances from beneath her eyelashes. From the expression on India's face, she already knew exactly what it was.

"You're bloody kidding me?" She looked at Nelly agog as she held the book in her hands, "Is this your one?"

Nelly nodded, her cheeks now a shade of ripe red. "No bloody way!" India grinned, leafing through the book eagerly. She looked at it as if it was nourishment, feeding her happiness. "Oh my God, Nel. This must have taken you forever!"

"What is it, then?" Spencer asked irritably.

India looked up at Nelly, almost as if for permission, and then back at Spencer. "It's a collection of poems. Nelly's favourite poems. *L'Allegria.*" She said this in a mock-Italian accent that made Nelly smile.

"Oh right."

"No. You don't get it. You see, they're in Italian. I'd always see Nelly sprawled about the house reading them over and over and over and I always said I wished that I could read them too, so as I knew what she loved about them so much. And she's translated them for me. Look." She held up the book, pulling the pages apart to reveal the wordy centre. There was small, scruffy handwriting scrawled around the edges of the pages. Oliver found himself staring at the tiny letters. The untidiness of them surprised him a bit, as if he'd subconsciously assumed that Nelly's handwriting would be an impressive cursive like his own. These notes were less the academic insights that he would have anticipated and more smatterings of consciousness. Eager. Impatient. Words he hadn't before associated with Nelly. As if she couldn't get her thoughts out onto the page quickly enough.

"It looks like a load of old tat to me," Spencer sneered, "What's wrong, Nelly? Mummy and Daddy couldn't afford to buy you a new edition?"

"Spencer!" India snapped from where she sat on the ground between them. The blush on Nelly's face began to mottle the skin of her neck like a rash. She looked down toward her knees and rubbed at the skin on the bridge of her nose self-consciously. Oliver looked at Spencer from across the circle. There was a small smirk playing on the edge of his lips, pleased at the tension that he had caused. He finished the last of his wine and dropped the glass onto the grass beneath him lazily. Oliver thought in that moment how intensely he already disliked his sister's boyfriend.

"She knows I'm only playing around, don't you, Nel." It was a statement, not a question. Nelly paused and then nodded absently, turning toward the house to avoid the eye contact that India was desperately trying to make with her. Oliver waited for a moment in the silence. Then he stretched forward and plucked the book from India's hand. Everyone turned to look at him in that moment and he suddenly wasn't sure what to do with the thin folio now that he was holding it. He felt curious about its contents, of Nelly's quips and comments, but yet it felt too personal to leaf through uninvited. So, he just sat with it in his hand for a moment. He looked up and saw Nelly's eyes upon him. "That's a really cool gift," he said finally. She smiled.

Nelly slept in his bed again that night. She had seeked him out after dinner, loitering on the front step with an unlit cigarette as if she hadn't planned on needing to light it. Oliver moved to stand next to her and pressed the bud of his burning cigarette against hers, allowing her to take several short breaths against it until hers was beginning to burn also. He stood back and leant against the wall of the house as he had been when she'd found him. He'd come outside for some time alone after his parents had arrived. They'd just come back from Cannes. They had been there for six weeks, but they hadn't made the trip to Paris to see Oliver when he was still there, even though they hadn't seen each other in over a year. Then again, Oliver hadn't made the trip either. It seemed strange to be back in such close proximity with them now after so much time apart. Claustrophobic, almost. He turned and looked at Nelly watching him from where she stood on the front step. She had changed for dinner and was wearing another of India's dresses. He had heard India insisting on it earlier on in the day. Nelly had given in, but only after much prodding. This one was slightly too big for her so as she had to keep scooping the straps back up toward her shoulders. She smiled at him, the colour in her cheeks beginning to show after the bottle of wine that they had all shared during dinner.

"I just wanted to say thanks. For being nice to me earlier," she said as if explaining herself. Oliver raised his eyebrows and she continued. "You know, when Spencer was being…"

"A twat," Oliver finished for her.

She smiled fully and Oliver noted that she forgot to hide her teeth. "Yes, a twat. A real nob, actually. But why break the habit of a lifetime?"

Oliver felt his mouth twitch into a smile. "What d'you think she likes about him?"

Nelly shrugged. "He's good-looking, I s'pose."

Oliver raised an eyebrow absently.

"I dunno. It's like he has her under some sort of spell, or something. She's blind to the fact that he's an utter cunt."

"Well, I wish she'd open her bloody eyes."

Nelly laughed lightly, as if trying to lighten the atmosphere. He turned and looked at her then. "He stares at you a lot, doesn't he?"

"Who? Spencer?"

Oliver nodded.

"Mmm. I think he hates me. I don't know why, really. Probably that I tell India what a twat I think he is every opportunity that I get," she grinned as if she was joking, but it didn't reach her eyes. She hesitated, "It's really sweet that you look out for her. I always thought you were a bit of a…"

"Go on."

She looked at him as if he was daring her. "Well, a bit of an arsehole, to be honest. You know, women flock all over you and you never seemed to give a shit."

"My famous prowess."

She rolled her eyes, pretending not to smile even though her cheeks twitched. "But you look out for India. I can tell. It's very redeeming."

"After the endless women and ill repute, you mean?"

Nelly nodded, "Exactly."

They smiled at each other and Oliver thought for a moment about trying to kiss her. She clearly liked him, but yet she was hanging back from him in a way that he wasn't used to. Protecting herself. Her strap fell down over her shoulder again and she left it there, as if she didn't notice. The skin on her shoulder was beginning to tan and Oliver found himself staring at it.

"Your parents are nice," she said finally.

Oliver nodded, putting his cigarette out under his shoe. He turned to look at her now, watching her watch him. She had an interesting colour to her eyes. Dark brown, but with a fleck of something almost black around the edges. "Do you fancy a drink?" He asked her.

She nodded.

They fell asleep together after sharing another few glasses of red wine. She had complained that India and Spencer were in India's room, and Oliver had shrugged and asked her why it mattered, as if knowing that she would stay with him anyway despite the pull-out bed that was made up in his father's study. He watched her as she slept. Her lips slightly parted. Her breaths long and deep. He gently pulled the strap of her dress back up over her shoulder and then let his hand linger there for a moment, the warmth of her body comforting against his hand.

1994
Nelly

Nelly awoke beside Oliver for the second time. He was beautiful as he slept. Even more so than he was awake, somehow. She had tried so hard not to let herself like him. Not to be one of the endless line of people that pined after Oliver Matthews. But yet here she found herself now. Curled up beside him under the quilt, his breath so close that she could feel it against her face. There was a tiny chicken pox scar underneath his left eye and she fought the urge to reach out her hand and touch it. Something about Oliver as he slept was so much more innocent than when he was awake. So much more fragile. Awake, he seemed like someone who could never care for a moment what any other person thought of him. Like an unmovable wall. Solid. Strong. But asleep, everything seemed different. Or perhaps it was just the fact that she was in his bedroom alone with him. When they were with everyone else downstairs, it was like two ships in the night. But together in this room, in this bed, it was as if there was nothing in the world that she couldn't share with him.

They had spoken for hours the night before. She had told him about her parents' restaurant and how they had always struggled for money and he had told her about his relationship with his father and how they had always struggled for closeness.

"I suppose I do with everyone, in a way," he had said.

"Everyone but India," she had corrected. He'd looked pleased about that. She had been absently resting her foot on the side of the windowsill and he had leant back and taken it into his lap. Casually. Naturally. As if he hadn't even thought about it. Being alone with Oliver was agonisingly easy in a way that Nelly had never felt with anyone else. In a way that she certainly had never felt with Henry.

Henry. Nelly's boyfriend, of sorts. The two had been seeing each other on and off for a few clumsy months. After that first encounter at The Punter, they had seen each other again at one of India's parties. Henry had asked Nelly for a date after an awkward, slightly painful kiss that had ended in him grabbing her breasts like he was juicing oranges. They had been on four dates over five months. He had left university the year before and had a full-time job in London. Which was the main excuse that they used for not seeing each other more often.

Of course, the main reason was really that Nelly wasn't very interested in Henry any more than she secretly assumed that he was with her. He was nice and funny, in a way. And India liked him. So she thought that she ought to like him also. But there was something missing. Something that Nelly couldn't quite put her finger on, but yet knew was absolutely crucial.

"At least you get a good shag out of it," India had told Nelly when she had confided in her.

Nelly had shrugged. The truth was that the sex was average at best. Not that Nelly was a particular connoisseur in the matter. But it was always awkward. Clumsy. Oddly jabbing. And Nelly was sure that something pretty fundamental was missing there, also. Something that she had never felt but yet craved almost animalistically.

She could feel it now as she watched Oliver sleep. She wondered what would happen if she crept into the crook of his shoulder and lent her face to his chest. How his skin would feel against her cheek. But she couldn't. Wouldn't. She already felt guilty about the situation, although she had no real reason to. And yet she wasn't quite sure who the guilt was directed toward. She had assumed that Oliver knew about her relationship with Henry. He had been there at the night when they had first met at the pub, after all. But he hadn't mentioned it and neither had she, not wanting to break whatever spell seemed to be sewing between them.

The noise of warm, bare footsteps on a wooden floor broke the silence of the morning just before the door clicked open and India burst into the room. "Hello sleepy heads," she sung as she hopped onto the bed, tucking herself under the quilt at the other end so as her feet were between Nelly and Oliver's torsos.

"Do you not knock?" Oliver asked irritably as he turned over, his voice thick with sleep.

India shrugged, "Why would I?" She grinned at Nelly and for a moment Nelly felt almost maternal toward her, like India was a child that had crept into bed with her parents after a bad dream. "Anyway, what do you two think about going to the beach today?"

"Mmm," Oliver responded through his pillow.

"Come on. It's glorious outside! And we could take a picnic. A couple of bottles of champagne. It sounds gorgeous, don't you think, Nel?"

"It sounds really nice," Nelly agreed.

"But?"

Nelly shrugged. "I don't really have anything to wear. I didn't realise there would be a beach."

"Can't you wear your shorts?"

"Yeah, but I mean…" she blushed awkwardly, feeling childish about not wanting to reference a swimming costume in front of Oliver.

"Oh, don't worry about that. You can borrow one of mine. Although my boobs are about ten sizes smaller than yours, so you might look a bit Pamela Anderson." She laughed and nudged Nelly's hip bone with her heel. Nelly felt her cheeks reddening. "I'm kidding. You'll look bloody gorgeous. Just like Pamela does. Oliver, what do you think? Will you join us? Come on, it'll be a good laugh."

"Will it get you to shut up?"

India looked thoughtful for a moment, "It might."

"Then fine. I'll come."

"Good. We needed you to drive!" India grinned mischievously, causing Oliver to reach up and make to swipe at her with his pillow. Nelly suddenly felt very conscious of the fact that Oliver was shirtless, his shoulder blades prominent on his back as he lent forward. He had removed his top and bottoms before getting into bed the night before so as he remained just in his underwear. He had done so absently, as if not even considering that he wasn't alone. Nelly had slept in the dress that India had lent her. But yet it had felt so intimate that she may as well have been naked. If India thought it was peculiar that her brother and her best friend were sharing a bed for the second night in a row, she didn't show it.

"Well, that's settled then. We'll leave at eleven-ish," she turned her attention to Nelly, looking pleased with herself. "Come on. Let's try on costumes."

The beach was as glorious as India had promised. She and Spencer were clearly experiencing one of their odd days of happiness, both infectiously giggling and tangling over one another at every opportunity. Spencer even laughed at one of Nelly's jokes at one point. From the outside, anyone would have suspected that they were no more than a group of friends enjoying each other's company. None wishing that any of them would leave and never return.

Nelly was wearing the swimming costume that India had lent her. It was black and plunging at the front in a way that meant that Nelly had to constantly fuss over it through the course of the day to make sure that she wasn't exposing herself.

"You look good in it, you know?" Oliver had told her when she caught him watching. He was leaning back on his elbows against the sand, his head tilted back so as he was studying her almost lazily. "You have a good body." He said it matter-of-factly, as if stating something about the weather.

"Thanks," Nelly said awkwardly.

Oliver shrugged, "I'm just saying you shouldn't be so self-conscious."

"I'm not self-conscious," Nelly lied, trying to see if there was a way of tightening the straps across her shoulders.

"Well, I wouldn't be shocked if you were."

"What's that supposed to mean?"

"It's a bit risqué for you, isn't it?" He grinned, his eyes now closed and his face pointed toward the sky. Nelly was pleased and disappointed at the same time that he was no longer watching her.

"It's your sister's," she jabbed back at him, hoping that this would cause him some embarrassment.

"Good job that you're the one wearing it and not her then, isn't it?"

She swiped a handful of sand toward him playfully and he grinned again, clearly proud of himself for ruffling her feathers.

"Can you two stop flirting and fuck already?" Spencer laughed, opening a can of beer.

"How about you fuck off?" Oliver responded lazily, not bothering to sit up.

Spencer laughed and rolled a beer toward him. He passed another to India and then held one out toward Nelly in offering, not quite close enough that she could take it without closing the gap between them. She eyed him dubiously for a moment and then bent forward on her hands and knees to take it, placing one arm over her chest to conceal her cleavage. "Oliver, I bet you wish you had the view I'm getting right now."

"Don't. You know she doesn't like things like that," India said, smacking Spencer playfully on the arm as if it had all been an innocent joke.

Nelly felt her stomach squirm and her cheeks go immediately red. She thought about responding, but found herself routed to the spot. Oliver stood up and took the beer from Spencer's hand, passing it to Nelly silently, then laid down on the sand just beside her with his eyes closed. The proximity felt reassuring, although she wasn't sure why. Nelly kept her eyes on Spencer, "Thanks."

He smiled, reaching over and pulling India onto his lap. "Well, you two had better get any shagging in over the next week before Henry makes his appearance."

Nelly looked up from her beer toward India. "Oh, Spencer! Sorry, Nel. It was supposed to be a surprise. We rang him yesterday. It was Spen's idea. Isn't that sweet? Who knew you were so thoughtful?" She nestled into the side of his face, but Spencer was still watching Nelly hungrily, eating her reaction.

"What's wrong, Nel? Are you not chuffed to be seeing your boyfriend? How long have you two been together now? Six, seven months?"

"Five," Nelly corrected. "Only just five. And I've not seen him in almost six weeks. I wouldn't really say that he's my—"

"That's exactly why I thought it would be a lovely idea for you. Four love birds under one roof. I hope you don't mind, Oliver mate?"

Oliver was quiet for a moment. "Why would I mind?"

"Well, being the spare wheel and all that. Although from what I've heard you are hardly short of women. I'm sure you'll be onto something a lot more exciting than our sensible little Nelly. No offence, Nel."

Nelly raised her eyebrows, "Course." Oliver didn't say anything but instead sat up and clicked the lip of his beer open.

"You sure you're alright, mate?"

"I honestly couldn't give a shit who Nelly's shagging, Spencer." He didn't snap. The words coated Oliver's tongue almost lazily. Nonchalant. But it still hit Nelly like a punch in the stomach. She knew that it shouldn't. She did have a boyfriend, after all. Sort of. Even if it was one that she didn't know if she really even liked very much. India knew this. The two of them had spent hours speaking about it. Nelly couldn't understand why her best friend would think it was a good idea to invite Henry to come and stay. Then again, India thought that everything that Spencer suggested was a good idea.

Henry arrived the following week. Whatever spell there had been between Nelly and Oliver seemed to have been broken in the seven days since. Whether it was because he now knew that she had a boyfriend or whether it was because she had imagined the entire charade, Nelly wasn't sure. She'd spent each night since on the futon in India's father's office, listening to the noise of India and

Spencer laughing or arguing down the hallway and inadvertently finding herself wondering whether Oliver was still awake on the floor above and whether he was sat on his windowsill looking out into the garden. One of the evenings, she had opened the window and peered up, daring herself to look. His window was open, but he wasn't there.

The next day Henry arrived. India had been beside herself with excitement, blindly taking her friend's quiet response as nerves and fussing over Nelly at every opportunity. Spencer also seemed quietly pleased with the situation. He and Henry weren't friends, but they knew one another from various parties that India had thrown and Spencer clearly felt that having Henry there would mean some sort of alliance for himself. Nelly also harboured a suspicion that Spencer was enjoying the discomfort that it was causing her to be with Henry and Oliver under the same roof. But then again, how could Spencer know this?

"So, what have you been up to over the summer, man?" Spencer clapped Henry on the shoulder as they sat down in the garden beneath the quince tree. Nelly often noticed that Spencer was like this around other men. Using terms that sounded foreign in his mouth. Desperate. He was one of them—posh, privileged—and yet she could tell that he felt like a fish out of water around them all the same. This would normally have endeared Nelly to a person, but instead it just made her dislike Spencer all the more. As if he were wearing a skin that didn't fit properly over his bones.

"Work mostly," Henry shrugged. "You know how it is."

Of course, none of them did know how it was, but they all nodded. Henry pulled the chair that Nelly was sitting on closer toward him and pinched the skin on her upper arm accidentally in doing so. "I've been working on this really stellar account lately. Very lucrative. Everyone is excited about it. I'm this close to sealing the deal," he held up two fingers to demonstrate how close he was.

Nelly moved to reach for the wine and Henry stood up automatically, plucking it from the table and filling her glass. "Of course, until then it's all corporate dinners and schmoozing the client. I tell you, if I have to hear him tell the story about how he made his first million again I might just self-combust."

"I bet you're all laughs around him though, eh mate?"

Henry grinned, "Tits and teeth!" He laughed and turned to look at Nelly, "You alright, babe? You seem quiet."

"I'm just a bit tired," she smiled weakly. "We were up late last night."

"Well, we certainly were," Spencer gestured toward India and then winked over at Henry.

"Spencer!" India giggled, rolling her eyes happily.

Henry laughed. His arm coiled over the back of Nelly's chair, feeling clunky and heavy around her neck. She wriggled forward in her seat, trying to find a more comfortable position to accommodate it. Just then, Oliver stepped out from the house and down the steps toward the garden.

"Well as I live and breathe!" Henry stood up, smacking his thighs happily, "How are you doing, mate?"

"Hey mate," Oliver smiled, padding forward over the grass toward Henry. He wasn't wearing any shoes and Nelly noticed the small streak of white just around the edges of his ankles from where his socks hadn't allowed the sun inside. Henry pulled Oliver into a hug and they tapped each other's backs jovially.

"God, it's been a bloody while, hasn't it?"

"Something like that," Oliver smiled. "How've you been?"

"Yeah good, mate. Really good. Probably not as bloody good as you, though. I heard tale of you chasing beautiful women around Paris. Or was that the other way around?"

Oliver smiled lopsidedly and moved with Henry to join the circle without actually responding. He took the seat the other side of Nelly and moved it so as it was slightly further away, his eye-line almost opposite. If he felt uncomfortable about the fact that he had shared a bed almost naked with Henry's girlfriend only nights previously, his countenance didn't show it. He sat back in his chair, placing both of his feet atop the round stone table in front of him and lit a cigarette. They sat there for the entirety of the afternoon; Henry was making everyone laugh with stories that Nelly suspicioned were half true, and India was drinking too much wine.

Eventually, after a particularly giddy fit of laughter, India said, "Nelly, why don't you show Henry where he'll be sleeping?" She eyed Nelly mischievously, raising her eyebrows into her blonde fringe. Spencer scoffed beside her as she perched atop his knee like a ventriloquist dummy. Henry raised his arms in mock fatigue, "Well I could use a kip." He winked at Nelly.

"I haven't finished my drink," Nelly said, holding her wine up to demonstrate. It was a feeble delay.

Henry plucked it from her hand and quickly downed the contents, "Ah, there you go. Problem solved." He laughed and looped his arm around her waist as she stood up awkwardly. "This way, is it?" He grinned at the group, gesturing toward the house.

Nelly showed Henry to the room where she had been sleeping for the past nights. The futon was already laid out ready for them, Nelly's bag of clothes tucked awkwardly to one side of the room. Henry held her face in his hands after closing the door, his palms warm and clammy on her cheeks. He lent down and pecked her lips firmly, the way that a grandmother might kiss a child. "I've missed you, Nel."

Nelly moved her chin downward away from him, "Yeah, me too."

Henry beamed, "Well then, shall we get you out of these wet clothes?" He started unbuttoning her blouse rhythmically.

"They aren't wet."

"Ah, don't tell a guy that," Henry laughed at his own joke.

When they had finished, Nelly sat up and put her blouse back on. She was still wearing her bra. Henry sat back against the pillows; his arm rested behind his neck as he watched her. "Hey, was that alright?"

"Yeah. Of course," Nelly replied quickly. She was lying, but Henry seemed satisfied by this. He bounced slightly against the mattress, testing the weight of it.

"Cor, this is a bit springy, isn't it? How've you been sleeping on this for two weeks?"

"Oh, it's been fine."

"Well, at least we won't be doing much sleeping for the next few days, eh?" Nelly must have looked uncomfortable, but he read her expression as disappointment, "Oh I'm sorry babe. Did you think I was staying longer? I'm sorry. It's just that I have to get back for work, you know? Woo my other girlfriend into investing all of his money in my father's firm." He grinned and rubbed the back of her shoulder as she buttoned her top back up.

"Of course. That's fine."

"Just as well really. I don't know how you've been sleeping on this every night. Although it can't have been as bad as the night that you slept with Oliver. I myself have done that more than once and for a pretty bloke, that man can snore, believe me."

Nelly's head spun toward him, "I didn't sleep with—"

He grinned, "Don't start panicking. I know nothing happened. You're my good girl. I'm just messing about."

"Oh good. Of course. Nothing happened. How did you—"

"Spencer just mentioned it. What d'you make of him, anyway? Is he always such a cunt, or is today a special occasion?"

"He's always a cunt," Nelly confirmed, "Why was he talking about me?"

Henry shrugged, "Reckon he was trying to look out for me, or something."

"Or he was trying to meddle to cause a problem."

Henry raised his eyebrows at her.

"What? He definitely doesn't like me. He makes that very obvious."

"Why d'you care? The bloke's a loser. Besides, Oliver's a mate. And I don't think you're exactly his type, anyway."

Nelly felt her heart sink in her chest. "What d'you mean?"

"Well, you know, Oliver's into that more bohemian thing, isn't he? Like his sister. Or, not like his sister, that'd be weird. You know what I mean though. Free spirited; a bit slutty; not too clever."

"India's clever."

"Of course. I just meant the bohemian thing."

"Oh yeah. Fine. Can you pass me my underwear, please?"

Henry plucked her knickers from the floor beside him and handed them over, "You know the phrase, one man's trash is another man's treasure."

"Am I the trash in this scenario?"

"You're the treasure. *My* treasure!" Henry kissed the bottom of her neck wetly, "I just mean that he probably thinks of you more as a little sister, or something."

"Yeah, probably," Nelly nodded her head. She could feel Henry watching her hungrily as she stood up to pull on her shorts, pulling her blouse down to cover the top of her buttocks as she did so. "Can you look away for a minute?"

Henry laughed, "I think it's a bit late for that." He still turned around, though. She pulled her shorts over her bottom and buttoned them quickly, suddenly feeling even more exposed than she had done naked. Henry turned back and reached, grabbing one of her bottom cheeks and squeezing slightly too firmly through the denim. "I like you in these, babe. They suit you."

"Thanks."

"A bit daring for you, aren't they? India must be rubbing off on you." Nelly moved so as she was just out from his reach. "Hey, are you in a mood?"

"No. Of course not. I just need the loo," Nelly replied, smiling weakly. Henry nodded and went back to resting against the pillow. Nelly clicked the door of the bathroom shut and counted out three minutes in her head, holding a hand towel over her mouth to muffle the sound of her crying.

1994
Oliver

Oliver wasn't sure which of the two couples were worse suited. His sister and the desperate idiot that she was dating, or Nelly and his friend from university. Both women seemed set on settling for less than Oliver thought that they deserved which, from Oliver's perspective, was a pattern that he was used to seeing in women. Nelly, his sister, his mother. All three of them too good for the man that they chose to stand beside. Not that Oliver thought himself much better than his father or Henry. He had certainly not always acted as a perfect example of how to treat women. Other men seemed to love him for it. Other women too, for that matter. He had snuck out from bedrooms, made promises that he hadn't had any intention of keeping, led girls into believing in something that wasn't there. And he never felt bad about it. But he didn't like seeing other people treating India and Nelly that way, either. His own double-standard. It wasn't that Henry was a bad person. He was a good laugh and Oliver had enjoyed his company in the time that they had spent together at university. But they had grown up and grown apart in the way that friends often do.

Oliver felt utterly baffled as to how Henry didn't appear to notice the fact that Nelly recoiled from his every touch and sunk further into her chair whenever he was near. What little light had begun to spark around her in the recent weeks seemed to be shrinking over the past days. Dimming like a bulb that's about to run out. At first, Oliver had imagined that she had just felt awkward. He and Nelly had been stoking a flirtation and she clearly fancied Oliver more than she did her boyfriend, which undoubtedly made Henry's arrival uncomfortable for her. But after a while, it seemed like there might be more to it, though Oliver wasn't certain quite what. Oliver had told himself that he didn't care about the fact that Nelly was seeing someone else; after all he had only just gotten to know her, and she definitely wasn't his usual type.

He knew that he enjoyed the challenge of her. The uncertainty of her glances. The nervous way that she chewed on the inside of her cheek when she was waiting for him to say something. But after a while that challenge developed into an interest. He found himself wanting her approval when he made a comment, or watching her from across the table, trying to read her expressions.

A certain bond had quickly begun to form between them in a way that made no sense to him, and Oliver found it brought out colours in him that he both enjoyed and loathed. Protective and yet somehow almost vulnerable. And so, when Spencer had announced that she was already taken by none other than his ridiculous friend from university, he had pretended to himself that this news hadn't annoyed him. That the only reason he had been slightly interested in her was the lack of other women around. And maybe this was partially true. But yet since the news, he had found himself changing his countenance in her presence. Deliberately avoiding her gaze during conversations and pulling back to his usual self. Unanchored. Untied.

This didn't mean that he didn't still notice her. The blush on her neck that she tried to hide with clunky jumpers, despite the heat of the summer. The way that she rubbed the lipstick on her lips on the back of her hand until it almost disappeared as if she were embarrassed to have put it there. Or the way that she prolonged the evening as long as possible each night since Henry's arrival, sipping on her wine slowly until it was completely drained, as if she was trying to put off going to bed. He noticed things about Nelly that he wasn't sure anyone else did. Even India. He found himself oddly concerned about her. And so, he was glad when India had announced that she and Nelly would be going on a girls day.

"We need some best friend time," India explained as she kissed Spencer's cheek in the garden.

"Is that what you're going to wear?" He asked, pulling at the hem of her dress.

"Yeah. Why, don't you like it?"

"You just look like a fucking stripper, that's all."

"You look gorgeous," Nelly had corrected, eyeing Spencer territorially.

"Thanks," India had said quietly. When they had left, she'd already changed into a pair of jeans.

"You the jealous type then, Spenny?" Henry clapped Spencer on the shoulder as Spencer pulled a chair up to sit beside Oliver and Henry in the garden. The two of them had been sharing a joint and Oliver felt the nerve in his jaw twitch as Spencer reached over to take it from him.

"She's a good-looking girl. I'm just looking out for her," he replied simply.

"She's definitely gorgeous," Henry laughed, looking at Oliver and adding, "Sorry, mate."

Oliver raised his eyebrows back at Henry, "Fancy a beer?"

"Cheers, mate," Spencer replied. Oliver clenched his teeth together a bit too hard, hearing a ringing in his ears as he did so.

"She does have a good pair of tits," Spencer was saying as Oliver walked back out into the garden with the drinks. Oliver glared at him and he finished, "Nelly, I mean."

Oliver put the beers down in front of them and pulled the cap off from his own, tossing the bottle opener onto the table.

"Yeah, I don't have any complaints," Henry grinned.

"Come on, Oliver. You must have noticed. I saw you staring at them at the beach the other day," Spencer grinned, cupping hands in front of his chest demonstratively.

"She's Henry's girlfriend," Oliver replied, feeling suddenly irrationally irritable.

"Well, sort of girlfriend," Henry replied. Spencer ignored him, responding to Oliver.

"Since when's that ever stopped you?"

Oliver clenched. "What d'you think my sister would say if she heard you saying that about her best mate?"

Spencer shrugged, "What she doesn't know won't kill her. Besides, I'm saying Nelly has good tits. Not telling her to sleep in my bed." He let his gaze linger on Oliver's for a moment challengingly and Oliver held it until Spencer was forced to look away. He had known that Spencer had told Henry about he and Nelly sharing a bed the first nights that she was there. Henry didn't seem to care though, which Oliver wasn't sure if meant that he didn't care about Nelly or didn't think that Oliver would be interested in her. Either option irritated him, although he knew that it shouldn't.

Oliver already disliked Spencer before he had met him. India had given her relationship glowing reviews every now and then over the phone when they had spoken about it, but Oliver had noticed that they were few and far between. He had asked her once what Nelly thought of him, her being India's closest ally, and

India had gone uncharacteristically quiet. That was the first time that Oliver knew he that Spencer was bad news. He was glad for that reason also when India had said that she and Nelly were spending the day alone. Spencer seemed to have a strange interest toward Nelly that Oliver didn't understand. He clearly loathed her, and yet he went out of his way to bring her name up in every conversation, or to seek her gaze when they were sat in a group. Oliver wasn't sure whether it was attraction or hatred or something more sinister. Spencer seemed threatened by Nelly's relationship with India as if it were a competition; Oliver wasn't certain which of the two Spencer was competing for, though.

No, Oliver did not like Spencer. He spoke and acted to other people, especially Oliver's sister, in a way that made Oliver want to crawl out from his skin. But Spencer's behaviour was never far enough out of line for Oliver to outwardly remark upon. Oliver knew plenty of men like Spencer and, besides, India was the type of girl that fell in love at the drop of a hat. She always had been. He was sure that this relationship wouldn't last long. It was just his bad luck that Spencer was lasting long enough for Oliver to have to spend another afternoon sharing his joint with him.

The girls walked back up the lawn that evening arm in arm, speaking closely into each other's ears as if sharing sweet nothings. Every now and then India said something that made Nelly smile and she only remembered to bring her hand to her mouth when Henry walked over to greet her.

"I'm afraid I'm going to have to steal this one for a little longer, Henry," India told him musically before he could get to her, steering Nelly away toward the stone steps. Spencer smouldered irritably and lit another cigarette, chewing on the bottoms of his cheeks. Oliver wished that Nelly and his sister would come back to the garden just so as he had a reason to get up and leave. But he also wanted them to stay away. The noise of India laughing loudly sung out from the bedroom window above them and Oliver saw Spencer tense at it.

"What d'you think they're laughing about?"

Oliver shrugged, neither knowing nor caring. He was studying the stone wall at the edge of the garden and thinking about the many afternoons that he had spent sat there. It was perfectly obscured by the quince tree so as it was out of sight from his father's office. He hadn't sat there in a long while.

"It'll just be girl talk, mate," Henry grinned. "They're probably comparing the size of our cocks or something." Spencer scowled and Henry laughed and smacked him on the shoulder. Shortly, Spencer stood up and stalked back into the house.

Henry waited until he was out from earshot and then caught Oliver's eye. "Cor, he's a bit hard going, isn't he? I was only having a laugh about the cock thing, but he seemed genuinely peeved. Don't you think?"

Oliver raised his eyebrows and nodded weakly. Henry seemed satisfied, "Bloody hell, mate. I don't know what your sister sees in him."

Oliver shook his head, still looking at the wall. "He's a twat."

Henry grinned, seemingly pleased that they were back on familiar terms. He lent closer in, "So then, mate, what d'you think about Nelly? She seems a bit off, doesn't she? A bit moody, I mean."

"I hadn't noticed."

Henry didn't seem to care about the response. He continued, "I was a bit concerned that she'd figured it out, you know? About Milly."

"Who's Milly?"

Henry shrugged, pretending to be blasé, "Oh, just this girl I've been seeing back in London. You'd like her. Smashing tits. Anyway, I was beginning to think that Nelly had cottoned on. She's been a bit off with me over the last couple of days."

Oliver took in a breath of nicotine and held it, "Why d'you care if you're seeing this other girl anyway?"

"Well, that's the thing. This other girl, Milly, well she's just a bit of fun. A lot of fun, if you know what I mean. But I just can't have Nelly finding out. Not now that things with her are just getting interesting. Did you see her in those shorts the other day? I think India's finally rubbing off on her," he laughed. "Anyway, d'you reckon you might be able to find out for me? Ask India if she's mentioned anything."

"Are you seriously asking me to spy on your girlfriend?"

"Come on, mate. You owe me. Remember that morning with Alissa and that other blonde? Hmm. Who helped you out then?"

Oliver rubbed his face. He suddenly felt tired. "Yeah, sure. Whatever."

Henry beamed, "Cheers mate. Hey, d'you fancy another beer?"

Oliver had no intention of asking his sister what was wrong with Nelly and whether it was to do with Henry. Just watching the two of them over the past days was enough for Oliver to know that Nelly's displeasure with Henry's visit had less to do with a burning secret and everything to do with the fact that she clearly didn't like him very much. He doubted however that she knew about the other girl that Henry was seeing, otherwise he was certain that India wouldn't have invited Henry to stay with them. Oliver pondered the idea of telling Nelly about Henry's indiscretion, but then thought better of it. After all, the two of them weren't really friends. And she had slept in his bed for two nights without even mentioning that she had a boyfriend. He was sure that, had he tried to, he could have kissed her. So, did that make her any better than Henry, really?

He thought about this that night as the five of them sat beneath the quince tree once more, drinking red wine and listening as India laughed loudly at a story that Henry was telling, her legs dangling over Nelly's as she perched merrily on the arm of her friend's chair. There were other seats vacant, but India seemed to want to be close to Nelly this evening. Every now and then she bent down to whisper something in Nelly's ear and they both shared long expressions that almost seemed like another language. Oliver felt certain that India was doing it on purpose, shielding Nelly from Henry as much as she could without actively warding him off. He found himself feeling pleased about it.

"What did you two do today?" Spencer asked loudly, throwing a cigarette butt towards India's bare calf. It missed.

"Oh you know, girl stuff," India smiled.

"See, mate?" Henry grinned at Spencer in an I-told-you-so fashion; his voice lifted slightly patronisingly as if he were reassuring a child. Spencer bristled.

"This wine's a bit shit, isn't it?" he stated coldly.

"Oh really? You don't like it? It's one of Dad's. It's supposed to be good."

"So now I don't know anything about wine?"

"No, that's not what I meant."

The group sat quietly as India and Spencer spoke. Oliver swilled the wine around his mouth slowly. It was a good wine. All of his father's collection was. If he could have been bothered, he might have told Spencer this. Offered the idea of Spencer fucking off and leaving his parents' house and his sister's bed. Offered the idea of him fucking off altogether. But as it stood, he had just about reached his limit of Spencer and his sister's bickering over the past weeks. He had already made plans with friends for the rest of the summer. He just needed to get through the next few days.

"Are there any others?" Spencer asked.

"I mean, yeah. I put a white in the fridge."

"Why wouldn't you bring that out as well?"

"Sorry?"

"It's a warm evening. I'm just saying, it's a bit poor of you to not have thought that someone might prefer the white. That's all."

"I'm sure you know where the fridge is by now Spencer," Nelly replied. Her voice was smooth and even, but so much so that it was as if her calmness was at an effort.

Spencer regarded her serenely, "You're right." He still remained sat on his seat, staring at the two of them.

"I'll go and get it for you," India said finally, getting up from the chair and moving past them over the lawn toward the house. Spencer watched her as she went and curled his lip over his teeth as if she had offended him. Henry lit another cigarette and they sat in silence, Nelly angling her body away from Spencer and slightly toward Oliver, so as he could see the mottled red rash that was beginning to tickle up her neck despite her outward poise.

"You're drinking a lot tonight, Nelly," Spencer said, regarding Nelly boldly from his seat. He was slouched off of it almost nonchalantly, his legs spread wide enough that he could trip someone that walked past.

Nelly raised her eyebrows but didn't bother looking at him.

"Oi, I'm talking to you," Spencer said, throwing a wine cork at her head. It missed her and landed by her feet. She breathed quietly through her nose and then turned her face to regard Spencer passively, the two of them holding eye contact as he brought his wine glass to his lips and took a long sip.

"I thought you didn't like the wine," Nelly remarked evenly.

"Clever," Spencer replied.

"Now, now, you two," Henry laughed, leaning forward and topping up his wine.

"Oh, we're just playing. Aren't we, Nel?"

Nelly smiled briefly back at Spencer, not letting it touch her eyes. India walked back over to the circle with the bottle of white in her hands, placing it down on the table in front of Spencer and then dragging a chair over to sit beside him. Nelly adjusted herself on her own seat as Spencer drained the contents of his glass and filled it with the new wine. India waited until he was finished and then picked the bottle back up from the table, standing up and going over to refill everyone else's glasses.

"Oops, not too much for Nelly," Spencer slurred from his seat.

"Why?" India asked, directing the question at Spencer.

"He's just being a twat," Nelly said to her glass. Henry laughed.

"What was that?" Spencer asked.

"Nothing," India replied quickly.

"I said you were being a twat," Nelly told him plainly. Oliver could see the rash beginning to travel down her throat.

Spencer raised an eyebrow, "Careful, Nelly."

Nelly rolled her eyes and turned her attention to the sleeve of her cardigan, tugging at a loose strand of wool.

"Is she always like this when she drinks?" Spencer shot toward Henry.

Henry smiled, "I quite like it when she gets fiery."

Oliver could see the rash spreading across Nelly's temples, her teeth clenching behind her lips.

"I bet," Spencer laughed, spreading his legs further apart. He watched Nelly for a moment and then said, "It probably loosens her up, doesn't it, a bit of drink. Wouldn't be the first time someone's found that, would it, Nelly?"

"Huh?" Henry replied.

"Spencer," India said nervously, her smile wavering. Henry leant forward in his chair. Spencer looked pleased with the commotion that he was causing, a smirk playing on the edges of his wine-stained lips. He cleared his throat, his eyes still locked onto Nelly's obscured profile, "Well, I mean after the whole sexual assault thing. That's what she likes to call it, at least."

"Spencer."

"Oh, Nelly doesn't mind my saying. We're all good mates here."

"Sexual assault thing?" Henry asked, forgetting his cigarette in his fingers.

"Yeah, you know? That time in Clacton when some lad put himself in Nelly without her saying he could. Although, you had had one too many shandies, hadn't you, Nel?" He laughed into his glass. Oliver could see the rise and fall of Nelly's chest beneath her jumper.

"Nel, I—" India began.

"Oh fuck. Was that a secret?" Spencer interrupted.

"What the fuck. Hang on. What do you mean someone raped you? When was this?" Henry asked, finally turning his gaze to his girlfriend. Nelly was silent.

"Like five years ago, wasn't it Nelly?" Spencer replied.

"Five years ago. And what, they fully raped you?"

"Henry, drop it," India said, her face paling.

"They just fingered her," Spencer shrugged impassively.

Henry looked relieved, "Oh, well thank God for that."

"What?" India shot.

"Well, it's hardly getting raped, is it? Not properly, I mean."

India bit down on her bottom lip, strangling a response.

"I'm just saying, it isn't that bad. It's not like she'd never done it before."

"Na. It would have just been a normal Friday for India," Spencer laughed.

"Shut your fucking mouth." Oliver heard the words leave his mouth before he'd realised that he'd said them. He dragged his eyes away from Nelly, who seemed to be rooted to her chair.

"Right, right. Sorry, mate," Spencer laughed, "I forget she's your sister."

"I'm not your fucking mate, mate," Oliver spat. He could feel the adrenaline pumping in his chest, filling his throat like warm bile, ringing in his ears.

"Calm down," India said nervously, "Everyone's had too much to drink, probably. Spencer, just say sorry to Nelly."

"For what?"

"For upsetting her!"

"He hasn't upset me," Nelly's voice spoke out suddenly. It was calm and even, despite her addressing it toward the ground.

"Nel—"

"*He* could never upset me," Nelly said, this time bringing her eyes up to meet Spencer's lurid gaze, "I would never give him the power." There was silence for a moment and then Nelly stood up from her chair. Oliver could see the imprints from the plastic on the backs of her thighs as she tugged her jumper down over her shorts, walking away from the group.

Oliver found Nelly later sat on his wall beneath the quince tree. She was sitting with her back to him, her curled head lulling against her left shoulder. Oliver had spotted her from his bedroom window. For about an hour, he'd watched her silently, chewing over the idea of going to her. He was still cross with her about the situation with Henry. But yet every fibre of him suddenly wanted to be by her side, pulling him toward her. Now that he was there, he wasn't even sure what to say. After a long moment, he allowed his trainers to crunch over the gravel toward her, easing himself gently up onto the wall so as his legs flopped over the other side.

When he'd been young, he used to let his legs swing out in front of him as he sat there, but now he could almost touch the ground on the other side. Nelly's legs were crossed in front of her, looped together by her ankles as she stared out at nothing. Goose-skin puckered the flesh of her thighs and Oliver had to tell himself to look away.

Neither of them said anything for a long moment. But then Nelly's voice spoke, "Do you think it's supposed to be this hard?"

Oliver turned his eyes toward her. He wondered if he should ask what she meant, but really, he already knew. He breathed in through his nose and then said, "No. Probably not."

Nelly nodded. The rash that had mottled the skin of her face earlier that day had faded, leaving the usual smooth skin of her cheek. Oliver wanted to reach out and stroke it and feel the warmth of her. He put his hand in his pocket.

There was silence for a moment and then Oliver said, "He's a real cunt. Spencer, I mean."

Nelly smiled toward her shoes, "Yeah. No change there."

Oliver nodded. He could feel the words curling over his tongue, wishing to be said. "I'm sorry that happened to you."

"Oh, it's okay. Spencer does that sort of thing a lot, trying to feel like he has something to hold over me."

"I meant the thing in Clacton," the words sounded useless as soon as they left his mouth.

Nelly paused for a moment, her body frozen still, and then loosened again and nodded.

"Did you tell anyone about it? At the time."

Nelly breathed through her nose and then let out a sigh through parted lips. She'd brought her gaze up to focus on the field in front of them, now blanketed in shadows. She looked pensive for a moment and Oliver wanted to break the silence, but then thought better of it. Sometimes, people just needed the time.

After a while, she said, "Do you know that feeling when you drop a glass and it smashes on the floor? That pit in your stomach when you realise that it's going to break?" Oliver watched her, but didn't reply. "And in the moment, it's scary and horrible and you feel like there's nothing you can do to stop it once it's started happening. And then afterward you feel sad and clumsy and somehow a bit ashamed that you've smashed the glass. Nobody else's glass got smashed. Maybe you should've dried your hands more thoroughly or maybe you gripped too hard. And by that time, it feels like there's nothing you can do about it anyway. Anyone you do tell says that it doesn't matter; it was just a glass. And even though it makes you want to throw up, you wonder if you have exaggerated it in your own mind somehow. So, you just clear up the mess and wash the blood off from your fingers and hope nobody notices. That nobody realises that it broke you a little bit."

She was speaking matter-of-factly, as if she really were speaking about a broken cup. As if she were numb to the pain, somehow. But he could tell that it was still there. The scar. Oliver nodded calmly, despite the fury searing up again inside of his chest. He could almost see the redness of it behind his eyelids. He felt angry. So irrationally angry. The fact that a man could hurt someone else like that—that someone had hurt Nelly—made him feel sick. The idea of a man touching her and forcing themselves inside of her made him want to tear away his own skin. He felt like he could kill whoever had done this to her in that moment. That the rage searing inside of his stomach could burn them both alive. He wanted to tell her that she wasn't broken. That she was beautiful and clever and kind and strong and that nothing that had happened to her was because of her.

But something inside of him, whether it was the rage or the fear that he was feeling, stopped him from doing so. After a long moment, he reached up and shrugged his jacket off from his shoulders. He hesitated for a moment and then leant over, draping the fabric over Nelly's bare legs. He let his hands linger there for just a moment and then retracted them. She smiled down at the place where they had been. The two of them sat like that for a while in silence; Nelly staring down at her feet and Oliver battling with the anger inside of his chest. That was the first moment that Oliver realised that he might have loved her.

1996
Nelly

"I'm telling you, Leo, it will fucking fit!" India's voice was clipped and irritable as the four of them tried without luck to shove the suitcases into the old mini-cooper. It was August and extremely hot as they stood outside of the Aeport de Marseille, the two o'clock sun beating down on Nelly's exposed shoulders. She could already feel the heat of it burning her skin in that beautiful, slightly painful way that she had come to love this summer. They had been travelling, she and India with their friends, Leo and Thomas. The trip had been India's idea, obviously. She had presented them all with it one afternoon at their flat as they trawled through past exam papers. Of course, the other three all came from money and had jumped at the opportunity.

Nelly, on the other hand, had to use what was left of her student loan and also borrow a small chunk from her parents. They had done it 'on the cheap', getting the least expensive train tickets that they could find and staying in grotty hostels, drinking cheap wine and eating cheap noodles. She had felt nervous about the money up until the plane had first taken off from Heathrow airport. But then something wonderful had happened and, for the first time in a long time, Nelly had felt all of her worries somehow melt away. So far, they had been to Amsterdam, Berlin, Prague, Madrid and Barcelona. Now, they were on their way to Provence.

"I cannot tell you how much I can't wait to see the pool," India said through gritted teeth as she shoved the back end of her suitcase into the back seat of the car.

"I can't tell you how much I can't wait to see a shower," Leo laughed, his smile lopsided against his cheek.

"Yeah. I can't wait for you to, either," India chirped, nudging him with her flip flop.

They all laughed as the case finally slid into the back seat, the car dipping slightly under the weight of all of their luggage. "How're we all gonna bloody fit?" Thomas asked, peering in via the exposed window.

"Fuck knows," Leo said, shaking his head. "Who's driving?"

"I can!" Thomas said quickly, plucking the keys from Leo's hand. He opened the front door and folded his long limbs inside, his knees almost touching the steering wheel. "Bloody hell, India. Can the cases not go somewhere else? I can't even push back the seat!"

"We're just going to have to have a bit of a squeeze for about twenty minutes, okay? It won't be half as bad as that brothel you guys made us stay in in Germany." India wrinkled her nose as if to punctuate her point.

"Seriously though, Ind. Where are we all gonna go?"

India rolled her eyes, "Just get in and stop your complaining, would you? Honestly, it's only gonna be a few minutes and I didn't see either of you offering to arrange the transport. Besides, this is stylish."

"Yeah, for a clown car," Leo smiled at Nelly comradely from out the passenger window. Nelly smiled and raised her eyebrows back, all too aware of what India's idea of a few minutes would likely turn out to be.

"Erm excuse me. What do you think you're doing in the front?"

"What d'you mean?"

India folded her arms over her chest, "I'm the one that knows the way, remember?"

"Oh bloody hell, India. I'm never gonna fit in the back!" Leo gestured toward the rear of the car where the majority of the two seats was taken up by the rucksacks and various luggage.

"Well, you're lucky Nelly is about two inches wide, aren't you?" India said, reaching forward and tugging open the passenger door, "Come on. Out with you. Thomas needs my flawless exploration skills."

"Exploitation skills, more like," Leo replied, rolling his eyes. Nelly grinned widely when India smacked Leo on the bottom as he moved around from the car. Leo laughed and opened the door, saying to Nelly, "Come on then. Master's orders."

"Cheers," Nelly replied. She stepped forward and ducked her head under the roof of the car, already feeling the heat from inside radiating out toward her. "Bloody hell, Ind. There really isn't a lot of room."

"Oh, not you as well. You're supposed to be on my side!"

The suitcase that India had forced into the vehicle was taking up the majority of the back seat, leaving just enough room spare for one set of legs to somehow contort themselves inside. "D'you mind if I just sit on your lap?" Nelly asked Leo over her shoulder.

"At this point, I'd strap myself to the roof if it got us to civilisation any more quickly," Leo replied, before grinning and throwing a wink in Nelly's direction. She backed out from the door and let him move past her, folding himself inside on the seat behind India.

"Fuck, the seats are boiling," Leo said, squirming on the leather as if he had just sat on needles.

"Oh, stop complaining. We'll be there soon and you can take those smelly shoes off and jump in a nice cold pool."

"There'd bloody better be a pool," Leo said under his breath to Nelly as she eased herself onto his lap, pulling the door carefully shut beside his knee. Nelly laughed.

"Right then. All present and correct?" India asked authoritatively over her shoulder.

"Yes, Mum," Nelly replied, flicking her friend's ear. India grabbed Nelly's fingers and kissed the top of her hand quickly.

"Okay then. Off we go please, driver."

"Right. Okay," Thomas responded dubiously, turning the keys in the ignition. The car started with a slow gurgle, groaning under the weight of the four of them.

"What time is it?" India asked.

"Twenty past two," Leo responded from behind Nelly's ear.

"Oh fuck. I told Oliver we'd be there at one."

Nelly felt the familiar twitch in her stomach at the mention of Oliver's name. It had been a year since she'd seen him last. Since the summer that she had spent at India's house, things had changed considerably. Unsurprisingly, Nelly and Henry had broken up. He had called things off just after the holiday at India and Oliver's house. He had seemed indifferent. Nelly had felt relieved momentarily and then hadn't felt anything at all, as if it had never happened. More surprisingly, India and Spencer had finally broken up too. At first, Nelly had assumed it was one of their regular tear-filled tirades and that it wouldn't last, but India seemed set on her decision and for once seemed to have stuck to her word.

The other thing that had happened was that Nelly and Oliver had become friends. She wasn't sure whether it was her that had reached out toward him or Oliver toward her, but somehow, they had both seemed to of gravitated toward one another in some inexplainable way. It had begun when he'd sent her a postcard from Lyon one day, where he had been on holiday. It had a picture of a black cat on the front with scruffy, fluffy dark hair and he had simply written on the blank side, *Reminded me of you.*

She wasn't even sure why it had reminded him of her really, or how she had known that it was from him. And yet somehow, she understood it all as easily as if it were her own name. They'd begun like that, sending one another silly pictures of animals and grotesque artworks; cats wearing bonnets or naked statues with oddly small or large genitalia. It had been very un-Oliver like. And yet it wasn't at all. After some time, they'd begun to write each other small letters on the backs of the cards. Letters that grew and swelled and then petered back down from time to time. Letters about what they were doing or what they were thinking, or about how badly Oliver hated the work at his dad's company. They felt almost like diary entries. Tiny snippets inside a relationship that had somehow begun to bloom without reason.

Nelly wasn't sure why, but she'd kept all of their correspondence hidden. They weren't secret, per se. And she was certain that India would think them either adorable or just utterly nondescript. But yet Nelly still hadn't wanted to share them. As if by keeping them just between she and Oliver, they could mean whatever the two of them wanted them to mean. As full of or empty of importance as they needed the letters to be. Now, with the prospect of seeing Oliver in the skin only hours away, the letters suddenly felt both ridiculous and weighty on Nelly's chest all at once. She fidgeted on the seat, her stomach churning beneath her vest.

"You alright?" Leo asked her from behind her ear.

"Yeah just… uncomfy," Nelly replied.

"You're telling me!" Nelly could hear the smile in Leo's voice from behind her. They had become close, the four of them. They had met during a team project at university. Leo and Thomas were living together on campus, both English students, and they had met in their American literature class. Nelly had liked Leo immediately. He had a kindness to him that made him seem almost vulnerable. Thomas was great, too. When they'd planned the trip, Nelly had worried silently that Thomas and Leo would think it some sort of hook-up opportunity. However, nothing of the sort had happened. Partly down to the fact that they had become good friends and none of them seemed to want to cross the boundary, and partly because it turned out that Leo was gay.

India and Thomas stoked a flirtation, but nothing had come of it so far. Nelly found herself hoping for India's sake that it might one day, if not right now. Thomas was nice. And kind. And protective of them in a way that was almost brotherly, as opposed to the possessive way that Spencer used to behave. But still, she was glad that it hadn't so far. She knew how India could be with men, after all, and she wasn't ready for the friendship to be ruined yet. Even though she felt guilty for secretly feeling that way about her best friend.

"Is your brother there on his own?" Thomas asked as he steered the car toward the busy dual carriageway.

"Mmm? Oh yeah. But I think he has his girlfriend there with him a lot," India replied lazily, turning a map around in her hands as if it might help with her comprehension, "You need to take the fourth exit."

Oliver's girlfriend. That was another reason why Nelly was nervous. She'd known that Oliver had a girlfriend for a couple of months, since India had mentioned it after being on the phone to him one afternoon. If it was strange that Oliver had never mentioned his girlfriend to Nelly, she had tried to not allow herself to fantasise about why he may not have. They were friends, certainly, but there was a sort of unspoken rule between them. As if there was some sort of illusion that could be broken if the other allowed it to be so. Or maybe Nelly had just imagined that. Now, faced with the prospect of seeing both Oliver and his beau in the next sixty-plus minutes, Nelly felt as if the insides of her stomach were squirming against her rib cage.

The sun beat down on them through the open window as Thomas drove the car along the winding country road toward the house where Oliver was spending the summer. The wind, hot and dry, beat against Nelly's face sending tendrils of loose dark curls across her forehead as she stared out the window. The house had a cobbled face and was made up of what looked like one level, with a curving stone staircase curling around the side of it toward a garden where a figure was stood, looking out at them with a hand cupped over their eyes, shielding the sun.

"Here we are! See. It wasn't too far, was it?" India beamed at Nelly over the headrest with all of the excitement of a child visiting a funfair.

"Yeah. Not too far," Nelly smiled back in agreement.

"Bloody hell, Ind! It's certainly better than the hostels, isn't it? Your dad's company certainly pays well."

"Thank Christ for that," Leo muttered behind Nelly's ear, making her laugh.

The figure at the top of the stairs stared out at them as the car pulled to a halt on the dry-earth driveway, making a small screech of protest as Thomas pulled up the hand-break. Nelly could see Oliver more clearly now. He was leaning against the face of the house, supposedly watching them from underneath dark sunglasses. As India pulled open the door and called out to him, he lifted the bottom of his shirt to wipe his brow revealing a tanned strip of stomach just above his belt.

"Oliver!" India beamed, bouncing out from the car and toward her brother.

"I guess we're getting the bags, then?" Thomas laughed, winking at Leo and Nelly.

"No change there!"

"Heya, Bug," Oliver smiled as India threw her arms around him. Nelly watched as Oliver reciprocated the embrace, picking his sister up slightly so as her toes dangled just above the ground. It reminded Nelly of the way that her dad used to hug her when she was small.

"Hey, mate. I'm Thomas." Oliver extended a hand to shake Thomas's offering, smiling at him from beneath his glasses. His faced looked more relaxed—easier, somehow—than when Nelly had last seen him.

"Hey, mate. Nice to meet you."

"And this is Leo and Nelly," Thomas introduced them politely as he slung a rucksack over his shoulder.

"Umm I think I can handle the introductions, Tommy." India prodded Thomas's rib lightly, a smile playing on her lips. "Besides, Oliver doesn't need introducing to my Nelly. She's practically his second little sister by now!" India stroked Nelly's arm as she glided past back toward the car to help Thomas with the bags. Leo raised an eyebrow at Nelly and then shook Oliver's hand before turning to help. Oliver moved to the car to join them, plucking a rucksack out and hoisting it over one shoulder.

"Oh, you don't need to—" Nelly began to say, but Oliver shook his head.

"It's fine," he smiled at her and then moved to stand just in front of her, "Anyway, hi."

"Hi," Nelly replied weakly, not really sure what to say. Now that they were together in real life, it was almost as if she were seeing him again for the first time. She suddenly felt very aware of the thin coating of sweat that was beginning to cling to her upper lip, or the way that her armpits smelled beneath her deodorant. Oliver stepped closer forward, closing the gap between them, and bent down to kiss her cheek.

"Hi," he said again, smiling at her. He was close enough that she could smell him. Tobacco and lemon mixed with something sweet and familiar.

"Oh shit!" A voice behind them said, breaking the spell. Nelly turned around to find India clutching a bottle of green liquid in her hand, Thomas and Leo both doubling over in varying degrees of cheek-splitting laughter beside her. "The shampoo exploded!"

Nelly watched from a cool stone seat in the garden as Oliver's outline shadowed around the window from the kitchen of the house. They had been there for a few hours now. He had given them a short tour when they had first entered. There were two bedrooms and a pull-out bed in the living room, then a small, rustic orange kitchen that split into a larder behind a beaded curtain. Oliver explained that he'd been staying at the house on vacation, renting it from someone at his dad's office. Nelly noticed the easy way that Oliver moved around the place and felt somehow jealous and happy at the same time, though she wasn't quite sure what about. He'd shown them all where the bathroom was soon after and they'd taken turns going in and washing themselves for what had felt like the first time in weeks.

When it had been Nelly's turn, she had twisted the dial down so as the water was tepid, easing herself in and then angling her face toward the weak downpour so as liquid trickled welcomingly over her skin. There was a bar of yellow soap placed on the bottom of the shower, breeding soapy white water around it. Nelly picked it up and smelled it, her mind wandering for a moment as she imagined Oliver rubbing the soap across his own body. When she had finished, she dried herself on the coarse pink towel that India had laid out over the toilet seat for her and then dressed again in fresh clothes in the bathroom. Now, sat on the cool seat in the garden just a couple of hours later, her hair was just beginning to curl and crisp against her bare shoulder.

India was sat beside Thomas on a similar seat, her pink cheeks flushing with the wine and the warmth. Nelly noticed Thomas's hand lingering around the back of her chair, brushing softly against the nape of India's neck whilst he watched her speak. It really was a surprise that the two of them hadn't gotten together yet.

"I'm telling you; I'd rather marry Mr Bingley!" India laughed over her glass of wine.

"You bloody liar," Leo jibed across the table as he refilled their glasses, "You above anyone else would marry Darcy."

"I would not!"

"Whatever you say, gorgeous," Thomas said, shaking his head. He reached forward to pick up his glass, "Go on then, Nel. What about you?"

"Mmm?"

"Who'd you rather, Bingley or Darcy?"

Nelly swallowed a gulp of wine, feeling the warmth of it in her cheeks. Without hesitation, she replied, "Darcy."

"Yes! Exactly," Leo applauded.

"Oh, Nel!"

"I know. I know," Nelly grinned at India, who had somehow managed to wriggle closer into Thomas's palm. "Okay. We all know we should want to marry Bingley. But in reality, we'd pretty much all end up with Darcy. Or George Wickham."

"You aren't wrong about Wickham," Leo nodded, pointing his glass toward Nelly. "That sexy scoundrel."

"What is it with women and the brooding, mysterious types?" Thomas said, shaking his head in mock disbelief.

"You'll never know," India jibed, causing him to grin at her like a chimp. India giggled, "Fine. Do you know what. On second thoughts, I'd take Elizabeth."

"Elizabeth?"

"Oh, you'd be the talk of the town!" Leo gasped, covering his mouth playfully.

"I should bloody hope so."

Nelly laughed along as India continued her rant. It was so nice to see her friend back to herself again. Glorious, actually. She wondered when the last time was before this summer that she'd seen India truly smile and then thought sadly that she wasn't sure she ever had. Which was a shame. She had the most contagious smile.

At some point when Nelly somehow hadn't noticed it, a body materialised beside her carrying a plate of meats and breads.

"Everyone alright for drinks?" Oliver asked breezily, placing the plate down on the table in front of them all. Without asking, he picked up the bottle of wine and topped up Nelly's glass before filling his own and sitting down beside her. She smiled at him and immediately felt the heat moving up the edges of her neck, creeping toward her cheeks.

"Really, cheers for having us here this week, mate," Thomas said, inching himself just far enough away from India's shoulder so that it didn't look as if she were falling into his lap.

Oliver smiled just enough so as the edge of his mouth twitched upward. "Pleasure," he said simply. He had taken his sunglasses off now and Nelly noticed the small white lines around the edges of his blue eyes where the sun had hit him. He stretched back easily in his chair, bringing his leg up to rest on top of his other one and Nelly saw a bare strip of lighter skin between his shoe and his ankle.

"Oliver, did I tell you about the place we stayed in Berlin?" India beamed across the circle.

"Oh, bloody hell," Thomas smiled, shaking his head, "It wasn't that bad."

India jabbed him gently on the leg, "That's the fib of the century. Honestly, Oliver, you'd have died. It was disgusting. The bed that Nelly slept in actually had blood stains on it!"

"Probably from that guy she murdered," Leo toyed from the other side of her. He tapped her knee gently with his thigh and she smiled.

"Yep. Another country, another killing spree." The group laughed and she quickly felt embarrassed, as if she might have spoken out of turn or too casually. Without thinking, she turned toward Oliver to see his reaction and found that he was smiling at her. Not completely, but just enough so as the edges of his eyes crinkled in a way that hid the faint, white lines that the sun had forgotten.

"I'll sleep with one eye open, in that case," he said casually, holding Nelly's gaze for just a moment longer than necessary before reaching forward and placing his glass down on the grass beside him.

That night as Nelly lay in bed beside India in Oliver's spare room, she found herself remembering what Oliver looked like as he slept. The opposite to his sister, awake he always seemed so guarded. So protected. Not necessarily standoffish, but just as if he was consciously making an effort not to let anybody in too close. But when he slept—or, when Nelly had seen him asleep beside her those two years ago—he looked so innocent and vulnerable. Lips slightly parted, eyes closed, arms wrapped around his own torso. Nelly felt a warm sensation begin to travel in the pit of her stomach as she remembered the feeling of waking up beside him. Of feeling the warmth of his breath on her nose, their faces laying close together. She wondered whether anyone else had ever noticed how perfect he was as he slept.

1996
Oliver

Oliver felt uncharacteristically nervous the next morning as he padded down the hallway toward the kitchen. He had heard the voices of his sister and her friends travelling down the corridor, all of them not yet accustomed to the French time or indeed to sleeping in a comfortable bed, by the sounds of things. When his sister had announced that they were coming to stay with him for a week, he'd been dubious. The hatred that he felt for her previous boyfriend, Spencer, still hadn't shifted from his chest and he had immediately been concerned that the men that she had mentioned were travelling with them would be like him. The thought of another man like that around his sister and Nelly made him immediately irritable. But then Thomas and Leo had turned up and been perfectly pleasant. His sister even seemed happy, for a change; genuinely happy.

Then there was Nelly.

His feelings about seeing her were more complicated. After the months of them exchanging letters, Oliver had felt curious about the prospect of seeing her in real life. He had wondered how she would behave with him when she saw him. He'd imagined the two of them together a hundred times over the past months. Sometimes he imagined them seeing one another and behaving like old friends. Others, he imagined her running to him when they saw each other, pressing her soft lips against his and parting her mouth for him. Sometimes he just imagined her as she was. Shy. Secretive. Witty. Lovely. He had been quietly pleased when India had announced that Henry had broken up with Nelly. He had hoped that she might reach out to him afterward. They had made a connection that summer at his parent's house; he was certain of it.

In such a short space of time, he was shocked by how thoroughly he had felt like he knew her, and she him. As if they somehow saw each other from the inside out. When she hadn't contacted him, he'd thought about ways to reach out to her. He could ring the flat when he knew India was out, so he could pretend he had called to speak to his sister. The thought had occurred to him numerous times. But he wasn't quite sure of what he'd say if the circumstance arose. Then he'd seen the postcard. He had pained over what to write for days, just letting the card lay flat against his trouser pocket. And then, after too much weed and too much wine, he found himself writing on it and posting it.

He'd been surprised at how thrilled he had felt when she'd written back. It had come three weeks later. A postcard of a dog staring miserably out of a window. *Right back at you*, her scruffy hand had written across the back. She must have known that he would be back from his holiday, because she had sent it to his flat in London. He couldn't remember the last time that he'd smiled so much.

The smell of coffee drifted down the doorway toward him as he made his way to the kitchen. India, Thomas and Leo were all there when he entered, laughing at something that India was saying.

"Oliver! Morning, love," India beamed. Her fringe was pinned back from her face, reminding Oliver of the way she had looked when she was much younger.

"Morning," Oliver replied, easing himself around the crowded table and toward the cupboard where the coffee mugs were kept.

"I made a pot of coffee, mate. I hope that's alright," Thomas said, jumping up from his seat. Oliver nodded, picking the pot up from the side.

"Oh my God, what it was to sleep in a proper bed last night, Oliver," India trilled.

"Was it okay?"

"God, you should have heard us. Nelly and I were both snoring away like steam trains," India beamed again and Oliver nodded back.

"Nelly doesn't snore," Thomas said, nudging India with his elbow.

"Umm, yes, she does. It's adorable. Like a little kitten. Back me up, Leo."

Leo swallowed his coffee, "Mmm. Yeah, she does. But only when she's had a few."

"See?" India said to Thomas defiantly.

Thomas leant in toward India's ear. "Don't embarrass her."

India pulled a face. "Who on earth would she be embarrassed in front of?"

Thomas rolled his eyes, pulling a face at Leo, who just laughed and shook his head. Oliver felt irritable for a moment about how Leo could have known about Nelly's sleeping habits, but then found himself forcing back a smile at the idea of Nelly snoring. He had slept beside her before years ago, but she had always been as silent as a cat. Almost like she had been holding her breath. That's what had reminded him of her on the postcard.

The idea of her completely carefree, drunkenly wheezing made him strangely happy. He wished he could have been there to see it. He hoped Leo hadn't been as close to her as he had. That he hadn't had the thoughts about Nelly that Oliver had done when watching her silently slumbering frame. Something inside of him told him that, even if Nelly and Leo had slept together, he doubted they had shared the same proximity that he and Nelly had done. He was just thinking about this as the bathroom peeked open.

"Ind, can you come in here for a sec?" Nelly's voice whispered out from behind the inched-open door.

"You aright, love?" India asked, jumping off from the side of the table where she'd been perched and making her way to the bathroom door. *Love*, Oliver noticed again. It sounded foreign in India's mouth, like something she'd picked up from Nelly's vernacular. They had begun to morph into one another ever so slightly, in the way that best friends or lovers did. It was sweet. India disappeared behind the bathroom door and the three men were left in the kitchen, suddenly silent. Oliver leant against the kitchen counter and swilled the coffee around his mouth, his ears oddly pricked to the noises coming from behind the bathroom door.

After a moment, India reappeared, closing the door quickly behind her and bustling out from the kitchen only to reappear a moment later carrying a small wash bag and then disappearing again into the bathroom. Oliver looked up to see Leo staring at him, who then looked away quickly. After a while, the bathroom door opened again and India re-emerged, closely followed by a very wet Nelly.

"Excuse me, boys. Eyes averted, please. Nothing you haven't seen before," India's voice spoke, leading Nelly out from the kitchen by the hand. Oliver couldn't help catching Nelly's eye as she walked past him. The freckles that appeared in the summer had begun to pepper the bridge of her nose, which was slightly pink from the sun. Her hair was wet and dripped onto her bare shoulders, scrunched up like tangled corkscrews. He pulled his eyes away quickly when she returned his gaze, feigning an interest in the contents of his fridge. The two girls disappeared out from the kitchen and into the spare bedroom, their voices just audible from behind the heavy door.

"So, India said we're gonna head into town this morning?" Thomas said to Oliver. Oliver dragged his gaze away from the spare room door.

"Mmm. Right, yeah. We can cycle in and get some stuff. I have spare bikes. Or, there were spares left here, anyway."

"Great. Sounds good," Thomas smiled. He picked up his coffee and carried on drinking.

The two girls re-emerged shortly after, both now dressed. Nelly was wearing a white vest-top and denim shorts that looked like the same ones she'd worn at his parents' house two summers ago. Her face was glowing and shiny and there was a thin line of white where she hadn't rubbed the sun cream in quite properly down the bridge her nose. Leo walked past her toward the sink, running his thumb over the cream on her nose playfully as he passed.

"Don't forget to do those pink shoulders too," he smiled, giving her scapula a small prod. Nelly smiled back and covered her shoulders with her two hands, as if this resolved the matter. Oliver turned, trying to swallow the jealous feeling creeping up his spine.

"Oh yeah. Hang on," India said excitedly, disappearing back into the bedroom and then reappearing with something thin and almost sheer that she draped across Nelly's shoulders. She planted a kiss on Nelly's left cheek and then rubbed the lipstick away. "This will keep the sun off of them," she said as she patted the thin scarf over her friend. Nelly smiled back at her.

It struck Oliver how tactile the four of them all were with one another. The easy way that they moved around each other's bodies and reached out, touching and kissing and holding. It was as if the four of them had an unspoken bond; the sort that only came between lovers, or maybe friends or family that you have lived in close proximity with for prolonged amounts of time. Oliver wished that he could behave the same way with Nelly as Leo did. That he could reach a hand over and rub the sun cream into her nose, or kiss her cheek or hold her hand as he brushed by and not have it mean anything more than that. Without it seeming deliberate.

Even with his girlfriend, Lorraine, he wasn't particularly affectionate. They had sex, obviously. Loads of it. But she wasn't someone who he wanted to hold the hand of or stroke her hair from her face. He wasn't sure that he was someone that she would want to do those things either. Lorraine. He had let himself forget about her almost completely for the last couple of days.

Nothing had ever happened with Nelly. Not really, anyway. And yet the idea of the two of them—Nelly and Lorraine—cohabiting the same area made him somehow unusually uncomfortable. Awkward. He wasn't sure even to himself what he felt about Nelly. He was fond of her, definitely. At certain points, he even thought he might be in love with her. But how could he be, really? They barely knew one another. They had barely exchanged two words since she had arrived yesterday, despite all of his fantasies about their reunion. And yet, he also felt as if she knew him better than anyone in the world. Like they had their own secret language that only she and he understood. He allowed himself to forget about Lorraine for a bit longer.

They reached the town at around ten o'clock that morning. It was quiet and peaceful, with very few people milling about. Oliver often cycled into town to get things for the house. Bread. Wine. Water. Citrus candles to try to keep the mosquitos at bay. But mostly he did it just to look around. He liked the quiet simplicity of it. The slow moseying ramble of the locals going about their days. It felt so removed from his life in London where he lived now, working for his father's company. He hated his job with a passion. But it paid very well, which lubricated the thought of having to return. He spent holidays abroad; in France, mostly. That was how he had met Lorraine.

Before her, there had been a string of others that he had referred to as *girlfriends*, although he really had no intention of forming any lasting attachments with them. They were distractions. Things to pass the time with. There was always another one. Always someone else eager to have their hearts mildly tarnished by him.

Then there was Nelly. She looked out of place now in the small French village that his life had been inhabiting, like a foreign object that didn't quite fit. It felt strange that she was here where he was. He was standing outside of the shop holding a bag of groceries and smoking a cigarette. It was already hot outside, the sun glowing down handsomely onto the top of his dirty-blonde hair. The till to the store was just left to his shoulder, behind the wall. He could hear the fan whirling from inside, the steady bustle of the woman working behind the counter as she spoke with the few customers queuing to by their daily newspaper.

"Bonjour," Nelly's voice muffled out timidly from inside. Her accent was clumsy, as if she couldn't quite shake the London from it. Oliver suddenly felt aware for her that she clearly didn't know the language. Not that it would bother him. He spoke French fluently, of course, but even if he didn't, he had the confidence in himself and his abilities—in his social etiquette—not to be embarrassed by it. To not feel nervous to give it a try. Nelly, on the other hand, clearly felt shy at the prospect. For some reason, Oliver found it oddly endearing. He turned his head against the stone of the wall, allowing himself to watch her from the inside. Her cheeks were pink at the tops in the warm, stuffy heat of the shop, her arms clumsily clasping at a basket filled with wine and various toiletries.

"Bonjour, mademoiselle," the woman behind the counter spoke back. Her tone was clipped and sharp, as if she didn't welcome the prospect of a foreigner in her midst. Something in Oliver felt immediately protective. He let his cigarette drop to the ground and blew out the last of the smoke from his lungs, stubbing the butt beneath his shoe before entering the shop.

"Bonjour, Madame," he said easily as he entered.

"Bonjour, Monsieur," the woman trilled, changing her tone almost completely. Oliver moved to stand just behind Nelly's shoulder, the warmth of her sun kissed skin radiating onto his chest where it stood. He reached forward and took the basket from Nelly's hands, placing it down on the till in front of her. She had seemingly strategically placed the bread and wine bottle over her other things and she looked away and stroked the top of her nose uncomfortably as they became visible.

"Est-il possible d'avoir un sac aussi, s'il vous plait?" He asked.

"Oui, bien sûr," the woman said, plucking a plastic carrier bag from a peg behind her and flapping it out toward Oliver.

"Parfait. Merci beaucoup."

The woman began to scan the items in Nelly's basket through the till, placing each one down into the bag that she'd opened up for Oliver on the counter. Oliver and Nelly stood silently, his chest just close enough to her back that he could feel her against him. The woman probably thought they were a couple, he mused.

"D'you get everything you wanted?" He asked Nelly from behind her.

"Mhmm. Thanks," she responded. She seemed quiet. He imagined she just felt embarrassed. Maybe because she couldn't speak French. Or maybe because she was buying tampons, although that seemed silly. She fidgeted with a curl that had come loose from her hair tie, trying to tuck it back in. He reached a finger up to touch it, tempted to close the gap between them, and then thought better of it and so just stood watching the woman scan the items. A baguette. A bottle of red wine and one bottle of rosé. Shampoo. Tampons. A small pack of ice creams.

Nelly glanced over her shoulder at him and he smiled down at her in what he hoped was a friendly way. She turned back around.

"Vingt-six francs cinq, s'il vous plait monsieur," the woman said.

"Ah. Bon," Oliver responded, digging his hand into his pocket.

"It's alright. I've got it," Nelly said, reaching forward with two very scrunched notes.

"Oh, it's okay. It's stuff for the house. I don't—"

"Merci beaucoup," Nelly said to the woman, taking the bag from her hands. The woman raised her eyebrows and then took the two notes, placing them inside the till and counting change into Nelly's palm. The way she pronounced beaucoup sounded as if she were complimenting an arse. It made Oliver smile. He imagined it was the same reason that the woman had raised her eyebrows.

"Merci, Madame. Bonne journée," he said as he left the shop behind Nelly, who had for some reason insisted on carrying the bag even when he had reached out for it.

Nelly walked quickly when they were outside toward the huddle of India, Leo and Thomas who were sitting at seats in a café smoking. She placed herself down on a red plastic chair beside Leo, pushing the bag beneath her feet. Oliver immediately had the impression that he'd done something to annoy her, but he wasn't sure what. He pulled out his own seat and pulled it in to sit beside Nelly, angling his leg slightly to the left so as to not let his knee touch hers accidentally.

"Did you get everything you needed, babe?" India asked when Nelly sat down.

"Mhmm. Yeah."

"Fab. I ordered you both a champagne."

"Champagne? But it's—"

"We're on holiday," India said, waving the comment away with her hand. The waiter brought over the tray of drinks and placed them on the table and Oliver reached forward impulsively to set a glass down in front of everyone. India and Leo were taking turns in recounting a story from the group's trip to Amsterdam, which they were doing so rather raucously. Thomas chipped in with a quip or a comment from time to time and Oliver noticed the way that he glanced over at Oliver for approval when he did so, or the way that he playfully nudged at India's shoulder as he teased her. Oliver let his knee sink to the side so as his leg pressed against Nelly's beneath the table. He felt relieved when she didn't move hers away immediately. He let it rest there, her knee warm against his thigh. She was very petite. Tiny, in fact. It was one of the things that he found sweet about her, although he was sure that she would be irritated if she knew this.

They ordered more drinks when they had finished and sat for some time, sharing the ice creams that Nelly had bought from the shop earlier that morning. Oliver noticed a small smudge of vanilla under the tip of Nelly's nose, congealing in the heat, and wondered whether he could reach over and clean it off for her. What she might say if he did. Whether she would blush in the way that he found so endearing, spreading over her cheeks like a rash. She wiped it away herself before he could find out.

"I'm gonna go find the loos," Leo announced at some point, inching himself out from the seat and moving past them. He placed a hand each on the back of Nelly and Oliver's shoulders as he squeezed past. India and Thomas were still deep in conversation; her inching closer into his lap as they playfully argued and his smile spreading further apart as she cajoled him.

"I think he likes you," Oliver said to Nelly after a moment.

"Hmm?" She responded, as if she hadn't been expecting him to speak. Their legs were still touching beneath the table, but above it they had shown no sign of sharing the proximity.

Oliver raised his eyebrows toward Leo's form, which was now stood at the door to the café and asking someone for directions to the toilets in French. Nelly's eyes followed his for a moment, squinting a bit in the sun. She was quiet and Oliver was concerned she really was annoyed with him, but then her face broke into a smile. She almost forgot to cover her mouth. He loved it when she forgot to do that.

"Leo?"

Oliver couldn't help but smile back, "Yeah. I reckon he might."

"Mmm. I very much doubt it."

"Why?"

Nelly just watched Oliver for a long moment, the grin still in her cheeks.

Oliver shrugged, "He's always flirting with you."

Nelly shook her head so as another curl escaped her hair band, "Flirting with me? Ah, you would think that."

"What's that supposed to mean?"

Nelly just rolled her eyes. "Let's just say there's more chance of Leo being interested in you than there is in me."

"Huh?"

"Leo's gay," she replied simply, taking another lick of her ice cream. Oliver let his eyes hover on her tongue. It was pink and shiny and coated ever so slightly with a layer of vanilla. He wondered if it tasted like ice cream.

"Oh right," he replied finally, remembering himself. They sat quietly for a second whilst India and Thomas continued to chatter. "Not flirting, then," Oliver finally said.

Nelly shook her head, looking down at her fingers, "Nope. Not flirting."

"Right..."

"Would it have bothered you if he had been?"

The question was bold. Especially for Nelly. It caught Oliver off guard and forced him to look straight at her. She was smiling, her cheeks pinked from the heat and the alcohol. She returned his gaze for a second, timidly, and then pulled it back away. Oliver allowed himself a small laugh and then shook his head in disbelief.

"Have you ever kissed a guy?" Nelly asked him.

"Mmm? No."

"Never?"

"Nope," Oliver reaffirmed. He shrugged, "I'm not against it. I just never felt the urge to."

"Fair enough."

"Have you kissed a girl?"

Nelly smiled, looking pleased with herself for how provocative she clearly thought she was being. Truthfully, he didn't think it provocative at all. "Yep..."

Oliver raised his eyebrows, "Really?"

"Mhmm."

Oliver nodded, watching Nelly's mouth as she finished the last of her ice cream and set the small wooden stick down on the matt on the table. It was darker at the top where her lips had been against it.

"Not India?" Oliver found himself asking.

Nelly shook her head, "No. Not India."

"Good. That would have been... weird. For me, I mean..."

"Weird for you?"

Oliver nodded, lighting a cigarette. He felt surprised at where the conversation had travelled between the two of them in such a short space of time, but hoped his countenance wouldn't betray him in admitting it.

"Ah well, of course. It is all about you, isn't it?" Nelly said after a moment. The laugh escaped Oliver's mouth before he realised. He had forgotten how Nelly challenged him. She returned his smile almost shyly, from beneath her lashes. "Don't worry. I'm only kidding. I know it's because we're both your little sisters."

Oliver raised his eyebrows again but didn't say anything. He hated what India had said about Nelly being like a second little sister to him. It was true, he felt a protectiveness over her that was almost brotherly. When he saw other men looking at her legs or the soft curves of her chest, he felt an irrational need to shield her from them. But at the same time, he found himself looking at her in the same way. Sometimes he found his mind wandering when he stared at her, imagining things that were anything but brotherly in nature. He felt like this now as she sucked the sticky vanilla off from the edge of her thumb.

"Those bogs are disgusting," Leo announced when he arrived back at the table.

"Where are they?" India asked.

Leo nodded toward the back of the café, "Through there. Behind the Callipo sign," he told her before adding, "Wear gloves."

India laughed and stood from her chair, stroking Thomas's arm as she walked past. Nelly followed her almost automatically. The skin of her thighs made a noise as she stood, as if they had been stuck to the plastic, and the façade of confidence that she'd let slip out only moments ago quickly washed away as she glanced back at Oliver, a blush forming over the tops of her cheeks. He winked at her and she smiled before leaving behind India.

1996
Nelly

Nelly had been irritated by Oliver earlier when they had visited the town. She had already felt conscious of the fact that everyone already spoke French and that she didn't. A hangover from their upper education and her lower. She spoke fluent Italian, so it was obviously no reflection on intellect. And yet it made her feel like an outsider. An imposter amongst the group. The feeling had been reaffirmed when Oliver had stepped in to speak for her in the shop that morning. He had done it so easily, as if he were breathing. So beautiful. So effortless. She had felt herself bristle immediately and she had wondered if he had noticed. She even hoped that he had, for a moment. She had caught him though, watching her from the corner of her eye. There was an expression on his face that she had seen once before; the expression that he'd watched her with two summers back when they had sat together in his window. He had been... not nervous, but perhaps apprehensive. As if he had been caught letting his guard down and was contemplating whether to regret it. The unease of his expression coursed through her chest as if it had been her own emotion. As if she felt what he felt. It was difficult to feel annoyed with him after that. Besides, she knew he probably had thought he was being helpful in the arrogant way that privileged people often do.

Maybe it had been the half a bottle of champagne that she had drunk. Or maybe it had been the headiness of the holiday and the way that India's compliments coated her like a blanket. It wasn't something that Nelly would normally do. But when India had pulled off her dress and dove into the lake in her underwear, Nelly had already known that she would follow eventually.

Thomas followed India almost instantly, tugging off his socks and tucking them into his shoes before diving in. Nelly wondered for the hundredth time how the two of them hadn't gotten together yet. Then Leo jumped in; boxers off, and all. His bottom was white where the sun had tanned the rest of his skin these past weeks. It made Nelly laugh when she saw it, glowingly pale. She saw Oliver looking at her from where she stood. He had already taken off his shirt without hesitation. His stomach was tanned and toned, and he held himself in the way of someone used to removing their clothes in front of people and being admired. He was very attractive. Almost irritatingly so.

Nelly, on the other hand, felt bloated and uncomfortable. She had gotten her period that morning and it had left a dark, tainted mark against the pink of the towel that India had left out for her. She had felt nervous about this. Anxious, that Oliver would think her disgusting for staining his things. She'd hidden the stain and snuck it into the washing machine when the boys left the kitchen and India had helped her.

"What if it leaves a mark?" Nelly had asked nervously.

India had shaken her head, "You really don't need to worry, bub. Oliver's basically your brother. He wouldn't care about things like that," she had told her. *Basically your brother.* Was that really how Oliver thought of her? Like a sibling?

That's why she had tested him earlier. The memory of herself saying it—the provocativeness of the words—made her cheeks redden beneath her skin. And yet, it seemed to be working. He was looking at her as they stood there. The taut lines of his mouth lay motionless, waiting for her to move. After a moment, he jutted his chin toward her.

"You coming?"

Nelly bit down on the inside of her cheek, contemplating her choices. Oliver removed the clothes from his bottom half, revealing a pair of striped boxer shorts. He adjusted himself under the fabric unabashedly and then kicked off his blue boat shoes, leaving them on the bank by the rest of the clothes. He had a small scar on his shoulder blade; pink and puckered, as if it hadn't ever really healed. Nelly watched it as he padded on bare feet toward the water. He turned to look at her once more as the water began to pool around his feet, as if checking whether she was following, but then turned back around and dove in.

"Hurry up, Nel!" India called out. Her blonde hair was wet against her head, pushed back to reveal the perfect pinkness of her face from the hours in the sun. She was grinning out at Nelly, dodging splashes from Thomas and Leo as they fooled around.

"Yeah. Come on, Nelly. Get your kit off!" Leo called out.

Nelly breathed in through her nose. She wished she'd just gone in at the same time as India so as everyone wouldn't be watching her. She hated that she always hesitated. Always assessed the situation before diving in. Now, stood there on the bank fully clothed, she was faced with the prospect of either refusing to join her friends and looking boring or unclothing in front of them all. She felt conscious of the fact that she was on her period and was glad for the tampons that she'd purchased in the shop earlier that day.

"Come on, Nel. Off! Off! Off!" Leo started chanting. India began to join in, laughing like she was having the time of her life. Oliver just watched her, an expression playing around his eyes as if he were trying to predict Nelly's next move.

"It looks cold!" Nelly called out, immediately cringing at herself.

"It's fine once you're in," Thomas replied.

"Come on, Nel. Stop making excuses. Get those gorgeous boobs out!" India called from somewhere behind Thomas's shoulders.

Nelly bit down on her cheek again and then said, "Fine. Alright. Alright." There was nothing else for it. She trod off the backs of her plimsoles so as she stood in bare feet, feeling the damp grass beneath her toes from where the water had lapped against it. It felt swollen and plump. She took off her shorts first, wriggling them down her legs and then placing them on top of her shoes so as they wouldn't get wet. Then she reached for the hem of her vest. She could feel Oliver's eyes on her as she did so, but when she looked up, he had already averted his gaze, swimming toward India from where she splashed around in the water.

"Wit woo!" Leo cat-called toward her from the water. Nelly rolled her eyes at Leo and grinned, pulling her vest back down over her stomach. She felt self-conscious of how her body looked today, swollen and uncomfortable from the alcohol and her period. She'd keep the vest on and then change later, she thought finally. As quickly as she could, she tiptoed over to the water's edge and ran in toward the cheers and trumps from her friends.

She felt the cool of the lake against her skin, immediately cooling her down. The rest of the four were slightly further out so as Nelly had to swim toward them clumsily, unpractised. India was splashing Thomas and Leo whilst the two of them chased her via front-crawl and the look of them all, bedraggled and sun-kissed and happy, made Nelly laugh as she swam forward, her mouth opening and letting in an enormous glug of murky water.

She coughed and closed her eyes, feeling the liquid bubbling up her nose. Before she realised it, there was an arm around her waist, adjusting her gently so as she didn't struggle.

"I bet it's better than the wine we had last night, at least," Oliver said, a smile playing gently with the edge of his lips. Nelly felt his arm retract from her waist and cupped her hand over her mouth as she coughed. Oliver loitered beside her, watching her as if contemplating giving her further support. She wasn't sure they had ever touched before. Not really. Not on purpose. Not in front of other people. It felt intimate somehow.

"Yeah," she smiled, brushing her hair back from her face. She was sure that she must look as bedraggled as the rest of them. Apart from Oliver.

He stared at her, the smile still resting at the edges of his cheeks. For a moment, it seemed as if he was going to tell her something important, but then he simply stated, "Your hair's so curly."

"Mmm? Oh. Yeah," Nelly agreed, running her hand over the front of her face so as the curls stuck back together. She was treading water now and sunk ever so slightly in the water again as she did so, but Oliver's arm came back out to steady her and then retracted almost as quickly, just long enough to stop her from another mouthful of lake. "A bit frizzy, really. Especially in the heat." She didn't know why she was talking about her hair and felt immediately self-conscious.

Oliver regarded her for a moment longer and then said, "I like it. I can't imagine it another way."

For some reason, that made Nelly smile.

The sound of India screaming playfully chirruped out away from them and Nelly turned to laugh at her again. Oliver nodded toward the shapes of his sister and Thomas and asked, "So, how much do you want to bet that you're kicked out of the guest room tonight?"

Nelly turned to look back at him, shaking her head. Oliver put his arm around her again, but she didn't dip under. He took it back away. "I don't think so. Nothing's happened with them so far."

"No?" Oliver asked, "That's very…"

"Unlike India?" Nelly offered, "Yeah. I know. She's been good, though. She's been happy."

"She seems it."

They both watched her for a moment quietly before Oliver said, "Well, if she does change her mind there's always space next to me."

Nelly couldn't stop her head from flicking back to him quickly. It was such a bold thing to say that she had expected him to look pleased with himself, but instead he just lay back in the water closing his eyes against the sun as if he hadn't said anything at all. As if he had been no more provocative than offering somewhere to sleep to a friend. Maybe that was all it had been.

"Oh. Well, thanks," Nelly replied. They were quiet for a moment and she was inwardly wrestling with something, almost daring herself to say it. What about your girlfriend? But then she didn't, not wanting to break the illusion. She would happily pretend that Lorraine didn't exist for a little longer.

They spent a while swimming together in the lake, splashing and playing like children and jumping in from the side. They were all tired when they finished, dragging themselves out and lulling down on the side of the bank as they let the heat of the sun soak into their skin. At some point, Leo stood up to fish a bottle of something out from the bag of groceries that Nelly had bought earlier in the day.

"Right. Who's up for a bevvy?" He asked. "Oh shit, there's no corkscrew."

"Here," Oliver said, reaching out toward the bottle. He didn't move to stand, so Leo had to cross over to reach him. Water dripped from Oliver's wet fringe as he tapped the bottle against his knee, inching the cork upward. Once it had peeked the top, he took it in his mouth and tugged at it with his teeth until it let out a small pop.

"Cor, Lorraine's a lucky girl," Leo winked, laughing. Nelly felt a twinge in her stomach at the mention of Oliver's latest girlfriend.

Oliver smiled but didn't say anything, taking a glug of the rosé from the bottle and then reaching over to hand it to Nelly. "It's a bit warm," he said, wrinkling his nose.

Nelly nodded, taking the bottle from him. She reached up and placed it to her lips, letting the warm, almost vinegary liquid gulp into her mouth. She must have tipped it back too far because a few droplets escaped down her chin and she rubbed them away quickly.

"Cor, save some for the rest of us, Nel," Leo laughed. He reached over to take the bottle and then said more concernedly, "Oh babe. You're bleeding."

"Huh?"

"You're bleeding," Leo repeated, pointing toward Nelly's leg. Nelly quickly sat and looked down, her heart sinking as she saw a thin, watery trail of blood beginning to snail down her inner thigh. She brought her legs together instinctively, pressing her knees tightly closed in an attempt to hide it.

"Nel, are you alright?" India asked, inching herself up onto her elbows.

"Yeah. I'm fine. I just…" Nelly stumbled. She felt suddenly sick.

"You probably caught it on a reed, or something," Oliver offered from beside her. Without hesitation, he reached over her lap and quickly brushed the blood from her thigh with the back of his knuckles. Nelly's heart beat inside of her chest. He must have known, surely. He had seen her buying tampons earlier in the shop. But then surely he wouldn't have done that. Unless men really were that clueless. She quickly crossed her legs and, when she dared, stole a glance over at him. He wiped his knuckle on the back of his wet underwear unaffectedly and then lay back down, closing his eyes once more against the sunshine. Nelly took the opportunity and wriggled quickly back into her shorts, plucking her bag from the side and tapping India's shoulder. She'd need to find somewhere to change.

1996
Oliver

The atmosphere in the house shifted when Lorraine arrived that evening. It was Thursday and she had come a day earlier than Oliver had expected her to, although if he was honest with himself, he hadn't really hoped she would come at all this week. She worked in the town at a restaurant where she and Oliver had first met and she tended to wander up to Oliver's house on Friday evenings to stay for a couple of days. She was beautiful and sophisticated and just the right amount of arrogant that Oliver had found he tended to enjoy in women. She was nothing like Nelly.

"Enchantée," she said to the newcomers when she arrived, lazily flitting her lips against their cheeks.

"Enchanté," Leo replied for the group.

"Est-ce ta premiere nuit ici?"

"Ah non. C'est le... je ne sais pas, en fait. La troisiemme?" Leo replied, directing his question at Thomas.

"Mmm. Ouais, le troisiemme."

"La troisiemme," Lorraine corrected.

"Ah, pardon. C'etait rapide, non?" Thomas responded, looking at Leo.

"Mmm. Vraiment rapide. Trop rapide. J'ai besoin d'une deuxième semaine."

"Ha. Moi aussi."

"Ah bon. Et où étiez-vous avant la Provence?" Her blue eyes settled on Nelly as she asked this. "Vous tous. Le groupe," Lorraine qualified.

Nelly swallowed, her cheeks already beginning to mottle. "Oh, I'm sorry. I..."

"It might be easier if we speak in English," Oliver said bluntly.

"Pourquoi?"

"Parce-ce que ce n'est pas vraiment facile pour tout le monde si on parle juste en français."

"Mais je n'aime pas parler anglais. C'est… ce n'est pas très romantique. C'est lourd, non?"

Oliver shrugged.

"Parler français est difficile pour qui?" Oliver didn't reply, and then Lorraine looked at Nelly. She raised her eyebrows. "You don't speak French?"

"Oh. No, I don't. I'm sorry."

"Then why did you come to France?" Lorraine replied curtly, raising an eyebrow as if the notion of not being able to speak French was the same as not being able to tie a shoelace. Perhaps she was too arrogant, after all.

"Oh. Good question," Nelly tried to smile.

Lorraine raised her eyebrows and shrugged.

"I'm just gonna go help India," Nelly announced quietly, excusing herself from the table. She'd changed out from her shorts and was now wearing a pair of baggy blue jeans, although it was far too warm for them. They made her look even smaller than she was. She still had on the vest-top that she'd swam in earlier and, although it had long since dried, the way the sun had crisped it meant that it was now clinging against her bra underneath. Oliver kept having to stop himself from noticing the small pink bow at the front of it. Lorraine sat down in Nelly's seat as soon as she was away from it, despite there being others vacant, and lit a cigarette all whilst reverting back to French when she spoke with Leo and Thomas. For some reason, Oliver found this unsettlingly irritating. After a few minutes, he stood up himself and followed Nelly's steps into the small kitchen.

India went silent when he came in, sitting on the top of the work surface whilst Nelly rubbed pieces of garlic over a toasted baguette. When India saw that it was Oliver, she quickly said, "Oh good. There you are…"

Oliver raised his eyebrows and then walked over to the fridge.

"So… that's Lorraine?" his sister said toward Oliver's back.

"Mmm. Yeah."

"Mmm," India responded pointedly. Oliver didn't say anything, but took a bottle of white wine out from the fridge and closed it behind him. After a second, India said, "She seems a bit of a twat."

"India!" Nelly hissed from the chopping board. Her cheeks were red at the tops.

"What? I said it, not you," India said, as if this was supposed to be reassuring.

Oliver didn't respond. He wanted to agree and say that, yes, Lorraine was rude and arrogant and actually quite annoying. But, despite the strength that he felt these things with, it was actually only the first time that he'd realised he thought them and he didn't know how he could admit this without it seeming disingenuous.

"Can you pass the tomatoes, please?" Nelly asked quietly. She directed the question toward India, even though Oliver was much closer to the fridge. He turned around and opened it, plucking the thin plastic bag of red fruit out from the tray and then placing them down beside Nelly's chopping board. "Thanks," she said quietly, as if speaking directly to the board.

"Where d'you keep the glasses, Oliver?" India asked as she began opening and closing cupboard doors. "Oh, never mind. I've got them."

"Do you want me to grab those?" Oliver asked as India balanced the bottle of wine between her arms, her hands now carefully cradling the stems of several glasses.

"No. It's okay. But can you bring out the water?"

"Yeah. Fine."

India began to move and then stopped and looked back at Nelly, "I'll be back in two secs?" Nelly nodded. Oliver was unsure why India had inverted her statement as if it were a question.

Nelly stood chopping the tomatoes silently, her lips pressed tightly together as if she were concentrating. She tipped the thin slices into a bowl and then seasoned them with salt and pepper and olive oil. Then she picked up a stalk of basil and twisted the top of it, tearing the leaves off and crunching them up into the bowl. Oliver watched as she mixed everything together and then began layering it over the bread methodically.

"Did your mum teach you to cook?" He asked her.

He saw her shoulders bristle slightly, as if she hadn't been expecting him to speak. "Mhmm. And my dad."

"Right. They have a restaurant?"

Nelly hesitated for a moment and then said, "Yep."

Oliver nodded even though she couldn't see him.

"Are you alright, Nelly love?" India's voice asked, her face appearing from behind the doorframe momentarily afterward.

"Mhmm," Nelly nodded, placing the toasted breads onto a plate.

"Okay," India replied. She turned to Oliver and said, "Did you find the water?"

"Mmm? Oh. Yeah," Oliver replied. He turned around to open the fridge. When he turned back, Nelly was already walking out the kitchen door behind his sister.

He found Nelly later that night sat on the floor against the face of the house. She was smoking a cigarette, the tip of it glowing orange against the dark evening air. Oliver padded over on bare feet to join her. She didn't say anything as he sat down. He hadn't been able to sleep. Everyone had gone to bed a couple of hours ago, Lorraine with him and Nelly with India in the spare room; the two boys on the settee in the living room. Lorraine had been all over him all night, seemingly marking her territory. Although Oliver wasn't sure who she was really trying to impress. Clearly having been informed of her rudeness to Nelly, India had taken an immediate disliking to Lorraine. Which was uncharacteristic for Oliver's sister. She usually liked everyone. It was her main downfall.

"Stuck up cow," India had mumbled just loudly enough for Oliver to hear when Lorraine had announced that she thought Italian food was heavy and oily. Nelly had looked at India under her eyelashes, biting her two lips together in a thin line of discomfort. India had only wrapped Nelly up closer into her lap, almost as if she were protecting a child from a storm. Oliver wished he could have wrapped his own arms around her. But he knew it wasn't his place. Since Lorraine had arrived that evening, Nelly seemed to be going out of her way to miss his gaze or angle her face away from him. She'd been oddly quiet. Even more so than usual.

Oliver knew that it was Lorraine's presence that was the cause of it. It seemed as if there had been something occurring beneath the surface between the two of them; a spark slowly stoking over the last days. And yet, she had known that he had a girlfriend that wasn't her. And nothing had really happened between him and Nelly. Not anything concrete, anyhow. If it had been another woman, Oliver might have pretended that he had never noticed the undercurrent to their glances or their touches; he had certainly done so with women before. Getting himself off of the hook for things that couldn't really be explained. But with Nelly, it was different. Like he could never lie to her. Or would never want to. She saw him for what he was. Naked. Vulnerable.

He looked over at her now smoking her cigarette.

"You hardly ever smoke," he told her as he lit his own.

She shook her head and blew out a puff of air toward the sky, "No. I don't, do I?"

"Mmm. Doesn't suit you, really." He had meant for it to mean because she seemed so innocent. But it had come out matter-of-factly, even though he hadn't meant for it to.

She raised her eyebrows, "Okay." She stubbed her cigarette on the floor and went to stand up.

"No. I wasn't—"

Nelly stood and brushed the bottom of her jeans. She made to move away, but Oliver found himself reaching out his hand toward hers. She looked down at where his hand was encasing her palm and stopped, as if frozen. He regarded her for a moment and then slowly let his fingers curl between hers. He tugged her gently, easing her back down. He was surprised when she indulged him.

Nelly sat back beside Oliver on the floor where she had been beforehand. He was still holding onto her hand and, as she sat, he let it rest down on the ground between them, adjusting his hold on her slightly so as they were both more comfortable. They sat there like that for a moment as if it were something that they did all of the time.

With his free hand, Oliver plucked a second cigarette out from his packet and then held the tip of it against his own, puffing on the end until the second cigarette began to cinder. He took it away and held it out toward her and then, when Nelly didn't take it, he placed it gently between her lips. She watched him as he did so, as if not quite trusting what he was going to do. Her eyes held his for a moment whilst she read the situation. Then, with her other hand, she placed the cigarette between two fingers and took a drag, assuming the same position that she had done moments before.

They sat like that for a while until Oliver said, "I'll be sad when you go."

Nelly nodded toward her knees, "You'll see India at Christmas, though."

"Mmm," Oliver replied. It hadn't been what he had meant. He swallowed something in his throat and then, after contemplating the weight of it on his tongue, said, "But I'll be sad when *you* go."

Nelly looked up at him. Dark eyes glinting in the blueness of the night. Freckles peppered the bridge of her nose, a small trail of them gliding down toward her top lip. He wanted to reach out and kiss it. She rubbed her thumb over the top of his knuckles and looked away. The silence was blissfully uncomfortable. The night was becoming cold and Oliver was aware that both of them weren't dressed for it. But he was also aware of the fact that if they moved from this spot, they probably wouldn't ever assume the same position.

"Why will you be sad when I go?" Nelly asked finally. She looked nervous, but the way that she mumbled the words slightly into her breath told Oliver that she had premeditated the question. As if she'd dared herself to say it.

He watched her for a moment, his chest full of an uncomfortable concoction of anxiety and self-consciousness that he rarely felt. "You know why, don't you?"

Nelly pressed her lips together, nervous. She nodded slowly, her curls bobbing gently with her head. She waited a moment and then said, "But why, though?"

Oliver opened his lips to speak and then thought better of it. He took a last drag of his cigarette and then stubbed it out on the ground. "Because you're..." He faltered.

"Because I'm what?"

"You're..."

The sound of someone moving in the house broke the spell.

"You two not freezing out here?" Leo asked, emerging from the kitchen wearing a hoodie and lighting his own cigarette.

"Yeah. It is a bit," Oliver agreed. He glanced down and noticed that they weren't holding hands any longer. He wondered who had let go first.

1996
Nelly

"It's shit, isn't it?" Leo had said to Nelly when he sat down beside her by the pool on the morning before they were to leave Oliver's house in Provence.

"What is?" Nelly asked, looking up from her book.

Leo raised his eyebrows. His face was full of freckles and he nodded it toward the kitchen where Oliver was washing something at the sink, Lorraine draping her arms around his shoulders as if she were putting on a show.

"What do you mean?" Nelly had tried to say, pretending to be engrossed in her book. She was reading *To the Lighthouse* and it wasn't holding her attention.

Leo watched her plainly, a sympathetic smile curling his lips. "You know, at first, I wasn't sure which one of them you were in love with. India or Oliver."

"What? I'm not—"

"But it's written across your face when you look at him. Clear as day."

Nelly sighed, closing her book on her lap. She allowed herself to look up at Oliver through the window. Her stomach squirmed as she saw Lorraine manoeuvring herself so as her back was against the sink, her face toward his. "Is it that obvious?" Nelly asked.

Leo shrugged, "Ah, only to me. But probably just because I'm psychic."

Nelly eyed him gingerly.

Leo smiled, "And probably just because I'm in a similar position."

Nelly raised her eyebrows. She was about to ask who, but then she realised she didn't need to. "Thomas?"

Leo nodded. He was smiling, his green eyes glittering in the sun. He didn't look upset about it. But the smile didn't really look happy either.

"Does he know?"

"Mmm. Probably. Maybe. Who knows. I've never said anything to him. But he'd be an idiot not to."

"Shit. I'm sorry, Leo."

Leo shrugged again, his attention turning to Thomas who was rubbing sun cream into India's shoulders. "It's okay. As long as he's happy, I don't really mind too much."

Nelly leant to the side, resting her head against his shoulder. They both looked out at the men that they loved but couldn't have; Nelly felt as if she could feel her heart curling.

"Anyway, it's alright for you. He feels the same."

"Hmm? No, he doesn't," Nelly shook her head.

"I think he does."

"Why?" She hated how desperate she sounded, but Leo didn't seem to think anything of it.

He shrugged, "The way he watches you. It's like you're a puzzle he can't stop trying to solve."

Nelly raised her eyebrows, "It's probably just because I'm the only girl that hasn't let him shag them immediately."

Leo laughed, "Can you blame them?"

Nelly smiled, "No. I suppose not." She was quiet for a moment before saying, "Wouldn't it be more simple if we could just be in love with each other?"

"Ah. Now there's an idea," Leo smiled into her hair.

Nelly laughed. "You know, Oliver thought that we were. Or that you liked me, at least. He told me so that morning at the café."

"Did he now?"

"Mhmm. He thought we were flirting."

"Jealous boy," Leo tutted. He sat up straighter and turned Nelly's shoulders so as she was facing toward him. He was very tall and even sat down her head still only reached the top of his shoulder blades. Without warning, he tilted his face toward hers and kissed her on the mouth. Nelly could feel herself laughing into his lips. Leo pulled his face away and then grinned at her before wrinkling his nose and shaking his head. Nelly mimicked him and did the same.

Leo sighed, "Oh well. We gave it the good British try."

Nelly laughed and let her head rest back onto his shoulder.

Later that day India emerged from the house looking very pleased with herself. She was carrying something heavy in her hands, rushing down the lawn toward them as if she had just discovered a wonderful surprise.

"Oliver, you have your camera here!" She grinned. She was gazing down at it as if it were going to show her something. Oliver bristled slightly in his seat, sitting up so as Lorraine had to shift slightly off from his lap where she had positioned herself.

"Prends-tu des photos?"

"Mmm. Ouais," he replied. He pushed her gently off from his lap and then moved toward India, staring at the camera as if it were something precious. "I'm just gonna put this ba—"

"Can you take a picture of us, Oliver?" India asked excitedly.

Oliver rubbed the back of his neck, squinting.

"Oh, go on. You're so good."

"Je pensais que tu étais banquier."

"Mm. C'est un passe-temps."

"Mon artiste!"

Oliver ignored her. He looked like he was battling with something. As if someone had just discovered his diary and he didn't want them to read what he'd written inside, even though it was poetic. He looked up to India. "Maybe later."

"But there isn't a later. We're leaving tomorrow!" India pleaded. "Come on everyone. Nel, Tom, Leo. Huddle up."

"I can't really be bothered right now, India."

"Oh, I'll do it then," India said, rolling her eyes. She took the camera from Oliver's hands and Nelly felt oddly surprised that he'd let her do so. India held the camera up to her face, closing one eye and directing the other toward the group. "Come on, get a bit closer," she said, waving her hand in front of her as if she were directing them.

"Come on then. Boss's orders," Leo whispered into Nelly's ear. She grinned despite herself as he hooked one arm around her shoulder and another around Thomas's.

"That's it. Gorgeous. Right then. Everyone, say cheese."

"Cheese," the group said in unison. The flash went off and Nelly began to move away.

"Oh fuck. Did I do it right?" India asked, looking at the camera as if she were speaking to it.

"Give it here," Oliver said, reaching out to take the camera from her hands. She handed it over to him. "Go on then. You get in too," he said, nodding to India.

She reached up and kissed his cheek before running over gleefully to join her friends. She stood beside Nelly, wrapping her hands around her waist and pressing her cheek against the curls of her head. "We'll do a topless one next," she whispered into Nelly's ear, making her laugh again.

The flash went off and Nelly hadn't had time to rearrange her face before the picture was taken. Oliver brought the camera down from his eye, standing still for a moment and holding it up demonstratively and saying, "I got a good one."

He turned and walked back toward the house, taking the camera with him.

1996
Oliver

The car pulled off from Oliver's driveway as quickly as it had pulled in a week earlier. He felt glum and oddly lonely as he watched the four friends pulling away out from his world. Lorraine had asked to stay for the day, but he'd lied and told her that he was busy. He didn't want her there. He'd be going back to England in four days himself, so there wasn't much point in carrying on the charade of being interested in her much longer, anyway. He could still hear the noise of their laughter and sibling-like bickering as they eased off from the drive, three tanned and freckled arms reaching out from the windows and waving at him. He waited, but the window that Nelly was sat in stayed silent. He felt as if his heart was aching as he quietly urged her hand to appear and wave him goodbye. But it didn't.

Oliver held up his own hand in solitude and then, when the car began to fade into the distance, returned back into the house.

1996
Nelly

The letter had already been there waiting when they had arrived home in Cambridge three weeks later. It was in a white envelope, stripes of red and blue chequered across the top.

Nelly Strapelli
24 Malcolm Street
Cambridge

She recognised the handwriting immediately. She felt desperate to tear it open and reveal its content. But she also wanted to savour it.

The letter stayed hidden in her sock drawer until she went to bed that night and she was certain that India had gone to her own room. Nelly sat with the letter on her bed, gazing down at the envelope before fumbling her thumb down the back of it to tear it open. She pulled out a single slip from the inside.

It was a picture. Small and black and white, almost like a Polaroid, although it had clearly been developed. It had been taken from the day before they left in Oliver's garden. The one that the group had posed for. Except for it was only of Nelly. Zoomed in, as if nobody else had been there. She looked down at the image, almost not recognising herself as the subject of it. Her face was angled upward, a smile spread across her cheeks toward India's chin that was just out from frame. Her skin looked tanned and olive-y, the sun hitting her face so as the right side of it was just in shadow. She had never thought of herself as beautiful. But, through the eyes of this lens, it was almost as if she could have been.

The paper was puckered slightly across the middle as if someone had written on the back of it and Nelly turned it over to reveal a simple line of words.

Because you are my Nelly.

1997
Nelly

"What time am I expected?"

"Half seven, India says. Although she really means half six. I think she's hoping you'll somehow telepathically know she wants you to help set up. And that you'll offer to pay for the drinks."

Oliver let out a breath on the other end of the phone that sounded like a smile, "Obviously."

Nelly smiled back. "And she said to tell you to bring champagne."

"Obviously again."

Nelly laughed.

Oliver continued, "Honestly, who asks guests to cater their own parties? Does she still have you on food?"

Nelly balanced the phone between her ear and her shoulder as she poured water over a tea bag, stirring in a heaped lump of sugar. "She does. But, in all fairness, I am her housemate."

"Mmm."

"So, I don't know that I really count as a guest. And you're her brother, so you don't really count either."

"I'll remember that next time I get told off for helping myself to biscuits."

Nelly smiled at him through the phone. It was India's birthday and she was throwing a party in her and Nelly's flat, with a lot of help from Nelly and Oliver. The theme was Icons and India had decorated the place accordingly, rolling out a very dishevelled red carpet that she'd found in the store cupboard at work outside the front door and stringing a glitter ball to the ceiling over the small, cluttered lounge. When Nelly asked India what she'd do about the carpet if it rained India had just shrugged and said, "It isn't allowed to."

Nelly thought it ambitious, since they lived in London. But then, why shouldn't it be sunny? Nelly was strictly in charge of the food, upon India's demand. She had managed to wrangle a rare day off from her work at Alfred Salter Primary School to prepare herself, getting up early to go to the market and spending a small fortune buying meats and tomatoes and cheeses and olives and anything else that she thought she might be able to stuff into pastry or over bread. Her parents, who had taken a particular shine to both India and Oliver in recent months, had provided a cake.

Nelly felt guilty about this, knowing that they didn't have a lot of money. But they had offered their services when India had mentioned the party over Sunday dinner one afternoon. They had misconstrued the mention as an invitation for themselves also and, when announcing this, Nelly had felt momentarily worried about her parents until India had hugged them both with one arm each and said that of course they were invited; they were family. It made Nelly's heart sing. Luckily, they were working that evening. Nelly wasn't sure that she wanted her parents to see one of India's parties yet.

"So, are you going to let me know who you're dressing up as yet? Or is it still a secret?"

Nelly chewed on the side of her mouth, already feeling nervous at the prospect of the fancy dress.

"Let me guess," Oliver's voice smiled down the phone, "Hmmm. Kate Bush?"

Nelly rolled her eyes.

"Alright then. Not Kate Bush? Okay. What about Dolly Parton? I'd quite like to see you in one of those dresses."

Nelly laughed, "No. Not Dolly Parton. I don't have the boobs for that, unfortunately."

"I think you might do."

Nelly blushed. "What makes you think it's a singer that I'm coming as?"

"Because India would murder you in your sleep if you didn't. You know she's banking on you to man the karaoke machine with her for the evening."

Nelly laughed. She and Oliver's relationship had developed since the holiday in Provence the summer previously. Firstly, Nelly and India had moved to London together which meant that they saw Oliver a lot more frequently than they previously had done. Secondly, and most surprisingly, Oliver and Nelly had become friends. And, whether it was the increased proximity or the decreased time between seeing one another, an ease had somehow lingered its way into their relationship. The anxiety that Nelly had once felt about him—the painful glances and stolen moments—was still there, but buried a little bit further down underneath a blanket of familiarity.

They saw each other often and she found that the more that they did so, the more that she understood him. He was still reserved and somewhat closed, but he was also sweet and generous and laughed more frequently than he had before. Or, than he had since Nelly had known him at least. She wondered idly whether it might have been slightly her influence, but then decided it was probably more India's. She was the one that was always smiling these days.

"Anyway, what about you? Who are you going to be coming as?"

"Ah. I can't tell you that, I'm afraid."

"Why not?"

"Because you won't tell me yours."

"That's very childish."

"Well, I didn't say I was proud of the reason."

Nelly laughed again. She could imagine the way that he would be arranging his face as he said this, one corner of his mouth inching up into his cheek as if he were pleased with himself.

"You better dress up."

"Or what?"

"Or…" Nelly chewed on her cheek again thoughtfully. "Or I won't let you over for Sunday dinner anymore."

Oliver gave a mock gasp on the other end of the phone, "Sunday without a Nelly Strapelli special?"

"Yep."

"Mmm. That is a predicament. Although I suppose worst-case scenario, I could probably get myself fed elsewhere."

"Oh yeah?"

"Mmm. There's a food truck just outside from my office that probably caters to a similar standard."

"Oi!"

He laughed and then was quiet for a moment before saying, "Don't worry. I'll dress up for you."

Nelly smiled, "Good."

Oliver sighed, "Anyway, I'd better be getting back to it."

"Yeah?"

"Mmm. Let India know I'll be over about half seven-ish."

Nelly opened her mouth to remind him that he was supposed to come to help earlier but he laughed and interrupted her, "I'm kidding. I'll be there at half six. Even earlier than that. Six o'clock. On the dot."

"Alright then. I'll see you later."

"See ya, Dolly."

Nelly smiled. She didn't want the conversation to end.

"Oh, and Nelly?"

"Mmm?"

"I was only kidding. Nobody makes meatballs like you do."

Nelly smiled, "Thank you."

"Apart from maybe your dad."

Nelly rolled her eyes and hung up the phone.

True to his word, Oliver arrived early to help the girls set up. He turned up wearing a red leather jacket, his dirty-blonde hair greased back from his face and a cigarette dangling from his lips. It irritated Nelly a little bit how good he looked, even when he was supposed to look stupid.

"James Dean?" She asked him when she opened the door.

He shrugged as if he wasn't sure himself. She fiddled with the clip in her hair that was pulling back one side of her curls. She was wearing a black Bardot top and tight black trousers that were made of a sort of shiny, stretchy material that was already beginning to dig into her stomach. When she'd tried the outfit on, she'd thought she looked good—a bit sexy, even—but now she felt self-conscious of her thighs and the way that the skin was puckering under her armpits where her bra was a bit too tight.

"And you came as?"

"Sandy. From *Grease*."

Oliver nodded, "Ah right." He was leaning against the doorway, his eyes trailing down Nelly's body to linger on her thighs and then quickly pull back up to her face. Smooth enough that she could convince herself she hadn't noticed. She turned around, feeling warmth beginning to rise in her cheeks. Oliver followed her into the flat and closed the door behind them. The place had exploded into some sort of bomb of glittering mayhem. Oliver eyed it dubiously, not saying anything.

"She got a bit carried away," Nelly said by way of explanation.

Oliver nodded.

"Is that my brother?" India's voice called out from the bathroom, "Tell him to come in and put the wine in the fridge. And can he go down and get the last box of party poppers from my car and bring them back up? I want them here when everyone arrives."

"I'm guessing she's coming as Stalin," Oliver said as he moved past Nelly toward the small, adjoined kitchen. Nelly smiled, crossing her arms in an effort to cover her bare shoulders a bit. She wondered how long it would be until she could get her cardigan. Oliver began to unload bottles of wine from a bag that he placed on the counter, pulling open the fridge and peering inside. He took himself out a beer and then called out to India, "There's no room in the fridge."

"Then make room!" India replied.

Nelly wrinkled her nose, "She's a bit nervous."

Oliver shook his head, but didn't argue. Nelly was just about to ask Oliver something when India appeared from the bathroom. She was wearing a white tutu over a black leotard, a pink bow perched on the top of her blonde hair which she was halfway through crimping.

"Ah. Barry Gibb?" Oliver asked plainly when he turned to look at her. India threw something at him that bounced off the fridge door.

"Nel, do I look okay?"

Nelly smiled, "You look gorgeous."

"Really? My hair isn't too…" she gestured around her head.

Nelly shook her head, "No. It's perfect."

India grinned, "Good. Thanks, my love. I'll be ready in two secs." She disappeared back into the bathroom and then returned again a few minutes later, her hair now finished. Oliver and Nelly were sharing a joke as she blew up balloons and passed them to him to tie onto strings, hanging them from the ceiling.

"Are you done with the streamers?" India asked Oliver over her shoulder as she dashed into the room. She was full of nervous, chaotic energy; her anxiousness radiating off from her and into Nelly's own stomach.

"Where are they?"

"Under the sink. Behind the vase," India instructed. She was brandishing something in her hand, which she reached forward with and started applying to Nelly's face. India drew the red lipstick around Nelly's mouth carefully, her pink lips parting slightly as she did so in concentration. "There you go. Officially perfect," she smiled, leaning back to admire Nelly's face.

Nelly rubbed her lips together, wishing that she could see herself. She stretched up onto her tiptoes to peer into the circular mirror that hung on the far wall, inspecting India's work. When she did so, she caught Oliver's eyes watching her. He smiled, then pulled them away and busied himself with looking under the sink.

1997

Oliver

By eight o'clock, the tiny flat was packed with people. Oliver had stationed himself by the window with the other smokers, leaning against the wall and listening to someone very boring telling him about all of the reasons why she loved Marilyn Monroe. She was wearing a white dress with a severely plunging neckline that she kept pressing together with her two arms in a way that she clearly thought seemed natural. Oliver couldn't imagine finding her less attractive.

"So, you're India's brother, aren't you?" She asked him, dangling her cigarette from her lips.

Oliver raised his eyebrows, "Yeah."

"Cool," she smiled, "I mean, I've heard loads about you. India and you are really close, right?"

Oliver blew smoke out from his mouth and nodded, "Yeah. I suppose so."

She clutched a hand to her chest, pulling a face. "That is so sweet! I've always wished I had a protective older brother to look after me." She reached out a hand and rubbed his arm, smiling at him with her wide mouth. It was almost shameless. He wondered how many glasses of wine she had drunk and noticed that it was the white; the cheapest one he had put into the fridge earlier that evening. What he was really doing was watching Nelly. She was standing by the kitchen counter holding a bottle of beer to her chest, her t-shirt pulled down to reveal her tiny tanned shoulders. She was standing with Leo and his friend—Tim or Tyler or something. Someone that Leo had brought with him from work.

"The guy I've been telling you about," he'd said to Nelly when he'd introduced them. Oliver had felt himself bristle immediately. Tim or Tyler was dressed in a purple shirt, unbuttoned to reveal a dark, mossy chest. He was standing next to Nelly, his hand leant against the counter just behind her back.

The three of them were laughing at something that Leo was saying. Oliver knew that he shouldn't feel jealous. He knew that he and Nelly were closer; more in sync. And it wasn't as if he wasn't sleeping with other women. But still, she was his Nelly. The idea of another man with her made him want to bite down very hard on the end of his cigarette.

"So, I'm one of three," the woman was telling him. "Three sisters, can you imagine? And I'm the flat chested one! I know right, my poor daddy." She laughed at her own joke and reached out to steady herself on Oliver's arm again. He raised his eyebrows, not making eye contact. Sometimes he wished that women wouldn't drape themselves over him so freely. What he really wanted was a nice girlfriend. Someone that he could talk with and watch television and cook with. He actually really enjoyed cooking. He liked how methodical it was; structured.

Nelly had taught him how to make lasagne recently. She had shown him how to get the sausages out from their skins and roll them up into hundreds of tiny meatballs, which she later fried whilst he watched her from just behind. She'd looked lovely as she'd done it. She looked lovely this evening, too. He wished he'd told her that when she'd opened the door.

The problem was, Oliver and Nelly's relationship consisted of the sort of uncomfortable concoction of clearly being interested in one another and yet not being able to do anything about it in case they spoiled things. They were too close and yet not close enough. So many Sundays when he was sat at the kitchen table listening to India and Nelly's chatter, he wished that he could reach out and hold Nelly's hand. Or that he could take her plate away and kiss the top of her head on his way to the sink. But he couldn't. Not when India was there. It was like an unspoken boundary. A rule. He wasn't sure which of them had made it.

"So, what do you think?" The woman asked him.

"Hmm?"

"About taking me out some time. India says you're a banker."

Oliver raised his eyebrows but didn't reply. The woman giggled. He wasn't sure what he was doing to make her behave in such a way.

Later that evening, the person that Leo had brought with him—Christian, it turned out—came over to Oliver where he sat on the settee. Oliver had been talking to his friends about something, but really, he was watching India and Nelly. They were singing along with the karaoke machine to *Like a Virgin*. India was so drunk that he was sure that if someone lit a lighter near her, she would go up in flames. Nelly also looked slightly worse for wear. She had let one sleeve of her top fall further down her arm to reveal a white bra strap, her red lipstick smudged slightly from where her mouth had been around the tops of glasses. Oliver couldn't help but laugh in spite of himself at the two of them. They seemed to have forgotten that anyone else was there, India's arm draped around Nelly's small frame as they both closed their eyes and swayed in unison. They were almost childlike. It made Oliver want to cuddle them both.

Leo wolf-whistled at them from the chair beside Oliver and clapped his hands loudly. "They're adorable, aren't they?" He said, clutching his chest like a proud parent.

Oliver nodded, forgetting himself momentarily. Leo and Christian exchanged a look.

"So Oliver, mate," the person—Christian—began to say.

"Mmm?"

"I wanted to ask you something."

Oliver lit a cigarette but didn't reply.

Christian continued, "See, I wondered how you'd feel about me asking Nelly out?"

The question hadn't surprised Oliver, even though it had annoyed him. He didn't return Christian's gaze but shrugged, saying, "You don't need my permission."

Christian exchanged a look with Leo, who was making himself busy with his beer. "No, of course not. I just mean…" Christian trailed off, but then said, "Well, you're close, aren't you? You and Nelly, I mean…"

Oliver blew the smoke out from his mouth.

"She talks about you a lot. So I was just wondering, like, bloke to bloke. Is there something going on with the two of you?"

Oliver looked up at Nelly, her face red from laughter as India rocked her in her arms.

"Like, are you a thing?"

Oliver stubbed his cigarette out in the ashtray perched on the coffee table. After a moment, he shook his head, "You'll have to ask Nelly, mate. I don't own her. We aren't sleeping together, if that's what you're asking."

Christian nodded, looking relieved. "Cool, cheers." He stood up, placing a hand on Oliver's shoulder as he moved by. Oliver could see Leo looking at him from his peripheral vision. He stood up and moved toward the window where the blonde girl was still watching him from.

1997
Nelly

"Oliver! Get Oliver!" India was saying from the bathroom floor, her head hanging into the toilet bowl.

"In a minute," Leo told her soothingly, stroking the back of her head as she vomited red wine and cheap vodka into the basin. Nelly thought that she might be sick too, in a minute. She wasn't sure how much she'd had to drink. The night was already blurry. She remembered people arriving. And people toasting. And singing karaoke with India. But the rest was already hazy. Like the kiss she'd shared with Christian. His cheeks had been rough and stubbly and his breath had smelled like smoke. Or maybe that had been hers. Either way, she hadn't enjoyed it.

"Oliver!" India shouted again.

"Alright. Alright."

Nelly could feel Leo's shape getting up from the floor and moving past her as she sat with her eyes closed against the bath. She heard the door open and the music from the living room pour in, Leo shouting something over the top of it.

"Oliver!" India called again between retches.

Nelly breathed in through her nose, feeling the room spinning around her. She wished she hadn't drunk so much. "Ind," she tried to say. Her voice came out whispered and slurred. "Ind. Are you okay?"

"Oh fuck," India replied, vomiting again into the toilet.

Nelly nodded.

At some point, she heard Oliver's voice coming into the bathroom.

"Jesus, you two."

"I think we might have overdone it," India said innocently, her face pressed against the side of the toilet bowl.

"I think you might have, mate," Oliver replied.

"I want to go to bed," Nelly announced. She turned her head and saw Oliver's frame swirling in front of her eyes. Perfect. So perfect.

"Mmm yes. Bed sounds good," India slurred back.

"Do you think you can stand up?" Oliver asked.

Nelly shook her head. It hurt.

"I have to stay here, Oliver," India told him.

"I thought you wanted to go to bed?"

"Nelly does! I have to stay here."

Oliver sighed. "Fine. Okay." He looked at India for a moment before she let out a fresh hurl of vomit. Leo dove back into the room and pulled her hair back just in time. Nelly watched vaguely as Oliver crouched down in front of her. He was watching her concernedly, his blue eyes slightly squinting. He was so handsome. She wanted to tell him so. To touch him. She reached out a hand and let it caress clumsily down the side of his cheek. He smiled at her.

"You're drunk."

Nelly nodded.

"Oliver, are you cross with us?" India asked. She had turned to sit with her back to the toilet.

Oliver shook his head, "Course not."

"But we're pissed."

Oliver shrugged, "It's your birthday. You're allowed to be."

"It isn't my birthday," Nelly said quietly.

"My birthday is your birthday," India replied, tapping Nelly's leg with her bare foot.

"Thank you."

"Oliver, do you still love me?"

Oliver turned to look at his sister, "Huh?"

"Do you love me? Even though I'm a pain and I made you bring the wine and everything."

Oliver smiled, "Yes. I still love you. Even though you're a little bit of a pain."

"Good. Now tell Nelly that you love her."

"Mmm?"

"Tell Nelly you love her, too."

Nelly watched as Oliver's head turned toward hers. He was still smiling, but sympathetically. Almost paternally. Nelly suddenly felt self-conscious of the lipstick on her mouth and she rubbed at it with the back of her hand. It felt sticky.

Oliver reached out and wiped the edge of her mouth, the ghost of a smile on his lips. She sat motionless, allowing him to look at her. She felt safe with him watching over them.

"Oliver! Tell Nelly that you love her, too!"

Oliver laughed slightly and shook his head. "I love you, too," he told Nelly.

1997

Oliver

"So, what d'you think I did next?" Felix was half-shouting from beside Oliver's ear. He was standing whilst everyone else sat, his hand gripped firmly around Oliver's shoulder, rocking him slightly as he spoke. Felix laughed, "I said to him, make me two more million and then we'll talk. And what did he go and fucking do?"

The rest of the table lifted beer bottles into the air, saluting and cheering. Felix grinned down at Oliver. He felt as if he should return the gesture somehow, even though he didn't feel particularly proud of himself. It was his job to make money, after all. He was good at it. Naturally good at it. But he also worked really hard, partially down to the fact that he was extremely conscious that he was working for his father's company and didn't want the rest of his colleagues to think he had a free ride. The truth was, Oliver hated his job every bit as much as he had done when he had first taken it. He also hated the version of himself that he had to be when he was there. Laddish. Chauvinistic.

In all fairness, he didn't actually change his countenance at all. But he also didn't say anything when the other men acted like arseholes, which he felt was almost as bad as actually being one. Long gone were the days where he sat in cafes in Paris taking pictures of dogs and pedestrians and lovers as they drank their morning coffee. Now he was a stockbroker. Just like his father had always wanted him to be. Still, he could leave if he really wanted to. He supposed it was the money making him stay. He did like the money.

Oliver's eyes tripped upward when he saw the shape of her walk into the room. She was wearing a pink dress; frilly at the shoulders and cut down just to the mid-way of her calves. He'd seen her wearing it before. There was a long zip at the back that he couldn't see at the moment and a tiny tear in one of the sleeves that she'd tacked back together herself, but it didn't matter. Nelly was beautiful anyway.

He stood automatically from his chair, not bothering to hear the rest of Felix's speech. Her eyes met his from where she was standing. Dark, full eyes. She looked a bit nervous. Nelly usually did.

He moved toward her automatically, kissing her cheek when he had closed the distance. She smelled like vanilla and something else he couldn't place immediately.

"Sorry I'm late," she told him as he drew back from her face, "I was at the restaurant. They're short-staffed again."

"Do you need to go back?"

She shook her head, "No. Nico's there now."

Oliver smiled. He was suddenly able to place the smell. A mixture of onions and tomatoes and meat. He would have loved to have been in Nelly's parents' restaurant with her eating Bolognese and drinking tap water rather than here drinking champagne and eating steak that was so expensive he may as well have bought the cow.

Nelly took a nervous breath and nodded toward the table. Oliver raised his eyebrows, "Yep."

She smiled, "Well, get it over and done with. Shall we?"

Oliver nodded, turning with her as she moved toward the table where his colleagues sat laughing. He allowed his hand to travel gently up the zip that he had known was there on the back of Nelly's dress for a moment, coming to rest on the small of her back. He pulled out the chair that he'd purposefully kept vacant beside his and she gave him a small smile as she sat down on top of it. He was glad that she was there. As if he could be a bit more himself.

"Here's the man of the hour," Felix said, smacking Oliver on the back as he pushed in Nelly's chair. "Hello, darling. Nice to see you," Felix winked at Nelly, bending forward across Oliver to kiss her cheek. Oliver watched him until he moved back away and then sat down. Nelly tapped her knee against Oliver's thigh underneath the table. He looked over at her, but she was looking at Felix as he carried on speaking. The proximity of her was reassuring.

They ate and listened idly to Felix telling more stories about work more and more loudly with the more that he drank. At some point, Nelly brushed her hand against Oliver's under the table and he stretched his fingers out, drawing her further in and stroking against the back of her knuckles. She had dry hands.

Always. Even when it was thirty degrees outside. He made a mental note to pick her up some hand cream the next time he was at Harrods. Nelly had come to one of Oliver's work events before. His colleagues often brought dates with them; wives and girlfriends and partners. Other-halves that, Oliver noticed, often were forgotten easily at the pub on a Wednesday afternoon when a better—or easier—prospect presented itself.

It seemed generally to be encouraged to bring a wife with you, as if the men that worked with Oliver were incapable of being able to be kept under control without them. Oliver hated these work events. It was just a lot of chauvinistic mingling and hobnobbing, all of which he was used to but found inherently draining. He had grown up in this world. Well aware that beneath the flatter and disingenuous compliments this was a group of people that, if the situation arose, would throw him to the wolves to save their own skin as easily as they would order a second round of drinks. And amongst all of the back-slapping and finger pointing, to have Nelly by his side was a sort of anchor back to reality; she wasn't the type of person that would ever be taken in by or take seriously the other men at the table. That was one of the things that Oliver loved about her. Anyway, it was nice to get to spend some time alone together. He felt her eyes on his now and turned to meet her gaze. She looked away quickly. A smile tugged at his lips.

A waitress stretched around Oliver's shoulder to place a plate of steak tartar in front of him and he leant back to provide her with enough room, automatically reaching to place his arm around the back of Nelly's chair.

"Can I get you anything else, sir?" The waitress asked him. She was attractive, with blonde hair that she flicked around her face as she spoke and a full, pink mouth. Oliver returned her gaze.

"I'm alright, I think. Thanks."

"Are you sure? A drink, or…" her voice trailed off, but she stayed standing in front of Oliver.

Oliver felt the smile tugging at the edge of his lips. He stroked Nelly's shoulder casually, feeling her skin warm beneath his fingertips. "I'm good, thank you."

The waitress was looking at him coyly, her mouth working beneath her lips. "Okay, well, if you change your mind." She winked and swayed away around the table, turning back to look at Oliver. He only returned her gaze because he knew that it would irritate Nelly. Her lips were pressed together in a thin line as she made a show of being very interested in her bread. Oliver smiled at the side of her face and she pointedly looked the other way.

They played this game a lot. But only when nobody else was around. Which was one of the other reasons that Oliver liked to bring Nelly as his date to his work functions. It was almost as if the charade of them doing grown-up, couple-like activities cajoled them into behaving as if they actually were an item. Or convincing themselves that they were one, for a time. There behaviour at such events was different than it would be under normal circumstances. And this was an unspoken rule that they both somehow knew. The boundaries, however, were titillatingly blurry.

"Think she might have liked you," Nelly told the air over her shoulder.

"Mmm?" Oliver replied softly, smiling into his glass.

Nelly turned and looked at him, her dark eyes shiny. She had a tiny mole on the very top of her lip that just cradled over the cusp of where her skin met her mouth. Oliver wondered what she would do if he reached over to her now and kissed it.

"You know she did."

Oliver shrugged, "I didn't notice."

"Yeah. Okay," Nelly replied, rolling her eyes. She looked away and then looked back at him, squinting her eyes almost accusatorially whilst her cheeks fought against her smile. Oliver was sure that she enjoyed their game as much as he did. He let his hand travel up her shoulder toward the bottom of her neck. They maintained eye contact until Nelly broke it, glancing at the people sat around the table beside them as if they had been doing something provocative.

Oliver smiled. He let his fingers spread across her shoulder blades. His hand was almost the width of her entire back when he let it stretch out. He smiled again and then let his fingers rest on her shoulder.

"So then, what does the missus think?" Felix asked him later on whilst Nelly engaged in conversation with the man to her other side. She looked somehow incredibly bored and also irrationally irritated at the same time. It made Oliver want to grin.

"Hmm?"

"Your missus," Felix said again, jutting his eyes to Nelly's frame. "She excited about it, or what?"

Oliver let his mind curl back to reality for a moment. "Oh. Yeah."

Felix looked pleased, "Yeah? That's good, mate. It's a bloody ball ache when they kick off about that sort of thing, isn't it?"

"Mmm," Oliver said noncommittally.

"So, you're gonna take it?"

Oliver took a swig of champagne. It was warm and almost completely flat. "Yeah. I'm thinking about it."

Felix clapped him on the back, "Good man. Good man. Listen, did I tell you about the office over there?"

Oliver let his eyes glaze over as he listened uninterestedly to Felix telling him about the New York office. He'd been offered the job earlier in the week. A year's transfer to the US. They were paying his accommodation and his relocation fee as part of the package; or, they'd offered to, at least. He hadn't made his mind up about whether or not he was going to take it. If he was honest with himself, he hadn't actually allowed himself to think about it at all. The reality of the situation was that, whilst they both enjoyed pretending to be a couple on occasions like this evening, Oliver was also certain that he and Nelly wouldn't be a possibility in real life. That was why they had their unspoken rule. That was why they had never really crossed any boundaries in their friendship. Not technically, at least.

To Nelly, her friendship with India would always come first. For Oliver, he knew that he was too selfish to ever really commit to one woman, as much as he liked to sometimes entertain the idea of being able to do so. Nelly was his friend. A friend that he adored. A friend that he hated hearing about being with other men. A friend that he lay in bed and fantasised about having sex with. A friend that he was pretty certain that he was in love with, and that was also in love with him. But a friend, nonetheless. And he wasn't willing to gamble on losing Nelly by fucking her and then inevitably also fucking everything else up in the process. He needed to get on with his own life. And yet, the idea of moving away from her again made his chest feel empty.

At some point during the conversation, Nelly turned around and rolled her eyes at the man she was talking to. She obviously thought that she was being discrete, blissfully unaware of how expressive her face was. Oliver smiled at her and she grinned back. He felt his heart swell inside his chest.

1997
Nelly

Oliver's hands brushed down the sides of Nelly's shoulders as he put her coat over them for her. She smiled, her back still to him. He was always so gentle when he touched her. Tentative and yet purposeful. Like he was being careful not to hurt her. Like she was to be handled with care. He made her feel precious. That was one of the things that she loved about him.

"Oliver, mate. You off?" Someone called from behind them. Oliver and Nelly both turned around to see Felix swaying forward, music blaring out overhead.

"Yeah," Oliver replied, reaching out almost automatically to place his hand on the small of Nelly's back. The feel of it there—the weight of it—was prominent and blissfully heavy through her coat. He often did this when other men from his work were around, as if he was marking his territory. Nelly enjoyed it, though she wouldn't have done if it had been anyone other than Oliver doing it.

Felix bent over and kissed her cheek, "Lovely seeing you, Nelly darling."

"Nice to see you too, Felix," she replied. It wasn't even a lie. As much as she couldn't stand Oliver's colleagues, Nelly loved coming to his work events with him. The first time had been India's idea. Oliver had mentioned that he had been told to bring a partner, and India had suggested he take Nelly. She said that Nelly would help him to make a good impression, but Nelly knew that it had partially been because India had been going on a date and she didn't want Nelly staying in on her own for another Friday night. India was like that these days. She only seemed happy to enjoy herself if she knew that other people around her were doing the same. Like she had a responsibility over them.

She undoubtably thought that both Nelly and Oliver would be indifferent to the suggestion, having a nice time at best. Nelly doubted that India knew quite how much the prospect of an evening alone with Oliver made Nelly feel both anxious and excited in extremes, or the way that her skin almost burned if Oliver's fingers so much as grazed over it. They had never really been alone together before – not officially, at least – and Nelly had been concerned that it might have been awkward. But the first time that she had met them, Oliver's colleagues had assumed without saying so that Nelly and Oliver had been romantically involved, and had spoken with and treated Nelly as if she were one of the other many wives and girlfriends dragged along to these events.

Nelly had been shocked when Oliver had also gone along with the charade. He held his hand to the small of her back as he introduced her and whispered jokes into her ear to make her smile when people weren't looking; he sat with his arm around the back of her chair and let his fingers dance against the skin of her shoulder as she spoke, his eyes trained against hers as if he was scared that he might miss something if he looked away. And she in turn reciprocated with her own version. When they were alone, Nelly allowed herself to be open with Oliver in a way that she never had been previously. They treated each other with a familiarity, as if they were used to touching and holding and talking in such close proximities.

Neither of them questioned what they were doing and why, because they both already knew. It was almost as if, free from their usual social circle, Nelly and Oliver felt as if they could play parts that they would normally never indulge. The more that they did it, the less Nelly was sure whether they were acting. It seemed natural. Easy. It was only when they left and resumed their real roles in each other's lives that it felt laboured. As soon as they went back to the real world, the charade ended. Nelly wasn't sure which of them had set the boundary or whether it had been mutual, but they both seemed to know it. That was why she hated when evenings like this had to end.

Felix shook Oliver's hand. "Congratulations again, son. Looking forward to your answer on Monday."

Oliver nodded, "Yeah. No worries."

Felix smacked Oliver's arm. He turned to Nelly and winked, "Do me a favour and convince him for me, Nelly?"

Nelly looked up at Oliver quickly but his face didn't give anything away. She returned Felix's smile and replied, "I mean, I'll do my best."

Felix laughed, "I'm sure you've got a few tricks up your sleeve." He winked again and Nelly had to tell her eyes not to roll. Oliver turned and led her out from the restaurant and into the quiet of the street without saying goodbye to his boss.

Nelly and India went round to Oliver's flat on Sunday because India's car was broken and she needed to borrow Oliver's. It was only three days since Oliver's work dinner, but the way that he and Nelly behaved when they saw each other couldn't have felt further apart. As usual, India let herself in when they arrived without knocking. Oliver was noticeably absent and Nelly could hear the shower from the bathroom. When he came out, he was wearing a pair of grey jogging bottoms and a slightly damp looking t-shirt, his hair tussled from where he'd clearly just rubbed at it with a towel.

"Do you have anything good to drink?" India asked him as way of greeting as she stared into his fridge.

He shook his head and then looked up at Nelly where she loitered behind the kitchen island. "Hey," he said.

"Hey."

"Oliver, can we have this?"

"Have whatever," Oliver replied lazily, reaching over India's shoulder and plucking a pack of beers from the fridge. He twisted the cap off from one and slid it across the island toward Nelly, smiling at her briefly as he did so. She felt herself blush and wished that she hadn't. From the outside, it was clear that the two of them had a strange relationship. Unhealthy, almost. For the most part, they acted as if they were friends. But then sometimes—like Thursday night—they behaved as if they were much more than that. Nelly remembered the feeling of Oliver's hand wrapped around hers. The sensation of his breath against her cheek as he'd kissed her goodbye and lingered around her mouth. She wished that one of them was more guilty than the other. If it had been purely him leading her on, then she could have known how to feel about it. But she was well aware of the fact that she was guilty of doing the exact same thing.

Whenever they were alone, they behaved one way and then when they were with anyone else—or, most prominently, when they were with India—they acted as if it had never happened. It was almost like they were having some sort of affair. And, even though they had never crossed any real boundary and she had never once lied to India about it, it made Nelly feel oddly guilty. As if she were cheating on her friend, somehow. The truth was, Nelly had known that she was in love with Oliver since the morning that she'd woken up in his bed three years ago after India's birthday party. She could still remember everything about it. The anxiety. The nervousness. The way that his face had been arranged as he'd rested and the way that his breath had smelled as it moved gently against her nose. At first, the feeling had been painful; agonising, even. But then it had ebbed into a familiar weight on her chest; not less or more, just somehow settled. She'd learned to live with it. Sometimes—times like Thursday night—she wondered if he felt the same way about her.

She knew that he liked her. He was kind and gentle and in some ways possessive over her in the same way that she disliked that she also felt over him. She noticed the way that he looked to her for reassurance sometimes or the way that he would go quiet if she mentioned another man asking her out. But then India would mention a date that he'd had or some girl that he'd slept with when he'd been out with his friends on the weekend and Nelly would feel as if she'd imagined the whole thing.

Besides, the situation was irrelevant, really. Even if she wanted to, Nelly didn't feel as if she could ever do anything about her feelings for Oliver. He was India's brother, after all. And, although she'd never said it, she knew that India would feel as if she had to choose between them when things inevitably went wrong. And she couldn't risk hurting India like that. Or losing her. Losing both of them.

"Do you want to go down together on the weekend, Ol?"

Oliver pulled his eyes away from Nelly's and turned to look at his sister. "Huh?"

"To Mum and Dad's. For the party."

"Oh. Mmm. I dunno. I've got something to finish at work on Friday so I dunno when I'll get off."

India rolled her eyes and shook her head at Nelly, "This boy, eh? Always working."

"Mmm," Nelly replied with a smile. She could feel her heart beating inside of her chest as if she had done something wrong. She swallowed a sip of beer. They needed to stop playing this game. She and Oliver. His eyes were on hers again when she looked back up. He winked at her, softly and quickly. She felt her cheeks begin to turn into a smile and looked back down at her bottle.

"Well, we can go down with you on Saturday morning, if you like?"

"Yeah? If you want."

"Saves getting the train," India shrugged at Nelly.

"Mmm. Yeah," Nelly nodded. A fresh pang of guilt stabbed through her chest.

"You alright, bub?" India asked, stroking Nelly's hair as she walked by.

"Mmm. Yeah. Of course." Nelly smiled, nodding a bit too enthusiastically.

India regarded her for a moment and then said, "It isn't about Christian, is it?"

Nelly felt her heart drop to her stomach. "No."

"Christian?" Oliver asked. His voice was flat and casual, but Nelly could almost hear her own breathing. She had gone on a couple of dates with Christian after India's party. They'd shared some more kisses and had sex clumsily under the influence of too much rosé. She hadn't had the heart to tell him that she preferred red. Nelly had been the one to end it. But she'd not told India this. It would have invited too many questions.

India's face looked at her now; the contours of her blue eyes soft and concerned. She stepped forward and pressed Nelly into a hug, stroking the back of her hair comfortingly.

"He's a twat if he doesn't want to be with you," she cooed.

Nelly smiled, "Thanks, Ind. I'm fine. Really."

"Only an idiot wouldn't be completely in love with you."

Nelly locked eyes with Oliver over his sister's shoulder. She wished she knew why she felt as guilty as she did.

1997

Oliver

Oliver hated going back to his parents' house. He visited as infrequently as he could, always blaming work and commitments with friends for his lack of involvement at familial events. He didn't have a great relationship with his father. He always made Oliver feel small. Inadequate. They seldom spoke. And when they did, Oliver found that they had very little to say, despite the fact that they had so much in common. He struggled with his father, and the fact that Oliver had begun using the same excuses for deprioritising his family as his dad had done all of Oliver's life made Oliver struggle with himself. He would have missed the anniversary party altogether had India not practically dragged him there.

They were going to be staying Saturday to Sunday; Oliver, India and Nelly. Nelly. She had come to be such a permanent fixture in Oliver's life that it didn't even feel strange to him that she would be involved so heavily with family functions and events. It didn't feel strange to him that he was as heavily involved in her family as he was, either. That Oliver had a permanent invite to Sunday dinner or that her dad rang him when his van frequently broke down on the way home from the market somehow seemed perfectly normal. The *second sibling*, India referred to Nelly as. Oliver hated that. But he loved that they were so often together, also. It was better than nothing.

"Do we think blue bunting or red?" India asked them as she stood on a chair in the garden, her bare feet balancing atop a very precarious plastic seat. Nelly moved behind instinctively, steadying the legs of it against the ground. They had become a sort of extension of one another over the past years; Nelly and India. Oliver wondered how India would ever keep from toppling over if Nelly weren't there to stop her. The idea of it pressed against his rib cage.

He knew it was selfish, the way that he felt for Nelly. It wasn't that he wanted her just for himself. It was more that he knew what the friendship was to India. The stability that it provided for her. And until he was sure—really, really sure—he knew that he couldn't compromise that. The problem was, the more time he spent watching Nelly from the corner of his eye, the surer that he was about his feelings for her.

He still hadn't given work an answer about the move to New York. It was more money. A lot more money. He would be working for a partner office, not technically part of his father's company. He would finally be able to prove that he wasn't just his father's son; that he had earned his place, as much as he had inherited it. His father was also pressuring him about it. That was one of the reasons that Oliver hadn't been looking forward to this weekend. If he was honest with himself, Oliver knew that it was a very good move professionally and that it would open doors for him that may not be available otherwise. It would be easy to say yes to and much more difficult to turn down. The problem was Nelly.

He watched her now as she moved away from India and toward the table that they had set up in the garden. She was standing with her back to him wearing a green dress that cut just above her ankles, her feet bare against the lawn. He could already tell how the shampoo in her hair would smell if he positioned himself behind her and allowed his face to tuck into her neck. He looked away when India jumped from her chair and did that exact thing.

1997
Nelly

She found Oliver where she'd known that she would that night. His back was to her as she wandered toward him over the lawn, the music from the party blaring out and fading away behind her. He was wearing a suit in a way that gave the impression that his body was almost rejecting it; the jacket lay splayed beside him on the wall whilst his shirt gathered untucked from his trousers, revealing a slither of skin above his belt as he leant into his knees.

"Come here often?" She asked as she sat on the wall beside him. She was unnerved when he didn't return her smile.

Oliver let a puff of smoke escape his lips, his rolled cigarette limp against his fingers. "India inside?"

Nelly felt her stomach twist as she nodded. He nodded back and offered her the cigarette.

"Are you o—"

"I've been offered a job," he said, interrupting her.

"Oh. That's great. Congratulations. Is it still at—"

"It's in New York."

The words lay on her chest like milk too cold from the fridge. She nodded slowly. Oliver turned to look at her. He watched her face for a moment and then sighed, looking back at his knees.

"Is it for a certain amount of time?"

"It's for a year. In the first instance, at least. They want someone from the London office to head up some new clients over there."

"That's amazing," Nelly said, trying to ignore the tears that were suddenly threatening in her throat. "You must be really proud."

Oliver shrugged.

"Mmm. Are you gonna take it?"

He shrugged again. They were quiet for a moment. "I've got to give them an answer by Monday."

"Ah."

She dragged on the cigarette, feeling the tears creep further upward. "Is that what Felix meant the other night?"

Oliver nodded.

They were silent for a moment.

Oliver turned to look at her. His countenance was resigned, as if he were sad, but his gaze was clear and held hers as he spoke, "I'll turn it down if you ask me to."

Nelly nodded. She bit down on the edge of her lip, feeling the sadness rise in her throat. "I could never ask you to do—" Her voice broke off.

Oliver sat up toward her as if responding instinctively to her pain. He wrapped his arms around Nelly and tugged her gently down toward him, her face resting on his chest. She could feel the teardrops escaping down her cheeks and didn't dare to say anything.

1998
Nelly

Nelly felt Oliver's departure the same way that someone might feel the loss of a limb. She knew that she could cope without it if she really had to, but yet the pain of it was almost torturous. This was also worsened by the change in India's circumstances in recent months.

Four months previously, India had arrived home to tell Nelly that she had seen someone from their past again. Spencer.

Nelly had almost tasted the bile in her throat as India had said it.

"He's changed," India had told her feverishly. Nelly had shaken her head. People like Spencer didn't change. They hid their scales and then shed their second skin when your guard was down. She wished India could have seen it for herself.

There had never been a distance between India and Nelly throughout their entire friendship up until this point. Before, whatever Spencer had done Nelly always felt like she and India were on the same team. However, now it almost felt as if something was shifting. She dreaded going back to the flat each night in case Spencer was there, leering at her from the settee. He had given all of the impression of making an effort with India's best friend. He had even presented her with a speech the first time that he'd come to the flat.

"We're all adults now, Nel," he'd told her, as if her hatred caused by the things that he had done in the past was childish. He smiled almost sympathetically at what he was about to do as he had draped his arm around India's fragile frame.

"That was nice of him. Wasn't it?" India had whispered to Nelly afterward.

"What?"

"His apology."

Nelly had shaken her head. "He didn't apologise."

India had just sighed. Nelly couldn't understand how Spencer had somehow managed to make Nelly feel as if she were the problem in all of this. As if she were the one creating a wedge between them. She hated him so intensely that sometimes she wondered if this were true. But that was what people like Spencer did to you. Poison.

It had almost been like a weight had lifted from her chest when she had heard India speaking on the phone to Oliver one evening. He had been gone eight months and Nelly had felt his absence more than she could ever have imagined.

"Who's that?" Spencer had asked, jutting his chin toward the landline.

"My brother," India had whispered back, her eyes lingering on Spencer as if asking for permission.

"You're allowed to speak to your brother," Nelly had told her.

"I know," India replied, frowning.

Spencer watched Nelly from where he sat. His grey eyes inspecting her coolly. Nelly turned around.

"Yeah. I... I think that would work," India said into the phone. "Let me just—no. Yeah. No, no. I get it. I'll just ask Spencer."

There was silence for a moment.

"Spencer. Yeah."

Nelly could feel her heart beating inside of her chest.

"What?" Spencer asked.

India's voice replied, "My brother's back for a week soon and he asked if we want to go for dinner? The four of us?" Nelly wished India hadn't posed it as a question.

"When?"

"Next Thursday."

"It's not a lot of notice, is it?"

"I'm sorry, babe. It's just—No, Oliver. I was talking to Spencer. Yeah. No, I get it. We'll be there. Yep. No, I just have to—" she chewed her lip. "No, there's no problem. We're looking forward to it. Yeah. Love you too."

She hung the phone up gently and Nelly could feel the tension of Spencer's glare behind her back.

"So, it doesn't matter if I'm free or not, then?"

"No. It's just—"

"No?"

"No. It does matter. But Oliver's only back for a week and—"

"Yep. Fine. It's always this way."

"You don't seriously have a problem with her seeing her brother, do you?" Nelly heard herself asking from the sink.

"What?"

She turned around to look at Spencer. She'd been expecting him to look furious, but somehow, he looked quietly pleased with himself. She wished she hadn't given him the reaction.

"Nel, just leave it, would you?" India asked from beside him.

Nelly picked up her bag and left the flat.

1998
Oliver

"I'll have another beer," Spencer told the waiter.

Oliver watched him from across the table. He'd never noticed how skinny Spencer was before. He looked almost juvenile beside them. Childlike. Weak.

"Can I get another wine, please?" India asked.

Spencer rolled his eyes and Oliver felt his jaw clench. The waiter took their orders and moved away from the table.

"Is that alright?" India whispered toward Spencer's frame.

Spencer scoffed, "It's not exactly like you need another one, is it?" He made eye contact with Oliver as he said this and the camaraderie that he was clearly seeking made Oliver want to throw the table at him.

"Have whatever you want, Ind," Oliver replied, not averting his gaze from Spencer's. He noticed that India didn't touch her wine for the rest of the meal.

"Is it like this a lot?" He asked Nelly later in the evening. India had gone to join Spencer outside whilst he smoked. Nelly was watching them out from the window. Her usually kind eyes were squinted, focussing in on Spencer's frame.

"He's a fucking cunt," she told him.

Oliver nodded.

Nelly continued, her eyes not leaving India. "I hate him, Oliver. I honestly hate him."

He could hear the anger in the back of her throat. She didn't wear it naturally, yet he could feel the strength behind it. He sat back in his chair, finding her hand beneath the table.

"Yeah. Me too," he stroked his thumb over her hand and then let it go, "Don't worry. It won't last long. It never does."

"What if it does, though?"

Oliver shook his head, "It won't."

1998
Nelly

The idea that things could have gone from bad to worse as quickly as they did would never have occurred to Nelly this time a year ago. India seemed to be deteriorating rapidly. Once the lightest spark in any room, she now seemed almost like a shadowed version of herself. The same shape. The same beautiful, sweet person. But smaller; faded, somehow. Like a candle flickering against the wind.

Spencer basically lived at their flat with them now, without actually contributing to anything. He seemed to somehow occupy the entire space whilst skulking in one chair beside India, his eyes always glaring at her. At first, they had argued a lot, the same way as they used to. But then slowly but surely, the arguing began to peter down. India seemed to have lost the will to fight. Now, all that Spencer had to do was glare at her and she would become immediately quiet. Silent. Silenced. Somehow, the arguing had been more bearable.

Then there was Nelly. Adrift in the flat that she had once thought of as her safe place—her home—she now wrestled between being there constantly to keep an eye on India and spending as little time there as possible. Spencer rarely actively antagonised her, but he also made her feel utterly uncomfortable. She hated being in his presence. She could feel the hatred soaking through the air from him toward her.

"He's jealous," Leo told her one night when they were discussing the situation.

Nelly sighed, "What of, though? It isn't like I'm competing for India, is it?"

Leo shrugged, "He sees you that way."

Nelly stirred the straw in her Coke thoughtfully. After a moment, she said, "Do you think India would pick us over him, if push came to shove?"

"Literally?" Leo asked.

Nelly returned his gaze.

Leo looked thoughtful and then said, "Only time will tell, mate. I hope so."

Nelly agreed. Leo had offered for her to move in with him on countless occasion. He lived alone but had a spare bedroom that Nelly wasn't sure how he afforded on his salary as a paralegal. She spent most nights there now, anyway. She even had a drawer packed with clothes and hair ties and sanitary towels. It would be so easy to move in with Leo and shut the door on the entire unpleasant situation with India and Spencer. But she knew that officially moving out from the flat would be officially leaving India—officially letting Spencer win. She wasn't ready for it yet.

"Why don't I come back with you this evening?" Leo asked kindly, stretching out to hold her hand over the table.

"Would you?"

"Of course. If it would help."

Nelly nodded.

"What does Oliver say about it all?" Leo asked. She could tell that he was making an effort to be casual in the way that he posed his question.

Nelly sipped her Coke slowly. "Mmm. I think he's worried about her."

"Yeah?"

"Mmm."

"Did you tell him about how much weight she'd lost?"

Nelly sighed, "I told him she's not doing that well. But I'm not sure he really gets how bad things have gotten. He keeps just saying that it won't last. I dunno. He rings the flat to speak to her most weeks, anyway."

Leo nodded slowly. "Is he still seeing that girl?"

"Kelsey. Yeah. I think so."

"Right. Cool."

"Mmm."

They were quiet for a moment, both focussing on their drinks. After a while, Nelly asked, "How did you get over him? Tom?"

Leo smiled slightly, his green eyes on the board of specials that the pub was offering that day. "I didn't."

"Never?"

Leo shook his head.

"God. It's shit, isn't it?"

"I'm afraid so, mate." Leo smiled coyly down at his drink, as if weighing something up on his tongue. "Did I ever tell you that we had sex?"

"What? No! You and Thomas?"

"Mmhmm."

"Wow. When?"

Leo laughed. "When we got back to Cambridge that summer after France."

"No. Just before he and India got together?" The memory of it fluttered through Nelly's mind. A simpler time. She had always assumed that India and Thomas's short-lived romance following their trip combined with his moving away had been the reason that none of them saw Thomas much anymore. She never suspected that he and Leo had actually gotten together also. Although, now that she thought about it, she wasn't sure why not.

"Yeah. Or, somewhere during. If I'm honest."

Nelly raised her eyebrows, "You never said."

"Well, you're India's best mate. And I fucked her over, really."

"But you were in love with him. She'd have understood."

"Yeah. Well. It doesn't matter now, anyway."

"So, what happened? How did it happen?"

Leo looked pensive. "It was… weird. We'd been back a couple of weeks and we were getting ready to leave the dorm in Cambridge, you know? And I'd sort of written the whole thing off. I'd been in love with him for two years already and he was straight and definitely obsessed with India. I'd made my peace with my place as his friend—his best friend. It used to kill me in the beginning, but after all that time, I didn't even really think about it anymore. Like, I loved him and he didn't love me in the same way and that was fine. But then one day he just knocked on my door and he was holding up a pair of my swimming shorts. You know, the orange ones that I wore all the time when we were away?"

He smiled, but Nelly knew it was just to himself. She sat quietly, letting him continue. "Anyway, he came in and said that they'd been in his bag and he'd just found them, muddled up with his things. He said he wanted me to have them back because we'd be leaving soon. And then he just kissed me. Just fully. As if he'd done it a thousand times. And it felt like the most natural thing in the world, the two of us."

Leo went silent. He twisted his pint glass on the table, watching the condensation drip in a ring around the edge of it.

"And then?" Nelly asked tentatively.

"Then… nothing. As soon as it was over, he acted like the whole thing never happened."

Nelly frowned, "What, he just pretended the two of you had never had sex with each other?"

Leo nodded, "Yeah. Basically. It was fucking weird. He just got up and put his clothes back on and told me that he was going to rugby. And then he just left. I tried bringing it up with him once a week or so later and he just stared at me blankly, like I'd fantasised the whole thing. Maybe I'd have thought that I had if I hadn't still had those swimming trunks on the end of my bed. And if I'm honest, it was almost easier that he did pretend we hadn't done it. I loved India and I felt shit for what I'd done to her, even though I knew she didn't really care about him. Not in the way that I did, I mean. And the idea of losing Thomas as a friend was just horrible. So, I played along with it, too. I just… pretended."

"Shit. Leo, that's awful. I'm so sorry."

Leo looked up at her. His freckled lips were smiling faintly, his green eyes welling at the edges. After a moment, he shook his head. "Don't be, darling. It was the best night of my life."

Nelly reached over and stroked his hand across the table. He had huge hands. Strong. Capable. Solid.

1998
Oliver

He wasn't looking forward to going home to England for Christmas. Despite all of his reservations, he'd actually come to enjoy his life in New York. The job was fine. Boring and stressful, but lucrative. The city, however, was amazing. Utterly alive; crawling with activity and prospect and vibrancy. He had a good apartment and a girlfriend—Kelsey. A curator. She was creative and sexy and clever and challenging, and he had come to really savour his time with her. She encouraged his photography and asked to see prints of his work, pouring over them with him for evenings at a time. She was great. Cutting and American and great.

It made him feel guilty every time he rang home to speak to India.

He felt worried about her, definitely. But also, somehow irritated with her at the same time. She was making this choice, after all; this choice to be unhappy that was impacting everyone around her. She could end it all, if she really wanted to. The problem was that she didn't. She clung to Spencer as if he were her only life force. The way she used to cling to Nelly.

Nelly.

Oliver didn't allow himself to think about her very often. She'd made her situation clear the last time that they'd been alone together. He loved her, definitely, and he knew in a way that he always would. And he knew that she loved him, too. But he also knew that she loved India more and that she had chosen her over him. She had said as much when she had let him go to New York. He'd had to draw a line under it. Walk away from it.

At least, he thought that he did.

When he arrived back in London the day before Christmas Eve and let himself into his old flat, he felt almost as if he'd somehow entered into a time-warp. It was empty and cold where the heating hadn't been on, but there was a photo stuck against the fridge with a tacky magnet of the London Eye. One that he would never have bought for himself, but that India had found hilarious two years ago when he had first moved in. It held down a string of pictures of the three of them in a photo booth. He, India and Nelly. The photos were all awful. Blurry and out of focus and unflattering. But they were also lovely. They had been at the carnival that day and had drunk more than their weights in cheap gin and tonics. India had shoved them all into the photo booth and pressed the button for the pictures.

"We won't remember it in the morning, anyway," she had laughed.

But he had known that he would. The feeling of being as happy as he had been in that moment could never be forgotten. He found himself oddly anxious that evening when he walked to meet them all. Nelly had asked him when he'd rung last week to tell India that he was coming back.

"You'll come, won't you?" She'd asked into the phone.

Her voice still made his heartbeat quicken.

"Please?"

He nodded against the receiver, "Yeah. I'll come."

Shouldering his way through the busy pub now he felt oddly like both a fish out of water and a local at the same time in only the way that someone who has been away from home for a long time can understand. Familiar and foreign. It was crowded and loud; people's spirits were high and their faces were pink from the cold and the beer. He saw Nelly perched on the edge of a table, her cardigan wrapped around her and her hair frizzy from where it had recently been muffled beneath a hat. She turned to look at him as he walked over and her face looked like home.

He hadn't expected her to run to him. Her body thumping against his as Nelly reached her arms around Oliver's neck, her face pressed against his chest. It caught him off guard.

"You have no idea how good it is to see you," her voice muffled into his jumper.

Oliver stroked the back of her hair. He knew exactly how good it was.

They spent the night pretending. Not in the way that they used to do where they acted as if they were together. But more as if they had never spent any time apart. Nelly laughed whilst Oliver told her stories about the idiots at his office and he listened and nodded when she told him about a programme that she was thinking about applying for in Rome.

"You should go for it," he told her as she sat beside him on the bench, people laughing and singing cheesy Christmas songs around them.

"Mmm. Yeah. Maybe. Probably."

Her smile shifted to the side and she looked away from him a moment. Oliver touched her without thinking, tipping her face back toward his so as she was facing him. He shifted on his shoulders slightly, forcing her eyes to look back at him. After a moment, Nelly smiled and shrugged. "I dunno, it's just. You know…"

"No. What?"

She sighed, "Well, the whole thing with India."

He nodded. "You're worried about leaving her?"

"I'm not worried. I'm scared." Her candour caught him off guard. Nelly shook her head, "It's awful, Oliver. It's honestly awful. He's there all of the time and he's just so hateful and horrible to her and he hates me so fucking much. I have no idea why, but he does. And she just lets it all happen. And I hate it. I absolutely hate being there with them. But I'm so scared about what will happen if I'm not, and—" The tears fell down her cheeks before she could stop them.

"Hey, hey. It's okay. I'm here," Oliver soothed, reaching out and pressing her into him. He could feel her breath warm and wet on his neck. Her chest was juddering in stolen breaths as if she was afraid to let it out.

"I'm so scared for her, Oliver," she told him.

He stroked the back of her hair, swaying her softly against his chest. In that moment, he had never felt so guilty for being happy away from them.

1998
Nelly

Oliver was going to come and meet her to go to her parents' house for dinner in just under an hour. She'd seen him last night for the first time in almost nine months and it had been wonderful—magic—like no time had passed. So wonderful that she almost hoped that she could now tell him how she really felt. That she loved him and that she was so sorry for letting him ever go to New York without knowing that. She wouldn't expect him to say it back, necessarily, or to do anything with the information. He had a girlfriend, after all. But at least then he would know. The feeling of it bubbled inside of her stomach as she stood in the bathroom, pulling the heat brush down over her curls as she watched herself in the mirror. She felt quite pleased with how she looked. She was wearing the new top that her mum had bought her for her birthday. It was black and glittery and fluttering at the sleeves, capped just above her shoulders. She was still stood in her underwear from the bottom-half down, waiting for the moisturiser that she'd just applied on her legs to sink in. She'd spent time on her makeup, too. Applying mascara to her eyes and rimming her mouth in the same red lipstick that India had given her a year ago. She felt unusually confident. Pretty, almost.

The sound of the front door closing made her jump. She turned her shoulders slightly, her body constrained by the wire of the heat brush.

"Ind, is that you?" She called out to nobody.

There was no answer. She heard the noise of the fridge opening and then slamming shut, the slight jingle of the wine bottles inside as they vibrated against the door.

"Ind?"

She suddenly felt a bit nervous. She had asked India to come to her parents' with her for dinner on Christmas Eve, as had come to be their tradition, but she'd told Nelly that she was busy with Spencer. She and Oliver would be travelling to the Cotswolds tomorrow morning to spend Christmas weekend with their parents. Although Nelly suspicioned that Spencer would try to talk her out of it, the way that he always seemed to. Nelly hoped that India wouldn't bail on her family and that her being in the flat meant that she'd come home to pack. Or that she had changed her mind and would be coming to Nelly's parents' with her, after all. A fluttering feeling began to buzz in her stomach as she anticipated her friend's response.

"Ind, are you okay?" She called out again. There was still no answer. Nelly sighed and placed the heat brush down on the edge of the bathroom counter, pushing the door open and peering out. "Ind?"

"Fucking hell," the voice replied scathingly from the kitchen.

Nelly's head shot to the side, settling on Spencer where he leant against the countertop. She backed behind the door, positioning her legs behind it as she spoke to him. She could feel the anxiety beginning to rise behind her sternum.

"Where's India?" She asked. She hated how nervous her voice came out sounding.

Spencer stared at her hatefully, his lip curling up over his top teeth as if she were something that he'd found on the bottom of his shoe. He moved purposefully toward her and Nelly had the sudden urge to slam the bathroom door closed.

"Where's India?" She repeated.

Spencer crossed the small flat in a matter of moments, regarding Nelly all the while. She reached out to push the door closed, but he shoved it open, forcing it to reveal her exposed legs. She stumbled back instinctively, feeling her spine press against the harsh rim of the counter. Her hands shook and she grabbed at the edge of it to steady herself.

"I'm getting changed." She said it as if she were justifying herself, but he didn't retreat.

Spencer raised his eyebrows, continuing to assess her. Slowly, he reached forward with his forefinger and plucked at the puckering of fabric between Nelly's breasts. She felt the breath catch in her throat.

"Bit slaggy for a night with Mummy and Daddy, isn't it?"

She tipped her chin toward him, desperate not to give him the satisfaction of seeing how frightened he was making her.

He smiled, seemingly enjoying the challenge. "I suppose that's what people like you think looks good, though."

She bit down hard on her cheek, tasting iron in her mouth. "Fuck off, Spencer." She felt the vibration of his hand smacking against the mirror behind her head before she saw him move. She could hear the rumbling of the neighbours' television in the next flat and wanted to scream out to them, but suddenly couldn't find her voice. Nelly's eyes squeezed shut instinctively and she hated that they had done so. When she opened them, Spencer's face was close to hers. She could smell the marijuana on his breath against her forehead. The blood was pumping in her ears.

"I know what you said to India."

"What?"

He smirked; his hand still pressed against the wall behind her head. "What you said about how she should leave me."

Nelly's mouth felt dry as she swallowed. "She should."

Spencer's lips curled up toward his cheeks. He barely moved, but his body pressed closer to Nelly's somehow. Uncomfortably close. "You know, it's pathetic really. How much you're obsessed with the two of them."

"I'm not."

"Oh, Nelly. Yes, you are." He shifted his groin toward her and she could feel his erection against her thigh. Nelly squeezed her eyes shut again, willing herself not to cry. "*I love you, India. I'd do anything for you, India,*" he mused, his voice mocking as he mimicked her accent. He laughed to himself. "Bloody good friend you are, when you secretly want to fuck her brother."

"I—"

"That's why you're all tarted up now, isn't it? Because Oliver's coming for you." He nodded at her patronisingly, "Yep, India told me. He'll be here in, what, half an hour?"

Nelly could see her chest heaving as her heart pumped beneath it. She was so close to Spencer that the proximity made her feel physically sick. He smiled.

"Don't worry. I'm sure he'll enjoy the way you look. Oliver likes a slut, doesn't he? Doesn't like to have to work too hard for anything," he let his eyes trace down her frame, lingering on her heaving chest. He chuckled as she snatched a hand up to cover it. "N'aww. That's a shame. I bet you won't do that for him, will you? I bet you'll let him stick his fingers inside your cunt, just like you let that twat in Clacton."

Bile began to rise in Nelly's throat.

Spencer bent in closer, his breath against her ear. Nelly held herself up as long as she could. Eventually, he breathed, "You deserved it, you know. You're lucky it wasn't more. You deserved to be raped."

Spencer retracted his hand from the wall behind Nelly's head and leant down, pressing his mouth against her cheek. He kissed her and then turned to move away. She shoved the bathroom door closed as quickly as she could, pulling the bolt shut atop of it. Locking herself inside.

She sunk down onto the cold tiles of the bathroom floor and hugged her knees to her chest, shaking as the tears stung down her cheeks. The panic attack was so awful that Nelly thought she was going to die.

1998
Oliver

Nelly didn't tell Oliver that she had changed her mind about the meal on Christmas Eve. He'd turned up at the flat to no answer, having left his key with them when he'd moved to New York almost a year ago. He had called the landline several times, his body pressed against the front door hearing the phone ringing from the flat within. When Nelly hadn't answered on the fourth time, he assumed that she had regretted asking him.

Maybe too much time had passed between them, after all. Maybe she had just been drunk last night and didn't even remember posing him the invitation.

He would be leaving for his parents' house tomorrow and then travelling back to New York on Boxing Day, having booked his ticket back in haste weeks previously.

He bent down, leaving the two parcels that he'd brought with him by the front door. Hand cream for Nelly and a ceramic platter for her parents. He'd picked them up at Selfridges earlier that day, his stomach fluttering at the idea of seeing them. Someone would probably steal the parcels, now. He turned away from the apartment and made his way back to the stairwell, feeling foolish for letting his heart bleed again.

1999
Nelly

She'd been living in Rome for four months and it was already all that she had hoped and more. The city was utterly breathtaking. The history; the canals; the people; the food; the language. As soon as she had landed, she had felt as if she was where she was supposed to be. At home. And not because of her heritage or because she spoke the language. That was part of it, obviously, but only a fraction. It was mostly because of the fact that, for the first time in her life since she had first moved to Cambridge for university, she felt as if she were doing something purely for herself. Something healthy. Something selfish. Something that was good for her.

She made friends easily. The majority of the other people in her cohort were also expats; mostly English, some Australian or American or German. They were all there to teach English as a foreign language to students who actually wanted to learn. It was refreshing, after years of living in London where people complained about making an effort in any language but their own.

Nelly lived in an accommodated flat that her work put her up in; not for free, but for a reduced rate. It was clean and comfortable and had an ensuite shower room, so it didn't really matter that it was situated in a less picturesque part of the city or that she could smell the scent of the sewers travelling through the cracks in her window at five o'clock in the morning. All of Rome was beautiful, after all.

Her world in Rome felt so far removed from her life in London that sometimes she didn't even think about it. About how the pizzerias reminded her of the places that she and India had visited on their holiday after uni, or how the coffee tasted nostalgically like a hangover after a night with her best friend. Rome was simple. Good. Lovely. Unlike the insidious mess that she had left behind.

The night before she had set out for Rome, Nelly had stayed at her parents' house in Clapham. She had moved out from her flat with India almost a month ago, the day after Boxing Day. Nelly had told India about what had happened between she and Spencer. She told her best friend how Spencer had threatened her and terrified her; how scared she had been in that moment and how afraid she was for India still. India had felt all of the pain that Nelly had stored up in her chest; it had been visible behind her eyes. Nelly had needed India to step forward for her in that moment. For India to admit that her relationship was Spencer was toxic and that she was better off without him. The worst part was, Nelly knew that India understood this. And deep down, Nelly had always thought that India would choose their friendship just as Nelly had done.

But then she didn't. India chose Spencer. It cut through Nelly's chest like a warm knife through butter. Her best friend was lost. Stolen. As if the lights were on, but India wasn't really home anymore. Nelly had never told Oliver what had happened on Christmas Eve or why she hadn't answered the door to him. She had heard him knocking for her, his voice calling through the wood. She had wanted to run to him and bury her head into his chest and let him hold her and make her feel safe again. But Spencer had still been in the flat, lurking behind the bathroom door like an animal. And Nelly couldn't bring herself to get up from the floor. And then, once she had moved out and moved away, telling Oliver about what Spencer had done to her had felt much like telling someone about what had happened to her in Clacton all those years ago. Benign. In-concrete. Humiliating.

"What can I do to bring her back, Mum?" Nelly had sobbed into her mother's shoulder in a way that she hadn't cried since she was a child. The tears choked at her throat, her chest heaving and gasping against them. She felt sick. Empty. Barren. As if she were grieving the loss of a person that was still, at least physically, alive. "If only she could just leave him for good, and not go back to him again and again and again. If only she was just strong enough to—"

Her mum sat her up straight, holding Nelly out in front of her with her arms outstretched. She regarded Nelly's dark eyes sternly, her own matching irises flicking between Nelly's as she held her daughter's gaze.

"Listen, my love. People like Spencer do not choose people like India because they are weak," she told Nelly, "They choose people like India because there is a light inside of them—a fire, burning hot—that the likes of Spencer will never know. And they are jealous of it and know that they will never have it for themselves. So, they make it their mission to take it from the very person that they saw it inside of." Nelly sniffed, feeling tears sting down her cheeks. Her mother continued, "Being abused by someone has nothing in the world to do with weakness. It has only to do with strength."

Nelly nodded, swiping her shirt sleeve over the sticky liquid pooling at the bottom of her nose. "What can I do to stop it for her?"

Nelly's mum wiped her daughter's tears with her thumb, "My darling, I'm afraid that if India is going to make the change, you cannot do it for her. This is something that she has to do for herself."

Nelly nodded. She already knew that it was true. She had flown to Rome the next day and she hadn't allowed the thought of India or the world that she had left behind in London to penetrate her mind since. That was, she hadn't until she had walked past a stall selling postcards. She had noticed the one of the cat smoking the cigar instantly. Like it had grabbed her with two hands. In that moment, there was only one person that she thought of.

1999
Oliver

The train pulled into the Roma Termini with a chugging noise that made Oliver's heart beating hard in his chest. He had received the call from Nelly a month ago. She and he hadn't spoken since Christmas, and yet when he had heard the jingling of the landline on the Sunday morning, he had almost instantly known that it would be her. Nobody else that he knew would ring him at eight in the morning.

"Shit. I'm sorry," she had said when he'd picked up, "I forgot about the time difference."

He smiled, "Don't worry about it. Are you okay?"

"Never better," Nelly had replied. He believed her.

Oliver felt oddly nervous as the train pulled in to the station in Rome that afternoon. He was only there for the weekend, the commute from the London office now making this possible again. For the entire ride from the airport to the station, he had imagined what he would say when he eventually saw her. Whether he would tell Nelly that he loved her and adored her or whether he would confess to her that she had broken his heart when she had stood him up on Christmas Eve. That every night since, he had laid in bed wondering what could have happened to make her change her mind.

Whether it had been something that he had said or done, or whether it was the opposite. He wanted to tell her that it was unfair of her to tug and pull at his heart strings like this just when he thought he might finally be okay without her. Of course, when he actually saw her none of these words managed to leave his lips.

Nelly was standing amidst the crowd waiting for him, her curly head at least five inches lower than any other that stood there. She was chewing on the inside of her cheek when he approached in the way that she often did when she was anxious. Other than that, not much about Nelly looked the same.

She was wearing a red camisole dress that cut off about mid-way through her thighs, the exposed skin of her arms and legs tanned and olive-y and speckled in delightful patterns of freckles that Oliver hadn't seen on her in years. She was holding a sign over her chest as she peered out into the crowd. Despite the empty feeling that had been sitting inside of his chest for the past months, the words that she was holding forced Oliver's face into an uncontrollable grin.

Posh English bloke.

She smiled back at him, seemingly pleased with herself. He felt in awe of her in that moment; the confidence in her that this new Nelly was exuding. She tucked a curl behind her ear and peeked down at the sign, shrugging at him slightly. That look. That glance back up through her eyelashes. Oliver already felt like he was home.

1999
Nelly

"Pecan, per favore, signore." Nelly was watching Oliver from the corner of her eye as they stood side by side in the gelato shop that afternoon. He was still carrying his rucksack, one shoulder of it slipped down so as it hung just to one side. His shirt was riding up slightly as a result of the bag, forcing a small slither of the skin around his waist to be exposed.

"E per te bella?"

Nelly's mind was pulled back to the gelato shop. "Cioccolato, per favore signore."

"Eccelente." The man scooped two large balls of chocolate ice cream and flattened them onto the top of the cone, pressing down so as he could fit more on. He smiled at Nelly as he handed her over her goods.

"Grazie mille," Oliver said as he thumbed through the notes in his wallet. Nelly had expected him to be a bit uncomfortable—to feel as she had done in the shop in France when he had been the upper hand; a fish out from water—but he didn't seem even the slightest part flustered. Irritatingly unflustered. Nelly felt herself eyeing him.

"No, no," Oliver said, waving his hand as the man went to give him his change."

"Grazie mille," the man smiled.

"Grazie mille," Nelly reciprocated, turning with Oliver as they moved to leave the shop. Oliver held the door open for her so as she had to duck just under his arm to get by.

"Buona giornata," Oliver said as Nelly dipped out from the shop. She turned and looked at him as the door swung closed behind them.

"Okay, then. Go on. How come you're so good at everything?"

"Hmm?"

"Well, apparently you speak Italian now?"

Oliver shrugged, "I don't speak Italian. Just the basics. It's pretty much the least you can do when you visit somewhere, isn't it?"

"Mhmm. Pecan is a very important word to know. Very offensive, otherwise."

Oliver grinned. He nudged into her slightly with his shoulder, pushing her ever so gently. She laughed at him. They moved toward a fountain which was partially shaded, each sitting down on the edge of it and looking out toward the busy square. Oliver let his rucksack fall limp off from his shoulder and moved it to settle between his feet.

"Alright. Do you want the truth?"

Nelly raised her eyebrows at him, "Always."

He grinned to himself and took a mouthful of ice cream, licking his lips before saying, "I don't even like pecan that much."

"Then why—"

"The names were written on the counter. It was the only one that I was sure I could pronounce."

Nelly's laughter caught her off guard. She tipped her head back slightly, allowing herself to close her eyes for a moment.

"Hey, there's no need for that." He sounded offended, but when she opened her eyes to look at him, he was still grinning at her.

"I would have ordered for you."

"Mmm. I seem to remember someone being extremely irritable when I did that same thing for them."

"Huh? Why would that annoy someone?"

Oliver raised his eyebrows at her, studying Nelly's face for a moment as if giving her opportunity for recollection. She widened her eyes at him and he laughed. "In Provence? When I spoke to the woman for you in that little shop," he shook his head, taking another mouthful of ice cream, "You were stroppy for hours."

"Um I was not stroppy, thank you very much."

Oliver held his fingers up in front of his face, squashing two together, "Little bit."

She smacked his hand away playfully, "No. I was not stroppy."

"It's okay. I get it. You don't like to be helped." Oliver was smiling smugly to himself as he bit further into his gelato. Nelly shook her head at him, wondering how he had been in the city less than two hours and already had managed to win the upper hand.

"I don't hate being helped. I just didn't *need* you to help me."

He shrugged, "But you didn't speak French."

"That didn't mean you had to waltz in like a posh prick and do it for me."

Oliver's grin stretched across his face, "Ah, so you admit it? You were pissed off."

"No—"

"And resorting to name calling. Very childish."

Nelly shook her head, the feel of the smile fighting against her cheeks. "Okay, okay. Maybe I felt a little bit insecure."

"Mmm. Little bit. Maybe," Oliver licked his ice cream and grinned to himself. He looked like someone who had just been proven right and was very pleased with themselves about it. It was very irritating.

Nelly rolled her eyes, her cheeks aching from smiling. "Well, I'm surprised you even noticed. You were normally too busy shagging every girl in the town to pay attention to my mood swings."

"Ahh, well it was a dry morning. Not too many townswomen around yet for me to pillage."

She shoved him in the arm and he laughed.

Oliver grinned at her and then let his smile fade. After a moment, he said, "You'd be surprised how much I've noticed about you over the years, Strapelli."

Nelly could feel her heart beating inside of her chest. "Oh." She tried to not let herself look too thrilled. "That sounds almost stalkerish. Should I be concerned?"

"Oh, I don't think so. Since when has a wall of photos been considered stalking?"

"Oh?"

"Mmm. Light touch, at best. Nothing to flatter yourself with. Now, if you knew about that towel you used that I've never washed then maybe you'd think differently. And there is that body in the cellar. But other than that..." He grinned at her as she laughed, small crinkles cradling his blue eyes. She allowed herself to rock slightly into his arm, her cheeks already aching. She had imagined this weekend with Oliver a thousand times over and in none of them had she let herself give into him so quickly. Perhaps she had been too generous with her own will power.

"Mhmm," he turned to look at her. His blue eyes locked onto hers, staring into them unabashedly for a brief moment before his eyes trailed downward. He nodded forward, "You're dribbling."

"Mmm?" Nelly looked down at her hand where ice cream was beginning to pool down the cone, "Oh shit."

"It's alright." Oliver leant forward casually and, as if it were the most normal thing in the world, bent in to lick the chocolate from Nelly's cone. His tongue flicked out quickly, tracing the liquid's path back up to the rounded top. There was a small moist stain where his mouth had touched it as he drew back, swallowing and then continuing to eat his own flavour.

Nelly had to tell herself to look away.

1999
Oliver

The two of them had stayed out all day exploring the city, not even bothering to go back to Nelly's flat to dump Oliver's rucksack. It had felt heavy on his shoulder and he had wished that he could leave it behind, but he hadn't wanted to seem pushy. Neither of them had broached the issue of the sleeping arrangements yet and, whilst Oliver was certain that he would offer to sleep on a settee or a floor or whatever Nelly had in her room, he also didn't want to fall back to reality quite yet. Not when the day had been so wonderful. Not when Nelly looked as beautiful as she did right now, sat beneath the dim lights of the restaurant.

Her hair was shorter than when he'd last seen her, perching perkily just on top of her shoulders so as it bounced over them as she laughed. Her cheeks were slightly pink, partially from the days spent in the sunshine and partially from the large jug of red wine that they were sharing between them. They had already finished one. Oliver could feel the warmth of the alcohol oozing comfortingly down the back of his neck as he sat and watched her, the wine settling in his stomach.

He felt as if he could watch her all day. He had thought of Nelly as beautiful for a long time. He couldn't pin-point the exact moment when he had realised it, but he knew that he had. But here, now, she seemed even more so. Attractive. Sexy. And it had nothing to do with the dress that she was wearing or the way that she had kept pulling her hair up to relieve herself from the heat during the day, revealing the nape of her neck—although those things were helping—it was more that she seemed so free, suddenly. Unanchored. Light. It was the first time that he had ever seen her this way.

Nelly moved to refill her glass when she finished recounting the story of how India had convinced a taxi driver in Budapest that they were visiting the city on official business from MI5, because they hadn't had enough money to pay the cab fare. Oliver had heard the story a hundred times before, but he smiled and nodded in all of the places that he knew Nelly wanted him to, anyway. He enjoyed hearing it. He loved seeing her so enthused. He sat forward across the table, plucking the jug and tipping it into Nelly's glass before refilling his own. It was warm and tasted faintly vinegary, but he didn't care.

"Thanks," Nelly smiled, taking the glass from him. She regarded it thoughtfully for a moment, twirling the stem of it in her finger so as it wobbled precariously on the table top. After a moment, she asked, "How is she?"

Oliver took a sip of his wine and then breathed out through his nose, swirling the liquid in his mouth. It was dry and a little bit bitter. "She's… not great," he replied honestly.

Nelly nodded as if this had been the answer that she'd expected.

Oliver watched her and then said, "She misses you."

Nelly nodded again. She moved back in her seat, rubbing the skin of her upper-arms subconsciously. She was chewing something over in her mind, as if toying with whether to confess it. Oliver allowed her the room to think. After a moment, she asked him, "Did she ever tell you why I moved out?"

Oliver regarded her and then shook his head slightly.

Nelly nodded in response. "It was Spencer, obviously." She rubbed her arms again and Oliver watched her, not wanting to interrupt. "Do you remember that Christmas Eve when I'd asked you to come to my parents' with me for dinner? The three of us, I mean."

Oliver swallowed his wine and nodded, placing the glass back down onto the table gently. He was making an effort to appear controlled, although he could feel his heart rate beginning to drum in the side of his neck. He looked down at his drink to compose his body.

"I never really told you what happened that night. Before you came round, I mean. With Spencer."

Oliver's eyes snapped up. "Between Spencer and you?"

Nelly nodded vacantly. She was still looking away from him. He hadn't been expecting her to say that and he suddenly felt his breathing becoming shallower in his chest as she spoke. "He came to the flat on his own. I was getting ready in the bathroom. I assumed it was India. That she'd changed her mind about coming. So, I went out to see."

Oliver could feel the adrenaline beginning to pump inside of his chest. He found himself balling his hands into fists underneath the table as Nelly continued.

"And he… said things to me. Horrible things, about you and India and the way that I feel about you both. He made me feel… dirty." She shook her head, her eyes beginning to pool. She continued, "He said that I deserved it. What happened to me in Clacton that time, when I was young. That I deserved for more to happen."

Oliver dug his fingernails into the palms of his hands, consciously focussing on not displaying the fact that he was breathing as if he had just run a marathon.

"He said things about you and the things that I would probably let you do to me and… he got really close. Right against me. Right here," she gestured in front of herself tearfully. "For a moment, I thought that he was going to… that he might…"

Nelly's voice trailed off as Oliver pushed out from his seat, his chair making a harsh scrape along the ground as he shoved it backward. People turned to look at them then and Nelly eyed them self-consciously, but Oliver didn't care. He moved around to the other side of the table and crouched down beside Nelly. Then he pulled the shirt off from his back so as he was just in his t-shirt, draping the material around Nelly's shoulders. She watched him tentatively, as if gauging his reaction. He felt furious. Utterly, irrevocably furious. But he didn't say anything. Instead, he crouched by her side silently, allowing her to continue.

"I told India about it," she said to him after a moment. "She cried and apologised and hugged me. And I asked her to please leave him. To please let him go. But she didn't. She still didn't." Nelly saw that she was beginning to cry and swiped furiously at her cheek.

Oliver reached out and took Nelly's hand from her face. It was cool and small. Just like he remembered.

"She chose him over me. Even after what he did. She chose to be unhappy over being my best friend," the words caught in her throat like a gasp. "And I couldn't forgive it. I just couldn't stay there anymore and watch her carry on doing the same thing to herself—to me. I couldn't. And I feel so awful about it. About all of it. She's suffering and I'm here. She's alone. And I'm not with her."

"Nelly," he realised that he was speaking before he'd known what he was going to say.

She was still looking out at where his space was at the opposite side of the table, now vacant. He reached out and tipped her face softly so as she was returning his gaze. He touched her chin for only a moment before telling his hand to drop back down, unsure of whether she'd want his hands on her. He felt rage; rage the like of he'd only felt once before in their house in the Cotswolds four summers ago. He looked down and realised that his hands were shaking. When he looked back up, Nelly's eyes were on his. Dark. Longing. Anxious. He realised that she was waiting for his response.

"Nelly, you deserve to live your own life. You deserve to be happy."

"I know. But if—"

"But nothing," Oliver's voice was purposeful, almost forceful. He swallowed, feeling like his heart was in his throat. He could so easily stop. He would normally stop. But he had regretted for years not having said more the first time. He looked back up, locking his gaze with hers. "You deserve to be happy. What you didn't deserve is any of the shit that Spencer has put you through. Any of the shit that that other cunt put you through, either. You didn't deserve for something so fucking shit to happen to you. You didn't ask for it, no matter what you did or what you wore or said or anything. And you didn't deserve for a cunt like Spencer to make you feel like you did. He should never, ever have been near you. Either of you. You are lovely. You are kind and beautiful and clever and if I'd known about this earlier—if I had been there, I would have—" Her lips were against his before he could finish his sentence.

She pulled back away from him; her mouth barely having brushed his. Nelly was staring at him nervously, almost as if she were a child asking for permission. Oliver swallowed the rage in his throat and leant into her.

1999
Nelly

Her hands shook as she pushed the key in to open the door of the flat. She was so distracted by what they had just done—what she was certain that they were about to do—that she could barely make the key fit in the lock. Oliver's hand rested on her hip as she fumbled, blissfully conscious of the weight of his body behind hers. His hold on her was gentle, as if he could retract it easily, should she ask him to.

She pushed the door to her flat open and moved inside, tugging at Oliver's hand to move with her. He pushed the door closed behind them and she turned to face him, waiting for something to happen. She could see the muscles in his jaw clenching as his eyes locked against hers, his fingers brushing the sides of her hips. When he didn't do anything, she reached up and kissed him again on the mouth and felt her heart flutter as his lips returned the movement. She pulled back and looked up at him, her head level with his heart.

"Are you sure?" He asked her.

She nodded. She reached up to kiss him again but, before she could, his mouth was already there. His lips pressed against hers and she opened her mouth, letting him inside. Their feet stumbled backward as their bodies locked together. His lips at first so chaste and gentle now pressed into hers greedily as if he were drinking her, devouring her. She wasn't certain which of them needed the other more. She reciprocated the intensity, opening her mouth and gasping against his.

His lips didn't leave hers as his hands travelled down her waist and clasped beneath her buttocks, picking her up and pressing her to his body. She wrapped her legs around him and slipped her hands through his hair as their mouths worked together, her fingers entwining and clutching at him desperately. She could hear him making a noise in the back of his throat as he moved them forward, resting her down on the top of the small table not a foot from the front door; guttural, animal. Nelly pulled her dress up over her thighs, feeling the hardness of him pressing into her through the material of his shorts. She wanted him. All of him. And she wanted him to have her. His hands moved up her legs to find her underwear, his thumbs hooking around the elastic and then hesitating. She reached her hands down to meet his, reassuring and guiding him as he pulled the underwear down her legs. She reached out for the front of his shorts and he helped her when her fingers fumbled with the buttons.

Oliver's mouth bit into her neck as he pushed himself inside of her. She came immediately.

They made love again the next morning. Last night had been passionate; years of built-up tension between them finally coming to a climax. This morning it was softer. They savoured each other; kissing, caressing, nibbling, lapping. She had felt self-conscious of the fact that she hadn't showered yet, but he had told her that he didn't care. Oliver licked along the inside of her thigh, softly inching her legs apart with his shoulders. He kissed her between her legs, his tongue moving gently and rhythmically until white dots appeared in front of her vision and her ears rang. He groaned as she ran her hands through his hair; she kissed the chiselled outline of his collarbone, her hands travelling over his taut skin and down his stomach as they had longed to do so many times before.

It was as if the two of them were each a puzzle that the other was finally solving. Like they were two pieces that finally fit together. When they had finished, she lay with her head against Oliver's chest listening to the steady drumming of his heartbeat. He moved slightly beneath her, shifting to let her closer in.

"Do you love me?" He asked her suddenly. His voice was even and steady, but Nelly could tell that he had been mulling over the question.

She turned over to look at him and his hand travelled immediately to her face, his thumb combing a curl away from her eyes as he watched for her response.

"You know I do," she told him.

"But can you tell me? Please. I need to hear it."

Nelly sat up slightly on her elbows, her eyes level with his. "I love you."

Oliver nodded, "I love you too."

1999
Oliver

The despair that he felt on the third morning at what he had done was terrible. He lay in the bed awake beside Nelly for hours watching her calm, beautiful face. Her lips were slightly parted as she breathed, the tiny freckle that peppered the top of her mouth taunting him, inviting him to kiss it as he had done the night before. He so badly wanted to. He wished more than anything that he could.

He had been turning the conversation over in his mind for half of the night. The past two days had been perfect; blissful. Nelly was with him, finally, and he was with her. It was all that he had wanted since the day that she had set foot into his bedroom and joined him on the window ledge. He should have felt happy. Ecstatic. And yet the gnawing of guilt in Oliver's gut was almost eating away at him.

He would have to tell her. She might even understand, maybe. She loved him, after all. And she knew that he loved her. He hoped that she knew, at least. Otherwise, he already knew that she wouldn't forgive him.

"Oliver?" Her voice asked sleepily as she stretched out in the bed behind him. He was sat at the foot of it, his elbows resting on his knees as he held his head between his hands. "Hey, are you alright?" She asked him. Nelly moved down the bed toward him beneath the thin sheet and wrapped her arms around his shoulders from behind, nuzzling her face into the side of his neck. Oliver smiled slightly despite himself and reached up to place his hand over hers as he turned his face to kiss her. He would allow himself one more kiss. "What's wrong?" She asked him. He stroked his fingers over the back of her hand absentmindedly, trying to force the courage to travel from his chest into his mouth.

"I—"

"Do you regret it?"

"What?" He turned to look at her fully, her dark eyes suddenly swimming in worry. He stroked her cheek as he kissed her lips again. He was already failing in trying to stop. She smelled sleepy and sweet and it made him want to wrap her up in his arms and go back to their bed beneath the covers. "I could never regret a moment of it."

"Then what's the matter? Is it about the long-distance thing? Because I could come back with you and we could—"

"It's not about the distance."

"Oh. About India, then?"

"No. It isn't India."

She paused. "Okay." He rubbed his hands over his face and clenched his teeth together, hearing a ringing noise in the edges of his ears. "Oliver, you're worrying me."

"I've not been completely honest with you," he told her. She sat on the bed looking at him, her hair fluffy from where she had been sleeping on top of it. He wanted to reach over and stroke his hands through it.

"About…"

"I've not been honest with you about my… about the situation." It was all coming out so badly. Nothing like the hundreds of ways that he had rehearsed it in his mind as he had lay awake the night before when she was sleeping.

"Okay," Nelly said carefully. She looked nervous; her eyes were suddenly wide awake as she watched him.

Oliver rubbed his hands over his face again and then turned toward her. He reached out and took her hand in his, feeling the cool of it on top of his skin. She was always cold. He watched his thumb rub over her knuckles and spoke to them, too nervous to look back up at her face as he said what he needed to say. "You know that I love you, don't you?"

Nelly watched him dubiously, "Yes."

"Because I really do. I've never felt this way about anyone and I don't want you to think that I meant to hurt you, ever."

"Oliver, you're scaring me. What haven't you been honest about?"

He sighed, then took a breath. "The situation with Kelsey."

"What situation?"

"Fuck," Oliver breathed nervously. "We're still together."

Nelly was silent for a moment and Oliver could barely force himself to look up from her hand. Eventually, she said, "Okay. But you're going to end it with her, right?"

Oliver nodded, "Yeah. I mean, I want to."

"You want to?"

"It isn't that easy," he rubbed his free hand over his face again. "She's moved to England."

Nelly pulled her hand back from his. He felt the absence of it immediately.

"She's moved to England?"

"Yeah."

"When?"

"Two weeks ago."

"Two weeks ago?"

"Yeah."

Nelly was silent for a moment, chewing on the side of her cheek as she watched him. He had never seen this expression on her face before. He wasn't sure how to gauge it.

"She's moved to England permanently?"

"Yeah."

"What? For work?"

Oliver shook his head slowly, "No. For me."

"For you as in she followed you there, or…"

"For me, as in I asked her to."

Nelly's voice began to rise, "You asked her to move to England for you? What, so you could be together?"

Oliver didn't expect his voice to catch in his throat the way that it did. "I transferred back to the London office and things had been so good between us in New York. With Kelsey, I mean. And when you stood me up on Christmas Eve, I just thought—"

"When I stood you up?"

He shook his head, "You know what I mean. That's what I thought you'd done."

"Apart from I was inside my flat being bullied by your sister's arsehole boyfriend."

"But I didn't know that, did I? I had no way of knowing that."

"So, she's moved to England for you. And where's she staying?"

Oliver didn't say anything. He reached out for her hand, but she pulled it away from his grasp.

"Where's she staying, Oliver?"

He took a deep breath through his nose and focussed his eyes on her hand where it sat balled on the bed. "With me."

Nelly shot out from underneath the sheets as soon as the words escaped his lips. She was naked and when he looked up at her she shouted at him. "Turn around!"

He turned away quickly, nodding. He could hear her pulling open a drawer beside her bed, shuffling for a moment before stepping angrily out from the bedroom and throwing the door open. He stood and followed her.

"Nelly, please. Listen to me. I—"

"Where does she think you are now?"

Oliver shrugged, his eyes seeking hers desperately.

"Where does she think you are, Oliver?"

He swallowed, "Visiting a friend."

"A friend? Just a friend. That's all I am to you?"

"No! Of course not. Not now. But before we left, we had never—"

"I tell you that I'm in love with you and you call me your bloody friend?"

"Nelly. I love you, too. You know I do. I'll go back and end things with her."

"Oh, that's good of you, Oliver. Well done."

"She's nothing to me compared with you. You know that. Please. I know that you know that."

"Oh my God. I feel like such an idiot!"

"No. You're not an idiot. You're lovely," he hated how desperate he sounded. But he was. Desperate. Desperate for Nelly to forgive him.

"I'm just like all of the other girls, aren't I? Do you lay in bed with them and tell them what they want to hear to make them feel special, too? Do you tell them all that you're in love with them? Or was that particular humiliation just for me?"

"Nelly, I do love you. I do. More than anything!"

Tears were streaming down her face and she pulled her hands up to her cheeks, covering them as she scrunched her eyes closed. Oliver moved forward and put his arms around her frame. She felt so small in his arms.

"Please don't cry. Please," he said into her hair. He kissed the top of her head and felt relieved when she let him. He kissed down the side of her face toward her ear and then bent and kissed her chin and her cheek where the tears trickled down them, leaving stained streaks across her perfect face. He kissed her cheek again and then slowly moved toward her mouth, kissing her gently and tenderly. She allowed her lips to kiss him back for the briefest of moments before shoving him away from her.

"I'm sorry. I—"

"You can't kiss me, Oliver. Not now. You don't get to tell me that and then just kiss me."

"I know. I know. I'm sorry. Nelly, I'm so—"

"Is that what I was to you? Just a notch on your bedpost? Some girl that your sister brought home with her that you saw as a challenging shag? Something to break up the summer with?"

"Nelly."

"Well?"

"Of course not! You know how I... I can't believe you'd even ask me that."

"And you couldn't have mentioned this earlier on? You've been here for three nights. We've had sex about ten times. You didn't think to mention at some point that you had a girlfriend that lived with you at home? You waited until the day that you're supposed to leave to tell me?"

"Well, I mean... I didn't..."

"What?"

Oliver sighed and shrugged, "I didn't want to ruin the weekend."

"Oh my God!" she shook her head again, seemingly searching for something in the air that she couldn't find. "I don't know why I expected anything different. I should have known that you'd do this."

"What do you mean?"

"Well, you don't exactly have the best track record with fucking women over, do you?"

"Nelly, that's not... that isn't what this is. I didn't come here to have sex with you. I didn't come here thinking that—"

"What, you didn't come all the way to Rome without thinking that fucking me might be a possibility?"

"No. I mean, yeah. Obviously, I thought about it. But I... Nelly, it wasn't just me."

"What?"

"It wasn't just me. I didn't come here having orchestrated the whole thing. *You* kissed *me*. Remember? Otherwise, I wouldn't have—"

160

"So, it's my fault?"

"No! Of course it isn't. I just mean that it was both of us. It was mutual. I wanted it and you wanted it." Oliver moved forward, attempting to close the gap between them, and then stopped himself when she moved backward from him. "What do you want me to do, Nel? Tell me. Tell me what you want me to do and I'll do it. Tell me what you want me to say and—"

"I want you to admit that you're a fucking prick."

"Okay. Okay fine. I'm a fucking prick."

"That you're a fucking prick and you never gave a shit about me. That this whole fucking connection between us has been a big fat lie."

"Nelly. But that's not... you can't really feel that way?"

"Yeah. I do."

"After everything. After the last years of me being so completely in love with you, you still think that I'd do that?"

Nelly breathed tearfully. She hesitated and then said, "Yeah... Maybe."

"Maybe?"

She shook her head in disbelief, "You're such a prick." She turned and faced the kitchen, angrily opening cupboard doors and then slamming them shut.

Oliver breathed deeply behind her. She was being unreasonable. Hurtful. He had omitted a truth, yes, but he had also admitted it to it now. He had confessed. Not just to Kelsey. But also to the way that he felt about Nelly. He had put his heart on the line for her, and yet it didn't seem to count for anything.

"Look," he said finally, "It isn't like you haven't probably been sleeping with other people whilst you're here, is it?"

"What?"

"You've been seeing other people, haven't you?"

She turned to face him, furious, "So now I'm a slut?"

"No! I just mean that I don't care that you have. I mean, it isn't nice to hear. But it isn't like we said we wouldn't see other people. I'm not having a go at you because of that."

"I don't have a fucking boyfriend, Oliver! A boyfriend that I convinced to move halfway across the world to live with me! I'm single!"

The words hit into his chest. He raised his eyebrows at her accusatorially, "You're single. Seriously?"

She stared at him and then shook her head, "Oliver, don't do that. You don't get to turn this around. You are the one with a girlfriend at home waiting for you.

A girlfriend that isn't me. I wanted you and nobody else. I'm not the one that's been lying."

"I haven't lied. I just didn't tell you."

"Oh, for fuck's sake. That's the same thing."

He sighed and shrugged lightly, "I didn't know this would happen, Nel."

"Well, that's what you're like isn't it? Both of you. You just do whatever it is that you want and sod the consequences for the people that you're hurting along the way. The ones that you drag through the mud with you."

"You mean India. Not me."

"You're as bad as her. You're narcissistic and egotistical. And you fucked me and you can go home now to your American girlfriend and tick me off from your fucking to-do sheet," her chest was heaving as she looked at him.

"Nelly. I love you."

She shook her head, "You both only love yourselves."

Oliver nodded. He drew his hand over his face once, watching her as she stood there in her tiny flat in Rome wearing a grey vest-top and plaid shorts. He took her in for one final time. His chest heaved at the thought of losing her. At the thought of her thinking the same things about him as he worried about himself. But he knew that it wasn't really just about him. He felt as if he could have done anything—said anything—and it would still be about his sister. It would still be about India. He would always come second place.

After a moment, he said, "If she had a cock would you have fucked her instead of me?"

Nelly threw the apple so hard that it smashed against the wall behind him.

Oliver left and got the next train to the airport.

2000
Nelly

Nelly didn't cry when she got the call. She supposed it was because she was numb to the pain. Because she had already grieved the loss of her friend two years ago. Because, deep down, she had somehow known.

It rained on her way to India's funeral. Buckets. As if the sky were also in mourning. As if the sun, normally so bright and clear in the sky on an August day, couldn't show its face amidst the grief. The windscreen wipers flashed across the front window as they stood still at a traffic light, letting commuters rush across the zebra crossing on their way to work. It seemed bizarre that people could still be going about their days as if nothing had happened, when Nelly felt that the world could well have stopped spinning. How could it carry on turning, when India was gone from it? She watched the rain drip down the side of her window, leaving a streak down the spotless glass.

"I wish it was sunny for her," Nelly told her mum as the car approached the church. Her mum squeezed her hand, wiping a tear from her own cheek.

"She's at peace now, my darling. She isn't hurting anymore."

Nelly nodded. She felt in her heart somehow that it was true.

The church was crowded when they arrived, so many people dressed in black and sporting large umbrellas as they attempted to shield themselves from the dismal weather.

She saw Oliver in the crowd of so many, stood beside his two parents as they greeted their visitors. Normally so tall and firm, he somehow looked crumpled and shrunken as if he needed someone else's arms to keep him upright. He stood with his arm around his mother's shoulders. His father nodded at people and shook their hands politely, all whilst clutching something firmly between his fist.

She didn't know what she was going to say when she saw them. She had thought it through in her mind on her flight over, but no words had come to her.

What could you say to someone who has lost part of themselves? She was sure that this was how they felt, because it was the same for her. No words could possibly suffice for such an agony.

"Nelly, sweetheart," India's mother said as they approached. She moved forward and wrapped her arms around Nelly's shoulders and Nelly felt herself move hers to reciprocate the action. "It is so good to see you."

Nelly nodded, "Mrs Matthews. I'm so, so sorry." The words felt oddly hollow.

Mrs Matthews nodded, drawing her face back from Nelly's and reaching up to cup her cheek. "Thank you, darling. I'm so sorry, too. Are you okay?" She tutted and smiled, "Stupid question really, isn't it? I've wanted to roll my eyes when people have said the same to me all morning. None of us are bloody okay today."

Nelly smiled back, "I'm—" Words seemed to fail her and Mrs Matthews nodded, understanding.

"It's so good of you to have come from so far, Nelly. You were such a friend to her."

Nelly sighed, feeling as if a weight were pushing down on top of her chest. Her eyes flicked toward Oliver's, who was already watching her. His mouth was slightly open, as if there was something that he was about to say. Mrs Matthews moved back from Nelly to greet Nelly's parents and Nelly turned herself toward him.

"Oliver, I'm so—"

He wrapped his arms around her, encasing her to his chest. She could feel his breaths shuddering against her ear, a small whimper escaping from above her head as Oliver's arms clung to her. She wrapped hers around him, feeling the shaking of his shoulders as he cried.

"She's gone, Nelly. She's really gone."

The service was as expected. The fact that India had taken an overdose in the bath on a Sunday morning was never mentioned and people sung tearfully and prayed to a god that most of them didn't believe in. Nelly felt almost as if she were drunk. The day hazed by before her like she had taken something to ease the pain of it all, as if she were somehow gliding through the motions of things.

She sat beside Oliver in the church. He hadn't asked her to. He had just taken her with him as if that were her place beside them. He held onto her hand throughout the service, gripping at it with an intensity that told Nelly that all of the pain that she was somehow miraculously numb to was rife somewhere inside of his body, eating him from the inside out. She had never seen Oliver cry. He seemed as if he hated it, tensing his jaw so as the tears fell silently down his cheeks and onto Nelly's and his entwined fingers. He kept his head turned firmly forward, never looking back at the people in the pews behind them. Like his sadness were only for her to see.

Later, they all gathered in a hotel for the wake. Nelly and Oliver sat in silence on a table with Oliver's parents. People came by to pay their respects and Oliver and his parents all nodded and smiled politely. His father's eyes were rimmed red and bloodshot, deep blue circles ringing them to compromise his attempt at maintaining composure. Oliver's mother sat quietly in her seat. Blonde and beautiful, India had been so much like her. She held onto her husband's hand throughout, rubbing her free hand over the top of their fingers reassuringly. Nelly marvelled at Mrs Matthews' strength. She wished she could find it herself.

Nelly stroked Oliver's hand too and he turned to look at her, the anguish of his feelings written across the perfect lines of his face. She could tell that he was battling with so much beneath the surface. She wished that she could take it away for him; suck it out, like poison from a wound.

"I wish we were back on that holiday in France. Do you remember?"

Nelly let her mouth smile slightly, "Of course."

He nodded. "Do you remember when India jumped into the lake and cajoled you into getting in with her?"

Nelly smiled, "Or when she made us all eat those tequila worms that Halloween?"

Oliver's face broke into a smile. He shook it away as if it had imposed, somehow. Unwelcome. After a moment, he said, "She had a way of making everything fun, didn't she?"

Nelly smiled at him.

He shook his head, "She would have hated this."

Nelly nodded, "Mmm. Not nearly enough drinking."

"Or dancing. She loved to dance, didn't she?"

Nelly nodded, "And sing."

"Badly."

Nelly smiled.

"What was that one that the two of you sung at her birthday?"

"The karaoke night?"

"Yeah."

Nelly sighed. "*Like a Virgin.*"

Oliver nodded. He sat still for a moment, his eyes fixed somewhere away from her, and then stood up suddenly and moved from the table. He adjusted his tie as he walked away from them, Nelly's and his mother's eyes both following him as he did so. He ignored the people attempting to catch his attention as he moved through the crowd, seemingly intent on something. Nelly sat and silently waited for a few minutes before the sound of something broke through the room.

Nelly found her cheeks spreading into a grin. She covered her mouth to hide it instinctively as Oliver made his way back over to the table. People turned and looked at him as he walked, looking baffled and slightly amused.

"Is that bloody Madonna?" Oliver's father hissed at him as he came back to join them.

"It is."

"Well get them to turn it the fuck off, Oliver. What do you think you're playing at?"

"No. No," Oliver's mum laughed, shaking her head. She turned to her husband, "She would have loved it." She reached over and stroked Oliver's hand gently. "She would have loved it."

The two of them went outside for a cigarette later on in the evening. It was only eight o'clock, but the sun was beginning to set uncharacteristically early for the season, like it was offering them a reprieve from the dreaded day. There were a few other people hovering around and they shuffled awkwardly when they saw Oliver and Nelly enter their proximity, but they both ignored them.

"Fuck, people hate death."

Nelly nodded, "Can you blame them?"

"Mmm."

Nelly took the cigarette from the pack that he wordlessly offered her and put it into her mouth.

"Nobody knows what the fuck to say. Neither do I, though. Everyone says that they're sorry and we say thank you and that it is okay. But it isn't okay at all, is it? It's fucking shit. My sister's dead and it's fucking shit. No amount of sorries or sympathetic handshakes or trays of bloody lasagne will make it any better."

"Oh," Nelly replied.

Oliver turned to look at her, "What?"

166

"Well, it's just," she hesitated. "It's just that my dad made you a lasagne this morning. It's in the boot."

"What?"

Nelly nodded toward where her dad had parked the car and Oliver's eyes moved to follow her.

"Oh," he said simply.

"Mmm."

He turned back to look at her, his face vacant, and then let out a loud laugh. His shoulders shuddered as he put a hand to his stomach, shaking his head. Nelly found herself smiling back, his laughter almost infectious. "Fucking hell, what a bloody shambles," he said as he pulled the lighter toward his cigarette.

"You're not wrong there," she replied. She bent in toward his cupped hand and let him light the end of her cigarette, taking a deep drag and watching the blue smoke blow out into the air in front of them.

"It's good to see you, Nel."

Nelly nodded at him, "It's good to see you, too."

Oliver crunched the gravel beneath the sole of his foot. "Listen, I really am sorry. About what happened in Rome and the things that I said and… I know you probably know this already. I mean, I must have left a hundred messages on that bloody answer phone."

"Oliver, I'm sorry. I wasn't ready to hear it. I was being stubborn. You don't need to say—"

He shook his head, "Just let me get it out. Please. I want you to know that… look, Kelsey and I aren't together anymore. I broke up with her the second that I got back to London. The second that I saw her. She told me she knew, anyway. She said she'd always suspected it. Apparently, I didn't hide being in love with you half as well as I thought that I did. I know that probably doesn't change anything now, but I just wanted you to know."

Nelly nodded, looking down at her cigarette. "Was she angry?"

Oliver laughed through his nose, "Nah. Turns out she was shagging someone from my work anyway. Felix, d'you remember him?"

"Felix?" Nelly asked, wrinkling her nose.

Oliver nodded, "I know. He always was a fucking tosser."

Nelly shook her head in disbelief. When she looked back up, he was staring down at her, his blue eyes squinted slightly as if he were concentrating. "Nelly, I want you to know that—"

"I thought I might find the two of you out here." Oliver and Nelly both turned as they heard Oliver's mother's voice come toward them. She was holding a bottle of white wine in her hand with three glasses dangling cleverly from the other. Nelly smiled as Mrs Matthews held the glasses out toward them. Oliver took them from his mother and poured each of the three of them a drink wordlessly, handing one over to his mother first and then Nelly. "What's the use of grieving if you can't use it as a good excuse to get thoroughly pissed, mmm?" She said to Nelly. Nelly laughed and nodded and then looked down at her hands, suddenly reminded of India by Mrs Matthews in a way that made her feel like a ghost was by her side. India's mother smiled as if she somehow understood and put her arm around Nelly, rubbing at her shoulder.

"Where's Dad?" Oliver asked.

Mrs Matthews smiled weakly, "He's gone upstairs for a lie down. He's not feeling too well."

"Shall I go and check on him?"

"No, thank you my darling. I think he just needs a moment alone. You understand."

Oliver nodded.

She sighed, "We just have to make it through the day, the four of us. Then we can be miserable in peace."

Oliver blew smoke out through his nostrils, "I wish everyone would hurry up and go home."

Mrs Matthews laughed lightly, "Mmm. They mean well, but I'm looking forward to not having to put on a bloody brave face so as not to make people too uncomfortable about the fact that I just lost my little girl."

"Oh, I'm sorry. I should leave the two of you alone," Nelly began to say, but Mrs Matthews shook her head and rubbed Nelly's arm.

"Not you, sweetheart. You're one of us. You meant the world to her, you know?"

Nelly pressed her lips together and nodded, "She meant the world to me, too."

"Mmm. And she knew that, my darling. Even at the end."

Nelly took a deep breath and then lifted her wine glass to her lips, the liquid cool against her warm face. She suddenly felt very hot, despite the weather. And guilty, for looking for reassurance from the person that must be suffering more than anyone today. Part of Nelly wished that she could feel something else.

Something other than utterly numb. The devastation must have been coming; it was scary knowing that it was enroute. Like knowing there will be pain when an anaesthetic eventually wears off.

They stood silently for a moment, their shoulders together in unity. All understanding and yet not understanding how the other was feeling in that moment. No one's pain is the same, but it is all painful.

"Are you two smoking? Awful things," Mrs Matthews said, wrinkling her nose. Oliver held out the packet toward her and smiled as she took one from it, signalling for him to hand her the lighter. "Don't tell your father," she instructed sternly.

Oliver smiled again and looked the other way. "You know, India and I used to steal your cigarettes when we were little."

"Mmm. I figured. Started young," Mrs Matthews nodded, rolling her eyes.

"Do you remember when Dad caught us and made us both smoke an entire packet each?"

"Mmm yes. If only it had bloody worked instead of fuelling the habit," Mrs Matthews mused. She turned and looked at Nelly, "They were two peas in a pod, those two. Even when they were small."

Nelly smiled at her. She had never thought of Oliver and India as similar. They were so opposite, in so many ways. But, now that she thought of it, they were also so very much alike.

Oliver smiled. "Hey, do you remember when—"

"What?"

Oliver's voice had trailed off as he looked out into the car park toward them. His gaze was focussed on something—someone—who was standing just far enough away from them for their face to be somewhat indistinguishable in the dusky light.

"Who's—" Nelly began to ask. She stopped as Oliver's body moved from the wall beside her, the sound of his shoes on the gravel crunching as he walked purposefully toward the figure in the distance.

"Oliver?"

Nelly moved behind him quickly, half running until she was close enough to see who it was that had joined them.

Oliver threw his glass onto the ground and grabbed Spencer by the front of his shirt, almost lifting him off from the floor.

"Oliver, don't!" Nelly called out behind him. Spencer looked so tiny in Oliver's arms. Minuscule, almost. Like an insect. It was startling to think how much of an impact someone so physically insignificant had managed to have on their lives.

"Have you not done enough?" Oliver shouted.

"Oliver!" Nelly tugged at his arm, trying to pull him back.

"Get off of me," Spencer squirmed. His voice was nasal and weak.

"I should kill you," Oliver spat at him. "I should kill you for everything that you've done. How do you have the fucking nerve to show up here today? How could you show your face where her family are?" He was so angry that his voice was almost ricocheting inside of Nelly's chest. Oliver was shaking Spencer as he shouted at him, rocking him like a baby with a weak neck.

"India would have wanted me here."

"Don't say her name! Don't speak about her, don't think about her, don't—"

"Oliver, stop!" Nelly called out. The few stragglers outside had begun to move toward them, sensing something interesting approaching. "Oliver, please. Please stop!"

Oliver continued to grasp Spencer in his hands.

"Oliver. You're scaring me. Please!"

Oliver's shoulders hung in mid-air for a moment, his entire body tense to Nelly's words. Eventually, he let Spencer go with a shove. "Stay the fuck away from us," he told him, moving backward and putting his arm around Nelly's shoulders. He pointed a shaking hand in Spencer's direction. "Stay away from us."

"Come on," Nelly told Oliver quietly as she tried to lead him away. Oliver's body shuddered as he eventually turned to move with her. He wiped a hand over his face, his grip on her shoulder firmer than it normally would have been. She gripped back into the fabric of his shirt, willing him to keep moving forward.

The noise of feet moving back toward them sounded and Oliver's body turned automatically, too strong for Nelly to hold onto. He looked utterly furious. Like something had taken over him and it was all that he could do to control it.

"Oliver, he isn't worth it," Nelly pleaded. Oliver looked back at her; his breathing heavy beneath his chest. "Please," she repeated. He closed his eyes for a second and then nodded, replacing his arm back around her and turning them away.

"You'd know all about not being worth it, wouldn't you, Nelly?"

Nelly was forced to let go of Oliver's shirt as he swung his body around to face Spencer again. But it wasn't he that got there first.

"What do you think you're doing here?" Mrs Matthews asked calmly, walking toward them with her elbow resting casually on the crook of her other arm. She stroked Oliver's shoulder as she moved past.

Spencer's cheeks twitched, as if assessing the situation. "She was my girlfriend. She would have wanted—"

Mrs Matthews' hand had smacked him across the face before he could finish his sentence. He stared at her, gobsmacked and furious. She merely blew the smoke out from her mouth and flicked her cigarette onto the ground, crushing it beneath her heeled shoes as if she hadn't moved an inch. Nelly might have thought that she had dreamed it had it not been for the red rash that began to spread across Spencer's cheek. Nelly could feel Oliver's body tensing beneath her hands. She held onto him as he moved to stand beside his mother, his shoulder edging just in front of her frame. Mrs Matthews patted him gently, her eyes still watching Spencer.

"Do you know, she used to collect cockroaches when we went on holiday, my little India. I hated it. She'd carry this enormous red bucket around the villa and plop them into it, carrying them around with her. She'd let them back outside later through the window and watch them go." She shuddered, "It used to revolt me. You see, I would have far rather stamped on them with my shoe or sprayed them to death with my L'Oréal. But she didn't want to do that. She was sweet, my India. Delicate. Innocent, despite her readiness not to be."

She laughed slightly and shook her head, flicking her blonde hair behind her ear. "I'll never understand how you managed it. She must have been told on a daily basis how lovely she was. She could barely walk down the street without someone falling head over heels for her. But even if you shut every window, cockroaches always find their way inside. You made her feel as if she were worthless. As if she didn't deserve the love that people felt for her. Like she was completely alone and isolated in the world. And, for some reason that I will never understand, no matter how many times we told her that it wasn't true, she didn't believe us. Not any of us. She believed you. Because you somehow succeeded in making her feel as if she didn't have anybody else."

She looked at Spencer again and shook her head as she surveyed him up and down as if she were critiquing his outfit rather than his soul. "You didn't deserve to breathe the same air as my daughter, Spencer. Get out from her funeral. Or I'll call the police."

Spencer stood rooted, furious. His eyes flicked from Mrs Matthews to Nelly and Oliver, pausing for a moment before looking back at her. His words came out spat between his teeth. "If you don't let me in, I'll—"

"You'll what?" Mrs Matthews asked curiously. She paused, as if allowing him ample opportunity to finish his sentence. When he didn't, she simply sighed, "Don't make the mistake of thinking that I'm afraid of you, Spencer. You've already stolen my daughter. What else could you possibly do to me?"

Without a moment's pause, she turned and moved away from him, her heels crunching calmly back over the gravel. She smiled at her son and linked her fingers between his, forcing him to turn away from Spencer as she led him away by the hand. Oliver hesitated and then went with her. Nelly stood and looked at Spencer for a moment, his jaw clenching beneath his skin.

"Nelly," Mrs Matthews' voice said calmly from behind her. Nelly turned and Mrs Matthews smiled understandingly. She held her other hand out toward her, "Come on, sweetheart. Let's go inside."

Nelly paused and then nodded. She looked at Spencer once more and then walked back toward India's family.

2000
Oliver

They had spent the night together after the funeral. Nothing sexual or romantic happened between them; not really, anyway. It had just been that they hadn't considered parting from one another. That they knew they should be together, in some way. Nelly had stayed at the hotel where the wake was with Oliver and his parents until the last stragglers had left. They had been nursing whiskeys quietly and Nelly had shuddered subtly each time that she had taken a sip, as if she didn't really like it but didn't want to say. It made Oliver smile a little bit. It was a very expensive drink.

"It's a good vintage, isn't it?"

"Mmm. Lovely," she took another sip as if to mark her point. Oliver smiled again.

"Don't drink it if you don't want to," he told her.

She nodded. His mum and dad were beside him, his dad's head resting against his mum's shoulder. He had never seen the man look so defeated. He had always seemed to Oliver like the strong one. Like the one of them that was void of affection. That didn't fit. Now, thinking about it, he fit perfectly. Oliver was more like him than he liked to admit. And his mother just sat there. Her face was staring out as the waiters and waitresses cleared away the leftover plates and glasses, her head swaying slightly along with the music that was still playing. Oliver felt very proud of his mother in that moment. He reached beneath the table and took Nelly's hand in his, bringing it up to his lips and kissing her gently on the knuckles. She glanced down at it only slightly, as if it were the most natural thing for him to have done in that moment.

They stayed up for most of the night, sitting on the balcony of the hotel room watching the moon rise and then be replaced by the sun. They drank an overly-priced bottle of Merlot and exchanged stories about India and the adventures that they had been on together. He told her about the time when India had flown over her handlebars and chipped her front tooth and Nelly told him about the occasion when India had thrown a glass of Chianti over a man for pinching Nelly's arse one Friday night in Cambridge. They laughed and they drank, each story bringing them closer toward one another; each tale entwining their fingers closer together. Nelly was wearing Oliver's suit jacket over her dress and she pulled it tightly around herself, hugging her arms against the cold as she chuckled at his story. The skin around her mouth was slightly purple from the alcohol, a faint violet line rimming her bottom lip.

Oliver imagined his were probably the same. He reached out without asking and found himself tracing his thumb over the ring where the bottle had met her lips, creating a circle. She sat still, letting him do so. He let his hand drop and bent forward to kiss her, not thinking about the consequences. He wanted her—needed her—close to him. As close as he could get her. She tasted like wine and cigarettes and home as she opened her mouth for him, meeting his tongue with hers. He moved off from his chair and went to kneel in front of her, his face now level with hers.

Oliver kissed Nelly's lips and her cheeks and then her neck and she rubbed her hands through his hair, pushing it back from his forehead. Her hands felt cool against his scalp. Refreshing. Like a moment of relief. He was about to move his hands beneath the suit jacket when the tears stopped him.

Sudden and violent. They chugged against his chest, forcing him to gasp for breath. He found himself resting his face against Nelly's breast, crying into her as she held him.

"I don't know what to do, Nelly," he heard himself gasp. He hated it. How weak he sounded. How pathetic. He wanted to stop—wished that he could stop—but he felt as if he had lost every ounce of strength inside of his body. All that he could do was give up to it and let her cradle him in her arms. The only place that he felt safe. The only place that he could feel what he felt.

Nelly stroked his hair, rocking him rhythmically against her. "It's okay. I'm here now."

2000
Nelly

Nelly went to meet Oliver at a restaurant on Bridge Street at eight o'clock on a Friday evening. It had been two months since India had died and every day since had felt oddly empty and full at the same time for Nelly; as if her body was so occupied with emotion that she couldn't quite access any of it. Like feelings didn't really fit into specific boxes anymore. Sadness. Love. Anger. Hurt. They all sort of merged into one in a horribly heady cocktail.

She had moved back to London almost a month ago. She'd known as soon as she had gotten onto the plane that Rome wasn't where she was supposed to be any longer. It didn't feel right, returning to a life of freedom and beauty after everything that had happened at home. Especially when Oliver needed her as she knew that he did. She had handed her notice in at her job and worked the three weeks that her contract specified she did, then packed up her few belongings and left her beautiful, tiny flat in Rome by the sewers and closed the door on that chapter.

She had wanted to cry when she handed the key over to the landlady, but the tears hadn't seemed to want to come. So, she had just shaken the woman's hand and thanked her and gone on her way. Back to London. Back to reality. Back home, whatever that was supposed to mean now.

Oliver was already at the restaurant when Nelly arrived. He was sat at the back at a small round table, twisting the stem of a wine glass in his fingers and watching it as it balanced precariously from edge to edge. He looked up when the waiter showed Nelly to the table and she could see soft blue rings cradling the bottoms of his eyes.

He stood up and kissed her on the cheek, pulling her chair out and resting his hand on her shoulder as she sat down. He faltered beside her for a moment, seemingly forgetting what he was supposed to be doing, and then sat back down opposite her. There was already a glass of wine waiting for Nelly in her place and she picked it up, taking a sip of it and letting the alcohol rub dryly against her tongue.

"It's good to see you," Oliver said.

Nelly smiled slightly, "Yeah. You too."

Oliver nodded, as if in agreement.

"So, how've you been?"

Oliver nodded again, "Yeah. Alright. Work's busy. But that's about it."

"Mmm." It hadn't been the answer that Nelly had wanted. She and Oliver had spoken most days since the funeral. Over the phone, always. Nelly called him first from Rome and then from her parents' house in Clapham. At first, he had spoken to her from his parents' house where he had been staying for a couple of weeks, and then from his flat in London. They rang each other and then listened whilst the other went about their business, either getting washing out of the dryer or pouring soup into a bowl for dinner. They spoke and yet didn't actually talk about anything, lately.

Like they wanted the company but also didn't want to have to engage with it. They both seemed fine with that, though. Another of their quiet agreements. That was until Oliver had asked if she wanted to go for dinner with him.

"Dinner tomorrow?" he'd asked her. She had been pouring milk into a cup of coffee when he had posed the question. *Dinner tomorrow?* So flippant, as if it was still a normal occurrence and the last time that they had seen each other hadn't been at his sister's funeral; or the time before that hadn't been an explosive argument that had torn both of their hearts in two.

"Sure," Nelly had replied.

Oliver had told her where to meet him. He'd offered to come and pick her up from her parents' house, but she'd said that she would meet him there. She knew that if he turned up at her parents', they would never let him leave. They'd want him to talk to them about the way that he was feeling. They'd want to hug him and feed him and tell him that he should never have gone back to work so quickly. That everything was going to be okay. Somehow, Nelly knew that this was the opposite of what Oliver needed right now. So, she'd come to meet him here, at the restaurant.

Oliver was wearing a blue shirt, unbuttoned at the top to reveal a tiny outline of his collar bone. It made him look vulnerable, although Nelly wasn't sure why.

He looked up at her and raised his eyebrows slightly. "Are you alright with that, or do you want something else?"

"Mmm? Oh, no. This is fine, thanks. It's lovely."

"Yeah? I wasn't sure if you'd prefer something sparkling."

"No, no. This is lovely."

"Mmm. I think it's a bit young. Look at the veins," Oliver replied, twirling the stem of his glass again and watching the droplets of purple bleed down the edges.

"Ah, right. Yeah," Nelly replied weakly, not really caring about the wine.

Oliver raised his eyebrows at her. "This is the part of the conversation where you call me a posh arsehole, remember?"

Nelly smiled weakly. "Ah. Okay then."

Oliver looked displeased.

She pressed her lips together and then said, "What about your parents? How are they doing?"

Oliver shrugged slightly, looking at his glass again, "Yeah. They're okay thanks."

"Oliver."

He sighed, his shoulders slightly deflating, and then looked up at her. She could see a faint tinge of red in the whites of his eyes. He nodded his head slightly, "Yeah, they're... Mum's joined a group."

"Oh yeah?"

"Mmm. For women that have been abused," he shook his head slightly, "I don't get how that can be helping her, really. I mean, she isn't the one that it's happened to. But she says that it is. Helping, I mean."

"Oh. Well, that's good. That it's helping."

"Mmm."

"And what about your dad?"

"My dad's being... my dad."

"Right. Yeah."

Oliver smiled slightly with his lips pressed together, his shoulders hunching toward the bottom of his jaw. "What about you, though? How've you been?"

"Yeah, I'm..." Nelly struggled for the words.

Oliver nodded. The waiter came over to their table and Oliver leant back in his chair, turning his face upward to meet the man's gaze.

"Good evening, sir. Madame," the man told them, leaning over the middle of the table to light the candle that sat in an empty wine bottle dripping wax.

"Evening," Nelly tried to smile, "Thank you."

"Now, we have some specials this evening. They're on the board to your right, sir. Just behind you. But I have to tell you that we've run out of the swordfish. Okay? I'm very sorry for this." His English was clearly in the process of being learned and the realisation warmed Nelly to him.

"That's fine. No problem," Nelly smiled again. The man nodded, his eyes anxiously watching Oliver for a response. Oliver turned his head to look at the board behind them, then turned it back and nodded without saying anything.

"Now, can I get you both something else to drink? Or something for the table?"

"Umm. I don't know, what do you—"

"We'll get a bottle of the Roederer," Oliver said, his head turned down briefly toward the wine list.

"Please," Nelly added automatically.

Oliver raised his eyebrows as he looked down at the menu, "Yeah."

"Of course. Of course. No problem. And anything for the table? Breads, olives, prosciutto?"

"You'd like some olives, wouldn't you?" Oliver asked Nelly.

"Oh, yeah. I mean, I'm not fussed, unless—"

"And we'll have some of the prosciutto as well."

"Prosciutto and olives. Very good," the waiter nodded sagely, "What else can you need, eh?"

Nelly smiled. She noticed that Oliver didn't. The waiter took the wine menu away from them and tapped his pen on his notepad to signal that he'd finished recording their order. He repeated it back to them and Nelly tried to smile at him when Oliver sighed loudly, clearly already considering the interaction as being too lengthy.

"I'll come back for your mains in a little bit," he told them, before adding, "And, if you don't mind me saying, you make a very lovely couple."

Nelly could feel her cheeks flushing. "Oh, we're not—"

"Thank you," Oliver replied again dismissively, still watching the wine bleed down the edge of his glass.

Nelly waited until the waiter moved away from the table before leaning in slightly and asking, "Are you sure you're alright?"

"Mmm? Yeah. Of course. Why wouldn't I be?"

Nelly chewed her cheek. "Well, you were a bit rude just then. To the waiter, I mean."

Oliver raised his eyebrows, "Was I? Oh well. I'll give him a good tip."

Nelly frowned. They sat quietly for a moment until the waiter brought them over their bottle. He twisted the top and smiled eagerly at Nelly when it popped, catching the cork into his hand. He poured a small amount into Oliver's glass and then waited for him to try it. Oliver picked it up, took a sip, and then nodded. The waiter poured Nelly a glass into a separate flute beside her wine and then topped up Oliver's, placing the bottle into an ice bucket in the middle of the table.

"I'll be back with your food in just a moment."

"Thank you. That's great," Nelly told him.

"Yeah. Thanks. That's… thank you," Oliver said. The waiter smiled and walked away and Nelly found herself reaching out her foot beneath the table toward Oliver's. She tapped the tip of her toe against his ankle and he leant his foot forward, as if meeting her there, but didn't look up to return her gaze.

"So, how's the house hunt going?"

Nelly sighed slightly, "I mean, it isn't really. I've got to get a job first before I can look for somewhere to live."

"Oh?" Oliver asked the question as if the thought had never occurred to him.

"Mmm. Yeah. And term's already started, so it's a bit difficult."

"Right."

"And. Well, I dunno. I just don't really… you know?" She wasn't even sure what she meant. But Oliver nodded as he swallowed his drink.

"Yeah. Sure," Oliver tipped his flute toward her, "The champagne's good."

"Oh," Nelly replied, picking up her own glass instinctively and bringing it to her lips. They were quiet for another moment and Nelly found herself chewing the fleshy part of her cheek, seeking something to say. It was odd for Oliver to be so quiet with her. So withdrawn. It made her uncomfortable. She found herself seeking his foot beneath the table again and was relieved when he looped his ankle beneath hers so as her leg balanced just on top of it. She smiled, "Well, if I don't move out of my parents' house soon, I think I'll explode. Mum's got me up at five every day helping with the deliveries."

"Oh yeah?"

"Mmm. She says that the routine is good for me. You know, with… everything."

Oliver nodded, "Yeah. Sounds about right."

Nelly hesitated, "I'm sorry. I probably shouldn't have said that."

Oliver shook his head, "It's fine. We're in the same boat."

"Mmm." Nelly bit into the side of her mouth again, feeling awkward. To break the silence, she said, "Anyway, I'll probably have to save up for ages before I can afford somewhere on my own. Everywhere half-decent is so expensive."

"You could always move in with me, if you wanted?"

"Huh?"

Oliver shrugged, "You could move in, if you like."

He sipped his champagne and turned to look at the specials board again behind him, as if what he had just suggested was the most normal thing in the world. Nelly felt lost for words. "Oh. No, I—that's not what I was getting at."

Oliver shrugged again, "Well, if you wanted. Would you like a starter?"

"Um, I—"

"I think I'm going to get one."

"Right. Yeah. Okay," Nelly watched Oliver drink his champagne, "Oliver, are you sure you're alright?"

He nodded, "Yep."

"Because it's normal, if you aren't. I mean, it's more than understandable if you're struggling."

"I'm fine."

"Are you, though? Because you don't seem it. You can tell me. I'm not fine, either. You can tell me anything."

Oliver sighed, "I'm getting on with it."

"Really? Because it seems like—"

"I'm getting on with it."

Nelly nodded, "Right. Yeah. Okay. I'm sorry."

Oliver sighed again and rubbed his face. He looked back up at her and then reached across the table, taking her hands between his. "No, you don't need to be sorry. *I'm* sorry. I'm being shit."

"No, you're just—"

"I'm being a shit," he told her. He smiled briefly from the edge of his mouth and it caught hers, tugging at the edges of her lips.

"Well, okay. You are being a bit of a shit. But you're allowed to be."

Oliver laughed then and she saw a glimmer of him in front of her. Shiny and lovely. He rubbed his thumbs over the edges of her knuckles and looked down at them.

"Why are your hands always so cold?"

"Mmm, are they?"

"Yeah. All of the time. Even when it's a like thirty-five degrees outside."

Nelly smiled and shrugged, "I don't know. Cold hands warm heart."

"Ah, that'd be it."

The waiter came back over and Oliver dropped one of Nelly's hands, holding onto the other one but allowing room for the wooden board to be placed down on the table.

"I added something a little special for you on there," the waiter told them proudly, "That's a fig liqueur with some basil-infused spirit. It will go nicely with the ham."

"That's great. Cheers, mate," Oliver told the waiter. Nelly smiled at him. He waited until the waiter moved out from earshot before nodding toward the fig liqueur and saying, "Are you feeling brave?"

Nelly laughed. She reached over and picked up the glass between her fingers with her free hand, bringing it to her lips. It tasted sweet and oddly warm on her tongue. She swallowed about half of the drink and then stretched over the table to hand it to Oliver. He took it from her, his fingers curling around hers for a moment as they exchanged.

Oliver watched her as he took the liqueur to his lips, placing the glass back down onto the table and then frowning slightly, as if in thought. "Mmm. That's strong."

"Yeah. It'll put hairs on your chest."

Oliver raised his eyebrows, "Well, I hope not yours. That might make things confusing for me."

Nelly laughed and moved to kick him beneath the table. He reached out and grabbed her ankle in his hand, as if anticipating her movement, cradling it in his palm for a moment before placing it gently on top of his knee. He nodded toward the vodka, "I'll do it if you will."

"Do you remember when she almost got arrested for sunbathing topless in the grounds at Kings?"

Oliver shook his head, "Honestly, who'd have ever thought that scholars at Cambridge could be so bloody uptight."

Nelly laughed. She could feel the warmth in her cheeks as she grinned for what felt like the first in a very long time. She wasn't sure whether it was the alcohol or the company or a concoction of the two, but it felt good. Finally, she felt as if she were feeling something.

"What about when she got banned from that bar for having sex on the fire escape?"

Oliver wrinkled his nose, "Yeah, I think you probably found that funnier than I did."

Nelly laughed and nodded. Oliver was smiling too. His cheeks were high on his face, one hand still stroking the skin of Nelly's ankle as it lay on his lap. At first, she had felt as if she had been stretching her entire body out to reach him. But now they seemed to have somehow gravitated closer toward each other through the meal, as if the table had shrunken or the chairs had pushed them closer together. Nelly felt as if she could reach out and jump right into him. Like they were sharing every feeling in their chests. It felt good to feel.

"She was always so lovely to me, you know?"

"Yeah?"

"Mmm," Nelly hesitated. After a moment, she said, "She was the first person that I ever told about... you know. The thing that happened in Clacton. I'd always sort of thought that..." she trailed off. Oliver waited. "I'd always sort of thought that it was my own fault, somehow. Which is embarrassing to admit. Because of course it bloody wasn't. But still."

Nelly sighed, remembering, "She'd come into the bathroom in my halls, looking for me. She wanted me to straighten her hair. But I was already in the bath," Nelly laughed a little, "She never knocked."

Oliver smiled and shook his head, "She never understood the need."

Nelly laughed. "Do you remember when she walked in on us that morning at your parents'?"

"Of course. Scuppered any plans I might have had."

Nelly laughed again.

Oliver smiled, "Go on then."

"Hmm?"

Oliver waited patiently.

Nelly nodded. "I tried to hide that I was crying, but she saw. And I just sort of blurted the whole thing out. And then it was out there, in the open. And she didn't judge me. She didn't even say anything. She just took her shoes off and stepped into the water and hugged me. She even still had her denim jacket on. And I felt like… I dunno. Like someone finally understood. Like someone finally saw me." She rubbed her eyes, "It's stupid, probably."

Oliver shook his head, "No. It isn't stupid." They sat quietly for a moment until Oliver said, "I'm really glad that she was that person for you."

Nelly nodded and smiled to herself, "She had such a big heart."

"Too big."

They sat for a moment in silence until Oliver said, "Did I tell you about what she used to do when we were little? At restaurants?"

Nelly shook her head, "No?"

Oliver laughed half to himself, "It was adorable, looking back. She used to be so chatty. I mean, that never changed. Always wanting to talk to the waiters and the concierge and the sommelier."

"Well, la di da."

Oliver squeezed Nelly's ankle and she smiled. "She'd just go on and on about whatever she was into at the time. Cartoons, or books that she'd read, or bugs that she'd collected. She'd just sit there and talk their ears off." Oliver laughed, "Dad couldn't stand it. He used to get so annoyed. So, Mum worked out that the best way to get her to shut up was to give her dessert. It was all that she was interested in, anyway."

Nelly smiled, "Why save the best till last?"

Oliver nodded, "Exactly. So, we'd always order India's dessert as soon as we got there. Chocolate mousse, she normally had. Or tiramisu, if it was on the menu. And she'd just sit there and eat her pudding whilst we all ate our mains, and then it would swap around." Oliver laughed and shook his head, "Fuck. I'd forgotten about that until just then."

Nelly reached over and took his hand in hers, "That's so sweet."

Oliver nodded. "She was such a lovely kid."

"She was such a lovely person."

Oliver nodded again, "Yeah. She really was, wasn't she? I mean, she was flighty and ridiculous."

"With a penchant for terrible men."

Oliver nodded, "Yeah. And she couldn't sing to save her life."

Nelly smiled, "But she really was lovely." Nelly stroked his hand and Oliver watched it. He stared at their fingers intertwined for a moment, as if deep in thought. Nelly let him. After a moment, he said, "I'm really sorry, Nelly."

She frowned, "Oliver, it isn't your fault. You've got nothing to be sorry for."

He shook his head. "No. I'm sorry for what happened with us."

"Oh. Oliver, I... it was a long time ago now. You've already apologised."

"But it still matters. To me, it matters. If all of this hadn't happened, you probably wouldn't even be speaking with me still." He shook his head, "Fucking ironic, isn't it?"

Nelly could feel her heart beating, "Oliver, I'm... none of it matters now."

"It does. I fucked up. I fucked it all up," he leant back in his chair and rubbed a hand over his face, breathing through his nose. "And the shittiest thing about it is that I so badly wanted it to all work out. I really meant it—everything that I said and we shared—I fucking meant all of it. I swear, I never lied to you. Not about how I felt, anyway. You're probably the first woman I have been honest with. Fucking hell. I mean, I picked the worst time to develop a conscience. But other than that, it was the best time of my life. Being there with you in that tiny room in that shitty block of flats was the best time of my life."

They sat in silence for a moment, neither knowing what to say. Eventually, Nelly spoke.

"My flat wasn't shit."

Oliver laughed through his nose. "No. Sorry. Yours was the exception."

Nelly smiled as they eyed one another. Oliver looked back down at their hands intertwined across the table.

"It was mine, too. By the way. The happiest time of my life."

Oliver looked back up at her and smiled again before sighing.

"That probably makes it worse."

"Why?"

"Because it just all went to shit, didn't it? I honestly still think about it now. About sitting on the end of that bed watching you sleep and knowing—just knowing in my gut—that everything was going to change and that you were never going to love me the same way again. That you'd never trust me. That you'd never forgive me. I've never felt like it before. That feeling, right here." He placed a hand over the top of his stomach. "Fuck—it felt awful. I felt like I'd lost a limb. And..." He looked thoughtful and Nelly let him. "And I don't want you to think that that was what it was to me. The stuff that you said it was, I mean. That you were just like the other girls. Because you weren't. You have to know that you weren't. I swear to you, it meant more to me than you'll ever know. It meant the world to me. And I kick myself every day about it. Just thinking that I could have handled it all differently. That, if I'd done stuff differently, things would be different now. If I could click my fingers and go back to that moment in the restaurant—that moment when everything happened—I would. In a heartbeat, I would. And I'm so sorry, Nelly. I really am so, so sorry."

Nelly nodded. She stroked her thumb over his knuckles as he watched her from across the table, "I'm sorry, too."

He frowned, "No, you don't need to be—"

"I do. It was both of us. You fucked up, yes. But I don't think that I was ready either. Really. I thought I was. And I wanted to be. But I don't think that I could have been. Otherwise, I'd have understood more. I'd have been pissed off still, obviously. But we would have worked it out. If we had both been ready to—if I had really been ready to—I'd have worked it out."

Oliver watched her quietly and then nodded. He looked down at their hands and then back up at her, "Do you think you're ready now?"

Nelly pressed her lips together, her heart thumping beneath her chest. She breathed deeply, trying to feel the feelings that she was somehow still numb to, and then breathed back out again. "I don't think either of us are ready right now. Not with... everything."

Oliver hesitated and then nodded. He picked up their hands and kissed her knuckles gently before setting them back down on the table and withdrawing his from hers.

"I can't lose you again, Nel," Oliver said all of a sudden. Nelly looked up at him, his eyes suddenly full with worry. He shook his head, "I can't lose you again. Not after everything. With India and with us and... I can't risk it. I have to have you in my life. I can't lose you. I don't know what I'd do if I really—"

"Hey, you won't," Nelly said, reaching forward and taking his hand back into hers. She looked him in the face, searching for his eyes. She brushed her thumb over his knuckles and nodded gently, "You couldn't, okay? I promise."

Oliver nodded quickly, pressing his lips together. He reached forward and took her hand in both of his, bringing it to his lips and kissing her on the palm. She watched him silently and then reached for both of his hands with her two when he set them back down on the table. They watched each other quietly for a moment and then the waiter came back over, interrupting their silent communication.

"And have we decided on a main?"

Nelly nodded at Oliver, forcing her eyes away from his for a brief moment. "I think we're going to start with dessert."

2000
Oliver

Meg Ryan's face flashed on the screen of Oliver's television, looking alarmed as she attempted to walk away from Billy Christel at an airport.

"And this is your favourite film ever?"

"Mmm. Yeah."

"Ever? In the entire history of cinema, your favourite film is *When Harry Met Sally*?"

"Yeah. Or *Dirty Dancing*."

Oliver snorted to himself as Nelly's voice answered down the telephone. He enjoyed irritating her. There was something satisfying about it. He could almost feel her rolling her eyes from her parents' living room in Clapham.

"What, would you prefer it if I pretended that my favourite film was something French and sophisticated, with subtitles?"

"I'm just saying, for someone whose favourite book is *Anna Karenina* I'm a bit surprised."

"Did I say that?"

"What?"

"That my favourite book was *Anna Karenina*?"

"Yeah. I think so. Years ago." Oliver knew so. He had gone to a bookshop and bought it the next day. He wasn't sure that he saw the fuss.

"Hmm," Nelly's voice mused, "I probably thought it made me sound interesting."

"And sophisticated?"

"Exactly. Probably."

Oliver smiled, "So then, what is it really?"

"Mmm. I don't know, to be honest. It changes. I suppose I've read *Emma* more times than anything else, probably. Or… mmm. No."

"Go on," Oliver was enjoying himself.

He heard Nelly breathe quietly on the other end of the phone, "Well, I really like *The magician's Nephew*. But that was more when I was little. You probably wouldn't know it."

"Digory and Polly. I'm familiar."

"Are you?"

"Mhmm. You don't have to sound so surprised. I had a childhood too, you know?"

Nelly laughed slightly, "Of course. I'm sorry. I suppose I just can't imagine you curled up reading books about magic."

"Technically more science, really."

"It's called *The* Magician's *Nephew*. Not the *scientist's* nephew."

"He's an inventor, though. And isn't science a sort of magic, really?"

"Mmm. Very profound, Mr Matthews."

Oliver laughed. "Go on then. What was it that you liked about it?"

"I dunno, really. I suppose the idea of vanishing away into another world," she was quiet for a second. "You know, when I was little—like, really young. About five or six—I got in so much trouble with my mum because I stole a pair of scissors from the kitchen and chopped holes all over my quilt. I was trying to find Narnia."

"And you didn't think to look inside the wardrobe?"

Nelly laughed, "Yes. Well, apparently, I thought it was more likely to turn up in my bed."

"I'm sure Freud would have a field day with that."

Nelly laughed. "My mum was furious. I ruined the whole quilt."

"You ragamuffin."

"Quite the rebel, eh?"

Oliver smiled, thinking of a tiny, curly-haired Nelly chopping her way through her duvet. "I wish I could have known you then."

"Really?"

"Mmm."

Nelly laughed, "I'm not sure you would have liked me very much. I was very… bookish."

"I can imagine. Did you have glasses?"

"Mhmm. Big round ones. I looked like a tiny librarian."

Oliver laughed.

"I bet you were a really cute kid. One of those blonde families that they put in the back of photo frames when you buy them."

Oliver smiled and shrugged, "I dunno. I suppose so."

"Were you always perfect?"

The question caught Oliver off guard slightly. He smiled, "I didn't realise that you thought that I was."

Nelly went quiet, then said, "Liar."

Oliver laughed. He took a sip of his drink, weighing up giving away some more personal information, then decided that he would. "I did have a bit of a spell when I was young where I had to wear a patch."

"A patch?"

"Mmm. Over my eye…"

"Did you?"

"Mhmm. The left one."

"That's really sweet. It makes me want to hug little you."

"If I'd have known that, I'd have dug the photos out years ago."

Nelly laughed, "Oh, I love this bit."

An elderly couple were on the screen, recounting a story to the camera of how they had first met. Oliver listened as the two went back and forth, talking about some sort of camp on Coney Island, and something vaguely metaphorical about melons. The mundanity of it was beautifully reassuring. He could almost hear Nelly smiling on the other end of the phone.

"I like how he introduced himself. I think I'll do that from now on."

"What?"

Oliver mimicked the man's New York accent, *"Oliver Matthews of the Cotswold Matthews."*

Nelly laughed and it made Oliver smile. "Mmm, it doesn't have quite the same ring to it."

"Mmm. It doesn't, does it? Thank Christ I'm so good-looking."

Nelly laughed again. It sounded like a bell gently chiming.

"Or perfect; that's what you said, right?"

"Alright. Alright. Don't let it go to your head."

"Too late."

Nelly laughed again, "How do you even know which melon is good?"

Oliver adjusted himself on his settee so he was sitting more comfortably. He was still wearing his suit, but he had taken off his tie and his shoes, his feet bare where they rested on the coffee table.

"Are we really talking about melons, or are you being facetious?"

"We're really talking about melons."

"Mmm. Shame. Well, who the fuck knows. Open it up and find out, I suppose."

"Mmm. Maybe that's where you're going wrong. You should be able to tell before chopping it apart."

Oliver frowned slightly, "I feel like we aren't talking about melons…"

"We are."

"Mmm. Okay. If you say so."

They were both quiet for a while, watching the film in companionable silence. They'd been doing this sort of thing a lot lately. It had been three months since India had died now, and the world seemed to be moving on. At first, people had tried to offer their condolences to Oliver to almost an irritating extent. He had left his parents' home after only a couple of weeks to go back to work in London, not able to stand the proximity of his and their combined pain. However, work hadn't been much better. People had turned up with cupcakes and back smacks and offered awkward, uncomfortable attempts at remorse for his sister, who most of whom had never met. But now, everyone that had first barraged him with their apologies seemed to have almost completely forgotten.

It wasn't even that he wanted to be reminded about it. He didn't need to be. It was more or less all that he thought about anyway, and he certainly didn't want to speak about his feelings with anyone. Apart from Nelly. She was the only other person that seemed to understand it. Not that her pain was the same as his; it seemed entirely different, strangely. Like each of them had lost a limb, but Nelly was refusing to admit that hers was missing whilst Oliver felt as if his was openly bleeding. She seemed as surprised by this as everyone else was. She had spoken to him about it before, saying that she supposed she had come to terms with losing India before the loss had actually happened. She had already felt the pain of it and was trying to let herself heal; to cope with her new life, without a part of her that she so relied on previously. She thought this was true, anyway. But Oliver knew differently. India had been more than just a limb to Nelly. Their friendship had been more than something external. They had knotted together, the two of them; coping with life by each propping the other one up. The loss of

India would actually hit Nelly at some point. And Oliver planned on being there for her when it did.

Just like she had been for him.

"Is that really what New York's like?"

"What d'you mean?"

"I dunno. It looks magical."

"*Magician's Nephew* magical?"

Nelly laughed. He imagined her covering her mouth and hoped that she wasn't. "No, I just mean… it looks really lovely."

Oliver nodded, "It is really lovely. I mean, the subway smells like piss and people wear a lot of caps, but it still manages to be sort of amazing."

"Mmm. I'd love to see it."

"Men pissing on the subway? I feel like you've probably seen your share of that in Clapham."

Nelly laughed again, "The whole thing. The loveliness."

"We can go. If you'd like?"

"Oh. Yeah. Maybe. I'd love that. Can we go to Coney Island?"

"Why would you want to go to Coney Island?"

"I dunno. I like the accent."

Oliver laughed, "Yeah. We can go to Coney Island. We can go wherever you like."

He adjusted himself on the settee again, shifting his weight so as he was laying down long ways, the phone balancing against the side of his face as he still watched the TV. He sat slightly, picking up his glass and lifting it to his lips. The ice in his whiskey was almost completely melted, laying forgotten on the table.

"Do you have a drink?"

"Mmm."

"Gin?"

Oliver sat the glass back down. "Whiskey."

"You sophisticate."

Oliver smiled.

"I've got a hot chocolate."

"Oh. Cosy."

"Mhmm. And I'm in my pyjamas."

"Are they silky and sexy?"

"Umm, no. Definitely not. They're comfortable and plaid and about six sizes too big for me."

"Mmm. Oh well. I can pretend."

Nelly laughed. "I've been in my pyjamas by about seven o'clock every day lately. Honestly, I don't think I've gone to bed so early since I was about eleven."

Oliver smiled again, "Well, that's being a lady of leisure for you."

"If you can call getting up at half four to help my dad with the market deliveries *leisure.*"

"Still loving staying with Mum and Dad then?"

Nelly sighed, "I mean, they're lovely. Obviously. But I am going a bit mad. If I don't find somewhere to live soon, I might never leave. I slapped my dad's hand away from the focaccia yesterday and realised I'm officially turning into my mum."

Oliver laughed at this. He had offered for Nelly to move in with him once, when they had first seen each other after the funeral. He hadn't expected to say it and was mildly shocked at himself when he had. She had said no, obviously. And he had felt strangely disappointed. Not that he thought it was actually a good idea either. He also didn't know why he'd said the thing about New York. It was like someone hitting your knee and it bending involuntarily. Or saying you will only stay for one drink and then accidentally having five. He swished the last of the ice around in his tumbler, thinking about his next statement. He'd been wondering when to breach the subject since work on Monday afternoon. He didn't want to come across as condescending or patronising, or—potentially worse—like he was trying to resolve her problems for her, even though that was really what he was doing. Nelly hated it when people tried to do that, so he had to be careful about it.

"You're quiet."

"Mmm. I just remembered something that this bloke at work was saying. Phil. D'you remember Phil?"

"Tall with glasses?"

"Mhmm. Yeah. Well, his wife's the head at a senior school and he was saying that she's looking for someone for the English department. Apparently the teacher is going on maternity leave, or something."

"Really? What, just for the rest of the term?"

"The rest of the school year, I think. Yeah." Oliver tensed and felt relieved when Nelly's voice sounded excited.

"Really? That's amazing. What school is it?"

"Mmm. I'm not sure. One in Notting Hill. So, a bit of a way for you, but—"

"No. I mean, I could get the tube. Until I find a place."

"Mmm. Exactly. Or you could stay here, when you wanted." He'd done it again without meaning to.

"Yeah. Maybe. Oh wow, okay. Are they interviewing at the moment?"

"Mmm. I'm not sure. I can ask him tomorrow for you, if you like? Or you could always swing by the office?" he felt as if he may have pushed his luck a little too far, but she didn't seem to notice.

"Yeah. That would be great! Unless it's a pain for you? I know you're busy."

"Mmm, no. It isn't a pain."

"Great! Shall I come tomorrow? Or…" she suddenly sounded a bit embarrassed. "Or whenever suits, obviously."

Oliver nodded, "Yeah, come by tomorrow. I'll finish about sixish and Phil's normally still about at that time, so he could give your CV to his wife, or whatever. We can grab dinner after, or something."

He could almost feel her smile radiating through the phone. "That's amazing. Sixish, okay. No problem. I'll let Dad know for the deliveries."

"Great."

"Oh my God. I need to think of what I'll wear."

Oliver smiled.

"Thank you, Oliver."

Oliver shrugged, "It's nothing." He smiled again to himself. He loved it when Nelly let him help her. He already knew that Phil's wife would give Nelly the job. He'd made up the bit about the interviews. If Oliver asked it as a favour, he was pretty sure that he'd get it. But he wouldn't tell Nelly this. Not when the prospect of getting it for herself would make her so happy.

"No, but really. Thank you. That would really help me out."

"It's fine. Honestly. Now, can you please stop grovelling? You're interrupting my favourite film."

Nelly laughed against the phone receiver and Oliver smiled back to her. It was strange how her happiness seemed to be so infectious.

2000
Nelly

Christmas had been strange. Nelly had spent the entirety of December secretly dreading it, and then felt sad when it was over too soon. Not because she would miss the festivities, but because the idea of starting a new year without India in it was unfathomable.

She still hadn't cried. Sometimes she worried that something inside of her was broken. India had been more than just a friend to Nelly; India had, in many ways, been the love of Nelly's life so far. They had been inseparable since the moment that they had met. Two halves of one whole. If you had one, you had to take the other. That was their deal. Or once it had been, at least. Maybe that was why Nelly hadn't cried about it. They had been split apart a long time ago; Nelly had already processed the loss. That's what Nelly chalked it up to, anyway. At first, when Nelly had moved to Rome, it had been agony. But now it was just numb. Painfully painless. Sometimes she bit hard into the fleshy part of her cheek to check that she could still feel. She hated the taste of blood.

She had spoken to Oliver on Christmas Day. Whatever pain was void so far in Nelly's chest was definitely rife in the Matthews' home. A non-event, was what India's mother had called it on the phone when Nelly had spoken to her. Nelly understood. Life was one big non-event these days.

Still, it had passed, like all other things had done. And Nelly's life was in ways moving forward. She had secured the job that Oliver had told her about. Although *secured* was a generous term for it. She had gone to Oliver's office to meet the man—Phil—that Oliver had told her about, and Phil had invited her and Oliver for dinner to speak about the role. They had eaten a catered meal of veal and dauphinois potatoes and Nelly had spoken with Phil's wife, Maeve, about the job whilst they ate.

"It's a lovely class," Maeve had told her, "Fourteen is such a nice age."

"Oh. I don't remember it being," Nelly had replied.

They had all laughed at this, although Nelly wasn't really sure why. She hadn't been trying to be funny. Oliver had rubbed her knee beneath the table and she had felt reassured.

Nelly was due to start working at St Mary's Secondary in the New Year, after the Christmas break. She had already been in for a staff training day to meet her team and had been surprised to see a faintly familiar face in the staff room. A woman named Tara, who Nelly recognised from India's birthday party a few years ago.

"I was so sad to hear of India's passing," Tara had told Nelly as they stirred spoons into coffee mugs together.

"Mmm. Thanks," Nelly had replied.

"She was such a lovely girl. It must be so painful for you."

Nelly had just nodded. She couldn't admit that it both was agony and yet also wasn't. Nobody seemed to understand that. Apart from maybe Oliver.

Nelly had also moved into a new flat in Shepherd's Bush, closer to where she would be working. It wasn't the nicest of areas and her dad insisted on her ringing him to let her know she was back safely each time she went to their house for dinner, as if he assumed she never otherwise left the flat, but it was comfortable and closer to work. So, it was fine.

The first time that Oliver saw the flat he hadn't outwardly told Nelly that he hated it, although it was as clear as the nose on his face. He had stood just loitering against the kitchen counter, both of his hands plunged inside of the pockets of his pea coat, silently casting his eyes across the room as if assessing for damp.

"It's alright, isn't it?" Nelly had asked him. She wasn't sure why she'd phrased it as a question, but Oliver didn't seem to notice.

He had nodded vaguely and said something about having a spare room in his apartment. He kept bringing that up recently, as if he expected Nelly to jump at the opportunity of it. As if them living together wouldn't make their already complicated relationship even more so. The trouble with Nelly and Oliver's relationship was that everything about it was complicated. They were just friends, but they were both also in love with each other in some way. They were just friends, but Oliver was still her emergency contact on the HR forms at work.

They were just friends, and yet Nelly didn't feel that she would ever be able to explain the boundaries of their relationship to anyone else. They were both more and less than at the same time; complicated and simple. Nelly wasn't seeing anybody else, and she hoped that Oliver wasn't either. Which was ridiculous, really, as it had been her that had told him they weren't ready to be together.

None of it made sense to anyone, apart from Oliver and Nelly.

"People think it's weird, you know," she'd said to him once on the phone late at night.

"What's weird?"

"You and me. The way we are with each other."

"Do they?"

She had hesitated, "Mmm."

"I couldn't give a fuck what anyone else thinks about us, Strapelli," Oliver had told her simply. That had satisfied her. And yet it also hadn't. It was all so complicated. So, when Oliver asked her what her plans were for New Year's Eve, she felt immediately both curious and dubious.

"I don't know. Probably a pizza and a beer and then bed by ten," Nelly had replied vaguely. She was trying to find the second to her pair of shoes in one of the ten boxes that Oliver had just carried upstairs for her.

"You wild child," Oliver had said plainly, "Well, if it isn't too hard to rearrange the pizza, I've got a better option."

"Oh really?"

"Mmm."

She studied him for a moment. He was holding the fridge door open, staring inside of it as if expecting something to materialise. After a while, he plucked out a glass bottle of milk and sniffed the top of it. "I think this milk's off."

"It can't be. I only got it yesterday."

Oliver swirled the milk around in the bottle.

"So, what's your better idea?"

"Mmm?"

"For New Year's?"

"Oh yeah. I've planned something."

"You've planned something?"

"Yep."

"What?"

"Cornwall," Oliver lifted the milk to his lips and then took a hesitant sip, "Mmm. It definitely is off."

Nelly walked forward, one foot still bare, and took the milk from Oliver's hand. She put the bottle to her own lips and took a sip before wrinkling her nose. Oliver smiled and took it back from her. "What do you mean you've planned something in Cornwall? For who, your family?"

"Yeah. For you and me."

Nelly stared at him, trying to ignore the fact that he had just referred to the two of them as family. And trying to ignore how that made her heart vibrate. "You've planned something in Cornwall for you and me? For New Year's."

"Why do you keep repeating everything that I'm saying?"

"Because it's…" Nelly searched for the word, but couldn't find it. What she wanted to say was that it was very out of the blue. And, to be perfectly honest, a ridiculous idea given the current status and non-status of their complicated friendship. The boundaries were already blisteringly blurry. To fade them any more than they already had would be dangerous. And yet it was also what she wanted.

"Lovely? Thank you very much for planning it, Oliver?" Oliver offered, raising his eyebrows at her.

"No. I mean, yes. Of course. Thank you. But… you've planned a weekend away for you and me?"

"If you keep just repeating everything I say, I'm going to have to call a doctor."

Nelly smiled and shook her head. She chewed on her cheek thoughtfully, "I dunno. Is it a good idea?"

"I think so."

"Obviously you do."

"Obviously."

"I just mean, is it just the two of us?"

"Mhmm. A little holiday."

"What do you mean?"

"Mmm. I'm glad you asked that. You see, a holiday is where people go away from the place that they live to have a bit of fun and relax. There's sometimes ice cream, although it might be a bit cold for that. There's also sometimes skinny-dipping, but it might be a bit cold for that too. Although I'm game for it if you are."

Nelly rolled her eyes, "You know what I mean. Is it not a bit weird for you and me to be going on holiday together on our own?"

"I don't see why it would be."

"Well, I mean… with us. With our… history. You know, we've set… boundaries and stuff."

"Nelly, are you insinuating that you couldn't keep your hands off of me if we're alone together outside of London? That's very flattering."

She pulled a face at him and he smiled, looking pleased with himself. Then sighed, and said, "Look, I don't fancy spending New Years Eve at my parents' house sitting together in silence mourning my sister. And I don't want to spend it at some shitty party where nobody is mourning her, either. So, I thought it might be a good idea, you know? Get away from London for a couple of days. A change of scene," he shrugged, "I'm gonna go anyway. It's up to you if you come too."

Nelly chewed on her lip. He turned his face away so as he was staring out of the small window above the sink, apparently inspecting the brick wall opposite. After a moment, she said, "Is it two nights, you said?"

"Mhmm. I've got to be back for work on Tuesday."

"Right," she thought for a moment, "Will it cost a lot?"

"In which sense?"

"Money-wise."

Oliver shook his head, "Don't worry about it."

"Oliver."

"It won't be expensive. I promise."

Nelly nodded.

"You don't have to come, if you don't want to."

"No, it isn't that."

"Well, you don't sound very happy about the idea."

"I am. I just… is it all planned?"

"Mhmm."

Nelly chewed her cheek. On the one hand, it was definitely not a good idea. She had said that they weren't ready to be together yet because she knew it was true. They were both grieving, in different ways, and to start something so monumental amidst that felt like a concoction for chaos. But on the other hand, she loved him. She knew that if he was asking her, it was because he needed her. Plus, the prospect of spending New Years Eve on her own in her flat thinking about the fact that her best friend had committed suicide was making Nelly's chest feel tight. She turned the idea over in her mind, reassuring herself that so long as they weren't sleeping together, they weren't really crossing any boundary. "Okay."

Oliver eyed her suspiciously, "Okay you want to go, or okay you're doing it because you feel like you have to?"

Nelly smiled, "A bit of both?"

He nodded, "I can live with that."

Nelly laughed. She knew what he was doing. He enjoyed teasing her, seeing how far he could push her. She knew he liked the taunt of it. She walked over, closing the distance between them.

"I'd like to come."

"You would?"

"Yes. Please."

"Okay, okay. No need to beg, Strapelli. It's very unbecoming."

She went to hit him on the arm with her spare shoe and he grinned, showing his teeth between his lips. He ducked out from her reach and picked up a box, "Good. I'm glad you finally owned up to how desperately you want to come away with me, because we're leaving in about twenty minutes. Which one of these has your bikini in it?"

Nelly had to tell herself to stop looking at Oliver as he sat in the driver's seat of the car, the motorway spanning out behind them. His arm was balanced on the lip of the window, his fingers just brushing the wheel as they tapped along with the radio. *Brown Eyed Girl* was playing. The way he was drumming his fingers was very distracting. Everything about Oliver was still very distracting. Not just the way that he looked. But that as well. He was wearing a blue shirt and he had the top of it unbuttoned, so as the hollowed area beneath his Adam's apple was showing. His skin was still somehow faintly tanned, despite not having been outside of England for a year.

Nelly wished that she could touch it. Although she absolutely mustn't. She had been very clear that the two of them were just friends, whatever that meant. Just friends who were in love with each other and had had sex previously. But still, just friends. For now, at least. She knew that neither of them was ready to be in a romantic relationship right now, both still too damaged from the loss that they had experienced. And it was also that Nelly knew she still didn't completely trust Oliver with her heart. Loving Oliver Matthews was dangerous. He was the only person left living in the world that could break her heart. And yet he was also the only person that Nelly felt completely safe with.

"So, what's the hotel like?" Nelly asked, busying herself with a map.

"Mmm. I'm not sure yet."

"How did you find it then?"

"Well, I haven't exactly."

Nelly put the map down in her lap and turned to look at him, "You said you'd booked it?"

"No, no. I said I had *planned* it. I was very careful about that."

"Oliver, saying that you had planned a holiday insinuates that you also booked it."

"Well, I'm afraid that wouldn't hold up in a court of law."

"I think it probably would."

"Not with the lawyers that I can afford."

Nelly rolled her eyes. "What, so we're just going to turn up and hope for the best? What if we can't find a hotel with space?"

"It's Cornwall in December. I'm pretty sure there'll be one spare room."

"Two."

"Pardon?"

"Two rooms."

Oliver frowned, "I don't follow."

"We're two people. We need two rooms."

Oliver turned to look at her briefly before looking back at the road, "We do?"

"Yes."

"We didn't all of the other times."

Nelly chewed her cheek, "That was... different. We weren't... you know? Things have changed since before." Before Rome, was what she wanted to say. But she didn't dare. Neither of them spoke about it. That was another of their unspoken rules. Don't bring up that they had slept together. Don't bring up that they'd confessed to being in love with each other. Don't bring up that they broke each other's hearts.

"Fine, we can have two rooms."

"Thank you."

"As long as mine has a sex swing."

Nelly hit Oliver's arm with the map and he grinned, showing his teeth again. She loved it when he did that. It was like a smile that was reserved only for her.

They arrived in Cornwall a little after five o'clock, the sky outside already beginning to morph into an inky-blue. Nelly gazed out of the window as the car pulled around a winding road, gazing out at the sea in the distance. Even in the half-light, it was beautiful. She wound the window down and breathed deeply.

"Don't you love that smell?" Nelly asked Oliver.

"Five hours of driving?"

"The sea."

Oliver smiled, "Yeah. I do."

It took them a while to find a hotel. Eventually, they pulled up outside of a hotel called Port Gaverne. It looked a bit like a very grand pub from the outside, with a white-painted stone face and wooden, round tables perched outside readily waiting for a warmer climate or a solitary smoker. Oliver stopped the car and opened the door, as if he had been expecting to arrive at this exact location all along.

He stood, stretching his arms above his head for a moment and then reached into the back of the car to get his coat, shouldering himself into it. Once snuggly inside, he said to Nelly, "Do you want to come in, or would you rather wait in the car?"

"Oh. I'll come in," Nelly replied. She quickly put her boots back onto her feet, which she'd taken off during the journey, and reached over the seat to locate her own coat, which was buried beneath a mound of scarves and woolly hats that she had thrown into the car as an after-thought. She pulled one of the scarves around her neck and a hat roughly onto her head, flattening her hair, and then clumsily shoved herself out from the door. Oliver watched her amusedly and then, when she moved to get her bag from the boot, said, "Don't worry. I'll get those in a sec."

"Oh. Okay. Yeah, I suppose we'd better see if they have room first."

"Mhmm."

Oliver opened the hotel door for her and Nelly moved inside, feeling the warmth of the place pinking her cheeks immediately. It was smart inside, and very cream. The type of place where Nelly felt constantly nervous about spilling something.

"It's... nice," Nelly said.

Oliver shrugged, "It'll do."

"Good evening, sir. How can I help you?" A man behind the reception desk asked cheerfully as Oliver and Nelly approached.

Oliver rested one arm on the counter whilst Nelly peered just over it, feeling conscious of her size beside him. "Evening. Do you by any chance have a spare room for a couple of nights?" He glanced at Nelly, "Or two rooms, rather."

"Ah, we actually have a wedding party over this weekend, sir."

"Ah."

"But they're only one-hundred and seven. Let me check for you."

"Excellent. Thank you."

Nelly made a face at Oliver as if to say, "One-hundred and seven?" He smiled at her from the corner of his mouth.

"Okay, there's nothing in the east wing. That's okay. Let me just check the West for you. Okay," the man tapped his finger against the mouse impatiently as he waited, "That's it. Let me have a check. Ah. Yes. You're in luck, sir. We've got one room in the West wing for you. Double bed with a spa bath and a balcony view. Now that's two hundred and thirty pounds per night, breakfast included."

Nelly felt her mouth gape slightly open. She glanced up at Oliver nervously, but he looked unfazed. "Great. Thank you very much."

"And, did you say you needed two? Or just the one?"

"Oh, we can just—" Nelly began to say.

"Two, please. If you have it."

Nelly tried to catch Oliver's eye, but he seemed very interested in the bar that was just visible down the corridor to their left. She was already worried about the money.

"Ah, perfect. There's another room on the east wing just down the hall. It's a bit smaller, but with a garden view. Would that be okay?"

"Mhmm. That's perfect."

"And that one is at two hundred and nineteen pounds per night."

"Yep. Excellent."

Nelly felt as if her stomach was going to drop out from her. "Oliver, it's fine. We could just share. We don't need to—"

He shook his head, "Nope. I'm not risking any funny business, Strapelli. No matter how much you try."

Nelly felt her cheeks blaze instantly hot. She stared at him appalled and the man behind the reception desk hid a smirk as he tapped away on his key board.

"Okay, excellent. Shall I get those booked in for you both, then?"

"Yes please."

"Great. Who's having the beach view?"

"You can just put them both under Matthews, thanks," Oliver said, leafing through his wallet and pulling out his card.

"Excellent, thank you sir. I'll do that." The man typed away on the computer and then said, "So that will be a total of eight hundred and ninety-eight pounds for the two rooms for the two nights. Do we want to put that on two cards, or…?"

"No, that's fine. You can just put them both on this," Oliver said, reaching over to hand his card to the receptionist.

"Oliver, I can get mine," Nelly whispered to him. He ignored her.

The man put the booking through and then found them their keys. He handed them both over to Oliver, who handed one to Nelly.

"I'll pay you back," Nelly told him as they walked away from the desk. She already felt anxious about the money, the rooms being far more expensive than she had imagined that they would have been.

Oliver shook his head, "Don't worry about it."

"But… Oliver, it was really expensive."

Oliver shrugged, "Not really."

"But—"

"It was my idea. It's fine. I wouldn't have asked you if I'd wanted to go halves on it."

Nelly breathed through her nose, "Mmm. But I was the one that asked for two rooms."

"Only because you can't keep your hands off me."

"That's not what I said."

"Well, that's how I took it. So, I'm more than paid back in ego."

Nelly smiled and shoved him lightly on the arm. "I really will pay you back."

"Mmm. Okay. If you insist, I've got an idea."

They wandered along the sea front, both wrapped up tightly in their coats against the chill of the December wind. They were each carrying a packet of chips in their hands, which warmed Nelly's skin through her gloves. Nelly had insisted on paying for the food, even though it was a measly amount in comparison with the rooms. Oliver hadn't seemed to want to let her, but hadn't refused either. The smell of vinegar and fish clung to the air until Nelly felt as if she could never smell anything but it. Oliver was chewing his chips quietly, watching Nelly as she rummaged in her own parcel with a small wooden fork.

"Do you not like the crispy ones?" He asked her.

"Mmm? Oh, no. Not really. I like them nice and mushy."

"Mmm," Oliver nodded. He reached in and plucked a particularly crisp chip from Nelly's handful, placing it into his own mouth.

Nelly smiled. "What made you want to come to Cornwall, then?"

"The topless sunbathing that you promised, mostly."

Nelly laughed and Oliver smiled to himself. "Mmm, we used to come here when we were little. Me, Mum and India."

"Not your dad?"

Oliver shook his head, "He was away a lot. But my grandparents had a house here. Down there on the peninsula." Oliver nodded forward and Nelly followed his gaze, as if she knew where he was referring to. "We'd sometimes come in the summer holidays. Or for Easter, sometimes."

"That's nice. Do they live here now?"

Oliver shook his head. "They're both dead."

"Oh, I'm sorry. I forgot."

Oliver shrugged.

Nelly chewed on a chip and then opened her lips slightly, sucking in some cold air to stop it from burning the roof of her mouth.

"Hot?"

"Mmm," Nelly nodded. "That must have been really nice. Did you come to this beach?"

"Sometimes. Yeah."

Nelly smiled, "I bet India loved it. Anywhere that had a slither of sun."

"Mmm. You should have seen her in the summer of 84. Sunburn up to her armpits."

Nelly laughed. Oliver smiled too.

"She was a lot fairer skinned than you are."

"Mmm. She got it from Mum."

"But she always wanted a tan."

Oliver laughed through his nose, looking out at the sea. "Yeah, she loved the sunshine," he said finally.

Nelly nodded, "She was the sunshine."

2000
Oliver

They went back to their separate rooms after their walk on the beach, both claiming to be tired from the journey. Oliver felt slightly disappointed. He'd asked Nelly to come with him so as he wouldn't be alone. Not to sit in a room in Cornwall depressed with his own thoughts for company. That was partially why he was so pleased when she turned up at his door at ten o'clock, holding a bottle of something pink and cheap-looking along with a packet of Maltesers.

"It isn't champagne," she told him, "But it's all that they had downstairs."

"Rosé from California is all that they had in the bar?"

Nelly shook her head, "Oh Christ no. Not the bar. I tried there, but on the menu, it said six pounds for a bowl of olives so I didn't bother. No, I went to an off-licence next door."

"On your own?"

She gave him a look like she was humouring a parent, "It was literally about a twenty-second walk."

Oliver nodded. He never used to worry so much about Nelly wandering around on her own. Not in Cambridge, or London, or on her and India's travels; not all of the time that she lived in Rome. It wasn't that he hadn't cared before. It was just that he had always assumed, without realising he did, that everything would be alright. But since India had left them, Oliver's perspective had changed a bit. Or since everything that Nelly had told him happened with Spencer and that boy in Clacton, also. He worried about his parents a lot. Even his dad. He hated ringing home, but also hated it if he didn't hear from them for a few days. He worried about Nelly a lot, too. More so, even.

He had begun feeling anxious if he knew that she was out on her own when it was dark. He especially hated that she had to walk back to that horrible flat in that shitty neighbourhood. He had awful fantasies about someone following her and attacking her and him not being able to get to her in time. Sometimes he invented excuses to ring her in the evenings when he knew she'd have gotten in, just to check that she was alright. He knew it was over the top, which was why he never mentioned it. She'd definitely be cross with him if she knew about it, too.

"I grew up in Clapham," she had told him sternly once when he'd offered to drive her home so as she didn't have to get the tube at night. "Besides, if one of us is going to be the target for a mugger I'm pretty sure it would be you."

She'd been referring to the fact that Oliver apparently looked posh. She didn't realise that it was something far more sinister than her getting mugged that gave Oliver anxiety at night.

"Right then. Do you fancy a drink?"

"I wouldn't say no."

"Do you think they have glasses?"

Oliver shrugged, "Mmm. They'll probably have mugs. By the kettle, wherever that is."

"Okay," Nelly hesitated by the bedside cabinet, "Can I have a look in there?"

Oliver raised his eyebrows, "I've not unpacked my suitcase of sex toys into there yet, if that's what you're worried about finding."

Nelly smiled and rolled her eyes before crouching down and opening up the bedside table. "Ah, jackpot."

She placed the two mugs on the table and poured wine into them, comparing them to check that they had the same amount.

"It's very sweet," Oliver said when he took a sip of it.

"Mmm. Delicious," Nelly replied, wrinkling her nose and smiling. Oliver was sat on one side of the bed. He'd already had a shower and changed into tracksuit bottoms, a grey jumper pulled on over the top of his t-shirt. Nelly, on the other hand, looked just as she had when he'd picked her up that morning other than the fact that her hair was fluffier than usual from where it had been hidden beneath her hat. She had clearly tried to tame it by forcing it into a ponytail at the back of her head, so as it puffed up from behind her face like a halo. Oliver had to try not to smile at it.

"Did you not want a shower?"

"Mmm, mine didn't have any hot water." She pulled her cardigan closer around herself, as if suddenly worrying that it smelled.

"Oh."

She smiled, "It's fine. I rang reception already. They're going to fix it tomorrow."

"Mmm." Oliver nodded. He wasn't completely surprised. In his experience, the more expensive the room the more chance there often was of something fucking up in it. "Do you want to use mine?"

Nelly shook her head, "No. It's fine." She blushed and looked the other way and it made Oliver want to grin. After all of this time, she still seemed to embarrass so easily, even with him.

"Are you sure? It is a spa bath, apparently," he teased, wanting to push it slightly further.

Nelly thought about it for a second and then shook her head, "No. It's really fine. Thanks."

Oliver shrugged, "Suit yourself."

"I shall." Nelly smiled with her lips pressed together and then loitered around at the end of the bed, seemingly looking for somewhere to sit down. Oliver laid back on the pillow, his head balancing on his elbow.

"Are you looking for something?"

"Mmm? Oh no," Nelly turned back to him, her mug of wine pressed to her lips. "Oh, are you tired? I can—"

Oliver shook his head, "I'm fine. Just getting comfy."

"Ah. Okay." She began flicking through a magazine that was on the small table in the room. *Hunters World,* Oliver had already seen that it was. He smiled. Once Nelly had referred to men hunting as *a posh man's pissing competition.* "Why would hurting something lovely make you feel good about yourself?" She had asked. He watched her flick through the magazine again now. He knew she was stalling.

"See something you like?"

"What?"

He nodded toward the magazine.

"Oh. No, not really." She put it down and went to the window, "These curtains are nice."

"Do you feel uncomfortable, or something?"

"Hmm?"

He raised his eyebrows at her.

She looked confused, "No."

"Really?"

Nelly began to say something, but then broke into an involuntary smile. The rash continued to mottle up to the tops of her cheeks, just beneath her eyes. She smiled and put her hand over her mouth, "Maybe a little bit."

Oliver nodded. He thought about asking her why, but was quite sure that he already knew the answer. "Do you want to watch something?"

Nelly nodded, "Mmm. Yeah. Okay."

Oliver picked up the remote control and flicked the television on in front of the bed, bringing up a news channel where someone was talking about something going on to do with tax. Oliver flicked the channel. "You'll have a hard time seeing it from over there."

Nelly looked at him quickly and then looked back the other way, seemingly weighing something up in her mind before coming to sit on the bed beside him. He was lying roughly halfway on the quilt, his head balancing just above one and a half of the pillows. He thought about moving up to give her more room, but then didn't. He understood why she felt uncomfortable being alone with him in a bedroom, after everything that had occurred between them. They'd slept in the same room only once since Rome, the night of India's funeral. Other than that, they had always parted ways before bed time. She even refused to sleep in his spare room, even though he offered for her to frequently. He knew that the balance of the situation was delicate. Truthfully, Oliver hated that Nelly had started to feel uncomfortable being alone with him. He understood. They had had sex. And she seemed intent on demonstrating to him that the two of them were strictly friends now, despite the fact that he knew she knew he was in love with her and that she was probably also still in love with him.

The only time they had ever spoken about it was when she had told him that she didn't think either of them were ready yet. Which was probably true, given the fact that India had just died at the time and neither of them were dealing with it particularly easily. Oliver did wonder though if Nelly would ever be ready. Because he was. It was frustrating. In Oliver's mind, they may as well be a couple anyway. They did everything that couples did, other than have sex with each other. And he knew very well that Nelly would be upset with him if she knew that he still slept with other people. The truth was, sex to Oliver just wasn't as big of a deal as it was to Nelly. Besides, it was her decision, after all. Still, he had never told her about the other women.

Nelly sat down beside him on the bed and picked up one of the decorative cushions, hugging it to her own body. She was so close that her curls touched his shoulder accidentally, betraying her efforts not to stray too near to him.

"Sorry," she said, moving up slightly on the bed. Oliver pretended to ignore her, looking at the television. They continued flicking through the channels for a few more moments until Nelly said, "Oh, stop!"

Oliver smiled, "*Jurassic Park?*"

Nelly nodded, "I love it." She picked her mug up to her lips and took a swig, "Mmm. Drink quickly. It's even worse warm."

Oliver raised an eyebrow at her and picked up his own mug, draining the contents. "Top up?" He asked, bending down to pick the bottle up from the floor. He refilled her glass without her answering. Nelly smiled at him briefly before returning her attention back to the television. The scene showed the three scientists in a truck, one flirting shamelessly with the female scientist whilst he dumbed down some scientific theory.

"What a twat."

"Excuse me?"

Nelly nodded toward the television. "I hate the way that he explains that to her."

Oliver nodded, "Mmm." She looked so personally offended by the scene that it made Oliver want to grin. He told his cheeks not to.

"She's a scientist, too. Why would he have to dumb it down for her?"

Oliver nodded again, "I think we're supposed to think he's a dick."

"Well, I definitely do."

Oliver laughed briefly through his nose. He took a gulp of the cheap wine and was glad that the bitter taste of it was starting to ebb away the more that he drank.

"Do you believe that?"

"What?"

"The chaos theory thing. That the same event could have a different outcome if it happened at a different moment?"

Oliver shrugged, "Mmm. Yeah, probably. But I imagine most things would stay as they had been the first time."

"Really?"

"Mmm."

Nelly sighed and nodded slowly to herself. She went to take a sip of her wine and then seemed to think better of it, stopping and just gazing down into the mug. She looked thoughtful, as if something was on her mind. Oliver watched her, waiting to hear what she had to say. Eventually, she just looked back up at the screen.

Oliver was sat in the hotel restaurant eating breakfast on New Year's Eve morning. He was at the table on his own, a small espresso and a half-eaten croissant in front of him. There was a woman sat a couple of tables away that kept turning her head to look at him, trying to catch his eye. She was attractive. If he had been on his own, he might have invited her over. But as it was, he couldn't risk Nelly coming down and seeing him do so.

She was upstairs in his room at the moment, using his shower. She'd confessed that the hot water still wasn't working in her room when he'd gone to find her that morning, saying something about a stand-up wash with the sink. It had taken several attempts to convince her to use his bathroom. Eventually she'd given in, taking a rolled up purple towel and her wash bag with her down the hall. It made him smile that she'd packed her own towel.

She had struggled to get the shower working and had popped her head out of the bathroom door to ask him to help her. She'd been wearing the purple towel that she'd taken out from her luggage, her hair already half wet from where she'd clearly attempted to brave the cold water. Oliver had followed her into the bathroom and pretended not to see when she quickly adjusted the small pile of her clothes so as her underwear was at the bottom.

"I just can't get it to go hot," she'd said to him, loitering by the toilet.

Oliver looked at the shower and then leant forward to it, adjusting the tap and then holding his hand underneath it. "Were you turning it left, or right?"

"Left. I think."

Oliver smiled. She'd been turning it the wrong way. He wondered whether she'd been doing the same thing in her own room. He turned it the right way and let his hand hover beneath the water for another moment, until it began to run warm.

"There you go," he said, standing back. He turned around and looked at her, stood there in her purple towel with her arms wrapped around herself. Her cheeks were blushed, even though she'd just been standing in the cold. She was very lovely.

"Thanks," she said, looking a bit awkward. Oliver realised that he'd been staring at her and then nodded. He moved to go out from the bathroom and told her that he'd meet her downstairs.

The blonde woman on the other table was just looking as if she were about to get up to speak to him when Nelly walked into the room.

"Hiya," she said, waving her hand as if she hadn't seen Oliver in a long time and then flattening it by her side as if she was embarrassed about having done so. She was wearing a green knitted dress with dark black tights, her cheeks rosy from where she'd clearly been rushing. Oliver noticed that she had lipstick on and she kept rubbing her lips together, as if she were trying to hide it.

"Good afternoon," he said. "All cleaned up?"

"All cleaned up, thank you." Nelly smiled and hovered her hand with the key card, offering it toward him. "I hope I locked it okay. I just put that in and then waited until it flashed red. That's right, isn't it?"

"Mmm. It'll be fine."

"Okay. Cool," she looked around the room at the buffet breakfast, "Have you been here ages? I'm sorry if I took too long."

He shook his head, "You're fine."

"Okay."

"Do you want something to eat?"

"Oh no. It's fine. You've already finished."

Oliver smiled, "I know you want something. You're doing that thing with your nose."

Nelly blushed. "Okay. Do you mind if I just grab a coffee?"

"Be my guest."

"Okay. I'll be two secs. Do you want anything else?"

He shook his head, "I'm all set."

"Okay. I'll be quick. I promise."

Oliver smiled. Nelly wandered off toward the buffet and Oliver watched her go. She started lining up for the coffee machine in a queue that she seemed to have formed of her own accord, and Oliver couldn't help but laugh at her when she frowned at a man for stretching in front of her as if he hadn't realised that there was a system in place. Oliver carried on watching Nelly for a little while and then glanced back at the woman at the next table. She was now watching Nelly, too.

They spent the day wandering around the village and then the beach, the majority of the shops closed because of the holiday. When they got back to the hotel that evening, the bar was already full to the brim with people dressed in suits and sparkling dresses. There was a sign in the front of it that read:

Congratulations, Mr and Mrs Cook.

"Ah, the elusive wedding party."

"Mmm. Yeah," Nelly had said, peering behind the sign awkwardly. "What shall we do? Do you want to go to the room?"

Oliver smiled to himself at the fact that she'd referred to it as *the* room rather than *his*, hoping that this boded well for the rest of the evening. He thought for a moment and then turned to look at her. "Do you have a dress with you?"

"Umm, I've got something. Yeah. I didn't know what you had in mind, so…"

He nodded, "I've got a plan."

Oliver changed into a suit in his room before going to knock for Nelly. It seemed strange, calling on her like this. He felt oddly like a teenager going to pick a girl up for a date or a school dance. Not that he had ever enjoyed that sort of thing. He had been surprised at what he'd found when Nelly opened the door.

She was wearing an olive-green dress that cut off just above her knees and down the centre of her chest to expose the spherical rounds of her breasts. Nelly tugged at the neckline shyly, as if not quite confident enough in it.

"India gave it to me years ago," she said, as if this explained things.

Oliver nodded, not bothering to hide the fact that he was staring at her.

"Does it look silly?"

Oliver shook his head.

"Are you sure? It's not too… I dunno. Slutty?"

Oliver shook his head again, "No. Just the right amount of slutty."

Nelly smiled and rolled her eyes at him. She was still loitering in the doorway. "You look nice."

"Thank you."

Nelly blushed and tugged at the straps of her dress again. "So, what's your big plan?"

Oliver raised his eyebrows, half-forgetting the fact that they were going somewhere, and then said, "Oh yeah. Come on. We're going to a party."

He could tell that Nelly was nervous as they wandered into the room where the wedding reception was in full swing. It was packed with guests, which only solidified Oliver's hunch that there would be far too many people who had already had far too many drinks for anyone to know or care that he and Nelly were gatecrashing. Oliver took a glass of champagne off from the table where rows of them sat waiting, handing it to Nelly and then taking another for himself.

"What if someone notices us?" Nelly asked.

"Then we'll tell them we know the bride."

"What if the bride notices us?"

"Then we'll say that we know the groom," Oliver shrugged, "Fool proof."

Nelly looked nervous, so much so that Oliver was mildly surprised when she took a sip of her champagne and nodded. "Okay, so what do I say if anyone asks me who I am?"

Oliver shook his head, "No, that's the thing. You don't wait for people to ask you."

"What?"

"Watch," Oliver looked around the room and spotted a couple of people roughly in their seventies, both eyeing up the wedding cake in the edge of the room. Oliver made his way over to them, Nelly in toe, and smiled as if he knew them. "Evening! So good to see you," he said, bending down to kiss the woman on the cheeks. He extended his hand to the older man and was pleased when the man shook it, looking only mildly bemused.

"Good evening," the woman said.

"Hey. Wow, it's been a really long time, hasn't it? What, five years? No, probably six?"

The couple exchanged looks and then nodded vaguely.

"I'm Hugo's son," Oliver said, as if by way of explanation. It was a gamble, but he was very willing to bet that there was at least one Hugo at the affair, from the accents that he had heard in the room thus far.

"Oh, you're Hugo's boy!" The woman said eagerly, nodding at her husband. "Gosh, you've changed a bit!"

"Ah, well I suppose it's been a while."

"Yes, yes," the woman said pleasantly.

"George, isn't it?" The man replied.

"George, yeah. And this is Freya," Oliver said, putting his arm around Nelly's shoulder and dragging her into the conversation. Her cheeks were already bright pink.

"Hello, nice to meet you," Nelly said meekly.

"Hello, dear," the woman said, smiling at Nelly. "That's a lovely dress."

"Oh, thank you. I love your hat."

"Yes. I wore it to Ascot."

"Ah."

Oliver smiled.

"And how do you two know each other?" The woman asked.

"Freya's my fiancée," Oliver replied quickly, smiling at Nelly's perturbed face. "We're getting married next autumn. You must have gotten the invitation?"

"Oh, no we didn't get it," the woman said, turning to her husband.

"That keeps happening at the moment, doesn't it?" The man said to his wife. "That bloody postwoman. Doesn't know her arse from her elbow."

"Mmm."

"Well, I bet your dad's pleased, isn't he?"

"Dad? Ah yeah, of course."

"Yes. He was always rather upset that you were a homosexual. But we did say, didn't we, John, those things are often just a phase."

"Mmm yes."

Oliver heard Nelly muffle a snort behind him.

"Oh, yeah. Absolutely. Yeah, I do still swing both ways, of course. Keeps things interesting, doesn't it, darling?"

Nelly had buried her nose into her champagne, trying very hard to not have to make eye contact with anyone.

"Yeah," Oliver continued, "I mean, why order a la carte when there's a tasting menu, eh?"

They moved away from the couple just before Nelly's champagne came out from her nose.

2000
Nelly

It was almost midnight and Nelly was in the hotel bathroom sponging champagne off from the front of her dress with toilet roll. She and Oliver had been at the wedding reception for a few hours, both drinking more than their share in free champagne and dancing very badly to the music as the DJ played Craig David three times in an hour. That was when Nelly had spilled the champagne down herself.

She looked down at the stain on her chest, her eyesight slightly fuzzy, and decided that it was probably the best that she was going to be able to do. She put the wet towel in the bin underneath the sink and stretched over the counter to look at herself in the mirror. She was wearing a red lipstick and it had become faded at the edges. She wiped it off with another piece of tissue paper and then rifled through her small handbag, trying to retrieve the rest of the stick. She wound it up and stretched forward again to see more clearly. She was just bringing the stick to her lips when she was reminded of the first time she had worn it. At India's birthday party, years ago. India had applied it for her, pulling her own pink lips into a circle, to mirror Nelly as she puckered.

Nelly looked down at the lipstick and felt suddenly sad at how little of it was left. She put the lid back onto it and then rubbed her thumb up and down the tactile ridge before placing it back into her bag. She'd save it for another time.

When Nelly emerged from the toilet, she saw Oliver leaning against the bar, waiting for her. There was a blonde woman there speaking to him that Nelly recognised as the woman from the breakfast room this morning. She was wearing a light-grey bridesmaids dress and running a hand along Oliver's chest as she laughed at something. Oliver was watching her, looking mildly amused.

He turned his face to look at Nelly almost automatically just when Nelly was wondering whether to go back into the toilet. Oliver stood up slightly from the bar, both hands in the pockets of his trousers, and raised his eyebrows at her. He looked very handsome this evening. Nelly had seen him wearing a suit a hundred times, and yet he somehow looked different now.

The woman stood straighter too, adjusting Oliver's tie as if she knew him well enough to do so. He didn't seem to notice. Nelly watched them for a moment and thought how suited they looked together. The other woman was tall and confident in the same way as Oliver was; in the same way that everyone in Oliver's world seemed to be. Whereas Nelly suddenly felt extremely aware of the stain on her dress.

Oliver pulled a face at her as if asking what she was doing and Nelly suddenly remembered herself, moving toward the two of them.

"You alright?" Oliver asked her when she had closed the distance. He leant down and kissed her on the cheek, as if he hadn't seen her five minutes before.

Nelly nodded and shuffled slightly away from him. "Hi, I'm Nelly," she said to the woman still draped around Oliver's side.

The woman looked down at Nelly and smiled, wrinkling her nose as if Nelly were a child, but didn't introduce herself. After a moment, she turned back to Oliver and said, "Well, I'd better go and find the bride. Maid of honour duties, and all that."

"Mhmm. Yeah."

She loitered, "Yeah, well. You've got my number." Oliver didn't say anything and the woman smiled, tapping him on the chest before walking away.

Nelly watched the woman go and then rubbed subconsciously at the stain on her dress where her skin was suddenly feeling sore beneath.

"I'm obviously not going to call her," Oliver said after a moment.

"Mmm," Nelly said, nodding.

"She just came over and—"

"Do you fancy a cigarette?"

"Huh?"

"I'm a bit hot. Are you hot?"

Oliver nodded, "Yeah, I suppose so."

"Okay. Great." Nelly turned away from Oliver and began moving through the crowd, toward where a glass door led out onto a balcony. It was cold outside, but she barely felt it as she elbowed her way through, smiling apologetically at people as she did so. Oliver followed her, right behind each step that she took.

There were several other people standing on the balcony, sharing laughs and cigarettes. Nelly turned and looked at Oliver and he tapped his pockets.

"I don't have any."

"Me neither," Nelly said.

Oliver smiled. He turned to a group of men beside him and said, "Excuse me, mate. Do you have a spare cigarette?"

The man nodded, "Yeah, sure."

"Cheers." Oliver plucked two cigarettes from the open packet and handed one to Nelly.

"Do you need a lighter too, mate?" The man asked.

"Ah yeah. Thanks." Oliver took the lighter from the man and flicked it open, lighting his own cigarette and then taking it out from his mouth and offering it to Nelly. She took it and handed the other one back to him, which he lit before returning the lighter back to the stranger. They both looked at each other for a moment, feeling the cold of the night air cooling their cheeks. Someone shoved into Nelly's back and Oliver frowned at the man when he slurred an apology over Nelly's shoulder. Oliver moved his mouth as if he were going to say something, but Nelly shook her head him. She suddenly felt very out of place.

"Shall we go over there?" She asked, pointing to a spot on the balcony that was slightly less occupied.

Oliver nodded. They moved toward the edge of the balcony, Nelly resting her forearms on the cold railing. The sky looked completely black from where they stood—inky and vast. Oliver moved to stand beside her and they both stared up at it, quietly smoking.

"What do you think she's doing up there?" Nelly asked suddenly.

"Up where?"

"In heaven."

Oliver smiled, "Right." For a moment, Nelly thought that he was going to tell her that heaven probably didn't exist. He looked amused by what she'd said, as if it were almost childish. But he didn't say that. Instead, he took a drag of his cigarette and replied, "I imagine she's having a whale of a time."

"Really?" Nelly asked. She wasn't sure why she was questioning it as if Oliver knew the answer.

Oliver nodded, "Of course. India and Jesus would get on like a house on fire. A bloke that can turn water into wine sounds right up her street."

217

Nelly laughed and caught it in her hand, covering her teeth. She looked back at Oliver and he reached out and pulled her palm gently away from her face. He placed it by her side and then reached up again, stroking her cheek softly with his thumb.

"You have a lovely smile."

Nelly pressed her lips together, her cheeks feeling hot.

Out in the air, she was suddenly aware of how drunk she was. She kept thinking about the last New Years Eve that she had enjoyed. The last one that she had spent with India. They had been at the pub near their flat in London. It had been crowded and Oliver and Leo had both been there, too. Before Leo had moved to Australia. They were all there. India had convinced them all to do round after round of sambucas and then, when the clock had chimed midnight, she'd kissed Nelly fully on the lips and held her face in her hands. Auld Lang Syne had been playing behind them from somewhere overhead. Nelly hadn't been able to stop laughing when India had pulled her face away from hers, but India had looked completely serious. She'd cupped Nelly's flushed cheeks in each of her hands and said, "Promise you'll never leave me, Nel."

Nelly had laughed, "India!"

"I'm serious! Promise that you'll never leave me and we'll spend New Years together for always until we're two old ladies with purple washes."

"Of course."

"You promise?"

Nelly had made a sign across her chest between them, "Cross my heart."

India had smiled back at her, "Good. You and me forever, okay? We don't need anyone else. Only each other. Nobody else understands."

Nelly had nodded and laughed, thinking her friend drunk and silly and India had gone back to laughing and dancing as if she hadn't a care in the world.

It hadn't been true, of course. None of it had. They both had ended up needing other people and they had never spent New Year's Eve together again. And now Nelly would never get to spend another one with India. Now, India would never get to grow old.

Nelly turned and looked at Oliver, her heart somewhere in her throat as people behind them started counting down from ten. Oliver watched her and then nodded slowly, placing his arm around her shoulder and bringing her closer to him.

"Happy New Year, India," he said as people cheered around them. He raised his champagne glass toward the sky and then took a gulp.

Nelly didn't trust herself to speak.

2001
Oliver

He wasn't sure which of them had kissed the other first. It had just passed midnight, still standing out on the balcony. Nelly had looked cold and he'd taken off his jacket, draping it around her shoulders. She had reached up to find his hands and he had found his face dipping toward her cheek, brushing it gently. She had turned her face to meet his, and then it had been happening.

Oliver pushed the hotel room door open from behind Nelly's back, his mouth still pressed to hers. She was so much smaller than him that he was almost forced to bend toward the embrace, his hands gripping and tipping the bottom of her chin to meet him. Her tongue against his tasted like champagne and cigarettes and he found it utterly delicious. He longed to taste more of her. Ached for it.

She pushed the door shut behind them and he picked her up, bringing her closer. Her legs wrapped around his waist and he thought about pulling her skirt up and fucking her there, against the hotel room door. But something made him hesitate. It was Nelly. She was different from the other women. She mattered to him.

Oliver stumbled forward, placing Nelly down onto the bed. He looked into her eyes as he undid his tie, silently asking her whether she was sure. She reached forward and started unbuttoning his shirt. Nelly stretched up and kissed Oliver's cheeks, his neck, his throat. He leant into her and he could hear her breaths against his face, longing and wanting. She moaned into his ear, the warmth of her breath on his skin, and he had to remind himself to not rush. To take it slowly.

Nelly reached up to the sleeves of her dress and pulled them down, exposing her chest. She glanced downward shyly—nervously—and he found himself moving forward instinctively to reassure her. They kissed and she pressed herself closer against him, their bare skin melting against each other's. Nelly led his hand up from her waist to her breast and Oliver felt something inside of him begin to take over. Something animal. Primal. He turned her around, moving to lie behind her on the edge of the bed. She was breathing heavily and quickly, as if she had run a race, and the sound of it was driving him crazy. He kissed her neck, tasting her skin against his tongue. She moaned and he reached down to her thighs, pulling her dress up to gather at her waist.

He could feel how wet she was through her underwear. He rubbed his fingers over her slowly, her moan intent against the side of his jaw. He kissed her again and pulled her knickers to one side, silently telling his fingers to hesitate until he knew that she was definitely okay with what was happening. Her hand reached out to take his and guided him inside of her. Oliver kissed Nelly's neck, her throat, her collar bone, her nipple; his teeth tugged at her gently and she moaned as he did so.

"I wish I could see you touch yourself," Oliver heard himself breathing into her ear.

"Now?"

"No. When you're on your own. I wish I could see you when you're on your own. I want to know what you look like. Do you touch yourself like this?"

She moaned as he rhythmically inserted his fingers inside of her and, when she didn't answer his question, he retracted them. Her face turned slightly at the withdrawal. He rubbed over her, hearing the breath catching inside of her throat. "Or do you do it like this? What do you think about when you do this?"

Nelly breathed in, almost gasping.

"Do you think of me?"

"Yes."

"Can you tell me?"

"I think of you. I always think of you."

"Good. I think of you, too."

Oliver kissed her neck and Nelly pushed herself against him, moving her hand to find him behind her hips. He heard himself groan as she pulled down his zipper, her hand finding him inside of his trousers. There was none of the clumsiness that had been there on the first night that they had slept together. Their touches were deliberate and certain; they already knew each other's bodies and what the other needed.

"I want you so badly," he told her as she stroked him.

"I want you, too. I need you closer. Please."

Oliver pulled his hand away from where he was touching her, moving to cup her jaw and pull her mouth to meet his. She moaned into his lips and he moved to take himself out from his trousers.

"I love you, Oliver."

Oliver groaned against the back of her hair as he pushed himself gently inside of her, "Fuck. I love you, too, Nelly."

That was when she started crying. He had stopped immediately, almost jumping back from her.

"Nelly, what's wrong? Have I hurt you?"

She shook her head, turning around to cry into his chest.

"Nelly?"

"She's gone!" Nelly's voice was almost a scream; he could feel the pain in it. He had known it would come. He grasped his arms around her, holding her to him. Nelly sobbed against his naked skin, "She's really gone."

He nodded gently against her head, holding her racked body as she cried. "It's okay. I'm here," he told her quietly.

He held her like that all night.

2001
Nelly

She hadn't spoken since they had gotten into the car hours ago. She had been thinking about a time a few years back when they had been in Budapest; India, Leo, Thomas and Nelly. It had been warm and the only place that they had been able to find a drink was a small bar that seemed to cater more to an older clientele. They had sat themselves outside, all huddled around a tiny wooden table, taking shots of rum and smoking cigarettes that were definitely illegal. At some point, Nelly had gone to the toilet inside. It had been one of those bathrooms where the toilet was separate to the sink, the cubicle so small that even Nelly barely had room to stand up properly inside of it. When she had gotten back to the table and began to move around back to her seat, her three friends had exploded into laughter.

"Oh, Nel," India had said between laughs. She gestured toward Nelly's bottom and Nelly glanced behind her.

"What?"

"Oh sweetheart," India had laughed, "Your arse is out."

Nelly glanced back over her shoulder and saw that, indeed, her skirt was tucked so high into her underwear that half of her backside was exposed. The three of them broke into more laughter.

"Oh my God! I walked the whole way back through the bar like that!" Nelly hissed. She fell back down quickly onto the chair beside India and tugged at her skirt, feeling her cheeks burn. She had always felt self-conscious about her bum.

India laughed and rubbed Nelly's leg, "You gave them an eye full!"

"Oh my God, don't," Nelly replied, covering her mortified face. "I'm so embarrassed. Do you think many people saw?"

"Mmm, probably," Leo replied, handing her a shot.

"Oh, we're out of drinks. Nel, come with me to the bar?"

"Are you joking? I can't go back in there now! Not when they've all seen…"

"Don't be so silly. You have a gorgeous little bottom!" India swiped for it beneath the table and Nelly shuffled away.

"No, I don't. It's covered in stretch marks and I've had the same underwear on for two days."

"Oi!" India snapped.

"Dirty girl," Leo laughed, pulling a face at Nelly in mock-disapproval.

"We've *all* had the same underwear on for two days!"

"Not him," Thomas laughed, nodding toward Leo, "He chucked his on the train on the way over."

Nelly buried her face into her hands. India pulled them away. "Oi, now you listen here young lady," the table exploded into more laughter at her sudden seriousness, "You aren't allowed to say those things about my best friend. Or you'll have me to deal with. Okay? If I had a peachy little bum like that, I'd be walking around with my skirt hooked over my hips all day long."

Nelly smiled, "That's easy for you to say. You haven't just flashed the old couple in the corner."

India sat for a moment and then said, "Right. Fine." She stood up and wiggled her hips as if she were doing the hula, catching the bottom of her long, pleated skirt and tucking it upward. When she turned around, all that was covering her pink bottom was a tiny white thong.

"India, no!"

"Nope. You asked for this." She darted out from behind the table before Nelly could grab her, moving quickly through the crowd and saying loudly in English, "Excuse me. So sorry. Coming through."

Thomas and Leo exploded into more hysterics and Nelly felt her own stomach beginning to hurt from laughing. "India! Stop! You don't have to do that!"

"Best of luck with that one," Leo had winked.

Nelly darted through the crowd quickly, following India, and caught up with her at the bar. She quickly wrapped her denim jacket around India's waist and, through fits of laughter, managed to tie it up. A man behind them tutted and gave them a dirty look, sending them into more giggles.

"Fucking hell. What's a girl got to do for a free drink around here?" India asked her. Nelly laughed and India hooked her arm around Nelly's neck, kissing the top of her head.

"You're so daft," Nelly laughed, shaking her head. Her stomach ached from how much fun she was having. How much fun they had all been having the entire holiday.

India shrugged, "If you look stupid, I look stupid. That's how we work, remember?"

Nelly looked at her best friend, a mixture of ridiculousness and pride on her lovely face. Nelly smiled at her and nodded, "That's how we work."

"And there won't be any further comments about you thinking that your little bottom is anything less than lovely?"

Nelly laughed again. India narrowed her eyes. "There'll be no more comments."

"Alright, excellent. Because I think we're about to be asked to leave."

The scene kept playing around in Nelly's mind now as the car moved down the motorway back toward London. She kept seeing Oliver turn to steal glances at her as they drove, his face a mixture of discomfort and concern.

She already felt terrible about it. The kiss on the balcony; the things that they had done in his room; the fact that she had broken down in front of him when it was him who had been the one that needed the holiday. The whole thing was such a mess. She was so in love with him. Truly, so in love with him. But suddenly all of the numbness that had been inside of her body for so many months seemed to have flushed away. Like a hangover once the paracetamol wears off. And she could feel all of it. Everything at once.

The pain of her and Oliver and what he had done in Rome. The horribleness of the fact that she loved him and yet didn't trust him. The agony of India being lost from the world and that Nelly hadn't been there for her when she was most on her own. She would never be able to be with her again. Her best friend. Her best person. It was all too much. Too agonising. Too painful.

She had spent the entire night crying until she had, at some point, fallen asleep. Oliver had stayed beside her, his arms still firm around her body as he slept. He was so beautiful asleep. He always had been. Feeling suddenly indulgent, Nelly had allowed herself to reach out and stroke his lips as he breathed, watching them gently pucker and part as he lay there. His eyelids had flickered and she had taken her hand away, laying back down against his chest. The only place that she really felt safe. And yet didn't.

They drove the entire way home in silence. When Oliver parked the car outside of her flat, he said, "Do you want to talk about it?"

Nelly had shaken her head, still looking out of the window. A man was sat at the floor of a bus stop making his bed for the night out of a cardboard box.

"Do you want me to come in with you?"

"If you'd like to," Nelly had replied.

Oliver looked uncomfortable. He so rarely looked uncomfortable. "Do you want me to?"

Nelly chewed on the edge of her cheek. Suddenly the fleshy part that she'd been biting into for months felt rough and grainy. She hated how awkward she had made things. Truthfully, all that she wanted was for Oliver to take her back to his flat with him and hold her in his arms again and tell her that everything was okay. She so badly longed to hear that everything would be okay. But she knew that she was being selfish. So, she shook her head slightly, "No, it's alright."

Oliver nodded. "Will you be okay?"

Nelly began to nod and then felt herself start to cry again. She brought her hands up to her face, cupping her palms over it. "I'm sorry. I don't know why I can't stop."

Oliver put his arm around her, pulling her toward him over the hand-break. "It's okay," he said into her hair, "It's okay. It was going to come at some point."

Nelly nodded, trying to steady her breathing. Her cheeks stung from the tears, as if she had been scratching at them. "I'm sorry," she said again, "I think I need to go."

"Yeah. Of course."

"I'm really sorry."

"Don't be."

Nelly nodded, fumbling with the handle to her door.

"Are you sure you don't want me to come up?"

Nelly bit her cheek and shook her head, "It's okay. I'll be fine. I'm just going to go to bed."

Oliver looked dubious, but then nodded. "Okay. I'll ring you later, yeah?"

"Mhmm."

Nelly pulled her handbag out from the car and held it in her two arms. She'd get her suitcase later. Oliver seemed to think the same thing.

She could tell that he was watching her as she moved away from the car, pulling open the door to the building and moving inside. She didn't trust herself to turn around. She knew that she'd probably run back to him and ask him to come with her. And that wasn't fair. Not when he was finally moving forward.

Nelly felt an instant relief when she pushed the door shut to her flat. She lay on her settee and pulled a blanket over her face, sobbing into it until her chest hurt. At some point about an hour later, someone rapped at her front door. She let it knock, her tear-stained face turning toward it nervously.

They knocked again.

She suddenly hoped that it was Oliver. Nelly was just going to force her body up when she heard the sound of a key turning in the lock. She turned to see her mother pushing the door open, her face already searching the flat anxiously.

Her mother rushed to her immediately, scooping Nelly up into her arms. Nelly heard the tears escape her throat and felt herself unwinding, like a ball of string that had been knotted for too long.

2001
Oliver

He had sat in his car outside of Nelly's apartment building battling with whether or not to follow her inside for almost half an hour. Her neighbour, a red-haired woman that wore the same wolf fleece every time Oliver picked Nelly up, watched him suspiciously as she smoked a pipe by the front door. People never smoked pipes anymore.

Eventually, he had called Nelly's parents' house.

"What's happened?" Her mother had asked as soon as she had heard Oliver's voice. Mother's seemed to do that. As if something was built into them to just know. He wasn't sure what exactly to tell her, other than that Nelly needed her.

He drove home and let himself into his flat and felt oddly lonely.

He wished that he could still be in the hotel room with Nelly, when they were watching Jurassic Park; before anything else had happened. He wished that she would call him to help her with the shower and that he could just smile at her as she stood there in her purple towel. She was so lovely. He had known that she would feel the emotion of India's death at some point. In a way, he was glad that he had been with her when she had. But he wasn't glad about how it had come about.

He had felt her watching him as he had laid in the bed that morning. Her fingers had stroked his forehead and he had needed to tell his eyes not to open, pretending to still be asleep. He wasn't sure what exactly to say to her, given what had happened the night before. Maybe they had had too much to drink. Maybe he shouldn't have kissed her, or shouldn't have let her kiss him. He still wasn't certain which way around it had been. Not that it mattered, really. Their platonic relationship was always going to have an expiration date. At some point, they were going to lay their cards on the table and give into the feelings that they both had for each other. Or one of them would give up waiting for the other and move on with someone else, which would almost definitely be too much for the other to bear witness to. The problem was that neither of them ever seemed to be ready at the same time.

It always seemed to come down to that. Timing.

He hoped that they hadn't fucked things up for good.

After a while, Oliver ran out of things to occupy himself with and began unpacking his suitcase, placing the items in the washing machine. He thought about the damp purple towel that must be in Nelly's and decided to take that out too, placing it in with his things. Before turning the machine on to wash, he dug his hands into his suit trouser pockets to check that there was nothing inside. He pulled out a ten-pound note and a folded piece of paper, which contained the blonde woman from the wedding's phone number.

Oliver turned the machine on and set the piece of paper on the side, next to his keys.

2001
Nelly

Nelly stood in the rain outside of an Indian restaurant, peering up and down the road. She was looking for Oliver. They had made the arrangement to meet for dinner earlier in the week. It had been three weeks since New Years and, despite speaking on the phone more than once, they hadn't actually really talked to each other. Not about anything that had happened, anyway. Nelly felt anxious as she waited. She was always feeling anxious lately. Her hands shook slightly as she held onto the stem of her umbrella, her lips pressed together tight.

After another minute, Oliver walked quickly around the corner toward her. He broke into a gentle jog when he saw her, his hair tousled and damp from the rain.

"Sorry, I couldn't find anywhere to park," he told Nelly, bending down to kiss her cheek. "You're freezing. Why didn't you wait inside?"

"Oh, I… I'm not sure…" Nelly shrugged, trailing off.

Oliver smiled gently at her, reaching up and brushing a stray curl behind her ear. "Come on. Let's get you in the warm before you turn to ice."

Nelly nodded limply and let Oliver steer her toward the restaurant. He opened the door and, when she fumbled with her umbrella, took it from her and let it down, shaking the excess rain out into the street. She waited for him to finish before going inside.

"We have a table under Matthews," Oliver told the woman behind the bar. She was pretty, with long straight hair that she flicked around her neck. Nelly hoped that hers hadn't gotten too frizzy in the rain. She suddenly felt compelled to flatten it. The woman led them over to their table and pulled Nelly's chair out for her.

"Would you like me to take your coat?" She asked sweetly, smiling down at Nelly.

Nelly almost missed the question, and Oliver replied for her, "Yeah, please." He moved behind Nelly and shrugged her out of her trench, taking her scarf with it and handing it over to the woman. He winked at her when she took them and Nelly felt oddly like a child being undressed for bed.

"I'll be back in a moment with your menus," the woman told them, "Can I get you anything to drink? Wine? Beer?"

"I think I'm just going to get a water," Oliver told her. He looked at Nelly.

Nelly swallowed, "Would I be able to have a water too, please?"

"Certainly," the woman smiled again and moved away. Nelly was looking at the crisp white of the table cloth, fiddling with it between her fingers. If she folded it just right, she could make a perfect point with it. It hurt a little bit when she pressed it against her palm. She did it again. Oliver was watching Nelly from across the table where he sat. There was a look on his face that Nelly hadn't seen in a while; one that she had never seen directed at her before. She didn't like it.

"Hey," he said, reaching across the table and taking her hand. He turned it over and looked at the palm where it was red from the point of the table cloth. Nelly looked the other way and was glad when he didn't mention it. "How are you doing?"

"Mmm, yeah. I'm okay," Nelly lied.

"Nelly."

She looked back at him and smiled slightly, raising her eyebrows and repeating, "I'm okay."

"Mmm," Oliver replied, still watching her. "Your mum said that you've been... a bit down. Which is absolutely normal, of course."

"When did you speak to my mum?"

Oliver looked at her and then shrugged slightly, "Just the other day. I called wanting to talk to you a couple of times. Just to see how you are, sort of thing."

"Mmm," Nelly nodded, "Thank you."

"You did the same for me."

Nelly smiled at him and nodded again, feeling the tears begin to prickle in her eyes. She quickly stole a breath and then turned her attention back to the table cloth.

"Hey," Oliver said, reaching for her hand again.

"I'm sorry," Nelly replied. She pulled her hand away and used it along with the other to cover her face. She wiped at the tears furiously, as if they didn't deserve to be there.

"Hey, you have nothing to apologise for."

Nelly nodded.

"Do you want to leave? I can take you home?"

Nelly shook her head, "No. Thank you. I'll be fine in a minute. I'm just being stupid."

"You aren't being stupid."

"Yes. I am."

Oliver watched Nelly concernedly, his blue eyes scanning from her face back to her hands. After a moment, he said, "Are you sure you don't want me to take you home? I've got the car."

"It's really okay. It's good to see you."

Oliver smiled slightly and nodded. His fingers twitched as if he was going to reach for her hand again, but he seemed to think better of it. The woman came back over with their glasses of water and looked at Nelly anxiously, but Nelly looked the other way. Oliver thanked her and smiled until she left. "My mum's been asking after you."

"Oh, that's nice," Nelly replied. She took a gulp of the water, her mouth feeling dry. "How is she?"

Oliver shrugged and bobbed his head from one side to the other, "She's getting there. You know? She's er... she's still going to her group. She said that that's helped her a lot. You know? Talking with other people that have gone through the same thing."

Nelly nodded, still focussing on anything other than Oliver's face. "That's really good. I'm glad she's coping."

"Mmm," Oliver replied. He hesitated and then said, "She did say that there's one similar in London that she's heard of. Near Liverpool Street, on a Tuesday at two o'clock."

"Oh right."

"Mmm. Well, I was thinking maybe... I don't know. Maybe it would be worth a shot? I could take you, if you fancy it?"

Nelly nodded, but then said, "I work at two on Tuesdays."

"I'm sure Maeve could give you the afternoons off, if you explained why."

Nelly shook her head, "I can't."

"Okay. Well, maybe there's others."

"Maybe." Nelly tried to smile, "So, how are you? How is work?"

Oliver smiled at her, "You must really be clutching at straws if you're asking me about work."

Nelly took a gulp of her water.

"Work's fine. Boring. I'm supposed to be going to New York again in a few months. I wondered if you fancied coming? You'll have half-term, won't you?"

"To New York?"

"Yeah," Oliver smiled, "You said you always wanted to go. It might be good for you, the change of scene. I'd even indulge Coney Island, if you really wanted."

Nelly tried to smile.

"It's okay," Oliver said. He took her hand and rubbed it with his thumb before placing it back down onto the table. "You don't have to make your mind up now. Do you want something to eat?"

"Oh. Yeah, okay," Nelly said, remembering that they were at a restaurant. She kept thinking about the last time that she had spoken with India. She had played it over and over and over again in her mind in a never-ending loop. It had been when Nelly had told India about the things Spencer had done in the bathroom. Nelly had been devastated. About the things that Spencer had done to her. About the fact that Spencer was coming between them and taking India away. About the fact that India had chosen him over Nelly. About the fact that she hadn't been able to go to dinner with Oliver and tell him that she loved him.

Now that she replayed the memory in her mind, she wondered whether she should have known then. Whether, had she not gone to Rome and left India alone in that flat with him, Nelly may have been able to change things. Her hands shook as she reached them up to cover her face, realising that the tears had started again.

"Okay. It's okay," Oliver told her, standing up from his side of the table and crouching beside Nelly's chair. He pulled her face toward him, nestling her into his shoulder. "Come on, let's go home."

2001

Oliver

Oliver half-carried Nelly up to her flat that evening. She felt thinner in his arms than she had done before; more fragile. She reminded him of an eggshell that he had rescued from an abandoned nest as a child. He had kept it on his windowsill, like a souvenir. Oliver pushed the door closed and locked it behind them, wondering whether he should have taken her back to his own flat. She had said no though, when he had offered that. Even though it was closer and, he was sure, would have been far more comfortable. Nelly's frame stood idly in the middle of the small kitchenette, as if awaiting further instruction. Oliver moved behind her and put his arm back around her waist, steering her toward her bedroom.

When they were inside, he pulled the duvet back for her and closed the blind as she submissively buried herself beneath the covers. Her face was pink and stained from crying and she looked almost childlike. Oliver stood beside the bed next to her, suddenly not sure of what to say or where to put himself. Would she even want him here with her, after what had happened between them at New Years? Or would she just want him to leave? Would she be safe if he did leave her? He wasn't used to Nelly being like this. She had always been the capable, dependable one. The stable one, out of all of them. And yet now she seemed as if something had begun to unravel. It made him nervous.

"Do you want me to—" he began to say.

"Am I a horrible person?"

"Huh?"

Nelly sniffed, "Am I horrible?"

"Of course not. Why would you—"

"I left her there, Oliver. I left her in that flat with him because I couldn't stand it anymore. I left her when she was unhappy so as I could go off and do something selfish—something just for myself. And I was so angry with her. She was dying and I was angry with her for being with him and I just keep thinking about what could have happened if I had never gone. If I had stayed and forced him to keep away from her. Forced her to listen to us. Maybe if I had never left her, she would still be—"

"Hey," Oliver said, forgetting all concern and moving to sit on the bed in front of her. He scooped her up into his arms and she let him, her face burying into his neck and her hands gripping at his shirt in tiny fists as she sobbed. Oliver stroked Nelly's hair, holding her against his chest. "Nelly, none of this is your fault. You could never have known. None of us could have. She wasn't well. She wouldn't have listened. She didn't listen, to any of us. Only to him. You didn't do anything wrong."

"But how will we ever know that? What if it could've been different? What if I had never left her there?"

Oliver stopped for a moment, unsure of what to tell her. "It probably wouldn't have changed anything," he said eventually.

He stayed at Nelly's flat with her that evening, her in the bed and him sat beside her on top of the quilt, her face nestled against his heart. When he was sure that she had finally fallen asleep, he eased himself out from beneath her arms and went to the living room. His phone had been vibrating inside of his pocket for over an hour, pining for him as he had rocked Nelly gently to sleep. He inched his head around the door, checking that she hadn't woken up, and then pushed the door gently to so as he was alone. He waited another moment and then took his mobile out from his pocket, seeing the six missed calls from a number that he hadn't bothered to save. He knew who it would be. He waited another moment before ringing it back.

"Hey stranger," the woman's voice said from the other end of the line. She sounded drunk and she was already getting on Oliver's nerves.

"Hey," he said, "You called me?"

The woman giggled, "I might have done. I was just in the bath thinking about you. About the last time when you were in here with me."

Oliver sighed, "I can't really talk right now, Tara."

She ignored him, "Do you want to come round? I'm sure I could get you nice and clean. Or a bit dirtier, depending."

"I can't right now. I'm… I'm doing something."

"Are you with someone else?"

"Mmm? No. I'm—"

"Because if you are that's okay. There's room for three."

Oliver breathed through his nose, rubbing his temples with his fingers. He was beginning to get a head ache. "I'm busy right now."

"Ugh, fine. Be that way. I'll just have to imagine what we could have been doing on my own then," she said. She clearly thought that she was being sexy, but her desperation was making Oliver's skin crawl. "Call me tomorrow?"

"Yeah, fine." He hung up the phone before waiting for her response. He heard something stirring from Nelly's bedroom and inched forward carefully to check that she wasn't awake. Oliver pushed the door slightly open and was relieved to see her as he had left her, resting silently against the pillow.

He walked back in and closed the door behind them.

2001
Nelly

"What's going on with the two of you, anyway?" Leo's voice asked over the phone.

Nelly shrugged against it, picking at a hangnail on her thumb; she hadn't been able to stop chewing it and it had started to bleed. "We're friends," she said quietly.

"Friends that shag?"

Nelly rubbed her lips anxiously. "We don't…"

"You don't what? Have sex?"

Nelly didn't reply.

Leo laughed lightly, "You're telling me that you have Oliver Matthews in your bed five nights a week and you aren't letting him have sex with you? Well, you have better will power than I would."

Nelly looked at the door to the bathroom, where Oliver was showering. He hadn't closed it but rather had pushed it ajar, the steam from the water eking out into her bedroom. Nelly still had trouble defining her and Oliver's relationship to people. Even to Leo. She and Leo didn't speak as often as Nelly would have liked, him now living in Australia with his boyfriend. But he still called to check in on her from time to time. He'd taken to doing so more frequently than usual of late, which Nelly suspicioned the person behind her bathroom door might be responsible for. She wasn't sure how that made her feel. Loved, definitely. But also like a liability. Or worse, a burden. Nelly wondered whether that was how she used to make India feel when she fussed over her. She scratched at her nail with her index finger.

"How are you?"

"Yeah, yeah we're good, thanks," Leo replied. She could hear the smile in his voice as he spoke. *We*. There was no singular since Leo had met Caspar.

Everything was joined; ensuite. Like they were one person. Nelly wondered whether he ever still thought about Thomas. She didn't ask him, though.

"Great."

"I keep telling you, you should come and stay with us for a bit. Melbourne's lovely."

"Mmm. Yeah. It's tricky, with term and stuff."

"Maybe in the summer holidays? You teachers reap the benefits then, surely?"

"Mmm. Yeah. Maybe."

"You should, Nel. I think it would be good for you."

Nelly nodded, although she wasn't sure how Leo would know what was good for her. He had no idea about the fact that Nelly blamed herself for India's death or that sometimes she wondered whether it would make a difference if she didn't get out of bed at all. Nobody knew about that. "Yeah, absolutely." She had no intention of going.

Truthfully, Nelly had no intention of making any plans of late. She thought it was just because she was grieving. The honest answer was that the idea of being happy or doing anything for herself made her feel so guilty that she felt her chest could cave in. That's what she had done when she went to Rome, and look what had happened then.

She was starting to think that she was a selfish person, although she really wasn't. But grief and depression does that to you; it makes you doubt things that you know to be true. One of these doubts was that Oliver liked taking care of her.

He had been so kind and understanding with her; for all of these months—years, even—he had treated her as if she were something special that he didn't want to break. But she did feel broken, now. Without her best friend, she felt as if she may never be whole again. And she was beginning to think that she might be a burden that he felt he had to tend to for India's sake. Like taking the washing out of a sibling's room when you know that they've forgotten it. Especially after what had happened at New Years. The memory of it was so humiliating that it made Nelly squeeze her eyes closed. She scratched at her thumbnail again.

"Nel, are you still there?"

"Mmm, yeah, I'm here. Sorry. Bad line."

"No worries," Leo chirped. "Listen, I've gotta go. But I'll give you a ring soon, yeah?"

"Yeah. That sounds great. Thanks," she wasn't sure why she was thanking him.

He laughed slightly, "Think about coming. Yeah? And bring that sexy man with you. I like the way he looks in his swimming trunks. Don't tell Caspar I said that."

"Mhmm," Nelly pretended to laugh at his joke.

"Okay then. Well. Love you, babe."

"Love you too, babe," she replied. He hung up the phone and she listened to the sound of the dialling tone until it cut off.

"Did you have a good chat?" Oliver asked as he stepped out from the bathroom. It was almost as if he had timed it for exactly when she had hung up the phone. He was wearing a towel around his waist, his body exposed. Nelly pretended to smile and nodded.

2001
Oliver

Oliver sat in his car outside of the school where Nelly worked, watching as she spoke to a child in a navy-blue uniform. Nelly was nodding her head as she listened to whatever the student was telling her, her eyebrows puckered slightly as if she were listening very intently. She told the child something in response and they beamed at her. Oliver smiled as he watched. One of the funny things about Nelly, from Oliver's perspective, was how little she noticed that others around her valued her opinion. She never seemed to realise quite how special she was to them. It was one of the things he loved about her.

Nelly noticed Oliver waiting in the car and looked up at him, raising her gloved-hand slightly in recognition. The little girl turned to look in Oliver's direction and then turned to look back at Nelly, to which Nelly smiled and shook her head, ruffling the girl's hair.

Oliver blew out a laugh and waved back. He was about to get out from the car to greet her when someone knocked on his window. Oliver turned to look as the woman named Tara rapped on the glass.

"Hey stranger," she said as he sat looking out of the window. It took him a moment to wind it down. Shit. He'd forgotten that she worked here, too. Or he'd probably never even asked.

"Oh, hi," he said. His eyes darted back to Nelly who was now speaking with another child, wrapped up in another conversation.

"Hey," Tara replied. She flicked her blonde hair out from her face and smiled at him, "Come to check up on me?"

"Mmm? Oh no, I'm—"

They were interrupted by Nelly walking over to them. Oliver sat up in his seat, moving to unbutton the belt and then seemingly thinking better of it.

"Hiya," Nelly said as she walked over. She was wearing the green gloves that his mum had given her for her birthday. They were suede and Oliver knew how soft they felt in his hands.

"Hello," Tara replied, inching back from the car. She eyed the two of them for a moment and then smiled at Nelly.

"Sorry about the class next Tuesday," Nelly said to Tara. "I just have a… thing. I really appreciate you covering year eleven for me."

"Yeah. Of course. No problem," Tara smiled. Her grey eyes glinted from Nelly to Oliver as she spoke and he pretended to be busy inspecting the steering wheel.

"Great. Well, I really do appreciate it," Nelly reiterated.

Tara smiled and looked at Oliver again. He didn't return her gaze.

"Cool. Well, are you ready, love?" Nelly asked Oliver.

He turned to look at her and nodded, "Mmm? Yeah."

"Great," Nelly moved around to the other side of the car and went to open the passenger door before saying, "I'm sorry. Tara, do you want a lift?"

"Huh?"

"Do you want a lift home? We're going to the cinema. In Bethnal Green. They're showing *When Harry Met Sally.*"

Tara eyed Oliver through the window. He still didn't look.

"You're welcome to join us, if you fancy it?" Nelly asked.

Oliver wondered if they could hear his heart beating inside of his chest. Tara regarded him through the window, seeking his gaze for one more moment before saying, "No, it's okay. I have plans. Thanks."

"Okay. Well, I'll see you tomorrow, then."

"Yep. See you then."

Nelly smiled at Tara kindly, giving her a small wave with her gloves. She got into the car and pulled the door shut, the belt giving a faint click as it slotted into place by her waist. Oliver pulled the car away almost immediately.

"Sorry about that," Nelly said, leaning over and kissing his cheek. "One of the year eights is having a problem with the others in her year. Girls can be so difficult at that age, you know?"

"Mmm. Of course. No problem," Oliver replied. He felt his heartbeat slowing down and reached over to take Nelly's hand in his.

"Are you alright?" She asked.

"Mmm," he replied, "Your gloves are so soft."

241

2001
Nelly

She stood waiting outside the door of her building on Wednesday evening, checking the time on her watch. It was her dad's birthday and she and Oliver were supposed to be going there together, but he was almost forty minutes late. She checked the time again and waited, pulling her jacket closer around her body. She was holding a present in her hand—a jumper, which she had wrapped in green paper—and it was cumbersome. She hoped that Oliver wouldn't be much longer. Nelly checked her phone again. She'd been standing out there now for almost an hour. She knew that Oliver sometimes wasn't able to leave the office until late or, less often, had to randomly work into the night. But he always let her know if that would be the case. They had been spending every evening together recently. She stayed at his most nights, apart from Tuesdays when she stayed at her parents' on account of it being close to her group. Oliver said that it cheered him up during the day, knowing that she would be there when he came home from work. He would drop Nelly at school in the morning and kiss her cheek, holding onto her hand as if he didn't want her to go.

Sometimes when he had to work late, even on Tuesdays, Nelly would let herself into his flat after work and make him dinner, which he'd later eat when he got in before slipping into bed beside her and wrapping his arms around her waist. Other times, they'd make dinner together; her cooking and him watching her slowly, as if contemplating something very complex. They didn't kiss or have sex and Nelly was very conscious of this. She knew that it was because of her; she still didn't feel ready for that. But she felt as if she were moving closer toward being able to again. Finally. Slowly. Nelly chewed her cheek as she wondered whether tonight was one of the nights that Oliver had to work late. She checked her watch again. It was almost five past eight. She was supposed to have been there at half seven. It wasn't like him. He would hate the idea of her waiting outside on her own at night.

Eventually, she left and walked for the tube.

Nelly had an anxious feeling in her chest as she walked from the underground station to Oliver's building. She wasn't sure why, but her breathing was increasing rapidly—almost as if she were panicking. She reached for the spare key that she had in her bag and then hesitated, knocking on the door instead. She wished she hadn't left her key on the coffee table before leaving earlier.

It took a while for Oliver to answer.

He pulled the door open dubiously, his face drawn and pale and his body doubled over as if he could barely stand.

"What's happened?" Nelly asked quickly as she walked forward, reaching out for him.

"Did you get my messages?"

"No?"

Oliver let out a breath and then winced, "I left you about a hundred messages. At your flat. And then with your mum."

Nelly shook her head as she closed the door behind her, "I didn't get them. I'm sorry."

"Mmm. Oh fuck," Oliver said, clutching again at his side.

"What's happening? What's wrong?"

Oliver gestured toward his stomach. His face looked sweaty and grey; his hair stuck against his forehead.

"Your stomach?"

"Mmm."

Oliver doubled over again and Nelly moved toward him, taking his weight on top of her shoulder. She was surprised when he let her.

"How long has it been like this?"

"Mmm, I don't know. A few hours, maybe."

"A few hours. You didn't go to work?"

Oliver shook his head again and Nelly sent out her second hand to support his chest as he flopped forward, catching him just in time.

"I think I'm—" Oliver began to vomit onto the floor by their feet just as Nelly held onto him. He reached up with a shaking hand and wiped his mouth. "Fuck. I'm sorry."

"It's okay," Nelly told him. She inched him forward carefully, "Come on."

She led him into the bedroom and went to pull out the duvet for him before realising that he had already vomited over it, a saucepan filled with yellowy liquid sat beside the bed. Oliver clutched at his stomach again and she felt him double back onto her shoulder. She was surprised at how strong she suddenly felt as she held him.

"Do you think a bath might help?"

"Mmm," Oliver clenched his eyes closed.

Nelly nodded and led him through his bedroom into the ensuite. He sat down on the edge of the toilet as she ran the bath for him, her hand hovering beneath the tap the entire time to check that the temperature was okay. He groaned every now and then and she turned to look at him, unsure of what to do for the best.

"You should be at your dad's birthday," Oliver winced from behind her.

Nelly shook her head, "Don't worry about that."

"But you should be. He'll be upset with me. I didn't mean for you to come here. I said that, in the messages."

Nelly shook her head again. She placed a hand on each of his cheeks and said, "If you need me, I should be here. Okay?"

Oliver watched her for a moment and then nodded slowly. He reached up and put one of his hands over hers. His skin was clammy.

"Okay. I think the bath is ready. Are you alright getting in?"

"Yeah. I'll be fine," Oliver winced.

"Okay, if you're sure." She moved to go to the door and then turned to look at him. He made to pull off his t-shirt and then doubled over onto the bath, clutching his side.

"Hey, hang on." She ducked beneath his arms quickly, her body pressed close to his chest. He smelled like vomit and sweat.

"You don't have to," he began to say.

"Shush."

Oliver winced as she pulled up the hem of his t-shirt, reaching to tug it over his head. His arms barely moved upward to help her, falling back floppily by his side like a rag-doll. He clutched his side again and Nelly moved to pull down his tracksuit bottoms, inching them carefully over his legs.

"I'm sorry," she said as he groaned.

He nodded and she inched his feet upward to pull the legs over his toes, holding onto his ankle to steady him. When he was in the bath, Nelly went to his bedroom. She already knew where he kept the spare sheets. Gingerly, she pulled the vomit-soaked cover off from the duvet and laid it down on the floor. Then she pulled off the pillow covers and did the same. As she was tugging off the bottom sheet, something red and lacy fell out onto the wooden floor. It was a bra. About the same size as hers. But she didn't have one in that colour.

Nelly stared at the underwear that didn't belong to her on the floor, feeling suddenly as if she might vomit too. She stood still, regarding it as if it might jump out toward her. After a moment, she picked up the bra and shoved it into the pile with the rest of the washing and carried it through to the kitchen. She shoved the linen into the machine and set it to clean before emptying the vomit in the saucepan down the sink and then placing the pan in the dishwasher.

Her heart pounded in her chest as she walked back to the bathroom. Part of her wanted to confront him there and then. But when she opened the door and saw him, any thought of doing so flew out from her mind.

Oliver was sat in the bath hunched over, his knees to his chest as he winced against the pain in his side. The room was hot, but he still shivered in the warm water. Nelly went straight to him, pushing the feeling of dread that was bubbling inside of her stomach to the back of her mind. He needed her. That was what mattered right now.

She knelt beside the bath, gently picking the shower head up from the wall and running it until it was the right temperature, holding it up over Oliver's body as he sat there letting her do so. She picked up the lemon-scented soap from the dish on the side and rubbed it together in her hands until it formed suds, running it over him. She lifted his arms one at a time and he winced slightly, but let her rub the soap beneath them. He leant on her shoulder as she helped him out from the bath, wrapping him up in a towel and then, when he couldn't dry himself, running another up his legs and over his back until the goosebumps on his flesh disappeared. She led Oliver back to his freshly-made bed and inched him down onto it, pulling the covers over him.

"You're supposed to be with your dad," he told her again as she placed the back of her palm on his forehead. He was very hot.

"Don't worry about that. Dad'll understand."

Oliver nodded, as if he did know that her dad would indeed understand that she would need to be there with him.

"How long has it been like this?" Nelly asked dubiously, feeling the heat of his skin against hers.

Oliver winced, "I don't know. About a day, maybe. I mean, I've felt a bit shit for a while. But it started getting bad last night." Nelly nodded. She made to move away from the room, but Oliver reached out and grabbed her hand. "Nelly, please don't leave me."

She hesitated, but then smiled slightly and shook her head, placing her hand over his. "Of course, I won't. I just need to use the phone, okay? My dad might be worried."

Oliver winced and nodded.

Nelly let their palms drop and then moved into the living room. She allowed herself a brief moment to gather herself, brushing the silent tear from her cheek and breathing quietly until she felt the crying ebb away. Then she walked to the coffee table, picked up the landline and dialled 999.

2001
Oliver

He was already at Nelly's parents' restaurant when she arrived. He had been standing at the bar speaking with her dad about a new wine that they were trying for the menu. It was an Italian one that Oliver hadn't heard of before and it tasted dry and delicious on his tongue. Nelly's dad had been so pleased when Oliver had said that he liked it, as if he valued Oliver's opinion. It made Oliver feel good.

"There she is," Mr Strapelli said as Nelly walked over to them. She was wearing a green trench coat over her clothes. Oliver loved that coat on her. It went with her soft gloves.

"Hey," he said, reaching out for her. He bent down and kissed Nelly's cheek, looping his hand around her to rest on her shoulder.

"Hi," she replied. She looked a bit dubious. Nervous. She always looked that way at the moment. Oliver imagined it was the grief; she still wasn't coping very well. They had seen each other a few times since his operation. She had come with him to the hospital, gripping his hand tightly in the back of the ambulance. Oliver had felt that it was all very dramatic; after all, it was just his appendix. But it turned out that it had burst, leaking into him. In a way, it was comforting to know that the pain in his stomach that he had been living with was only temporary.

At first, he had felt a bit ridiculous for the way that Nelly had seen him when she had found him at his flat. He knew that he'd vomited all over the bed, and probably onto himself. He also knew that she had changed the sheets for him and replaced them, folding the old ones away without a mention into his drawer. It made him love her even more, if that was possible.

"You alright?" He asked her into her hair, planting another kiss on her head. She nodded. He squeezed her shoulder slightly and her dad smiled at the two of them. "Your dad and I were just trying out a new wine," Oliver told her, handing her his glass.

"Yes, try it. Oliver thinks it's good," Mr Strapelli smiled.

"Really good."

Mr Strapelli beamed.

Nelly took the glass from Oliver and sniffed at it delicately before taking a small sip. They both watched her as she swallowed it and she said, "Mmm, yeah. It's good."

"Great, yeah?"

Nelly nodded. Her dad clapped his hands, "Let me get you a glass, Trofie."

"Oh, no. It's alright, Dad. We're gonna make a move in a sec."

"Are we?"

"Mmm," Nelly replied, turning to Oliver. She looked up at him and something in her expression seemed anxious. "I thought we could go somewhere else."

"To eat?"

She flitted her eyes toward her dad, "Mmm."

"Oh, don't be silly, Trofie. Why bother going somewhere else and paying for food that you can have here for free?"

"Oh no, Mr Strapelli, I wouldn't dream—" Oliver began to say, but Nelly's dad held his hand out, signalling for Oliver to stop.

"Family eats for free. That's our rule."

Oliver felt his cheeks twist into a smile. He felt as if his heart had just swollen. It was an odd feeling.

"Dad."

"I won't cramp your style, Trofie. Don't worry. Your mum and I have enough to be doing without watching you two's date."

Nelly breathed through her nose, glancing up at Oliver and then back at her dad.

"Is something wrong?" Oliver asked her, brushing her hair away from her shoulder so as he could better see her face.

Nelly swallowed and then shook her head. "No, it's fine. We'll stay here."

Nelly's dad clapped his hands together, "There you go then. That's settled. I'll get you a glass, Trofie." He moved slightly away from them to where the glasses were kept on the shelf.

Oliver smiled at her, "Trofie?"

Nelly nodded slightly, "It's what my dad calls me sometimes. It's a curly pasta. Because of my hair," she gestured to it.

Oliver laughed, "Yeah, I made that connection."

Nelly nodded and blushed.

"Trofie. I like that. I might steal it."

Nelly nodded and said again, "It's what my dad calls me."

Oliver smiled and kissed the top of her head.

Nelly's dad took the two of them over to a table in the corner, bending between them to light the tall candle that was stuck inside of a wine bottle.

"Oh, Dad. You don't need to do that."

"Hush, it's nice."

"Thanks, Mr Strapelli."

Mr Strapelli placed a hand on Oliver's shoulder before moving away from the two of them. Oliver enjoyed that. They had always been kind to him, Nelly's parents. As if they trusted him with their daughter. It made him feel good about himself, like he had earned it. He smiled at Nelly and reached for her hands over the table. She let him take them, but only held his limply. He stroked her knuckles.

"How was school? Have you had a bad day?"

"Mmm? No, work was… fine. There was a bit of a thing with some of the year eights, but it's all sorted."

"Is that girl still picking on Miranda?"

Nelly nodded, turning her head around and scanning the tables behind them as if she were concerned that one of the children from her school would miraculously have appeared. Oliver smiled at her. She was so kind.

"Girls can be really nasty," he said.

Nelly nodded, "Mmm. Boys too."

"In a different way, though."

"Mmm, yeah. In a different way."

Oliver smiled again and then inched his eyesight over Nelly's head, peering at the specials board. "What do you think you're going to have? I'm starving. I think I'm going to get the steak."

"Mmm," Nelly replied.

Oliver looked at her, "Are you sure you're okay?"

She chewed the edge of her cheek and then suddenly asked, "Have you slept with someone else?"

The question caught Oliver off guard. She wasn't looking at him as she said it, her eyesight trained onto the table cloth. He felt her fingers twitch in his and thought he might have misheard her.

"What?"

"Have you slept with someone else? Please, just tell me."

"I—" Oliver wasn't sure what to say. His stomach was suddenly beginning to feel painful again. "Nelly, what do you mean? What are you talking about?"

"Someone said something to me. One of the women at my work."

Fuck. Tara. Oliver swallowed a gulp of his wine, buying himself time.

"Who said something? What did they say?"

Nelly looked up at him, "Does it matter who?"

Oliver pressed his lips together. He felt suddenly sweaty.

"Oliver, please just don't lie to me."

He nodded again. "Fuck," he heard himself say out loud this time, "Nelly, can we not do this here? Please."

Nelly glanced over her shoulder toward where her dad was stood behind the bar, speaking with a customer. "I didn't want to. But it's happening now. He can't hear us."

"Fuck," Oliver said again. He wasn't sure what choice he had at this point. It was Tara. It had to be. And if she had said something to Nelly, he knew he probably wouldn't get away with outwardly lying. He was a good liar, but he still wasn't even certain that he would be able to lie to Nelly convincingly. After a moment, he said, "I've… what did Tara say?"

"Tara?"

He felt his heart stop in his chest.

"Tara?" Nelly asked again.

"Yeah, I… assumed Tara was the one that said something to you. Because you know her," his heart thumped as he grappled for an excuse for what he had just almost admitted.

"What do you… it wasn't Tara. It was Maeve, actually. She said Philip had told her about you going home with some woman after drinks the other night. What, do you mean Tara knows?"

"Mmm. I—"

"How would Tara know what you've been doing? She barely even knows you. I've never even seen you speak to her. You're actually pretty rude every time that you do run into her. I never really—" Oliver avoided her gaze as the

250

realisation dawned on Nelly's face. "Oh, no Oliver. Tell me you've not been sleeping with Tara?"

Oliver's heart was thumping beneath his shirt. He was sure that it was loud enough for the people behind them to hear it. He turned his head toward the bar, checking where Nelly's dad was. "Nelly, please. Please don't do this here."

"You've been having sex with Tara?"

"I—"

"For God's sake, Oliver!" She took her hand away from his and placed it over her face. "Fucking hell. I cried to her about it in the staff room. She hugged me and said you were a piece of shit. That's because you've been having sex with her as well, isn't it?"

Oliver didn't know what to say. "I... it hasn't happened in months. Not since I found out that she works at—"

"This is so fucking embarrassing!"

"No, Nelly. It isn't."

"How isn't it?"

"I mean, you shouldn't be embarrassed. You're the woman that I'm in love with. They don't mean anything to me."

"I'm so embarrassed! I told Tara that I was in love with you and that we were basically together. And all the while you've been fucking her behind my back! Oh fuck, and I have to see her on Monday and look at her and know that— What did you just say?"

"Nelly, please."

"Did you just say *they*?"

"What?"

"You just said *they*. *They don't mean anything to me.* They as in Tara, or they as in more than one?"

Oliver tapped his foot underneath the table, "Nelly."

"How many other women have there been?"

"What?"

"How many other women have you been having sex with?"

"I mean... I don't know."

"What? It's such a high number that you can't count to it?"

"No! It's... what are you asking me exactly? Since when do you mean?"

"Okay. Since New Year's."

Oliver's stomach dropped. He had been hoping that she would pick a timeframe less monumental. "I don't know."

"Well, is it two? Five? Ten? Twenty?"

Oliver shook his head, "Nelly, please. I—"

He reached for her hand again, but she took it away.

"Does the number even matter?"

"Of course it matters!"

Oliver sighed, "Fuck. I don't know. Five, maybe." This was a lie. It had been far more than five.

"You've had sex with five women since New Year's Eve?"

Oliver's mouth suddenly felt very dry.

"You're a fucking arsehole."

"No. I mean, yes. I am. I'm an arsehole. But—"

"But what?"

Oliver sighed, "Please, Nelly. Can we go back home? Can we talk about this in private?"

Nelly shook her head, "I don't want to go back to yours. Not when other women have been there with you."

"They haven't. They never have. I swear. I wouldn't let them go where you sleep."

Nelly sighed, shaking her head. She looked like she was trying very hard not to cry. "Please, stop lying to me. Please, don't treat me like the other women."

"I'm not. I swear."

Nelly sighed again, "I found their underwear in your bed."

"What?"

"Christ. That sounds like such a fucking cliché. I mean, I wasn't looking for it. When I changed your bed when you were ill, there was some other woman's underwear in there."

Oliver's stomach twisted painfully again. Fuck. He had genuinely forgotten about that woman.

"Fuck. Okay. Yes, there was one woman. But…" Oliver grappled for what to say next to justify himself. He rubbed a hand over his face, "You found this when you changed the bed? What, when I saw ill?"

"Mmm."

"That was weeks ago. Why didn't you say something then? Or since then, even. Why did you wait until now?"

Nelly sniffed, "I suppose I was trying to ignore that it had happened. I thought maybe it was just the once and that… I don't know. But then Maeve told me about it at work and it became real and I couldn't ignore it anymore, so I thought I'd ask. I hoped it would just be one stupid mistake. I didn't think it would be this." She shook her head, her eyes welling and red. "I really didn't think you'd do this to me again. After everything."

Oliver breathed. He was beginning to feel nauseous. He reached for her hand, but she took it off of the table and placed it in her lap. "Nelly, I… I know that I've fucked up. I've messed up. I know that. But it's only sex."

"Only sex?"

"I mean, you're acting like I've cheated on you. We aren't together. I want to be, but you constantly remind me that we aren't together."

"So, it's my fault?"

"No, I'm—that's not what I'm saying. Please don't do that. Don't put words in my mouth that I don't mean. I'm saying, you tell me—tell *people*—that we aren't together. You tell me that we aren't ready, then that I'm not ready, and then that you aren't ready again. And I get it. I know you aren't at the moment. Not with everything else that's happened. So, I'm okay with it. I deal with it. But then you still treat me like I'm your boyfriend. We still do everything that a couple does, apart from… that. We sleep next to each other every night and I know the names of all of the kids in your class. I take you to dinner three times a week and secretly prefer it when we stay in and you cook for us and we watch a film on the settee.

"I pick you up when it's dark outside, because I don't like you walking to the tube on your own, even though you tell me constantly that you're fine. I hate you going back to that fucking flat at all, and not just because of the mildew, or the damp, or because it's fucking tiny. I hate it because I wish you lived with me. I have to lay beside you wishing I could touch you and kiss you, but knowing that I'm not allowed to. I'm your husband, without any of the rewards."

Nelly nodded. She looked suddenly calm, as if she understood what he was saying even though she was crying quietly. "And sex would be the reward?"

"No. Well, yes. In a way. I just mean, we do everything that a couple does even though you tell me I'm not your boyfriend. So, I get that part from somewhere else. It doesn't mean anything to me."

"But that does mean something to me. The fact that you're fucking someone—other people—and then coming home to me, means something to me."

"Nelly, I—"

"And I get what you're saying. It's unfair of me to think that I can have all of those things, the things that you just said, and then not give you what you need."

"But *you* are what I need."

She shook her head, "No. It isn't. I'm not. And you've proved it. With five different women, apparently. And I'm so sorry, because I want that too. I want that for us, too. But I just can't... I'm not able to be that way right now. I don't know why not, but I just can't."

"I know. I know that. And I'll wait. Just ask me to wait."

"I shouldn't have to ask you to! You should want to wait for me, and you don't."

"That's not fair. I have been waiting. I *am* waiting."

"No, you aren't, Oliver. You're fucking other women. And you're right; I don't actually have any right to ask you not to. But I can't carry on like this, either. Knowing that you're out with another woman and then coming home to me. I can't just ignore it after we've said all of this." She shook her head, tears dropping down her face. "It's not fair of you to ask me to ignore it. And I'm not being fair in what I'm asking of you."

"But I want it. I want to be with you."

"I do, too. But—"

"But what?"

She looked at him, tears trickling down her cheeks. "But I don't trust you! How can I? You're already having an affair, and we aren't even together properly."

"That's what I mean! How can I be having an affair when we aren't together? It doesn't make sense."

Nelly shook her head, holding it in her hands. "Fuck. This is all too complicated."

"But it could be simple. We could just be simple."

She shook her head again, facing the table. After a long moment, she looked back up at him, "I don't trust you not to fuck it up though, Oliver."

"I won't. I'll be good!"

She shook her head, "But you probably won't be. We both know that you probably won't be. And I'm so scared that we'll do it—that we'll really get together, and then you'll do the same thing to me again. Because how would I ever be enough for you?"

"You *are* enough for me."

"No, I'm not, Oliver. That's the problem. I'm clearly not. And I'm too scared to lose you. To properly lose you. If we got together, we'd fuck it up and then we wouldn't have each other at all and… I just don't think my heart could take it." She clutched at her chest, as if protecting it. "I love you so much, and I couldn't bear to lose you, too."

Oliver nodded, reaching across the table for her hand once more. She didn't let him. "Nelly, I—what do you want to do, then? Do you want us to, what, set a time limit or something? What?"

"I… I think this is just too complicated. I think we should just… we always say we're just friends. Maybe we really should be just friends. Like we used to be. We should stop all of this before we start hating each other."

Oliver scoffed, "We've never been just friends."

"Maybe we should be."

Oliver shook his head, "And what would that look like? What would we be like if we were just that?"

"I don't know. Like, it breaks my heart knowing that you're with other women. But it shouldn't, because you aren't my boyfriend, as you said. Maybe that's what we need to do to make it normal. See other people, or something."

"You want to see other people?"

"I don't know. Maybe. I mean, you already are, aren't you?"

"No. I've had sex with a few other women. That didn't mean anything to me. It isn't the same. You're telling me that you want to be with someone else?"

"No! I'm not saying that. I'm just… it's too painful for us both like this. Maybe if we take that part away, we can—"

"Who do you want to be seeing, other than me? Who the fuck is it?" His temper had risen far more quickly than he had expected it to. Oliver clenched his fists together on the table, feeling adrenaline pumping behind his skin.

"No! There's not anyone else. I don't even—"

"Then why are you saying this? You aren't ready to be with me, but you're ready to be with someone else that you don't even know yet?"

"No! I'm not ready to be with anyone. I just mean when we are, one day. You already are. And I want to be able to be in your life still. For that to not break my heart."

"Has someone else asked you?"

"That's irrelevant."

"No, it isn't. Tell me. Now."

Nelly sighed, "What, asked me out? Yes, other people have asked me out, believe it or not. But that isn't why I'm saying this."

"Who?"

"Oliver."

"Who!"

"I don't know. Just men. It doesn't matter. I don't want to go out with any of them. I've said no, every time. I'm just saying that maybe one day we will, and—"

"Fucking hell. I don't fucking believe this."

"Oliver. You're not understanding what I'm saying. I don't want to lose you. I don't want—"

Oliver shook his head. All he could think about was the fact that Nelly might start seeing other people; other men. That they might get to sit with her and speak to her and touch her in the ways that he did—the ways that only he did. The ways that she didn't let even him, at the moment. It made his stomach cinch painfully where his scar was. He shook his head again, clenching his jaw. "What a fucking waste of time."

"Oliver."

Oliver stood up from the table and pushed his chair away, moving away from Nelly and out of her parents' restaurant without even looking back. He ignored her father's stare as the door closed behind him.

2001
Nelly

I feel overwhelmingly sad at times: Definitely agree, Slightly agree, Slightly disagree, Definitely disagree
When I think of the future, I feel hopeless: Definitely agree, Slightly agree, Slightly disagree, Definitely disagree
I feel guilty about something most of the time: Definitely agree, Slightly agree, Slightly disagree, Definitely disagree
Sometimes I think the world would be better without me in it: Definitely agree, Slightly agree, Slightly disagree, Definitely disagree

Nelly sat in the waiting room of the doctor's office looking down at the form that she had been given at reception.

"Nelly Strapelli?" A voice asked from somewhere to her right. Nelly looked up and saw a male doctor scanning the waiting room. It took her a moment to find her feet before walking toward him.

The doctor closed the door to his office behind them and gestured toward the empty two chairs in front of the desk. "Please, take a seat."

Nelly regarded the two chairs uncomfortably until she chose one, placing her bag onto the floor beside her. "I'm sorry, I didn't get to finish," she said, holding the form out toward him.

He looked at it and then said, "Ah."

Nelly chewed her cheek.

"It would have been helpful if you had completed the questionnaire first."

"Yes. I'm sorry."

The doctor nodded. "Why don't you tell me a bit about what you think the matter is."

Nelly nodded, "Well, I suppose I've just been feeling a bit down."

"A bit down?"

Nelly nodded.

"Okay. And is that a bit blue, a normal feeling? Something you've experienced often. Or something abnormal?"

Nelly rubbed her lips together. She wasn't sure what was supposed to be normal. "I don't know. I've been feeling very unhappy. And I've been having panic attacks, I think. At least, I think that I have. Quite a lot. Most days, at the moment."

"What do those feel like? The panic attacks."

Nelly chewed on the edge of her cheek. She wasn't sure how to describe them. Like she was outside of her own body. Like she wasn't sure what she might do. Like she thought she might breathe so fast that her heart might stop beating and she would die. She didn't want to sound dramatic.

"Could it be premenstrual?"

"Sorry?"

"Related to your cycles."

Nelly wanted to tell him that she knew what premenstrual was, but that it was his statement that she had found ridiculous. But instead, she shook her head, "No. I don't think so."

"Are you on birth control?"

"No. But... it isn't to do with that."

"Okay. Why don't you tell me what you think it might be to do with, then?"

Nelly rubbed her lips together, "I lost someone recently. My friend. My best friend. And I suppose I've been feeling a bit sad about it. Very sad about it. And, well... guilty, maybe."

"I'm sorry to hear that. When did this loss occur?"

"August the twelfth."

"Of this year?"

"No, last year."

The doctor nodded. He wrote something down on his notepad. Nelly rubbed the edges of the clipboard that she was still holding.

"And things have been out of balance since then?"

"Mmm, yes."

"Continually, or in ebbs and flows?"

Nelly thought about the past thirteen months. She thought about the days when she hadn't been able to get out of bed in the morning and the days where she felt so sad that it physically hurt. But she also thought about the days that she had spent with Oliver, laughing together or cuddling on the settee; holding onto his hand beneath the table as they ate orecchiette. Feeling loved. That was gone now, though. "Ebbs and flows, at first. But it's more constant now."

"What about sleep? Have you been able to get a normal amount of rest each night?"

Nelly thought for a moment and then shook her head. She couldn't remember the last time that she had slept the entire night through. Actually, she could. But she was trying not to let herself think of him. It would likely bring on one of the episodes of panic that she had been experiencing since that day at her parents' restaurant.

The doctor nodded again. "And what about friends and family? Is there anyone close to you that you can speak with about how you've been feeling?"

"I—" Nelly began to say. An image of Oliver darted into her mind again. She blinked it away. "Not really anymore. Not anyone that understands."

The doctor nodded again. He sighed and rested his hands on the table, cupping them in front of his notebook. There were very few notes written down. "It sounds like you might have onset grief disorder. It's basically when the grieving period tends to worsen over time rather than get better, following an initial phase of denial. It's normal, when something very traumatic occurs or when a person loses someone particularly close to them. You often find it in mothers. Or romantic partners."

Nelly chewed into the side of her mouth. Something about his wording made her feel judged. Silly. Like she was being over-the-top.

"There are a few things that I can recommend. There's grief counselling; some people find that really helpful. Or there are support groups."

Nelly nodded. "I've been going to one of those. It hasn't seemed to have helped very much. For me, anyway. I know it does for other people."

"Okay. Well then there are things like anti-depressants and sleeping tablets. Do either of those sound like an avenue you might be interested in pursuing, or do you not feel that you need those? Apologies, it is difficult for me to make an assessment without your form."

Nelly nodded. "Would they make me feel better, the tablets?"

The doctor shrugged slightly, "It's different for everyone. Some people have a lot of success with anti-depressants. Others say that they make them feel a bit unlike themselves, so they don't like to take them for a long course of treatment.

Sleeping tablets, on the other hand, would be similar to a heavy anti-histamine. They would just help you get to sleep, which in turn might help you feel like you could cope."

It was a strange turn of phrase, *feel like you could cope*. As if it would all just be a charade, whatever the decision.

"Do you think that might be the best course of action for you, at this time?"

Nelly thought for a moment, weighing her options. She wasn't sure why the doctor kept asking her what her opinion was; she had come to see a doctor to be told the best course of action, not to work it out on her own. After a moment, she nodded.

"Okay. We'll get you started on some sleeping tablets and then, if things don't get better, come back and see me again and we can speak about some other course of treatment. Maybe take the form home with you, so as you can have it ready should you need to come back. In the meantime, I'd also recommend grief counselling, as I say."

Nelly nodded again. "Okay, thank you."

The doctor nodded, "There are some leaflets that you can take from the waiting room with the information that you'll need. Other than that, if you just ask reception to print your prescription, you'll be able to pick that up from a chemist."

Nelly nodded again. It was all over so quickly.

2001

Oliver

He went to New York that September, as planned. Nelly didn't join him. It had now been three months since they had last spoken. He had officially lost her twice. He wasn't sure which of the two of them he was more angry with about it.

Oliver thought about Nelly every day. He thought about her when he drove to work in the morning; he thought about her when he sat on his settee at night, watching TV; he thought about her every time he opened his kitchen cupboard and saw the bottle of Worcester sauce sat there, which she used to put on her cheese on toast that he'd sometimes make her on a Sunday. She'd joke about it being the only thing that he could cook and he'd pretend to be offended so that she would cuddle him and say he made a great steak. He loved those Sundays. With her. With them. He loved every day with her in it. Now, the bottle just sat waiting to be used. Oliver didn't like Worcester sauce. He had just bought it for Nelly.

When he was in New York, Oliver took the train one day to Coney Island because he was thinking about Nelly. It took just over an hour to get there. Oliver wandered around for a bit and then spent some time looking at postcards in a small shop at the sea front. He bought one that said *Greetings from Coney Island* in big, vintage-style letters on the front. He thought about sending it to Nelly, but then wasn't sure about what he would say. There were too many words and too little space, and yet he didn't know how on earth he would fill all eight inches of it. He put the postcard in his back pocket and left it there. The rest of the time that Oliver was in New York, he worked on the weekends.

2002
Oliver

He hadn't planned on staying at Tony's birthday party very long. It was at a pub in Notting Hill, not far from where Oliver lived. He didn't know Tony particularly well, having met him at a rugby club that Oliver had recently joined, but he'd been invited to the party anyway and thought he may as well stop in. The pub had been busy when he'd turned up after work, music playing loudly and a large hand-written banner saying *Happy 29th Tony* strung up across the bar.

Oliver elbowed his way in and moved toward the cluster of people that he recognised, planning on saying a quick hello and then leaving. The last person that he expected to see tonight was Nelly.

She had straightened her hair so as it lay long and sleek over her shoulders, her mouth rimmed with red lipstick. She looked almost as shocked as he felt when she saw him approach.

"Oliver, mate. How are you?" Tony asked, hugging Oliver and smacking him on the back. Oliver couldn't take his eyes away from Nelly's.

"Hey," Oliver replied, "Happy birthday."

"Cheers, mate," Tony grinned. He handed Oliver a bottle of lager and Oliver took it, taking a swig. "You've met everyone, haven't you?"

Oliver nodded, "Mmm, yeah. I think so." He nodded at various faces that he knew around the circle, some nodding back and others giving him smacks on the arm or shoulder; the men at rugby liked him, like men normally did. Oliver let his eyes dart quickly over and away from Nelly. "Hey."

"Hi," she said, looking back at him. She looked as if she were waiting for him to say something, but he wasn't sure what.

"Oh shit, sorry. This is Nelly," Tony said, stepping slightly back and putting his arm around her shoulder. Nelly carried on looking at Oliver.

"Right. Hiya," Oliver said. He wasn't sure why he had said it like that. He kept looking at her straight hair. It was different. He wasn't sure he liked it.

"Hi," Nelly replied, she turned to Tony and said, "We actually know each other. Oliver's India's brother. You remember, my best friend?"

Tony looked surprised, "Oh, right. Fuck. I didn't know. Sorry, mate."

Oliver shrugged, "No problem."

"Wow, small world, eh?"

Oliver raised his eyebrows. India's brother. So that was what he had been reduced to. He was sure that it was a purposeful understatement, but it felt like a kick in the stomach all the same.

"Oh shit, sorry. My cousin just got here. I'll be back in a minute, yeah?"

Nelly nodded and smiled at Tony, "Yeah. No problem."

"Alright. See you in a minute, mate," Tony said. He tapped Oliver on the arm and then walked off to greet someone else behind them. Oliver stood and looked at Nelly.

"I can leave if you—"

"No," Nelly interrupted quickly. She shook her head, her strangely straight hair swinging on her shoulder. "It's nice to see you."

Oliver raised his eyebrows, "Really?"

Nelly smiled, covering her mouth, and nodded.

The two of them were sat at a small, round table in the pub whilst other people stood around them. Nelly was drinking a bottle of lager and she kept picking the label off from it, laying it down carefully on the beer matt on the table as if she were going to tidy it later.

"So, you and Tony?" Oliver said to her as she picked the last of the label free.

She looked up and nodded, "Mmm, yeah. I didn't know you knew each other."

Oliver shrugged, "We don't, really. We only met a couple of months ago, at rugby."

"Ah, yeah. Us too. Not at rugby, obviously."

Oliver smiled, "Yeah, I would have been surprised."

Nelly smiled back and then shook her head, "I'm sorry. It's weird talking with you about this."

"What?"

"About other men."

Oliver shrugged, "It was going to happen at some point, wasn't it?"

Nelly looked at the table and nodded, "Yeah. I suppose so."

"So, is it serious then?"

Nelly shrugged, "I wouldn't say serious, no. But he's nice, isn't he?"

"He's nice to you?"

"Mmm. Yeah, he's nice to me."

Oliver nodded. He felt oddly relieved.

She rubbed her lips together and then looked away.

"So, what else is new? You've changed your hair."

She looked back at him as if he had said something peculiar, then replied, "Oh, yeah. I straighten it now."

"Ah."

She tucked a piece of it away over her shoulder as if self-conscious of it and he saw her blush slightly. It made her look more familiar. More like his Nelly. "It goes curly every time it gets wet, though."

"Ah, right. I always liked it. Curly, I mean."

"Oh. I've always hated it."

"You shouldn't."

"Mmm," she chewed her cheek and then looked out at the bar for a moment before picking up her bottle and taking a swig of beer. She set it back down and asked, "What about you? How are things? How are your parents?"

"Yeah, they're alright. Mum's started volunteering at this charity, which she's enjoying."

"The one she used to go to?"

Oliver shook his head, "No. A different one."

"Ah. Sorry. I assumed."

Oliver smiled, "Don't be. And Dad's... fine. I mean, he still can't say India's name, but we're trying to trick him into it with take aways."

Nelly laughed, "Good plan."

"Mmm."

They sat for a moment, quietly drinking their beers. Oliver was about to say something, but Nelly interrupted. "It really is good to see you. It's been ages."

Oliver nodded, "Almost two years."

"Mhmm. That's a long time."

"Mmm."

She leant her head to one side and then leant it back, "I missed you. I hope you don't mind me saying that."

Oliver nodded, "Yeah. I missed you, too."

"That's nice of you to say."

"I wasn't saying it to be nice," Oliver frowned, "Why would you think that?"

"Mmm. I dunno. Things have just been weird since we last saw each other. I've felt a bit... I don't know."

"Like you wanted to cut my dick off?"

Nelly laughed and then looked surprised that she had, covering her mouth with her hand. "No. Well, yeah. Obviously. A little bit. I'm not made of wood."

Oliver laughed.

"But I was going to say that I felt a bit lost, I suppose. As well as wanting to chop your dick off, obviously," she laughed and covered her mouth before turning back toward him. "I suppose I wasn't myself without India. Without you, to be honest. I know it probably isn't fair of me to say that now, after all of this time. But I just want... it wasn't that I didn't want to reach out over these past months. It was just more that I didn't know what to say. I don't think I was very well. I *know* I wasn't very well. I wasn't coping. You already knew that, obviously. That I wasn't coping."

He watched her, but didn't say anything.

She continued, "I suppose I just don't want you to think that I hated you."

Oliver nodded. They sat quietly for a beat. "You must have hated me a little bit?"

Nelly smiled, "Well..." she laughed and covered her mouth again. Oliver laughed back.

"I've missed you, too," he told her, "So badly. And, if it makes you feel better, I probably hated myself enough for the two of us."

She nodded. "I really am sorry."

"What for?"

"For lots of things. I feel like I wasn't the version of me I wish I had been for you. For us. And I don't want you to think that I was just stringing you along, or something."

"I didn't think that."

"Really?" She looked relieved, "Because I wasn't. Not intentionally, anyway. I really did want us to..." she sighed and shook her head, "I just couldn't. You know? And I still feel so awful about it."

Oliver frowned, "Nel, it wasn't like I was a bloody saint."

"Yeah, but you were suffering. She was your sister."

Oliver watched her again.

"I'm sorry. It's probably the beers talking. I'm not making sense."

"You make sense to me."

"I really am so—"

"You can stop saying sorry now, Nelly. You've officially used up your quota."

"Oh." She looked suddenly embarrassed. He was glad that she was happy to see him, and even that she had acknowledged the pain that she knew he had felt. But he also was extremely aware that the reason for them not speaking for almost two years had been his fault, in the majority. She always apologised when she didn't really need to, putting blame onto herself for things that weren't actually her fault. He had seen her do that with so many people; India, Henry, Leo. He didn't want her to do that with him. If it had been anyone else, he would have. But not her. Not Nelly.

"Besides, I'm pretty sure I'm the one who should be apologising. And, for what it's worth, I'm sorry too. I've never been more sorry for anything in my life. I'm sorry that I didn't tell you that earlier."

She nodded, "It's okay. I kind of already knew."

He smiled at her, "Telepathic now?"

She shrugged and looked away from him.

He grinned. He knew she was hiding that she was blushing. He continued, "Honestly, to be fair I wouldn't have spoken to me either. I expected you to do far worse when we eventually saw each other. The first time that I saw Maeve at a work's thing she threw a glass of red wine over me and called me a cheating cunt."

Nelly chuckled, "Oh?"

"Yeah. Ruined a perfectly good shirt."

Nelly laughed, "I always liked Maeve."

Oliver smiled back. "Me too, to be fair."

Nelly smacked his arm.

Oliver grinned. "And she might have had a point."

"Oh?"

"Mmm. A tiny bit. Maybe. About this much," he held his fingers up in front of his face. Nelly laughed and then looked back down at the beer bottle again. He could see the tiny perfect freckle above her lip.

Oliver found himself reaching out and brushing her hair from her shoulder and then had to tell his hand to stop. She smiled and looked away from him for a moment and then turned back, her cheeks mottled with red blush.

"Did you really expect me to do something like that?"

He shook his head, "No. Not you."

She nodded slowly. "Anyway, what about you? Are you seeing anyone?"

Oliver swallowed his beer. "Mmm. Yeah. I have a girlfriend, actually. Catharine."

"Oh?" she looked surprised at this, her beer hovering between the table and her mouth.

Oliver smiled, "You don't need to look so shocked."

"No, it's just… I didn't know, I suppose."

Oliver nodded, "Mmm. Yeah. I get it. I didn't know either. About you and Tony, I mean. Sort of let myself believe that would never happen. Kick in the balls, isn't it?"

She smiled again and he returned the gesture. He stretched his legs beneath the table and felt them unfold more comfortably. Nelly drank her beer and then glanced back at him, wrinkling her nose. "Fuck, I hate that this is awkward."

"Is it?"

She rolled her eyes.

Oliver felt something twinge in his chest. "Some might say this was your master plan all along."

"You what?"

Oliver grinned. Her accent still sometimes surprised him when it came out of her mouth. It seemed more prominent suddenly; thicker, like it had been when they had first met. Or maybe he had just gotten used to it before. He raised his eyebrows, "When we last saw each other, you said we should both see other people and then we could be friends."

"Ah. Right, yeah."

Oliver shrugged, "So, how about now?"

Nelly moved her mouth as if she were chewing her cheek, thinking. "Are you asking me to be your friend, Oliver?"

"Mmm, I suppose I am. I've had an opening these past couple of years."

She smiled, "Mmm. Me too." She swigged her beer and nodded her head from one side to the other, as if thinking. "Okay. I think that could work. On a trial basis, of course."

"Yeah? That's good of you."

She laughed.

"Look, if you're worried that you'll fall in love with me again I promise to do something utterly cuntish at least once a year to stop that from happening."

She laughed again, "You shouldn't have any problems there."

"Mmm, exactly. My forte."

"And what if you fall in love with me?"

Oliver sucked air through his teeth, "Excellent question."

"Thank you."

"To be honest, that is a bit of a risk. But, if it were to occur, I could always just think about how you broke my heart when you were the only woman I've ever loved."

Nelly looked suddenly serious, "Oliver. I—"

"Or the way your breath smells in the morning."

She smacked him on the arm and Oliver grinned. He held out his hand to her, "So then, just friends? A gentleman's agreement?"

She let a smile creep back into her cheeks. "I'm guessing I'm the gentleman in this scenario?"

"Obviously."

Nelly nodded, "Obviously." She held her hand out toward his and then shook it.

"Nice doing business with you, Strapelli."

The two smiled at each other for a moment before letting go of each other. Hers felt exactly the way that he had remembered that it had in his palm.

2002
Nelly

"I don't understand why you always get so nervous before we see them. He's supposed to be your mate."

"I know. I just… want things to go right, you know?" Nelly was quickly cutting and stuffing artichokes ready for when her guests arrived this evening. She had been held up at work and was running a bit behind, so was beginning to rush. She hoped that Oliver would magically be running late too. The buzzer for the oven went off and Nelly pulled it open to take out the pastry cases that she had been cooking.

"It will all be fine."

"I just hope Catharine likes it. I feel like she doesn't like me very much."

"Really?"

"Mmm. Do you think she doesn't?"

Tony shrugged, his eyes still watching the television where he was playing a game on the PlayStation. He'd brought it round to Nelly's flat about a month ago and hadn't taken it back home with him since. It annoyed her, although she wasn't very sure why.

"Tony."

"I dunno. What's not to like?"

"Mmm," Nelly replied. She didn't like to say that it could well be the fact that she and Oliver used to be in love with each other that could be the reason why his new girlfriend might not like her very much. *New* was a funny term for Catharine, really. She and Oliver had apparently been together for five months now, which she liked to remind Nelly about often. Nelly supposed that Catharine being in Oliver's life would always be new for her, though.

Sometimes Nelly wondered what exactly Oliver had told Catharine about her, or about her and his past together. For the most part, she assumed that he probably wouldn't have told the whole truth. Not just because that was what Oliver was like, but also because she had found herself doing something similar with Tony. She had told him that Oliver was India's brother and that the two of them had had a bit of a thing a long time ago, but nothing specific. She hadn't, for example, told Tony about the weekend in Rome or the fight that she and Oliver had had after Nelly had found out that he had been living with Kelsey.

About the fact that they were more or less a couple for almost a year before she learned that Oliver was sleeping with other people, because she had felt so guilty about potentially being happy without India that she hadn't allowed Oliver to have all of her. Or the fact that she sometimes thought about him when she was in bed on her own at night. Or, even worse, when she was in bed with Tony. It wasn't that she was lying, per se, it was more that she didn't even know how to express most of it. And because she didn't want Tony to know everything, obviously. Otherwise, she was sure that he wouldn't want Nelly and Oliver being such close friends. What partner would want that, after all? And she loved Oliver's company. Nelly loved Oliver, in so many ways. Still. Despite everything.

Their relationship had grown into something different over the past few months. They had met up a few times as a four, never on their own, and they had spoken with and treated one another with a familiarity that one might treat a family member that they had grown up with but haven't seen in a long time. They knew everything that there was to know about one another, and yet still had new things to learn all of the time from the months that they had missed out on when they had been apart. Things that they both clearly in some ways begrudged not knowing. Oliver understood Nelly like nobody else did, which was one of the main reasons that it was so easy to talk to him. She could say things to Oliver that she couldn't say to other people. Like the fact that she still couldn't sleep without taking her sleeping tablets. Or he could tell her about how his dad told people that India's death was an accident and how it made Oliver utterly furious.

They didn't judge each other. They just understood. They accepted each other, in a way that nobody else ever seemed to be able to. Which, again, was probably one of the reasons that Catharine didn't like Nelly. Or perhaps Nelly was just imagining this.

The bell to Nelly's flat rang and Nelly turned around toward it, then turned back to the artichokes that she needed to have put in the oven twenty minutes ago. Something in the air smelled faintly like burning and it was adding to Nelly's anxiety. Tony was still playing on the PlayStation. "Do you think you could get that?" She asked.

"Yeah. In a sec."

Nelly rolled her eyes and put the artichokes down on the work surface, rushing to the front door. She pulled it open to see Catharine and Oliver stood there quietly. Oliver looked as he always did; impassive, confident, unfazed. Catharine on the other hand looked remarkably irritable, as if she had been caught mid-way through and argument. Nelly tried to smile kindly at them both.

"Hiya, how are you?"

"Evening," Catharine replied. Her voice was clipped and short. She stepped forward and offered a bottle of wine to Nelly. "This is for you."

"Oh, that's really kind. Thanks so much."

"Mmm, it's French. So hopefully you still like it."

"Oh, lovely. Yeah, I love French wine."

Catharine shot Oliver a look over her shoulder that he didn't reciprocate. She turned back and smiled at Nelly, "Can I use your loo quickly?"

"Of course. It's just—"

Catharine walked past her toward the bathroom. Tony was still sat on the settee.

"You alright, Tony?" Oliver called over.

"Hiya mate. Sorry, two secs."

Nelly rolled her eyes and Oliver smiled at her.

"Hey," he said, bending down to kiss her cheek. She stood on her tiptoes to let him. He smelled nice, like cedar wood and something beneath it. Lemon soap.

"Heya," she replied, "You alright?"

Oliver raised his eyebrows as if it were a response and replied, "You?"

"Yeah. All good, thanks. A bit rushed, to be honest." She led Oliver over to the small kitchen and was about to offer him a drink when she said, "Oh fuck!"

She suddenly remembered the oven beeping a moment ago and moved to take the pastry cases out, then remembered her oven gloves. She pulled the cases out quickly, sat them on the worktop, then replaced them in the oven with the artichokes. She turned around and saw Oliver quickly lifting the tray of pastry, a tea towel wrapped around his hand. A large, circular burn tarnished the surface. "Oh fuck, I'll never get that out," she said, looking at the black ring of burn on the work top.

Oliver smiled, "Mmm, yeah. You'll have a job. Here's a novel idea. Why don't you move?"

Nelly rolled her eyes. Oliver had always hated her flat.

"You know why I can't move. It's cheap. It's close to work."

"Ish."

"And—"

"Yep, yep. I've heard the spiel before," Oliver reached behind her and lifted four glasses from the cupboard where she kept them, hesitating and saying over his shoulder. "Tony, are you having wine?"

"Mmm? Oh, na. I'm on the tinnies, thanks, mate."

"Right," Oliver replied, turning back to Nelly. She sighed and opened the drawer to pull out the corkscrew.

"Thanks," she smiled when Oliver took it from her and began opening the bottle. "Is everything alright?" Nelly asked, tilting her head toward the bathroom door.

Oliver shrugged slightly. "Sorry about her."

"Oh, no. It's fine. I just—"

Oliver pulled the cork out of the bottle and lifted one of the glasses, filling it with wine. He handed it to Nelly and then began filling the others.

"I just wanted to make sure she was alright. She seemed a bit…"

"Doesn't she always?"

"Oh, well I don't know. I just meant—"

Oliver looked up and smiled slightly before placing the third glass on the side.

Nelly smiled and sipped her wine. It was very dry. "Tony, are you going to come and say hi?"

"Yep. I'll be there in a sec, babe."

Nelly sighed again, trying not to be irritated. Oliver looked amused. Nelly was about to ask what he found funny when he reached out and rubbed her upper arm. His hand on her skin was pleasantly warm and firm.

"Are we starting with wine, then?" Catharine's voice broke out from across the room. She stood watching them from outside of the bathroom for a moment before walking the few steps over to the kitchen. She was very pretty; tall, with grey eyes and straight blonde hair that she had worn up in a twist at the nape of her neck. She made Nelly feel frumpy and very conscious of the fact that her knickers were digging into the side of her hips.

"Yeah, if that's alright? Thanks so much again for bringing it."

"Mmm. I just thought we'd have something sparkling to start?" She phrased it as a question.

"Fucking hell," Oliver hissed beneath his breath.

Nelly pretended that she hadn't heard him. "Ah, of course. No problem. We've got some Prosecco in the fridge? It's nice. It's Sicilian."

"Prosecco?" Catharine asked, her small nose wrinkled. "Mmm, I'll stick with the wine thanks, on second thoughts."

Nelly smiled, "Of course. No worries."

"It's too sweet for me, Prosecco. It gives me a headache."

"Ah yeah, it can be sweet, can't it?" Nelly smiled again. She felt her cheeks beginning to flush.

Tony got up from the settee and walked over to them, his tin of Amstel in hand. "Hey guys," he grinned as he walked over, "Sorry about that. I was just in the last minutes of the game. You get how it is."

Oliver raised his eyebrows and smiled.

"Hi," Catharine replied, offering him her cheek. Tony looked confused and then gave her a hug. Nelly could see Catharine's hand tapping his back lightly.

Oliver smiled slightly and raised his eyebrows at the pair of them. Nelly suddenly felt very warm. She moved to open the window above the sink, but Oliver reached over and did it for her, bringing a wave of fresh air into the small flat.

"Well, something smells tasty," Catharine said, nodding toward the entrees on the work surface.

"Ah yeah. Sorry, I'm such a scatter brain tonight," Nelly said. She had forgotten about her pastry cases. She moved toward them and quickly placed them all onto a round, decorative plate. "Here you are." She smiled, holding the plate toward Catharine, "So there's tapenade and then those are tomato and mozzarella."

"Lovely. Thank you," Catharine trilled, her fingers hovering over the plate. She picked up a tapenade-covered tartlet and then stood with it in her hand. "Gosh, I'm starving. I've not eaten all day."

"What, not a thing?"

Catherine shrugged and shook her head at Tony. He laughed.

"Cor, I can't imagine you doing that. Can you, babe?"

Nelly felt her stomach squirm. "Mmm, oh. No. Definitely not."

Tony laughed and nodded toward Nelly, "This one's on about four meals a day."

Catherine laughed at Tony and then turned toward Nelly, "Gosh, I suppose we just have different figures. You know?"

Nelly smiled and nodded, "Mmm. Yeah. Of course." Nelly turned her face and hoped that it didn't show that her cheeks were burning. She offered the plate to Oliver, who plucked two of each and popped one straight into his mouth. He pulled an appreciative face and then winked at her, eating the second. Nelly smiled, trying hard to ignore the icy look that Catharine was giving Oliver at him doing this. She offered the plate around again and Tony reached forward and also took a handful, leaving just one solitary tapenade left for grabbing.

"Good job you had a big lunch, eh?" Catherine giggled.

Nelly wanted to roll her eyes at her and tell Tony that he should have left more for other people, but didn't. She hadn't had any yet. Oliver looked at the plate and then put one of the pastry cases that he was holding back on top of it.

"Oh, no. You don't have to—"

He waved his hand at her before she finished her comment. Catharine was still holding her food. Nelly smiled, "Well, the artichokes should be ready in about twenty minutes now. Sorry, I had meant for them to be done when you got here. But I had a bit of a nightmare day."

"Oh?" Catharine asked politely.

Nelly smiled, "Mmm, yeah. One of the year tens reversed the plumbing in the boys' loos so as the water flushed back out whenever someone pulled the chain."

Oliver laughed and so did Tony.

"Was that Connor?" Oliver asked.

Nelly nodded, "Mmm. Yeah."

"Well, he's got a promising career in plumbing, if nothing else."

Catharine scoffed, "Oliver, that's not funny. It's disgusting."

Nelly nodded, "Really gross." Nelly actually thought that it was quite funny as well, but she often found herself agreeing with Catherine even when she didn't really. She wanted her to like her.

Catharine eyed the tartlet that she was holding and then put it back onto the plate.

Nelly smiled again, "Anyway, it is really nice to see you both. Thanks for coming."

Oliver nodded, "You, too. Cheers."

"Cheers," they all said, chinking their glasses together. Nelly noticed that Catharine avoided Oliver's.

"What about you Tony, money or love?"

"Money!" Tony replied quickly, before laughing and wrapping his arm around the back of Nelly's chair. The air was beginning to feel increasingly more stifling. Nelly wondered whether she could reopen the small window above the sink that they had shut because Catharine was cold. "I'm only kidding. Love, obviously, if push came to shove."

"Aww, that's sweet. Isn't that sweet, Nelly?"

Nelly pressed her lips together and nodded in what she hoped was a convincing way.

Catherine smiled, "Well, I'd pick love too." Somewhere between her third and her sixth glass of red wine, she had begun to relax a little bit. Nelly noticed her swaying slightly in her seat, her smooth cheeks beginning to pink.

"Oliver?"

"Mmm?"

"Money or love, mate?" Tony asked. He laughed when Oliver didn't respond immediately, "This twat would obviously pick money, wouldn't you?"

Oliver smiled and shrugged. Tony laughed at his own joke.

"Stop it! No, you wouldn't," Catherine chided.

"Wouldn't I?"

"Of course you wouldn't. Money can't buy you happiness, can it? It can't keep you warm at night."

"If you have enough of it, it can."

Catherine smacked him on the arm.

Oliver continued, "It can't buy you happiness. But it can certainly buy you things that make you happy."

"But it can't make you happy like love can make you happy," Catherine said it as if she was explaining something very simple to a child.

Oliver shrugged, "In my experience, happiness from love is very short-lived anyway."

Catherine frowned, "What's that supposed to mean?"

Tony laughed again and shook his head, "You're gonna be sleeping on the sofa tonight if you aren't careful, mate."

Oliver shrugged, "I have a comfortable sofa."

Tony laughed loudly and clapped his hands together. He nudged Nelly, "Has he always been like this?"

She smiled, picking up her glass and drinking the last of her wine. She really did feel very hot. Oliver reached over and lifted the bottle to refill her glass before topping up Catherine's.

"I bet you two have all sorts of dirt on each other from back in the day. Go on, spill the beans, Nel. He must have had some gorgeous girl break his heart at some point? Someone must have turned him into the arsehole that he is today."

Oliver smiled slightly, blowing out a laugh through his nose. He turned his face to look at Nelly's, watching her expectantly. "Good question, mate," Oliver said to Tony. He was still watching Nelly. She opened her mouth to speak, but then wasn't sure what to say.

"Does anyone want another slice of the tart?"

"I will, cheers babe. There's always room for another tart from where I'm standing," Tony laughed. He winked at Nelly and then smacked her on the arse as she walked over to the work surface. She wanted to throw the dessert straight at him, but pretended to smile as if she found his comment humorous. It seemed like she did that a lot with Tony lately. She cut another slice from the dish for each of them and placed them onto plates. When she turned back around, she noticed that Oliver was watching her amusedly. He took the plate from her and then raised his eyebrows, as if still waiting for her to say something.

"Do you want cream?"

He shook his head, "Nope."

She nodded, "Okay." Nelly sat back down in her chair beside Tony and picked up her fork, placing the lemon tart onto her tongue. She wasn't even hungry.

"I thought I'd find you out here," Nelly said as she walked over to Oliver. He was stood against the front of the block of flats smoking a cigarette; one foot placed on the brick of the wall and both hands planted into the insides of his pockets, the cigarette balancing between his lips. He raised his eyebrows when she approached, but didn't turn to look at her.

"Well done, Poirot."

Nelly smiled. "I'm going to make coffee for everyone. I came to see if you wanted something?"

"Something?"

"A coffee."

Oliver nodded, but then said, "I'm alright, thanks."

"Ah, okay." Nelly turned to go back inside, but Oliver reached out and gently touched her arm. It was only slight; a graze, at most. But it made the hairs on the back of her neck stand on end. She turned to look at him, but he was still staring forward. "I should probably go back inside," she told him. He didn't reply. Nelly waited a moment, then moved the couple of paces forward until she was stood beside him, her back pressing against the cool of the brick. Oliver held the packet of cigarettes out to her wordlessly and she regarded it for a moment before taking one. "I hardly ever smoke anymore."

"Mmm. It doesn't really suit you," Oliver replied. Nelly turned to look at him, wondering whether he remembered that he had said this to her once before a long time ago. She smiled.

"Thanks for that."

He smiled back, offering her the lighter. She took it and lifted it to the cigarette at her lips, letting the orange flame flicker before her until the paper crackled and burned. She took a long drag, letting her lungs fill up with nicotine, her head feeling pleasantly dizzy.

"I think you might have pissed her off before. Catherine."

"Mmm?"

"With the money or love thing."

Oliver shrugged, "She'll get over it."

"Mmm."

"Or she won't. It doesn't really bother me either way."

Nelly turned to look at him again. Her face clearly portrayed her surprise, because he shrugged and said, "It isn't like she wouldn't pick the same thing, if she actually had the choice. She just thinks saying love makes her sound good."

"Really?"

Oliver nodded, "I'm pretty sure she's not with me just for my personality, let's put it that way."

"Well, who would be?"

Oliver smiled, this time showing his teeth and letting it touch his eyes. That smile that was reserved just for Nelly. It made her cheeks feel warm.

"She has a good job though. Why would she be with you because of that?"

Oliver shrugged. "Money likes money."

"Maybe it's ambition she likes."

"No. That's you. You like people to feel like they have a purpose. Catherine just likes the money," Oliver took a drag of his cigarette and held it in his mouth. "You don't have to pretend to like her, you know. Especially when it's just us. She can't hear you."

"I'm not pretending."

"Mmm. Right."

Nelly smoked her own cigarette and stood quietly for a moment before saying, "You didn't mean it, though. Did you? That you'd choose money over love."

"Mmm," Oliver swayed his head slightly from one side to the other as he took a drag of his cigarette, "I dunno. Money solves less problems than it causes."

"That's a controversial opinion."

"Not really."

"And love causes more problems?"

Oliver shrugged, "In my experience. More problems than money has, anyway."

"Mmm. Maybe that's because you've always had money."

"Yeah. Maybe."

Nelly rubbed the skin of her arms where goosebumps were starting to form. She was only wearing her dress, having not intended on staying outside for very long. She saw Oliver's eyes flicker momentarily toward her as she did this. "I'd better go back in."

"Yeah."

"I'll see you in a sec."

She was about to walk away when Oliver said, "You aren't much better though, are you?"

"What?"

Oliver shrugged, "Than me, I mean. You're having a go at me for saying money over love—"

"I'm not having a go at you."

"—but you're with Tony."

Nelly frowned, "What does that mean? I'm hardly with Tony for his wallet."

"You're with him because it's convenient."

"That's not true."

"Well, you don't love him. Do you?"

"I… it's too early for that. We haven't—"

"It's not too early. It's been, what, five months now?"

"Well, still."

Oliver shrugged, "You know whether you love someone or not."

"You do?"

"Yes."

Nelly rubbed the skin on her arms again, hesitating. "I don't know. He's nice to me. He's a kind person."

"That doesn't mean that you love him."

"Oliver, what do you want me to say?"

"Does he make you come when you have sex?"

"Excuse me?"

"When you have sex, does Tony make you come?"

Nelly shook her head in disbelief, "Oliver, how dare you! I'm not talking to you about that."

Oliver smiled and nodded, "Ah, so that's a no."

"Stop it. I didn't say that."

"You didn't have to. I've seen the way that you cringe when he touches you. You can't stand it. But surely he must notice? Oh. Or do you fake it, when you sleep together? You are a bit of a people pleaser."

"Stop it, Oliver. I don't want to talk to you about that kind of thing."

"Okay. Fine."

Nelly stood, suddenly furious. She watched Oliver watching the car park, smoking as if he hadn't just asked her something utterly inappropriate. "What does an orgasm have to do with loving someone, anyway?"

"Absolutely nothing, for most people. But I seem to remember it being a big deal when you were with me. Or rather, me giving other people one was the big deal."

Nelly shook her head.

"Oh, my mistake. When you weren't with me, rather. If semantics are important in this."

"Why are you being like this?"

Oliver took a drag of his cigarette, "I'm just trying to figure out why you're with him. Because if it isn't money and it isn't sex and it isn't because you love him, I don't get why you'd do it. Is it because he's safe? You know he won't cheat on you or do horrible things to you, so you just stick it out because it's easy and comfortable? Because you think being comfortable is what you deserve, rather than being happy?"

"No. Of course not. I'm not just using him. I'm not a horrible person."

Oliver shook his head, "No. You're the best person I've ever met. But I'm just saying, that can be the only reason. It's true, isn't it?"

Nelly shook her head, "No."

"I think it is," he shrugged passively, his voice even.

"Well, you don't exactly look like you're crazy in love with Catherine these days."

"I never said that I was."

"Well, neither did I."

"I don't pretend to be, though. Catherine knows where she stands. She doesn't like it, but she knows that I don't plan on her being a permanent fixture in my life. She's just convenient for the moment."

Nelly frowned, "That's not kind."

"I'm not the nicest person in the world. I don't think that's a shock to anyone."

"You can be nice. You can be really kind."

"Well, being nice didn't get me anywhere. Did it?"

Nelly took a deep breath, "I'm not getting into this with you right now, Oliver. Don't take it out on me just because you're pissed off with your girlfriend."

"I'm not taking anything out on you. I'm just asking you a question."

"Fine."

"And Catherine's only pissed off because she's jealous."

"Of what? Of us?"

"Mmm. She suspects something. She always has. Apparently I look at you strangely." Nelly must have looked anxious, because he added, "I haven't told her anything. Don't worry. I know you had a bit of a panic about that earlier, during dinner. Clearly Tony doesn't know anything either. Can I ask you though, what did you tell him? Because he must have had the same questions."

"About us?"

"About what we are to each other."

Nelly bit into the side of her cheek, looking down at her cigarette. It was only half-burned. "I told him that we are friends and that we... had some history. But that it's over and now we're just good mates. I told him the truth."

"Oh really?"

"Yes."

"Yes, you told him what you just said that you did, or yes, you told him the truth?"

"Oliver."

"Come on. I'm curious. Did you tell him that I'm just India's brother and that we're old friends? Or did you tell him the truth, like you say? Did you tell him that I'm the only person you've ever been in love with and that you're the same for me? Did you tell him that I broke your heart when I fucked other girls behind your back and that you broke mine because you chose India over me? Did you tell him about how you used to moan my name into my ear when I made you come? Because I know you used to come when you were with me."

"Oliver! Stop it. You're drunk. I don't want to have this conversation."

"Stop what? That's what the truth is, isn't it?" He watched her for a moment, as if he had asked her what her favourite colour was and was curious to know the answer. Nelly turned to look up at the window to her flat behind them.

"No. Obviously I've not told Tony all of that."

"Why not?"

"Oliver, stop it. You're being mean."

"I never want to be mean to you. I'm just being honest. And I want you to do the same. I want to know why you haven't told your boyfriend the truth. I mean, I think I know why. But I want to hear you say it to me."

Nelly sighed, closing her eyes for a moment. "You bloody know why not. The same reason you haven't told Catherine, I imagine."

Oliver shrugged, "I haven't told Catherine because I know that she would refuse to see you, and you'd refuse to see me without a third and fourth party involved. Because you don't trust yourself with me."

"Oliver."

"But that's not the same reason as why you haven't told Tony. I could hazard a guess why, of course. Probably because you know he wouldn't let you see me anymore. That's probably the reason you tell yourself, anyway. And I wouldn't blame him. I wouldn't want you to see me anymore either. But really, it's because deep down, you know that Tony will never make you feel the way that I made you feel, and telling him about us would be admitting to that out loud. And you settle for being with him because he's nice and safe, and you know that he won't hurt you like I did. Like I still could, if you'd let me close enough for us to try again."

Nelly moved away from him, the cold air putting distance between them. She was breathing heavily, her cold arms suddenly burning hot. "Why are you being like this?"

"Being like what?"

"An arsehole."

Oliver shrugged, "I suppose that's who I am."

Nelly shook her head at him. She breathed, letting her chest deflate. She felt shocked and angry and afraid all at the same time. Not of Oliver, but of the weight behind the things that he was saying to her; of the way that her stomach contracted when he told her these things, and the fact that it made her want to reach out to him and let him take her into his arms in the way that he had done years before. The dare of it. Dangerous. Lethal. This was why she never let the two of them be alone together.

"Just tell me that you don't still feel the same way about me as you used to, and I'll stop. Tell me that you don't think about me when he fucks you, or when you touch yourself, and I'll settle for just being your friend. Tell me that you're really one-hundred-percent happy living in this flat and being with Tony, and I won't bring it up again."

"I—"

"Because if you tell me now that you aren't one-hundred percent happy, I promise you that I'll take it all away. All of the unhappiness and the uncertainty. If you gave me a second chance or a third or a fourth chance, or whatever we're up to now, I would make it work."

"Oliver—"

"I'd look after you and I'd marry you and I'd take care of you forever. I'd have children with you, if you'd let me, and I'd grow old with you and I'd hold you every night whilst you couldn't sleep. Because I know you still don't sleep. I know everything about you and you know everything about me. You'd never have to fake anything again. It would just be you and me. If you tell me that's what you want."

Nelly breathed slowly, feeling her heart beating inside of her chest. It was everything that she longed to hear and yet everything she hadn't wanted him to say. He was dangerous. Her feelings for him were dangerous. Without India, he was the one person left in the world that could break her apart. And she didn't trust him not to.

"It isn't that simple."

"Why not?"

"Because it never worked before. We both fucked everything up every time that we tried. And we used India as an excuse when, really, we were both too damaged to make a real go of things."

"Okay. So, we won't fuck it up this time."

"But we probably will! You probably would. Or I probably would. And there are other people involved that we'd be hurting. Tony and Catherine."

"I couldn't give a fuck about either of them. I don't care about anyone, apart from you," he turned to watch her, his cigarette burning orange in his fingers.

"And I don't think that I could bear it if I lost you again."

Oliver sighed, taking a drag of his cigarette. He adjusted his footing on the wall and turned back to the car park, "I think you're just too scared."

"Stop it!"

"You're scared of the fact that I could hurt you. Because I have already. Because I know that I am right now. I'm hurting you now, aren't I?"

"Yes."

"Tell me that you want me to stop, and I'll stop it."

"Oliver—"

"Tell me that you don't love me anymore and I'll stop tormenting you. I'll let you live a loveless life with an average twat that doesn't know your clitoris from your elbow, and I'll go off and have my life. And we'll be just friends, like you say that we are. I'll stop caring about you like I do and I'll treat you like I treat everyone else. I'll make myself stop caring about you. You'll just be another ex-girlfriend. Even though you never really were."

Nelly could feel tears prickling behind her eyes. "Oliver, you're being mean."

"That's not an answer."

Nelly shook her head.

He regarded her again, then sighed, frustrated. "Tell me you don't still feel that way about me."

Nelly felt like she could cry. She clenched her fists, digging her nails into her palms. It was too much. Too risky. Too selfish. She couldn't trust him with her, or she with him. "I don't still feel that way. Okay? Is that what you wanted to hear?"

Oliver smiled, but didn't reply. Nelly wiped a traitorous tear from her cheek and turned around, moving back toward the door.

"Liar."

"Fuck off!"

Nelly turned back around to see Oliver smiling. The grin that was only for her. It made her angry.

"I'm gonna do you a favour and pretend when we get back upstairs that you didn't just say those things to me, okay? Because I know you're just being a twat because you've had too much to drink and that you'll apologise tomorrow."

Oliver laughed slightly and then nodded, blowing smoke out into the air in front of him. "Is that what you want me to do?"

Nelly hesitated. "Yes."

"Okay then."

Nelly nodded, then pulled open the door and stepped back into the ground floor of the building. She only realised that she was still holding onto the cigarette when it almost burned her fingers halfway to her flat.

2002
Oliver

"Are you fucking joking?" Catherine stood behind the island in Oliver's flat, in front of the work surface, staring at him over the fruit bowl. He had just told her that he wanted to break up, and she seemed utterly shocked by it. Oliver wasn't sure why. The most shocking part of the interaction for him was that he had a fruit bowl. He wondered when that had materialised. It must have been his mother. Or Nelly, at some point.

"I'm sorry," he told her, without particularly meaning it.

"You're sorry? You're fucking sorry?"

Oliver shrugged. He could feel the beginnings of a headache behind his eyes.

"So what, this just came out of the blue? You woke up this morning and decided you'd break up with me after five months?"

"No, not exactly. I've been thinking about it for a while."

"How long?"

"A few weeks, I don't know. Does it matter?"

"You were thinking about it when we were at my brother's wedding?"

"Mmm. I suppose so."

"You're a fucking cunt."

"Okay."

Catherine shook her head, aghast. "This is literally bizarre. I can't believe this."

"Really?"

"What do you mean, *really*?"

"Well, I don't think it's that shocking, is it? We argue every day of the week. And I hardly think we're the most compatible people in the world. Have I ever once made you laugh? Can you think of a time when we've ever had fun together that didn't involve sex?"

"We argue because you're a fucking arsehole most of the time."

"Fine. That's fair enough."

Oliver wasn't really sure why Catherine was finding this all so perplexing. Last weekend at brunch she had thrown a glass of orange juice over him because she thought that he had been looking at the waitress. It was strange to comprehend that she hadn't seen this coming.

"You didn't seem to not think we were very compatible last night when you were fucking me."

"Mmm, yeah. I probably shouldn't have done that. Sorry."

"You do realise that *I'm* the one that's too good for *you*, don't you?"

"Mmm."

"Do you have any idea how many men wish I was with them? I get asked out by different men every single week."

"Sure. You're probably right."

She scowled at him, "Is this a fucking joke to you?"

"I'm not laughing."

"Because it isn't fucking funny."

"Mhmm."

"You're a cunt."

"Yep. Okay."

"Is this about her?"

"Who?"

"Who do you fucking think? Her! Your precious little Nelly."

Oliver hesitated, weighing his options. He thought that he may as well be honest at this point. "Yeah, sure. Partially."

"What do you mean *partially*?"

"In part."

"I know what partially fucking means, Oliver."

"Okay then."

"So what, are you fucking her or something? You want to fuck her? You want to put your cock in that little slag?"

"Which one of those would you like me to answer?"

"Have you fucked her?"

Oliver sighed, "I have fucked her, yes. Or Nelly and I have fucked each other, rather. A long time ago. But we aren't doing that anymore."

"What, and you're hoping to start things up again?"

"In an ideal world, yes. But I don't think it's going to happen. That's not what this is about."

"Are you serious? You'd rather be with that common little whore than me?"

Oliver raised his eyebrows, trying to ignore the pounding beneath his skull.

Catherine scoffed, "She isn't even pretty! She's a common, chubby little bitch."

"Don't speak about her like that. Nelly hasn't done anything wrong."

"Oh, you're sticking up for her now?"

Oliver sighed. He picked up his glass of wine and took a sip. It didn't help. "What do you want me to say, Catherine?"

"Are you in love with her?"

"Yes."

"You fucking piece of shit."

"Yep. Okay. I'm sorry about that."

Catherine leant back against the work unit; her arms crossed over her chest. Oliver was very aware that the kitchen knives were stacked in a wooden holder behind her. "You piece of shit. You would seriously choose her over me? Nobody in their right mind would look twice at her compared with me."

"Well, there you go then."

"It's actually insulting how ugly she is. How could you go from me to that? Talk about a fucking downgrade."

Oliver took a deep breath through his nose. "Like I say, we're not getting back together."

"But you're still breaking up with me over her?"

"Partially, like I said."

Catherine shook her blonde head. "You wanna play this game? Okay. I'll play. Do you remember your Christmas party when I came with you?"

"Mmm. Sure."

"Well, did you know that Felix told me that night that he wanted to fuck me? Hmm, yeah. Feels shit to know that, doesn't it?"

Oliver shrugged. It wasn't surprising. Felix wanted to shag everyone.

Catherine seemed to get the wrong impression from Oliver's silence, so she continued. "Mmm, yeah. Maybe I'll let him now. I bet he's got a massive cock. Bigger than yours. Maybe I'll let him finish in my mouth, as well."

Oliver had to stop himself from laughing. It was all so pathetic.

"How would that make you feel?"

Oliver sighed, "Are we done yet, Catherine?"

Catherine snorted and then picked up her glass of wine, throwing the contents of it over the island toward Oliver. It spattered red stains all over his new blue shirt. He breathed deeply through his nose, feeling his head pound.

"That chubby little slag over me?"

"Please can you stop now? It's done, Catherine. We're done."

"Oh, so now you're kicking me out?"

"I'm not kicking you out. You don't even live here. I'm saying that I'm pretty sure that we've said everything that we need to say. You're just upset that someone is breaking up with you. You don't actually care that it's me doing it. Let's not pretend that this was something that it wasn't."

Catherine scoffed and then moved forward. She walked slowly around the island toward Oliver until she was standing right in front of him. Holding his gaze, she reached out and plucked his glass of wine from the surface and then poured it all over his groin. Oliver sighed again. He was pretty sure that she was enjoying how dramatic she was being.

"Excellent. Do you feel better now?"

Catherine wrinkled her nose, "Mmm. Not really. No." She tapped her cheek, pretending to think, and then threw the glass onto the floor. It shattered by their feet. "There. That feels a bit better."

Oliver nodded, "Lovely. You can leave now, please."

Catherine laughed. She walked away from him and picked her handbag up from the side. Oliver let his eyes close for a moment before she turned back around. "Do you know, you'll regret this?"

"Mhmm."

"You're nothing special. You're just another good-looking banker that thinks he can get away with being a cunt because he gets a half-decent bonus. But it won't last forever. And one day you'll wake up and realise that you're completely alone. Because I don't love you. And even Nelly probably doesn't love you. And nobody else in the world will fucking love you. And you'll die alone and depressed like your pathetic sister."

Oliver felt his jaw clench beneath his skin. "Get the fuck out of my flat, Catherine."

Catherine smiled. "Ooh, that one stung a bit, didn't it? Still, good to know that you do have a heart in there somewhere."

The door closed behind her and Oliver was left alone in his flat. He looked down at the stains on his clothes and the glass on the floor by his feet before walking to the fridge and taking out a bottle of beer.

Tony had phoned Oliver at two o'clock in the morning three weeks later. Oliver had been asleep, his alarm not having been set to go off for another four and a half hours. But he had shot out of bed, as if he had been awake all night. He had known instinctively that it would be about Nelly as soon as he had heard the phone ring.

"What's wrong? What's happened?"

Tony's voice had breathed down the phone. He sounded nervous. Scared, almost. "I dunno, mate. I came round to hers a couple of hours ago and she was locked in the bathroom. I can hear her crying from the inside, but I can't get her to come out. I thought she was just upset about something, so I left her to it. But it's been ages and—"

Oliver had been dressed and out of his front door before Tony could finish his sentence. The drive over to Nelly's flat was a blur. If anyone had asked him about it later, Oliver wouldn't have remembered getting there. He just knew that he had to reach her. She needed him. One moment he had been in his bed asleep, and the next he had been hammering his fist against the front door. Tony had opened it wearing a football shirt and looking utterly helpless.

"She's in the loo," he said as Oliver was already walking past him toward the bathroom.

He knocked on the door and then tried the handle. "Nelly, can you let me in?"

He could hear her crying on the other side of the wood.

"Nelly, it's me." Something inside of him was making Oliver panic. The memory of a similar phone call in the night three years ago. He braced himself to slam his shoulder against the door when he heard the soft noise of metal dragging backward. Nelly pulled the bathroom door open, her hair curly and her cheeks red and mottled with crying. She was wearing pyjamas, her hand clasped around something wet and papery.

He knew that she was having a panic attack before she even opened her mouth.

Oliver moved forward, taking her into his arms and pressing her against his chest. He could feel her breaths fast and urgent against his skin; panting, like she was struggling for air.

"It's okay. What's happened? Tell me what's happened."

Nelly's words were barely audible through her gasps, "She thought I was angry with her."

"Who?"

"India. She thought I hated her. She died thinking that I hated her and that I was angry with her, and I wasn't there and I should have been with her and—"

Oliver held Nelly against him, feeling her sob into his shirt. He stroked the back of her hair, half holding her up with his other arm to stop her from crumbling to the floor.

"It's okay," he told her, "Breathe. Just breathe. I'm here now. You're safe. I won't leave you. I'm here."

2002
Nelly

The letter had been from India. It had been the one that had arrived at Nelly's flat in Rome four years ago, after she and Oliver had spent the weekend together. Nelly had never opened it. She had assumed it was one of Oliver's many letters or postcards or answerphone messages apologising for what he had done. They had all said the same thing, and Nelly had been too devastated at the time to listen to what he had to say. After a time, she had stopped opening them at all. She had kept them, though. Every single one of them. Unopened. Untainted. Until now.

She had been thinking about what Oliver had said to her in the car park three weeks ago. He had told her that he still loved her and that he wanted to make things work. At least, that is what Nelly thought that he had been saying. At the time, she had been too scared and too shocked to say anything much in response. She had been taken aback by it. The brazenness of it all. And she had felt guilty, too. Guilty to Tony and to Catherine. Guilty for feeling the things that she did about a man that wasn't the person she was with. Guilty at the prospect of being happy. She was still scared. But she was also tempted. She had never been in love with anyone but Oliver in her life. Not like this. And everything that he had said had been true.

So, she had opened the letters. She wasn't sure what she had thought that she would find there. An answer, maybe. Something to tell her once and for all whether it was wise to risk everything and gamble on him once again; to gamble her heart on Oliver. She hadn't expected to see India's handwriting scrawled across the page.

My Nelly,

I'm so sorry. Please don't hate me. I can't bare it that you are somewhere in the world angry with me.

Please forgive me.

I

It had broken Nelly's heart more than anything that Oliver had done or might do to her ever could.

2002
Oliver

"So, I'm sorry about what I said that night a few weeks ago. At your flat. Or, in the carpark of your flat, rather."

Nelly pressed her lips together, looking down at the tablecloth and then back up to his face again. It had been two days since Tony had called Oliver in the night because Nelly had been having a panic attack in the bathroom. She had opened a letter from India and, even though he didn't understand quite the weight of it, Oliver knew that it had pealed Nelly's heart apart like a tin of baked beans.

"Oliver, you don't have to. I should be the one saying—" she broke off, her eyebrows knotting in the middle as she tried not to cry.

"Come on, it's okay. It's fine," Oliver tried to smile at her from across the table. Her eyes were ringed and black, as if they were bruised. It made him nervous. He never felt nervous. "I've been thinking about things a lot. You and me, we were... something that I put on a pedestal. But in doing that, I've made things weird for you. For us. And I hate that it's weird between us."

"Oliver—"

"I hate that you had a panic attack and you didn't call me, because you didn't feel like you could. I know it was because you didn't feel like you could. Because you know that I'm still in love with you. And just because I think you're still in love with me too, that doesn't mean that it's okay for me to keep pushing you when you've asked me to stop."

Nelly nodded, looking down at the table.

Oliver sighed, "I've never been as scared in my life as I was when I got that call."

"I'm so sorry."

"No. You don't need to be. I'm the one apologising. I hate that I wasn't there when you needed me. And I don't want that to ever happen again. So, I'm taking it off of the table, okay? I'm done making a fool of myself."

"You haven't made a fool of yourself."

"I have. I feel like I have. But I can be okay with that. What I can't be okay with is you needing me and me not being able to be there for you because of my feelings. Or not being in your life at all. We've both tried that and it doesn't work. And we've tried being together, and that doesn't work either. So, I'm taking it out of the equation, like you asked me to. I'm done with it, for both of our sakes."

Nelly pressed her lips together again and nodded. He could tell that she was trying very hard not to cry. "Oliver, I don't want you to think that I don't love you too."

"Hey, don't," he reached out over the table and took one of her hands into his. It was chilly. He was glad that she had a cardigan with her. "Everything's okay, alright?"

She nodded, looking away and wiping a stray tear from her cheek.

Oliver smiled, "So, I'm gonna tell you what we're going to do. I'm going to tell you that I'm moving to New York for six months."

"For six months?"

"And you're going to tell me that you're happy for me and that it's a great opportunity, like you did years ago. And I'll tell you that you're right. Because it's a fuck load of money."

Nelly laughed lightly through her sobs and looked down at their hands on the table.

"And then I'm going to go to that bar right there," he pointed at the bar behind Nelly's head, "And I'm going to order us two glasses of champagne, and maybe some chips, because I bet you're hungry. I'll let you have all the mushy ones. And then when I come back, you're going to tell me a story about some little twat in your class who drew a penis on the whiteboard in permanent marker, or who reversed the plumbing in the loos, or something."

Nelly laughed again and nodded.

"Yeah?"

"Yeah. Okay."

Oliver smiled, "Great. And there's one more thing."

"Mmm?"

Oliver hesitated, taking a breath. "I think you should move in with Tony."

Nelly's eyes shot back up to his, "What?"

"I think you should move in with him. Look, he's not who I'd pick for you. Obviously. But he's not a bad guy and... I don't think that I could go away not knowing that someone was there to look after you. In case something else like the other night happens again."

"It won't. I've been back to the doctors and I—"

"I couldn't do it, Nel. Please. I'm scared for you."

Nelly pressed her lips together and then nodded. Her lashes were heavy with tears. Oliver squeezed her hand and then stood up and walked away from her. He could feel her crying from behind him, but knew that he couldn't look back.

2002
Nelly

"Let's talk about the letter."

"Okay."

"Tell me what it said. You don't need to tell me verbatim. Not if you don't want to. But what was the gist of it?"

Nelly picked at the stray stand of wool that was dangling astray over her wrist. It was June, but the weather outside was still chilly in the mornings. Oliver had been gone for two months. Nelly swallowed, trying to arrange her face in a way that made her look as if she were less sad than she actually felt. "It was from India. Asking me to stop being angry with her."

"Right. Okay. And was the letter from a long time ago?"

Nelly nodded, feeling the tears beginning to gather in her throat. She felt angry at them.

"Before her passing?"

Nelly nodded again. "Yes. When I lived away."

"Right. Okay. And you hadn't read the letter before?"

Nelly shook her head. "No."

The therapist nodded, regarding Nelly softly over the front of her mug. The therapist was always drinking tea. The sessions were forty minutes long, but she still always drank the same mug of tea. Nelly's had been cold for ages. "That must have been very difficult for you to read, after all of this time."

"Mmm. Yes. I suppose so," Nelly felt a tear catch in her throat, "I'm sorry."

"That's okay."

Nelly breathed and concentrated on her fingers, like she had been instructed to do. Move the smallest one first, then work in toward the middle. It reassured her that she was still real. Still actually there.

"Why now, do you think?"

"Sorry?"

"Something must have compelled you to open it, when you never had done beforehand?"

Nelly swallowed, "oh, I… I'm not sure, really. I suppose I wanted to know what it said." Nelly hadn't mentioned that she had previously assumed that the letter had been from Oliver and that was why she'd never read it. She didn't want to give that part of herself away, too.

"Do you think that you could have been looking for answers?"

Nelly's eyes flicked up and then back down toward her fingers. "Yes. Maybe."

The therapist nodded. "It's normal for us to look for answers after we lose someone close to us from suicide. It's natural to wonder whether you could have done something differently, or whether there were signs that you should have seen."

Nelly nodded and then swiped a tear from her face. They seemed to keep coming. "I just loved her so much. And I hate that she isn't here anymore and I… I suppose I hate that she reached out to me and I didn't realise and just the idea that I could maybe have done something to stop it all and—"

"Nelly. Breathe."

Nelly nodded, feeling her chest beginning to pant. Focus on the little finger. Just the smallest one.

The therapist nodded, "India's actions were not your fault. It is very important that you realise that."

Nelly nodded, not really believing what she was being told.

The therapist regarded her again, waiting. Then said, "Do you think that one of the reasons that it was so difficult for you to read that letter is because you actually were angry with India?"

Nelly swallowed.

"Angry with her for the life choices that she was making, because you cared about her. You wanted her to be safe and happy, and you knew that the choices she was making would mean that she wouldn't be."

Nelly swallowed again and then nodded. "Maybe. But that's an awful thing to admit. To feel, even. What sort of a person could feel angry with someone who isn't here anymore?"

The therapist nodded, waiting for Nelly to stop crying.

"She was so lovely. She would never have meant to hurt anyone."

The therapist nodded again.

Nelly swiped a tear from her cheek. They always betrayed her.

"Anger is a valid emotion, Nelly. You are allowed to feel the things that you feel."

Nelly nodded, "Thank you."

"You don't need to thank me."

Nelly nodded again.

"You were angry because you cared about her. Not because you didn't. And that feeling is allowed."

"But I wasn't with her when she needed me. I was being selfish by being away and—" Nelly shook her head.

"What part of living your own life do you feel was selfish?"

"I suppose being away from her when she needed me."

"But she made it clear that she didn't want you there. You aren't responsible for anyone else's happiness, or the decisions that they make or made."

Nelly nodded.

"Do you think that it could be more that you feel guilty that *you* were happy. Not all of the time, of course. But for a portion. And you feel guilty that you could have felt happy when India was unhappy?"

Nelly swallowed. "Maybe."

The therapist nodded. "Do you think that's something that you're still holding onto now? That feeling of not being allowed to be happy because you feel guilty about the fact that India wasn't?"

Nelly pulled at her jumper again. "I'm not sure."

The therapist sipped her tea. "Could you please tell me about a time when you have felt happy recently? It doesn't need to have been in the last weeks or months. But the last years. Since India's passing, can you think of a time when you've been happy?"

Oliver's face as they drove to Cornwall flashed into Nelly's mind. She chewed her cheek.

2002
Oliver

"And what are your colleagues like? Are they nice?"

Oliver shrugged. He was sat across the table from his parents, at a large restaurant in Manhattan. They had flown in yesterday for a long weekend. It had been a surprise, which was surprising in itself. Oliver had to work for most of the time that they were going to be here, but he had committed to spending the evenings with them. And Sunday. His mother wanted to go shopping, and apparently that required their assistance.

"They're fine," Oliver told her, "Much the same as the ones at home."

"But American."

"Mmm. Yes."

Oliver's mother smiled and nodded, as if she now understood completely. His dad was still eating his steak.

"Have you spoken to anyone else from home since you've been here?"

"Mmm?"

"I don't know. Your colleagues from London. Or Nelly, maybe?"

Oliver smiled slightly. It was a terrible segue, even for his mother. He raised his eyebrows at her and she sipped her white wine as if she hadn't been waiting to ask him that exact question. "A little bit. Not a lot."

"Oh?"

"Mmm."

"And is she well?"

Oliver sighed, "Yeah. Sure."

"Don't say sure. Say yes, darling. You might be in America, but you aren't American."

Oliver smiled.

"So, you have spoken with her a little bit?"

"Yeah, a bit. Do you want another drink?"

"Mmm? Yes, actually. But in a moment. There's no rush," she placed her now empty glass on the table and then looked over at her husband eating his meal. She rubbed his hand as if he were doing something utterly adorable. "I bet she's looking forward to seeing you when you come back. You will come back, won't you?"

"Mmm. I don't know. Probably," Oliver replied.

"Probably?"

"Mmm. I'll see. The job's going well."

"Oh."

Oliver nodded.

"Well, maybe she could come out here and visit you?"

Oliver sighed, "Mum, I don't want to go over this again."

"What? I'm only asking."

"You know you aren't only asking. I've told you. Nelly is moving in with Tony."

"Because you told her that she should."

Oliver shrugged, "She's a big girl. She can make her own choices."

"She listens to you, though. She's susceptible to what you tell her."

Oliver shook his head, "She can think for herself. She could have not done it, if she didn't want to."

"So, you were testing her?"

"No. I just wanted to make sure that she was okay. She's had some stuff going on, since India."

"So, it was because you care about her?"

Oliver sighed, "It doesn't matter. It's happening."

"But sweetheart—"

"And I'm here, anyway. It's done. I'll see Nelly when I'm back, whenever that is. We're going to be friends. But that's all."

"But—"

"Mum."

Oliver's mum nodded and then sighed. "I just want to see you happy, sweetheart."

"I'm fine."

"Are you?"

"Sure," Oliver began to say, then corrected himself. "Yes."

His mum nodded. "Okay. I'll stop interfering, then."

"Thank you."

She sighed again, "What will be, will be, my darling."

Oliver raised his eyebrows at her and she smiled, as if she had told him something very wise.

"I'm just going to go and find the lady's. Would you order me another drink when the waiter comes back round, darling?"

Oliver and his father both nodded.

"But don't call them over, or anything like that. I hate the way that Americans do that. Like the French."

Oliver smiled, "I thought you liked the French."

"I do. But not with waiters."

Oliver nodded and she winked at him before standing and moving away from the table. Oliver watched as his dad watched her go, as if making sure that she had found her way okay. Oliver wasn't sure quite why he did this of late. He had never seemed so attentive when Oliver was younger. Or perhaps Oliver had just never noticed it before.

Oliver sighed and checked the time on his watch. "I'll go to the bar," he told his dad.

His dad nodded, then said, "You don't believe in that hippy bollocks any more than I do."

"Sorry?"

His dad looked up at him. Everyone told Oliver how alike the two of them looked, but he had only been able to start seeing it now that he was getting older. "That *what will be, will be* rubbish," his dad told him. "I love your mother, but that sort of shit is what I can't get on board with."

Oliver was surprised that this made him smile.

His father seemed surprised, too. "Your mother seems to think that if you want something badly enough, it will come to you. Just land right in your lap. And who knows, maybe she's right. She seems to get the things that she wants, in the majority. But I don't put any stock in it myself. If you want something— whether it's a job or a house or whatever—you go out and you make it happen. Life doesn't just give you what you ask it for. It isn't your parent; it doesn't owe you anything. You need to make it happen for yourself. You have to *make* life know."

Oliver raised his eyebrows, "Yeah, sure."

"I want you to tell me that you understand."

Oliver nodded, "I understand."

His father regarded him and then nodded back at him; his blue eyes were oddly soft. "If you want something, make fucking sure that that something knows that you want it. Work for it. Be brave for it. Never beg for it, unless you have to. But make it fucking known. And then if it doesn't happen, fine. That's the outcome and so be it. At least then you know that you tried. You need to know that you tried. Because things don't just happen because you want them badly enough."

Oliver nodded. He pretended that he didn't understand exactly what his father was trying to say to him.

"Oliver?"

"Yes."

"Do you understand me?"

Oliver nodded. He wasn't quite sure how his father always managed to make him feel so childlike. "Yes, I understand. The problem is that I have tried, though."

"Have you tried hard enough?"

"I think so."

His father shrugged, "Then that's all you can do."

Oliver shrugged back. "I'll go and get Mum's drink."

"I know that you think I'm made of stone. Your mother was always the nice one. The kind one that got all of the cuddles and the laughs and that. And she deserved it, don't misunderstand me. She's love in a person. That's what she's made for. Not me, though."

"Mmm."

His father watched him and then nodded plainly, as if in agreement with Oliver's non-commitment. "There're some things that I've been wanting to talk to you about. We don't get many opportunities to talk just you and me. Man to man."

Oliver regarded his father from across the table. He wasn't sure that they ever really had spoken before. Never properly, anyway.

His father nodded, "You see, I've been having a bit of a hard time of things, to tell you the truth. We all have. You included. And this isn't easy for me to admit to you. You, of all people. I know you always thought of me as the tough one, but I know that illusion has probably crumbled in the last few years. You've had to be the tough one for us. Your mum has had to be the tough one."

"Dad—"

He held his hand up, beginning to look frustrated. "Just let me get this out. Please. You see, I was always the one that had to have a go at you both when you drove your mum up the wall. I was the one that shouted at you when you got suspended for smoking weed on campus. I was the one that had to shout at India for stealing the car to go on nights out, or for trying to sneak that fucking French lad into the villa at three in the morning when she thought we were in bed."

Oliver blew a smile through his nose.

"I'm glad you think it's funny. Honestly, I am. I might not have done at the time. But I'm glad for it now. I'm glad that you have those things to look back on and laugh about. Things about her that you can look back on and remember the two of you laughing over behind my back. You both being happy. Her being happy." He adjusted his knife and then continued, "But I was always the ogre. And, to be honest with you, it never bothered me. I was away most of the time anyway, and my biggest concern was making sure that you had the tools to look after your own family in the same way one day. That was my biggest concern for *you*, anyway. And I know I'll be called old fashioned for it, but I am who I am. I wanted you to look after your own the way that I thought that I was looking after you all. Because I hope you realise that I did think I was looking after you. I did it for myself, in part; I'd be lying if I said that I didn't. I like the cars and the houses and the money. And I know that I wasn't the best husband or the best father. But I was mostly doing it for you, at the very end of things. For the three of you. And I hope that was known, even throughout it all. Because it breaks my heart—I know you might be shocked to hear that I have one—but it breaks my heart to think that might not have been known."

"Dad, India knew it. She knew that you adored her."

"I don't just mean India," Oliver's father said, clearing his throat. He took a sip of his wine and composed himself before he let slip more emotion. Oliver waited patiently, feeling slightly uncomfortable. His father took a second sip and then nodded again, "I just had to say it, you know? I wanted you to have heard it from me at least once. Do you understand what it is that I'm trying to say?"

Oliver swallowed his own wine and then nodded. It was the closest his father had ever come to saying that he loved him.

"There's something else that your mother wanted me to talk to you about."

"Oh yeah? I should have known she was behind this."

His father smiled briefly and raised his eyebrows at his glass. He cleared his throat. Oliver waited. "About Nelly. Are you in love with her?"

Oliver almost smiled at his father's brashness, "Mhmm."

"Right. And she makes you… happy? Not just fine, but actually happy."

"Yep. Most of the time."

"Right. And you've made that known to her?" His face looked irritated, betraying every inch of how much Oliver's father detested having to have this conversation.

"Yeah, Dad. I've made it known. She doesn't want it."

Oliver's dad swallowed his wine and then shrugged, "It doesn't look that way from where we're standing."

Oliver shrugged, "It is that way."

"Okay," he sighed, "Your mother worries, you know? *We* worry."

"Mmm."

Oliver's father smiled at him slightly. "We're the same, you and me. It seems like our lot in life is to be in love with women that are too good for us."

Oliver nodded, "Far too good."

"Still, at least we can afford to drown our sorrows. Eh?"

"Ha. Yeah." Oliver was shocked that he was enjoying himself. He nodded and then looked away from the table to where his mother was walking back over to them. She sat down, regarding them both for a moment before rubbing her husband's hand and then reaching over the table to hold Oliver's. It was a speech that had clearly been rehearsed, in part, but it didn't make it any less meaningful. To Oliver, the conversation with his father was almost like hearing a second language that he didn't use often enough to be completely fluent in; he understood the message because he'd been around it enough, but his grasp of the different tenses was patchy. It was almost the way that he felt about love in general.

2002
Nelly

It was strange to see her flat packed up, reduced to eleven brown boxes of clothes and kitchen utensils and bathroom products. She had less baggage than she had thought that she had, when it had come down to it.

"Cheers, mate. You're a lifesaver," Tony was saying into his mobile. He was on the phone to one of the boys from his rugby team who had offered to lend them his van for the move. They were due to be moving today, to a slightly larger flat in the city. It was further away from Nelly's work, but closer to Tony's. She looked around her flat now and thought how she would miss the small window above the sink.

"What about this, mate?" Tony's friend, Greg, asked Tony over his shoulder. Tony seemed to have a lot of friends around all of the time. Nelly felt awkward about the fact that she hadn't recruited anyone to help them. Then again, she could have asked her parents. But they didn't seem to think that the move was a very good idea.

"Chuck, I reckon," Tony replied, "That alright, babe?"

Nelly nodded in agreement instinctively before turning to check. It was a small green shoebox that had been stored beneath Nelly's various beds for the last five years. "Oh, no. There's room for that, isn't there?"

Tony sighed, "Really?" Greg pulled the top off from it and peered inside, his hand rummaging around. Nelly felt her stomach squirm.

"It's just a load of old post," he told them.

"Oh, yeah. It's mine," Nelly moved toward him quickly. She reached out for the box and Greg offered it to her.

"You don't need all of that old tat, do you?"

"It isn't tat, really. It's just letters and stuff. I can keep it in my drawer. It won't take up much room."

Tony rolled his eyes, "Girls, eh? You're such a hoarder. I've chucked half of my football cards and stuff. It isn't like we're moving into a mansion. You've gotta make compromises, Nel."

Nelly nodded, gripping the box in her hands. The truth was that she already felt she was making too many compromises. "Still, I'd rather keep it. If that's okay?"

Tony sighed, "What's even in it?"

Nelly stood still as he moved toward her and pulled the lid from the box, rooting his hand around. It felt strangely like his hand had plunged into her stomach. "It's stuff from India, and... I dunno. Just things."

"Come on, babe. That's for the chuck. You have to admit."

Nelly pressed her lips together. She glanced over at Greg who was now sorting through her bathroom products. "It's stuff from my life."

"But you have a new life now, babe. With me. You don't need any of this old shit."

Tony took the box from Nelly's hands and she nodded. She watched him put the box back on top of the pile labelled *rubbish*. He was tired, she knew, and frustrated with her for being difficult. But he was still making an effort to be nice. He was always nice to her. That's what Nelly liked about him. Or what she had thought that she liked, anyway. Suddenly though, it didn't seem like *like* was enough. Suddenly, Nelly didn't feel as if she was being difficult.

"Reckon we'll be due a beer after this, don't you?" Tony grinned toward Greg.

"Cor, you're telling me," Greg agreed. Tony winked at Nelly.

"Would you mind, babe?"

"Oh. Yeah. Of course."

Nelly moved over to the fridge that was empty other than for Tony's six-pack of Amstel and plucked two from the cardboard. It tugged at her finger sharply.

"Do you want glasses?"

"Na, don't bother. You'd just have to wash them before we pack them again," Tony said. Nelly nodded.

She placed more of her things onto various piles, cramming wooden spoons and spatulas into cardboard boxes and watching as Tony and Greg slowly sifted the pile labelled 'Rubbish' out from her flat. Tony looked shocked when Nelly's voice called out behind him.

"Are you sure that I can't keep that one?"

Tony sighed and Greg nodded at him, moving out into the stairwell. "Babe, we've been over this. You don't need this crap."

Nelly nodded, "Mmm, yeah. Right. Apart from…" her stomach churned. Nelly bit into the inside of her mouth and then stopped herself. "Apart from I think that I do need it."

2002
Oliver

"Do you think you might come home at all this summer?"

"Mmm, I'm not sure. I've got a lot of work on here at the moment."

"Ah, yeah. Of course."

"It's a difficult time to leave, you know? With the new clients and all that."

"Mmm. Yeah, sure."

Oliver smiled, noticing the way that *sure* had begun to creep into Nelly's vernacular. "I'm sorry," he found himself saying.

"Oh, no. Don't be. I get it. You have a lot on."

"Mmm."

"I was just hoping to see you, is all. But no worries. We'll see each other at Christmas, maybe?"

"Mmm. Yeah. Probably."

"Cool."

Oliver swirled the ice in his tumbler around, watching it dissolve slowly into the tequila. He had never previously enjoyed this particular liquor, but now he seemed to be developing a taste for it. "Or you could come here, if you liked?"

"To New York?"

Oliver smiled at Nelly's incredulousness. "It isn't a different planet."

"I know. But I just… I'd love to. But I have school and it's difficult taking time off during term and stuff. And, I dunno. Flights are really expensive. Like eight hundred quid."

Oliver raised his eyebrows, "You say that like you've looked into it."

"Well…"

Oliver blew a smile through his nose. "I can pay for it for you, if that's the problem?"

"No. It's fine. Honestly, it's fine. I wouldn't feel right you doing that. Besides, like I say, I don't know how I'd get the time off. Especially with the interview and everything."

"When is it again?"

"Tuesday the eighth, at three o'clock."

"Not like you're counting the days."

"I am! I've done a dummy-run there on the tube already. And I've bought a new notebook for it. Is that sad?"

Oliver smiled, "Why do you need a new notebook for an interview?"

"I'm not sure really. To look professional, I suppose. It's moleskin, so I felt like it looked a bit sophisticated. So far, I've just been using it to write down the weekly shop." Nelly took a gulp of something that sounded tea-like on the other end of the phone and Oliver felt as if he could smell the sugariness of it from across the Atlantic. It was funny how something like that can make you feel so far from and yet so close to a person. He looked down at his tequila and thought about how it had been a while since he'd last drank tea.

"Are you out for dinner tonight?"

"Mmm. I'm supposed to be meeting them at nine."

"Nine seems very late for a work dinner."

"Mmm, I know. It's the way here, apparently. I could do without it to be honest."

"You're always out. It sounds very glamorous. New York, I mean."

"Mmm. It is. You should buy a plane ticket and come and see it for yourself. Or let me buy it for you. We could get you to Gatwick now and you could be here tomorrow. Have I mentioned that?"

Nelly laughed slightly, "Do you ever just stay in and cook? Or do you not have an oven in that fancy hotel suite of yours? What is it, ten bedrooms? Twelve?"

Oliver smiled, "Three. And, again, if you bought a plane ticket you could see for yourself. I'd have them put chocolates on your pillow and everything, if you wanted."

"You'd *have* them?"

"I'd ask them to."

"Mmm, right," he heard Nelly run a tap on the other end. It squeaked as she turned it off. Oliver found it strange, the fact that Nelly lived on her own somewhere that he'd never seen. He couldn't quite visualise it, even though she had described her new flat to him more than once. It was green, apparently. The colour suited her. Oliver wondered whether she felt the same way about where he was living now. When he had heard that she had called things off with Tony, he'd felt shockingly relieved. Even though the two of them moving in together had been his idea. It had all been to keep her safe. But it was like he'd had something pressing on his chest that he hadn't known had been there. He finally felt like he could breathe again. "I've never understood the chocolates on the pillow thing. Who eats chocolate in bed, anyway?"

Oliver raised his eyebrows, "I'm sure there are plenty of uses."

"But you know what I mean. What if you didn't know it was there and then you smushed it all over the quilt? It would be a better idea to leave something like a mint. Or a polo."

Oliver laughed, "You forget that I've seen you eating chocolate in bed."

"When?"

"At my old flat. When we watched *Dirty Dancing*. You devoured that entire box of Maltesers."

"Alright. Alright. Fine. Red handed."

Oliver sipped his drink, feeling like he had given too much away. He was prone to doing that with Nelly. "Anyway, I do have an oven, but I've not used it. I'm not much of a chef, as you know."

"You know how to make lasagne."

"Ah, yeah. That's true."

"And meatballs."

"Only with scrupulous supervision."

Nelly laughed. "Well, call me boring but I'd hate to eat out every night. I'm making pork medallions this evening and I'm already counting down the hours."

"Mmm. I miss your cooking."

Nelly hesitated and Oliver wondered again if he had overstepped, but then she replied, "I miss you too, Oliver."

Someone patted Oliver on the back and he turned his head to see a man named Alec from his office sit down on the stool beside him. Quite a few of them from the office had been put up in the same building. Oliver nodded his head and gestured to his drink. Alec gave him a thumbs up. "Hey, can we get two more of these please, mate?" Oliver asked the barman.

He nodded. Oliver felt aware of how British he suddenly sounded and wondered whether that was the way his voice usually came out, or whether it was more pronounced now that he was speaking with Nelly.

"You're feeling thirsty."

"Mmm. Someone from work just got here."

"Ah. No worries. I'll leave you to it."

"It's fine. I can stay."

"No, it's okay. I've got to get ready for work anyway."

"Mmm. What if I want you to stay?"

Nelly laughed softly. "Ring me again soon? I can tell you all about my medallions. I'm sure you'll be on tenterhooks, what with your reclusive life in such a drab city."

Oliver smiled, "Yeah. Definitely."

"Okay. Well, bye then."

"Okay. Bye."

"Oliver?"

"Mmm?"

"Nothing. Just... no. It's okay."

"You sure?"

"Mmm. Yeah. I'll tell you next time."

Oliver nodded, feeling slightly disappointed. Their goodbyes were always difficult, partly because he didn't know quite how he was supposed to sign-off. What was the etiquette for saying goodbye to a friend that you were secretly still in love with? Or, not so secretly, he supposed. The barman handed over the drinks and Oliver raised his eyebrows in thanks, holding his credit card out toward him. "Okay. Bye."

"Bye."

He hung up the phone and placed it back inside of his pocket, pushing the empty glass of tequila to the edge of the bar and pulling the full one closer.

"That the better half?" Alec asked, nodding toward Oliver's mobile.

Oliver smiled. "Mmm. The better, definitely."

2002
Nelly

She got the job at The Perse secondary school. Assistant head-teacher. Nelly couldn't quite believe it. Not long ago she had barely felt like an adult; she still got ID'd the majority of the time when she bought wine at the local supermarket. For so long being a grown-up had felt like trying on a pair of shoes that didn't quite fit yet, when she had already thrown away her old ones. But her toes seemed to have found the edge now.

She had been surprised at how light she had felt after breaking up with Tony months ago. Immediately lighter, like the feeling when you notice that you've been holding your shoulders tense and then release them. She hadn't even realised that she felt he had been weighing her down. Or, not Tony precisely, but the relationship itself. She felt as if she could admit those things now. Partially because she knew that she shouldn't feel guilty anymore for wanting to be happy, and partly because she sensed from their conversation that Tony hadn't felt wholly differently about the whole charade. It was just something that they had both gone along with, it seemed. Neither of them had wanted to hurt the other, and then neither of them had actually been hurt. Sometimes that happens. If she hadn't learned from it, it would likely have felt like a huge waste of time. But she had. She knew what she wanted now.

Nelly sipped on her small plastic glass of red wine and looked out of the window. It was night time, but she hadn't pulled the blind down. She was enjoying looking out into the pitch-black of the sky; seeing it so vast and full and empty. It made her feel small, in a nice way. The magnitude of the world was reassuring. Seeing the largeness of it helped Nelly to rationalise her own life and her own worries and how small, in the grand scheme of things, her world was in comparison with the rest of it. Everyone had their own lives and concerns and heartbreaks. Everyone was the main character in their own story. It was a comforting notion.

It had been a long time since she had last been on a plane. She had bought the ticket when she had found out that she had got the job at The Perse, having been asked when her start date could be. She hadn't even planned it, but had found herself telling them a date two weeks from her last day at her current school. She had felt anxious about it immediately, but the woman at Human Resources had barely batted an eyelid, saying that this was fine and then going on to ask her about something else. It was strange the number of times lately that Nelly realised most people cared about things far less than she worried that they might.

Nelly twisted her neck from one side to the other, feeling the ache of it in her joints. She regretted that she hadn't invested in one of those foam pillows. She hadn't wanted to fork out the additional seven pounds for one. Oliver had offered to pay for her to fly business class, but Nelly had refused. She had wanted to do this for herself. Still, she regretted not buying the pillow when she'd had the chance.

They had been flying for almost eight hours now and Nelly was beginning to ache, along with becoming increasingly aware of her own body beneath the clothes that she had been wearing for almost twelve hours. She wondered whether she would have time to change in the toilets before seeing Oliver. She wasn't certain whether he would be meeting her at the airport or not, although she suspected it. She had told him what time her flight would be arriving and he had said that he'd already known.

"I looked up flights from London to JFK," he admitted when she asked him, "It was the only one coming in that day." He had sounded sheepish, which was unlike him. It had made Nelly smile.

She wondered whether he was nervous about seeing her, but then thought that he probably wasn't. It was rare for Oliver to be nervous about anything, and the things he was nervous about usually involved him being caught doing something that he shouldn't have been. Not spending a weekend with an old friend, or whatever it was that she was to him these days. She twisted her neck again, feeling it twinge. Or maybe that was just because she was feeling increasingly anxious with the prospect of seeing the love of her life in the next few hours.

She had been thinking about what she would say when she saw him. Would she tell him as soon as they were together in person, or would it be better if she waited for a dinner, or even until the end of the holiday? Thinking about it, she wasn't even certain that he would also have booked days off to spend with her. She brushed her tongue over the rough part of her cheek as she thought, mulling over her options. She was making a conscious effort not to bite it, but the skin was still mottled where it was healing. She wished that she could brush her teeth.

The idea of telling him made her anxious. She had told Oliver before that she loved him, obviously. But so much time and history had passed between them since that she wasn't sure whether she would just be pulling open an old wound. She was concerned about this. But also aware that wounds could heal, and she knew now that she wasn't ready for this one to scab over entirely. Still, the prospect of rejection was somewhat terrifying. In the lead up to the holiday, Nelly had comforted herself with the knowledge that Oliver would likely be accepting the offer to stay in New York for an additional twelve months and that this meant that, in the worst-case scenario, at least there would be an ocean between the two of them to ebb the humiliation if he turned her down.

But now, sat on the plane toward him, the ocean between them suddenly felt both larger and smaller all at once. There was so much beneath it that couldn't be seen from above; so much depth that nobody had yet reached. It was scary, but beautiful at the same time.

"Excuse me, ma'am. Would you be able to lower the blind, please? We're going to be landing shortly."

"Oh. Of course. Sorry," Nelly replied to the flight attendant. She turned and took one final look out at the abyss of the night before pulling the blind down over it. It was comforting to know that it was out there waiting for her behind the window. No matter what.

2003
Oliver

It had been pouring down all day; the rain stifling and warm and heavy. The air was the type that felt so close that you could almost grab it. The windscreen wipers on Oliver's car darted up and back over the screen, smearing the rain across it so as it cleared and then blurred again. He needed to remember to take the car to be valeted. Or he could clean it himself, he thought idly. He never did, though. He probably would if he really cared about it.

It had been a very long day. He had left the house at five am, the drive into the city taking him the best part of two hours. It was almost a quarter to nine in the evening now. He felt tired as he watched the road outside through the windscreen wipers. He always felt tired on the journey home. Oliver pressed the button to let the window down slightly, allowing in some fresh air, then changed his mind and pressed it again to make it go back up.

The car ground over the gravel of the small driveway, crunching satisfyingly to a halt. It was strangely quiet when Oliver turned off the engine, plucking the key from the ignition. Still. Like he had interrupted the world. He held the keys in his hand and was about to open the car door when something caught his attention.

He could see Nelly through the kitchen window. He already knew what she would be doing before he saw her doing it. Reading essays whilst she cooked. It's what she was always doing when he got home from work. It surprised him that he found the routine of this so comforting.

Oliver was always telling Nelly that she should close the curtains when she was home on her own in the evenings. She had a terrible sense of not knowing when someone was watching. She was blissfully unaware of her effect on people or how interesting she was to observe. She always had been. It was one of the things that he had always found so intoxicating about her.

Oliver found himself watching her now. He could tell exactly what she was thinking as she read. Her eyebrows knotted toward one another, forcing a very small crease into the centre of her forehead; she pouted her lips out slightly, as if she were getting ready to rebuttal the essay's opinion. It made Oliver smile. She rubbed her hand over her swelling stomach subconsciously as she continued to read.

Oliver loved seeing Nelly pregnant. Mostly because he loved her and the idea of them being a family made him happy, although he also found it slightly terrifying. But a part of him also thought that he liked it so much because there was a visible reminder of her being his, in a way. Part of him was inside of her and everyone could see it. It was the same feeling he had had when she had first worn the engagement ring. It was a masculine, possessive notion that Oliver wasn't necessarily proud to admit that he felt; he would never confess to it out loud to anyone. Apart from to Nelly, of course. He could tell her anything. He always had been able to. What was more odd was that Oliver enjoyed the same notion on himself. He liked knowing that people saw his wedding band and knew that he belonged to someone. That he was already claimed.

It wouldn't really matter, obviously; Oliver didn't need a ring to stop him from doing things that he shouldn't anymore. But, like the routine of Nelly's reading, marriage was something that once would have seemed stifling but now felt oddly reassuring to Oliver. The permanency of it. Solid. Final. At least, that was the plan. It had all happened quickly once the two of them had finally gotten together. They had been engaged within a month and married within four. Partly because of the pregnancy, but mostly because they both knew that it was right. Ten years seemed like long enough to have been mulling the notion over, after all.

The baby would be with them in three months now. They still didn't know what it was. They had decided that they wanted the surprise. Oliver secretly hoped that it was a girl. Sometimes Oliver stood against the sink whilst Nelly was in the bath and they spoke about names that they liked. Nelly liked Annabelle for a girl or Mark for a boy.

Oliver liked Annabelle but said that Mark Matthews sounded like a children's presenter. Nelly reminded him that he had said the same thing about her name the first time that they had met and the memory had made him smile. For one brief evening they had played with the idea that, if it were a girl, they would name the baby India. But then they had both separately decided that this wasn't a good idea.

"We already have an India," Nelly had told him when they had confessed to one another.

Oliver had nodded.

Sometimes it felt strange knowing that their baby would come into the world and never meet Oliver's sister, or that India would never meet his and Nelly's child. Their worlds had aways been so interwoven. It was their love for India that had brought Oliver and Nelly together, and the same love that had at times kept them apart. Now, they would both love another person that India would have never met. Life was cruel in that way. It also felt strange that India would never truly know what Nelly and Oliver had meant to each other over all of these years; how much and how deeply they had always loved each other, despite it all.

"I think she probably did know, deep down," Oliver told Nelly one day when she had been feeling sad about this. Nelly had looked anxious, but had then agreed.

"I hope she did."

They both still struggled with their grief. There were times when the two of them could sit together and laugh over shared memories, or memories of India that the other hadn't heard before. Times like that were special. Precious. And becoming more and more regular. But there were also still times in the night when Oliver knew that Nelly lay awake, silently feeling guilty about no longer feeling guilty for being happy without her best friend. And there were still circumstances when Oliver felt unrealistically anxious about bad things happening to people that he loved, like about Nelly being at the house on her own at night when he was away. Or the fact that she always forgot to close the curtains. But for the most part, they were happy.

Their scars may never truly heal, but they had both made their peace with that. It was the scars that meant they would never forget. Nelly must have read Oliver's mind about the curtain, because she looked up out of the window at that moment. She smiled at him and tilted her head, as if asking wordlessly what he was doing sat in his car in the rain. He shrugged at her and then smiled back.

Oliver watched Nelly in their home for another brief moment and then opened the car door and stepped onto the driveway, reaching over and dragging his coat out from the back seat with him. The rain spattered down onto his hair and down his forehead. Now he was home, the downpour felt refreshing on his skin.

317

Printed in Great Britain
by Amazon